EMILY FORBES

MARGARET WAY

LEAH MARTYN

MILLS & BOON

TAMING HER HOLLYWOOD PLAYBOY
© 2019 by Emily Forbes
Australian Copyright 2019
New Zealand Copyright 2019
First Published 2019
Second Australian Paperback Edition 2024
ISBN 978 1 038 90126 2

OUTBACK HEIRESS, SURPRISE PROPOSAL
© 2009 by Margaret Way Pty.,Ltd.
Australian Copyright 2009
New Zealand Copyright 2009
First Published 2009
Third Australian Paperback Edition 2024
ISBN 978 1 038 90126 2

OUTBACK DOCTOR, ENGLISH BRIDE
© 2008 by Leah Martyn
Australian Copyright 2008
New Zealand Copyright 2008
First Published 2008
Third Australian Paperback Edition 2024
ISBN 978 1 038 90126 2

Published by
Mills & Boon
An imprint of Harlequin Enterprises (Australia) Pty Limited
(ABN 47 001 180 918), a subsidiary of HarperCollins
Publishers Australia Pty Limited (ABN 36 009 913 517)
Level 19, 201 Elizabeth Street
SYDNEY NSW 2000
AUSTRALIA

Printed and bound in Australia by McPherson's Printing Group

CONTENTS

Taming Her Hollywood Playboy

Emily Forbes

Books by Emily Forbes

Harlequin Medical

The Christmas Swap

Waking Up to Dr. Gorgeous

The Hollywood Hills Clinic

Falling for the Single Dad

Tempted & Tamed

A Doctor by Day…
Tamed by the Renegade
A Mother to Make a Family

A Kiss to Melt Her Heart
His Little Christmas Miracle
A Love Against All Odds
One Night That Changed Her Life
Falling for His Best Friend Rescued by the Single Dad

Visit the Author Profile page at millsandboon.com.au for more titles.

Dear Reader,

Coober Pedy in South Australia is an amazing place. It is famous for its opals but, over the years, numerous movies have been filmed there, too, so that's where I decided to send my Hollywood playboy when he needed to stay out of trouble. Where better than the middle of nowhere—the Australian outback?

But, when it turns out that Coober Pedy isn't far enough away and Oliver finds himself in trouble once again, Kat is the person he turns to for help. A gorgeous, sensible paramedic, born and bred in the outback, she should know better than to fall for a movie star, but Oliver is nothing if not charming!

To Damien, Dean and Roger—thank you for showing me your town and for lending me your names. And to Dave Reed—I hope you enjoy seeing your name in a romance novel!

I had fun with my characters and I had a lot of fun trying to capture Coober Pedy on the page. If you'd like to see some photos of my trip you can visit my Facebook page, Facebook.com/emily.forbes.5855.

Best wishes,

Emily

For Deb,
the most amazing big sister.
I was so lucky to have you in my life.
I miss you every day.
xx
6th October 2018

Praise for
Emily Forbes

"*A Mother to Make a Family* is a lovely story about second chances with life and love…. A well written, solid tale of sweet love and charming family."

—*Goodreads*

PROLOGUE

'Toto... I've a feeling we're not in Kansas any more.'

The familiar phrase from *The Wizard of Oz* popped into Oliver's head as he sat in the all-terrain vehicle surrounded by nothing but red dirt. The heat in the vehicle was stifling but he knew it was worse outside. He could see the shimmering mirage of the heat as it rose off the baked land. A trickle of sweat made its way down his back, sliding between his shoulder blades as he looked out of the window and wondered what he was doing at the end of the earth.

He wasn't in Kansas, and he sure as heck wasn't in Hollywood either. Hollywood was clean and tidy, ordered and structured. A lot of the work on movie sets in today's world was done indoors, with air-conditioning and green screens, and any dirt, gore, murders, blood and disasters were manufactured. Here the dirt and dust and heat were all too real. Too authentic. It made him wonder about everything else—the murders, blood and disasters—it was too easy to imagine all kinds of skulduggery occurring in this seemingly endless land.

He shrugged his shoulders; they were sticky under his clothing as he returned his focus to the task at hand. He'd always had an active imagination but he was sure he'd be able to handle this place—it was only for six weeks. The dirt and dust would wash off at the end of the day, he was used to a certain level of discomfort in his job, and he certainly wasn't precious—although the heat was a little extreme, even for him. It had a thickness to it which made breathing difficult, as though the heat had sucked all the oxygen from the air. It felt like the type of heat you needed to have been born into, to have grown up in, to have any chance of coping with it. Of surviving.

It must have been well over one hundred degrees in the shade, if there was any shade. The place was baking. Hot, dry and not a blade of grass or a tree in sight to break the monotony of the red earth. The landscape was perfect for the movie but not so great for the cast and crew. Adding to Oliver's discomfort was the fact that he was wearing a flame-retardant suit under his costume in preparation for the upcoming scene. But it was no use complaining: he asked to do his own stunt work wherever possible and he was sure his stunt double would be more than happy to sit this one out.

The sun was low in the sky but the heat of the day was still intense. He closed his eyes as he pictured himself diving into the hotel pool and emerging, cool and fresh and wet—instead of hot and sticky and dripping in sweat—to down a cold beer. He would love to think he could have the pool to himself but he knew, in this overwhelming climate, that was wishful thinking; he'd just have to do his best to avoid sharing it with any of the single women from the cast or crew. He didn't need any more scandals attached to his name. His agent, lawyer and publicist were all working overtime as it was.

He started the engine as instructions came through his earpiece. It was time to capture the last scene for the day's shoot.

The stunt required him to drive the ATV at speed towards the mountain range in the distance. A ramp had been disguised in the dirt and rocks that would flip the vehicle onto its side for dramatic effect. The whole scene could probably be done using CGI techniques and a green screen but the film's director, George Murray, liked as much realism as possible and he had chosen this part of the world for filming because of its authenticity and other-worldliness. It was supposed to be representing another planet and Oliver could see how it could feel that way. He had grown up all around the world but even he'd never seen anywhere that looked as alien and hostile as this.

The setting sun was turning the burnt orange landscape a fiery red. The shadows cast by the distant hills were lengthening and turning violet. He knew the dust thrown up by his tyres would filter the light and lend a sinister aspect to the scene.

He waited for the call of 'action' and pressed his foot to the accelerator. The vehicle leapt forwards. He waited for the tyres to gain traction and then pushed the pedal flat to the floor. The ground was littered with tiny stones, making it difficult to maintain a straight course. He eased off the speed slightly as the vehicle skidded and slid to the left. He corrected the slide without difficulty and continued his course but, just as he thought he'd succeeded, there was a loud bang and the steering wheel shuddered in his hands.

He felt the back of the vehicle slide out to the right and he eased off the speed again as he fought to control it, but the tail had seemingly picked up speed, turning the vehicle ninety degrees to where he wanted it. To where it was supposed to be. He let the wheel spin through his fingers, waiting for the vehicle to straighten, but before he could correct the trajectory the vehicle had gone completely off course. The front tyre dropped into a trough in the dirt and Oliver felt the wheels lift off the ground.

The vehicle began to tip and he knew he had totally lost control. All four wheels were airborne and there was nothing he could do. He couldn't fight it, he couldn't correct it, and he couldn't control it.

The ATV flipped sideways and bounced once. Twice. And again.

It flipped and rolled and Oliver lost count of the cycles as the horizon tumbled before him and the sun's dying rays cast long fingers through the windshield.

Had he finally bitten off more than he could chew?

CHAPTER ONE

OLIVER MASSAGED THE lump on the side of his head. He'd taken a couple of paracetamol for the dull headache but fortunately he'd escaped serious injury yesterday. The bump on his head and some slight bruising on his shoulder were minor complaints and he had no intention of mentioning those aches and pains. The ATV had taken a battering but could be fixed. The repairs meant a change in the filming schedule but nothing that couldn't be accommodated. A serious injury to him would have been far more disruptive.

Despite his luck, however, the incident had made George, the director, wary and Oliver had agreed to hand over some of the stunts to the professionals. The movie couldn't afford for anything to happen to its star and he didn't want to get a reputation as a difficult actor. George had been good to Oliver; he'd worked with him before and he'd been happy to give him another role when other directors had been reluctant, but Oliver knew that being argumentative, disruptive or inflexible wasn't a great way to advance a career. He wasn't stupid, he knew actors were a dime a dozen. He wasn't irreplaceable. No one was. A reputation as a ladies' man was one thing; a reputation as being problematic on set was another thing entirely.

He stretched his neck from side to side as he tried to rid himself of the headache that plagued him. He knew it was from the accident yesterday. He hadn't had that cold beer and had gone to bed alone, so there were no other contributing factors. He knew exactly what had caused his pain.

The schedule change caused by his accident meant he wasn't required for filming this morning, but now he was bored. He wandered around the site, knowing that the heat was probably compounding his headache but too restless to stay indoors.

A whole community had been established temporarily in the middle of the desert just for the movie. Transportable huts were set up as the production centre, the canteen, the first-aid centre, lounge areas for the cast and crew, and Oliver, George and the lead actress all had their own motorhome to retreat to. Marquees surrounded the vehicles and more huts provided additional, and much-needed, shade. The site was twenty miles out of the remote Australian outback town of Coober Pedy, which itself was over three thousand miles from the next major town or, as the Australians said, almost five hundred kilometres. No matter which way you said it, there was no denying that Coober Pedy was a mighty long way from anywhere else.

He'd been completely unprepared for the strangeness of this remote desert town. He'd imagined a flat, barren landscape but the town had sprung up in an area that was far hillier than he'd expected. The main street was tarred and lined with single-level shops and a few taller buildings, including his hotel, with the houses spreading out from the centre of town and into the hills. Along with regular houses there were also hundreds of dwellings dug into the hillsides. He'd heard that people lived underground to escape the merciless heat but he hadn't thought about what that meant in terms of the town's appearance; in effect, it made the town look far more sparsely populated than it actually was.

He knew he should hole up in his trailer and stay out of the heat but he wanted company.

Generators chugged away in the background, providing

power for the film set, providing air-conditioning, refrigeration and technology. He was used to having a shower in his trailer but because of water restrictions apparently that was a no-go out here in the Australian desert.

If he moved far enough away from the generators he knew he would hear absolute silence. It should be peaceful, quiet, restful even, and he could understand how some people would find the solitude and the silence soul-restoring, relaxing, but it made him uneasy. He needed more stimulation. He wanted crowds, he wanted noise, he didn't want a chance to be introspective. He was an extrovert, a performer, and as an extrovert he wanted company. He needed company to energise him and as a performer he needed an audience.

He wasn't required on set but he decided he'd go and watch the filming anyway. It would kill some time and give him someone to talk to.

He turned away from the transportable huts that formed the command centre for the movie set and headed towards the vehicle compound. His boots kicked up puffs of red dust as he walked. Everything was coated in dust. It got inside your mouth, your ears, your nostrils. Everything smelt and tasted like dust. It even got inside your eyes—if the flies didn't get there first. Which reminded him that he'd left his sunglasses in his trailer. He spun around; he'd retrieve them and then grab a four-by-four and head further out into the desert to where filming was taking place.

He slipped his glasses on as he stepped back into the heat. Rounding the corner of his trailer, he heard an engine and noticed a dust cloud billowing into the air. He stood in the shade at the corner of his trailer and watched as a car pulled to a stop beside the mess hut. It was an old four-by-four, its brown paintwork covered in red dust, like everything else out here. A haze rose from the bonnet of the car, bringing to mind the story about it being hot enough in Australia to fry an egg in the sun. He believed it.

The car door opened and he waited, his natural curiosity getting the better of him, to see who climbed out.

A woman.

That was unexpected.

She stood and straightened. She was tall, slender, lithe. Her hair was thick and dark and fell just past her shoulders. He watched as she scraped it off her neck and tied it into a loose ponytail, in deference to the heat, he presumed. Her neck was long and swan-like, her limbs long and tanned.

She was stunning and the complete antithesis of what he'd expected, judging from the car she was driving. She reminded him of a butterfly emerging from a cocoon.

He blinked, making sure it wasn't the after-effects of the bump to his head causing his imagination to play tricks on him.

She was still there.

She wore a navy and white summer dress, which must have been lined to mid-thigh, but from there down, with the morning sun behind her, the white sections were completely see-through. He wondered if she knew but he didn't care—her legs were incredible. Magnificent.

Oliver was literally in the middle of nowhere with absolutely nothing of interest to look at. Until now. The middle of nowhere had just become a far more attractive proposition.

He watched as she walked towards him. Graceful. Ethereal. Sunglasses protected her eyes but her skin was flawless and her lips were full and painted with bright red lipstick. The shade was striking against her olive skin and raven hair.

He'd seen plenty of beautiful woman in his thirty-two years, he was surrounded by them on a daily basis, but he didn't think he'd ever seen a woman as naturally beautiful. The ones he worked with had all had some help—a scalpel here, an injection there—and he'd swear on his father's grave, something he hoped he would be able to do sooner rather than later, that she hadn't had any assistance.

He watched, not moving a muscle, scared that any movement might startle her, might make her shimmer and disappear, mirage-like, into the desert.

Maybe his headache was affecting his thought processes; maybe he'd been out in the sun for too long, or simply in the outback for too long. Other than the cast and crew he'd barely seen another person for days. The hot, dusty streets of Coober Pedy were, for the most part, empty. The locals hunkered down in their underground dwellings to escape the heat, venturing out only briefly and if absolutely necessary, scampering from one building to the subterranean comfort of the next. But perhaps many of the locals looked like this. Perhaps that was the attraction in this desolate, baked and barren desert town.

She had stopped walking as her gaze scanned the buildings, looking for something or someone. Looking lost. His curiosity was piqued. His attention captured.

Her gaze landed on him and she took another step forward. Belatedly he stepped out of the shadows and walked towards her; he'd been so transfixed he'd forgotten to move, forgotten his manners, but he wanted to be the first to offer her assistance.

'Hello, I'm Oliver; may I help you?'

She stopped and waited as he approached her.

'Thank you,' she said. 'I'm looking for George Murray.' Her voice was deep and slightly breathless, without the broad Australian accent that he'd heard so many of the crew speak with. She glanced down at her watch and his eyes followed. Her watch had a large face, with the numbers clearly marked and an obvious hand counting off the seconds. Her fingers were delicate by comparison, long and slender, with short nails lacquered with clear varnish. He was trained to be observant, to watch people's mannerisms, to listen to their voices, but even so he was aware that he was soaking up everything about this woman. From the colour of her lips and the shine of her hair, to the smooth lustre of her skin and the inflection of her speech. He wanted to be able to picture her perfectly later. She lifted her head. 'I have an interview with him at eleven.'

'A job interview?'

She nodded. 'Of sorts.'

'Are you going to be working on the film? Are you an extra?'

'No.'

'Catering? Publicity?'

'No and no.' Her mouth turned up at one corner and he got a glimpse of perfect, even white teeth bordered by those red lips.

He grinned. 'You're not going to tell me?'

Her smile widened and he knew she was enjoying the repartee. 'No, I don't think I am.'

Two could play at that game. 'All right, then,' he shrugged, feigning disinterest, 'George is out on set but he shouldn't be long. Filming started early today to try to beat the heat, so they'll be breaking for lunch soon. Let me show you to his trailer.' He'd take her to where she needed to go but he wouldn't leave her.

He bounced lightly up the two steps that led to George's office and pushed open the heavy metal door. He flicked on the lights and held the door for her. She brushed past him and her breasts lightly grazed his arm but she showed no sign that she'd noticed the contact. She stopped just inside the door and removed her sunglasses, and he caught a trace of her scent—fresh, light and fruity.

He watched as she surveyed the interior. An enormous television screen dominated the wall opposite the desk, which was covered in papers. A laptop sat open amongst the mess. A large fridge with a glass door was tucked into a corner to the left, and a couch was pressed against the opposite wall with two armchairs at right angles to it and a small coffee table in between. He wondered if this was what she'd expected to see.

'Have a seat,' he invited as he waved an arm towards the chairs. She sat but avoided the couch.

'Can I get you something to drink?'

She nodded and the light bounced off her hair, making it look like silk. 'A water would be lovely, thank you.'

He grabbed a glass and two bottles of mineral water from the fridge. He twisted the tops off and passed her the glass and a bottle.

'I'll be fine waiting here,' she said as she took the drink from him. 'You must have something you need to do?'

He shook his head as he sat on the couch. He leant back and rested one foot on his other knee, relaxed, comfortable, approachable, conveying candidness. 'I'm not busy. The scene they're filming doesn't involve me.'

'You're an actor?'

He looked carefully at her to gauge if she was joking but her expression was serious. Her mouth looked serious, her red lips full but not moving. But was there a hint of humour in her dark eyes? He couldn't read her yet. Perhaps she was an anomaly, someone who didn't immediately recognise him, or maybe he just wasn't famous out here in the middle of nowhere.

Should he tell her who he was?

No. That could wait. She still hadn't told him what she was doing here. She'd said she wasn't publicity but she could be a journalist. He didn't need more reporters telling stories about him. But if that was the case, surely she would recognise him.

Unless she was a better actor than he was, he was certain she wasn't a reporter.

He settled for vague. 'I am,' he said as the door opened again and George entered the trailer.

'Kat! Welcome.' He was beaming. Oliver was surprised; George never looked this pleased to see anyone. George was a little rotund, always in a hurry, and seemed to have a permanent scowl creasing his forehead. Seeing him so delighted to see another person was somewhat disconcerting.

He crossed the room as the woman stood. Kat or Kate, Oliver thought George had said, but he wasn't quite sure. Oliver stood too; manners that had been instilled in him, growing up as the son of a strict military man, remained automatic.

George greeted her with a kiss and Oliver was more intrigued. There was obviously some history here that he wasn't privy to. Who was she?

'I see you've met our star, Oliver Harding.'

'Not formally.' She turned to him and extended her hand. 'I'm Katarina Angelis, but call me Kat.' Her handshake was firm but it was the softness of her skin and the laughter in her eyes that caught Oliver off guard. 'It's a pleasure to meet you.'

He realised she'd known exactly who he was. Which put him at a disadvantage. He still knew nothing about her. But he did know her name seemed to suit her perfectly. He was sure Katarina meant 'pure', and Angelis had to mean 'heavenly'.

'The pleasure is all mine,' he said.

George cleared his throat and Oliver realised he hadn't let go of Kat's hand. He also realised he didn't want to. Beautiful women were everywhere in his world, but there was something more to Kat. Something intriguing. Something different.

Her skin was soft and cool. Flawless. She looked like a desert rose, a surprising beauty in the harshness of the outback, and he found himself transfixed by her scarlet mouth. Her lips brought to mind ripe summer cherries, dark red and juicy. He wondered how they'd taste.

'If I might give you some advice, my dear,' George said to Kat as Oliver finally let her hand drop, 'you should stay away from Oliver.'

'Hey!' he protested.

'You don't have to worry about me, George,' Kat replied. 'I can handle myself.'

George shook his head. 'You've never met anyone like Oliver.'

Kat was looking at him now. Studying him, as if sizing him up and comparing him to George's assessment. Oliver smiled and shrugged and spread his hands wide, proclaiming his innocence. He had to take it on the chin; he couldn't remonstrate with George in front of Kat—it would be better to laugh it off. He couldn't afford to show how she'd affected him. It was safer to return to his usual persona of charm and confidence, of not taking himself or anyone too seriously. She had floored him and he needed to gather his wits and work out what to do about it. About her. But, for now, he'd play along. 'George is right, Kat, I'm the man your father warned you about.'

She laughed. 'Don't go thinking that makes you special. My father is always warning me about men.'

He cocked his head and quirked one eyebrow. This was even better. He had never been one to back away from a challenge.

'Don't make me regret hiring you.' George eyeballed them both. 'Either of you.'

Oliver laughed; he was used to being told off, but he was surprised to see that Kat was blushing. She looked even more delightful now.

'I mean it, Oliver—don't mess with Kat.' George looked him straight in the eye. 'There aren't too many places left for you to run to and if you hurt her you'll want to start running, believe me.'

So now they were both going to put a challenge to him. Of course, that only served to entice him even more. George could warn him all he liked but Oliver had never been one to steer clear of a challenge. But he knew he had to tread carefully. He couldn't afford any more scandals.

'Go and find something to do,' George told him. 'I need to talk to Kat.'

Oliver left but he knew it wouldn't be the last he saw of Kat Angelis. He was glad now that she hadn't admitted that she recognised him, that she hadn't said his reputation preceded him. Perhaps she'd have no preconceived ideas about him and he could try to impress her without any rumours or innuendo getting in the way.

He was still none the wiser as to her actual reason for being on set but, if George was hiring her, he'd make sure their paths crossed again. If he was going to be stuck in this town for the next few weeks he might as well have some fun. He knew it was his choice, almost, to be here—George had made him an offer that his publicist thought was too good to refuse—and timing was everything. But that didn't mean he couldn't enjoy himself. He wouldn't misbehave, but even if he did he doubted anyone would ever hear about what went on out here. Coober Pedy and the Australian outback seemed to exist in its own little time capsule. It really was a whole other world.

Kat watched on as George shooed Oliver out of his office. Of course she'd recognised him—Oliver Harding was a star of multiple Hollywood blockbusters. He had been the lead actor in several recent box office hits and he played action heroes just as well as he carried romantic leads. He was in the news regularly, if not for his movies then for his off-screen exploits with his leading ladies or other Hollywood 'It' girls. Kat may be a small-town girl, living out in the desert in the middle of nowhere, but she had television, magazines, the internet and the local drive-in movie theatre, which showed new movies every Saturday night. Oliver Harding was famous and she would have to be living under a rock not to know who he was. The thought made her smile. She did actually live underground, like so many of the local residents, but that didn't mean she didn't know what went on in the rest of the world. Oliver Harding appeared in a new movie every six months, and with a new woman far more frequently. Having met him now, she could understand why. He was handsome on the silver screen but incredibly gorgeous in real life. He had charm, charisma and a twinkle in his bright blue eyes that had made her lose her train of thought on more than one occasion already.

'I'm serious, Kat,' George cautioned her again. Had he mistaken her smile to mean she wasn't paying attention to his warning? 'I've seen that look in his eye before. You really don't want him to set his sights on you. Stronger women than you have fallen for his charms. He loves the thrill of the chase and he hates to let a pretty girl go unappreciated, but he has a tendency to leave a trail of broken hearts behind him.'

He had a cheeky appeal and amazing eyes and his smile made her stomach tumble, but Kat wasn't about to succumb to his charm. She'd met charming men before and didn't intend to be another notch on his bedpost. And she hadn't been kidding when she'd said she knew how to handle herself. There was no denying Oliver Harding was gorgeous and charming but she was *not* the type to fall for charming and handsome. Well, that wasn't technically true but she wasn't the type to have flings with famous men who were just visiting. That was something irresponsible people did. Spontaneous people. And she'd learnt not to be either of those.

'Don't worry about me, George. I really can handle myself.'

'He has a reputation for seducing women, but, in his defence, don't believe everything you read or hear. He's a nice guy but still a flirt and definitely incorrigible.'

'I'm here to work, not fool around with the staff,' Kat stated, reminding herself of her obligations as much as she was reminding George. 'So, what exactly did you want to see me about?'

George sighed. 'Oliver has it written into his contract that he gets to do a proportion of his own stunt work. A large proportion. But yesterday things didn't go quite to plan. He was involved in an accident. The vehicle he was driving was supposed to crash but instead of going into a controlled sideways tip it flipped at speed and ended up on its roof. He seems to be fine.'

Kat thought back—she hadn't noticed a limp or any bruising or protective postures, but she hadn't been looking for signs of injury. She'd been too focused on his mesmerising blue eyes and on trying not to act like a star-struck fan.

'But,' George continued, 'since the incident our first-aid officer is refusing to be responsible for Oliver's safety and I must say she has a point. We have a stunt coordinator who is also Oliver's double but...sometimes things go wrong. I think it would be prudent to have someone on set who has more experience than just a first-aid qualification. Not full-time, just when we're doing the stunts. Do you think, if I gave you the filming schedule, you might be able to work with us? Would you be interested?'

'I think so.' George had outlined his thoughts on the phone to her last night but she needed more details. 'Can you give me a basic idea of what would be required, mainly how much time?'

She listened as George ran through the filming schedule with her.

'I'd still need to be available for ambulance shifts—even with the volunteers we don't have enough staff to allow me to give those up,' Kat said. Getting qualified paramedics to work in rural and remote areas was always tough and Kat knew she would have to make sure she didn't put her colleagues under any additional pressure by requesting time off in order to do something that was purely to satisfy her own desires. As tempting and exciting as it was to think of working on a movie set, not to mention with Oliver Harding, her commitment to her career had to be her priority.

'We could work around your schedule to a certain degree. As long as you could be on set when we're doing the stunt work. Would that be possible? I don't want to wear you out.'

From what George had described to her last night, the movie wasn't really her cup of tea—she preferred drama and thrillers to science fiction—but she had to admit it would be exciting to work on a film set, and getting to work with Oliver would be an added bonus.

'I reckon I can work something out. I'll see if I can swap some of my day shifts for nights. We're on call overnight. With a resident population of just over two thousand people there's not usually a lot to keep us busy. It's tourists that swell our numbers and keep us occupied.'

'That's great. I'll get a contract drawn up; you'll be fairly paid for your time.'

'I don't need—'

'Don't argue,' George interrupted. 'I need it to be all above board and your wages will be a drop in the ocean that is our budget. Think of it as spending money—put it aside and treat yourself to something.'

Kat couldn't remember the last time she'd treated herself to something. She couldn't even begin to imagine what she would do, but it was easier to agree.

'There is one other thing,' George added. 'A favour. I need some extra locations. The cave where I wanted to shoot is apparently sacred Aboriginal land and I can't get permission to film there. You don't happen to know of anything else around here?'

'I do know something that might do,' Kat replied. 'It's on my godfather's land about ten minutes out of town. I can take you out to see it later today if you like. Shall I meet you at the hotel?'

Kat picked up the copy of the film schedule that George had given her, kissed him goodbye and made arrangements to meet at five. She stepped out of the trailer and found Oliver waiting for her.

'Now are you going to tell me what you're doing here?' he asked as he fell into step beside her. His voice was deep and pleasant, his accent neutral. She'd expected more of an American flavour. Had he been taught to tone it down?

'I live here.'

'Really? Here?'

She could hear the unspoken question, the one every visitor asked until they got to know Coober Pedy. *Why?*

She never knew where to start. How did one begin to explain the beauty, the peace, the wildness, the attraction? She loved it here. That didn't mean she never entertained the idea of travelling the world and seeing other places, but this was home. This was where her family lived. And family was everything.

She had no idea how to explain all of that, so she simply said, 'Yes, really.'

'But you know George?' He was walking closely beside her

and his arm brushed against hers every few steps, interrupting her concentration.

She nodded.

'Are you going to tell me how?'

'It's not my story to tell.'

'At least tell me why you have the filming schedule, then.'

She stopped walking and turned to look at him. She had to look up. She wasn't short—she was five feet nine inches tall—but still he was several inches taller. 'Are you always this nosy?'

'Yes.' He was smiling. 'Although I prefer to think of myself as having an enquiring mind. It sounds more masculine. I'm happy to be in touch with my feminine side, but only in private.'

'I'm going to be working on the film,' she said, hoping to surprise him.

'Doing what?'

'Keeping *you* out of trouble,' she said as she continued towards her car.

'Trouble is my middle name,' he laughed.

She didn't doubt that. She'd only known him for a few minutes and regardless of George's warning she already had the sense that he was trouble. But she couldn't help smiling as she said, 'So I hear.'

Kat reached her car and stretched her hand out to open the door, which she hadn't bothered locking, but Oliver was faster than she was. He rested his hand on the door frame, preventing her from opening it.

'And just how exactly do you plan to keep me out of trouble?' His voice was deep and sexy, perfect for a leading man.

She turned to face him. He was standing close. Her eyes were level with his chest. He was solid—muscular without being beefy, gym-toned. He didn't look as if he'd done a hard day's work in his life, and he probably hadn't, but that didn't stop him from being handsome. With his chiselled good looks, he could have come straight from the pages of a men's fashion magazine.

He smelt good. He looked even better.

His blue eyes were piercing, his square jaw clean-shaven. His thick brown hair was cut in a short back and sides, slightly longer on top, like a military-style haircut that had been on holiday for a couple of weeks. She wondered if it was to fit the movie script or if it was how he chose to cut his hair. It suited him. It emphasised his bone structure.

'I'm your insurance policy,' she said.

He frowned and raised one eyebrow. She wondered if that came naturally or if he'd cultivated that move. Was it possible to learn how to do that?

'I'm a paramedic,' she continued. 'I'm going to be on set for the stunt work. Just in case.'

She'd expected him to object but he took it in his stride.

'Good,' he said simply before he grinned widely. 'I'll be seeing plenty of you, then.'

He was so confident, so comfortable. She wondered if he'd ever been told he couldn't do something. She imagined that if he had he would have chosen to ignore the instruction.

His arm was still outstretched, passing beside her head as he leant against her car. 'So, Kat, tell me your story.'

'Why do you want to know?'

She was caught between his chest and the car. She could step out, away from the boundaries he'd imposed, but she didn't want to. She didn't feel threatened. He was smiling at her. He looked genuine, friendly, but she needed to remember he was an actor. He was probably trained to smile in a hundred different ways. She remembered George's warning but she chose to ignore it. Just for a moment. She wanted to see what would happen next. She felt as if she was in a movie moment of her own.

His smile widened, showcasing teeth that were white, even and perfect. His blue eyes sparkled. 'Because I want to make sure I'm not overstepping any lines when I ask you out.'

He looked like a man who was used to getting his own way and she didn't doubt that; with women, at least, he probably did.

But she did doubt that she was the type of woman he was used to meeting. 'And what makes you think I'd go out with you?'

'I didn't say you would, I'm just letting you know I will ask you to. The choice is completely yours.'

'What did you have in mind?' She shouldn't ask but she wanted to know. She should heed George's warning and get in her car and drive away but it had been a long time since she'd been asked on a date and she was interested to hear his thoughts. She was interested full stop.

He smiled. 'I don't know yet but I'll think of something.'

There weren't a lot of options in Coober Pedy and Oliver, not being a local, would know even fewer.

Kat couldn't remember the last time someone had flirted with her or the last time she'd met anyone she wanted to flirt with. She couldn't deny she was flattered by the attention. She'd need to be careful. She'd been hurt before; a monumental break-up had left her questioning her own judgement and she'd avoided getting romantically involved ever since. She wanted her own happily-ever-after but she'd been scared to go out to find it. She'd focused instead on her career and her family and it had been a while since she'd even thought about going on a date. George's warning repeated in her head again but she had no idea if she was going to be able to heed it.

The touch of Oliver's hand had set her pulse racing and the look in his eye had made her wish, just momentarily, that she was the sort of girl who would take a risk, take a chance.

But that wasn't her. She'd learnt that taking risks was asking for trouble, and Oliver Harding had trouble written all over him.

CHAPTER TWO

KAT PULLED INTO the courtyard in front of the Cave Hotel. She found a spot to park under a gum tree in the shadow of the hill, seeking shade out of habit rather than necessity at this time of the evening. The air was still warm but the searing heat of the day was beginning to dissipate.

The sun was setting behind the hotel, turning the sky orange. The hotel was the town's only five-star accommodation. Kat doubted it could be compared to five-star indulgence in Paris, London or New York but it was luxurious by Coober Pedy standards and all that Kat knew. She'd never travelled outside Australia and had never stayed in anything rated above three and a half stars.

'Do you have a little more time up your sleeve?' George asked as Kat switched off her car. 'As a thank-you for showing me those caves I'll buy you a cold drink and introduce you to the cast. I imagine they'll gather in the bar before dinner and it would be a good chance to meet them before you start work.'

'Sure,' she replied. 'I'll just make a call and then I'll meet you inside.'

Like a lot of the dwellings in town, the hotel had been built into the side of a hill. It had newer wings that extended out from the hill but Kat always recommended that people book an underground room as a preference, for the atmosphere and experience plus the fact that the rooms were bigger and cooler. The original, subterranean floorplan had been designed to enable the rooms to maintain a constant temperature year-round, a bonus in the scorching heat of summer and during cold winter nights, but it meant that cell phone reception could be erratic inside.

The hotel had air-conditioning, an excellent restaurant and shops, and the courtyard parking area had been covered in bitumen, which, in contrast to the dusty streets, was perhaps all that was needed. More importantly it had an outdoor pool, secluded behind an adobe wall and surrounded by palm trees. Kat had always thought the palms a bit incongruous, considering the environment, but they seemed to thrive.

She stepped under the covered walkway that ran from the pool to the hotel foyer, seeking the shade. She called her father, letting him know she'd be late and checking that he was happy to wait for dinner. As she finished her phone call she heard the pool gate slam shut behind her. She turned her head and saw Oliver walking her way.

He had a beach towel slung over his right shoulder but he was still wet. He was bare-chested, his skin smooth and slick and golden brown. Damp swimming trunks hugged his thighs.

Kat's mouth went dry as she tried not to ogle him, but it was a difficult task. Eventually she lifted her eyes and saw him smiling at her. His smile was incredible. It started slowly; one corner of his mouth lifted first and then his smile stretched across his lips before they parted to reveal perfect white teeth and a wide, engaging smile.

'This is a pleasant surprise. I didn't expect to see you. What are you up to?'

He stopped at her side, took the towel from his shoulder and started to dry his chest. There was a purple bruise on his right shoulder and Kat was going to ask about it, but that was before she got distracted. Oliver's arm muscles flexed as he rubbed the towel over his body, diverting her attention. He ran the towel over his abdomen and she couldn't help but follow his movements. His stomach muscles rippled as he twisted to reach his hand behind his back and Kat's heart skipped a beat as she forced herself to concentrate. She was yearning to reach out and run her hand over his shoulder and down his arm. To feel his biceps tense and flex under her fingers. If she thought he was attractive fully clothed then he was something else altogether when he was partially naked.

She swallowed as she tried to rein in her imagination. 'I've just brought George back—we went to scout some locations.'

'You've already got the lingo, I see,' he said as he slung the towel back over his shoulder. 'What are you doing now?'

'I'm having a drink at the bar. George is going to introduce me to a few people.'

'Great, I'll see you inside.' He started walking towards the hotel and Kat focused on walking beside him, on putting one foot in front of the other.

He held the lobby door open for her but stopped at the entrance to the bar. 'I'm not dressed appropriately—I'll get changed and come back. Are you OK to go in by yourself?'

Kat wasn't used to people checking on her; everyone in town knew her and the locals expected people to look after themselves. On the whole women weren't treated any differently to men but she stopped herself from giving a short reply of 'of course', as she realised he was just being polite. He was just treating her with courtesy, showing some respect. It was something her father would have done for her mother.

Her father would have been horrified if her mother had gone into a hotel unaccompanied. When they had been courting there would have been separate bars for the men and women, and women would never have been permitted in the 'public' bar, but times had changed and no one now would bat an eyelid at a woman going into a bar alone. Kat knew she would feel uncomfortable in a different setting, in a different town, but everyone knew her here; she still appreciated Oliver's manners though. She nodded. 'Yes, I'm fine, thank you.'

The bar was cool and softly lit. It was in the original part of the hotel, dug into the hill. Its walls and ceilings were the colour of ochre, the same colour as the land, but the walls had been coated with a clear lacquer to stop the dust that would otherwise coat everything in its path. It was a large room and felt spacious even though there were no windows. Indoor plants helped to delineate the space, creating smaller areas and a sense of privacy while helping to disguise the fact that they were several feet under the surface.

George was waiting for her and introduced her to several of the cast and crew as she nursed the drink he had purchased for her. She tried to focus on who everyone was but she was constantly scanning the room, waiting for Oliver to return. She hated knowing that she was waiting for him, looking forward to seeing him, but she couldn't help the feeling.

She did a slight double-take when a tall man walked in—his build and even his gait were so similar to Oliver's that it wasn't until he removed his cap that she registered that not only was he not Oliver, but he also had a shaved head and was not nearly as good-looking. But his movements had been similar enough that she'd had to look twice, so it was no surprise when George introduced him as Chris, the man who was Oliver's stunt double. Kat shook his hand, noticing his brown eyes even as she noted that the touch of his hand didn't set her heart racing. He was pleasant enough, fit and young, but very definitely not Oliver.

'When you see Oliver,' Chris said to George after shaking Kat's hand, 'let him know I'll meet him in the gym for his training session.' He turned to Kat. 'Good to meet you, Kat; I'll see you on set.'

When Oliver finally entered the bar, Kat wondered how she could have mistaken Chris for him. There was an aura about Oliver, something drew her to him and she found it almost impossible to turn away.

'Hello, Kat.' He was looking at her intensely. Did he look at everyone like that? she wondered.

She felt as though he could see inside her, see all her secrets. Not that she had any. Something about him made her wish she was a little mysterious, wish she wasn't so ordinary. She wished there was something about her that could intrigue him.

'Chris is waiting in the gym for you.' George was speaking to Oliver and his voice brought her back to the present.

'That's OK, I promised Kat a drink first. Chris will wait.'

Kat opened her mouth to object—Oliver hadn't promised her any such thing—but before she could speak he winked at her and grinned and she kept quiet.

George's assistant, Erica, came to the table and spoke softly in George's ear.

'If you'll excuse me, I need to speak to Julia. It appears she is having a crisis.' George stood before adding, 'Behave yourself, Oliver.'

Oliver just grinned in reply, apparently brushing George's warning aside without a thought as George left the table, leaving them alone and leaving Kat a little nervous. To fill in the pause in conversation she asked, 'Will she be OK?'

'Have you met our leading lady yet?' Oliver replied.

Kat shook her head.

'Julia is always in the middle of a crisis,' Oliver told her. 'I attract scandals, she attracts crises. We probably shouldn't be allowed to work together. There's always a danger of too much drama.' He laughed and Kat found herself relaxing. 'Now, tell me, what are you drinking?' he said.

'Are you sure you shouldn't be meeting Chris?'

Oliver shrugged and shook his head. 'Not yet.'

'Won't you be in trouble?'

'I'm used to it. Trust me, you are far better company than Chris, not to mention better-looking, and I might not get this opportunity again.' He smiled his slow, drawn-out smile and Kat's stomach flipped and fluttered in response. It was almost as though his smile kept time with his thoughts but she felt at a distinct disadvantage because, while she could hazard a guess, she actually had no idea what his thoughts were.

'Besides, I told you trouble is my middle name.'

Kat smiled back. There was no denying his charm. 'Maybe trouble should have been your first name.'

Oliver laughed as he stood up and even his laugh was perfect. Deep and rich, he sounded like someone who laughed often. 'Chris will make me sweat for making him wait. I might as well enjoy a beer if he's going to take his revenge in dead lifts and push-ups anyway.'

'OK, thank you; a beer sounds good,' Kat said, accepting his invitation.

'Explain to me how the stunt double thing works,' she said when Oliver returned from the bar. 'I get that Chris has a similar physique to you and even moves a bit the same, but he doesn't look like you. Is that a problem? Is that why you're doing some of your own stunts?'

'No. Chris has been my body double on several movies and he wears a wig if needed, but in this movie he's often wearing a helmet, so his hair, or lack of it, is irrelevant.'

'What about his eyes?' Oliver's were such a distinctive, vibrant blue, Kat couldn't see how they could work around that.

'He's not in any close-up shots, so we don't need to see his eyes, but he could probably wear coloured contact lenses if necessary. The make-up girls are good and nowadays there's always CGI.'

Oliver was distracted by something over Kat's right shoulder. She wondered if Chris had come to force him into the gym and so was surprised when she heard her name.

'Kat?'

She turned to find her cousin, Dean, and his wife, Saskia, standing behind her. While she knew almost everyone in town, she hadn't been expecting to see any familiar faces in this particular bar. The Cave Hotel was expensive and usually frequented exclusively by tourists.

Kat stood up and greeted them both with a kiss. 'Hi. What are you doing here?'

'Dean is taking me to dinner at Mona's. It's our wedding anniversary.'

The hotel restaurant, Mona's, was the best in town and was the one drawcard for the locals, who often chose to dine there to celebrate special occasions.

'Of course it is,' Kat replied. 'Happy anniversary.' But Saskia had turned her attention to Oliver by now and was looking at him with interest.

'Hello. I'm Saskia and this is my husband, Dean.'

Oliver was already on his feet. 'Oliver Harding,' he said as he shook Saskia's hand and then Dean's.

'What are you two up to?' Dean asked.

Kat could see the look of approval on Saskia's face but, whereas her expression was one of appreciation, Dean looked wary. That wasn't unexpected—Kat, Dean and his brother, Roger, were more like siblings than cousins and the boys had always been protective of Kat, particularly when it came to who she dated, but she didn't need Dean trying to rescue her from this situation. There wasn't a situation at all. This was just a work meeting.

To his credit Oliver didn't seem fazed by Dean's abrupt question but Kat jumped in before Oliver could say anything that could be misconstrued. She didn't need any rumours getting back to her father. 'Oliver is an actor in the movie that's being shot in town. I'm going to be working with him.'

'As what?' Dean asked. His piercing gaze would have pinned a lesser man to the spot but Oliver seemed completely unperturbed by the attention.

'The emergency response officer,' Kat replied.

'That sounds appealing,' Saskia said with a slight smirk. Kat glared at her but Saskia just smiled, while Dean continued to size Oliver up.

Kat watched them both. Oliver was squaring up to Dean and she wondered if she'd need to step in between them. As fit as Oliver was, she wasn't sure he'd be a match for her cousin in a physical confrontation.

The men were much the same height, both a couple of inches over six feet, but Dean was probably twenty kilograms heavier with a hardness about him that Kat knew came from growing up in this environment. Oliver's muscles came from gym work, which was different from the muscles gained from working outdoors in the heat and dust of the Australian outback. Dean was neat and tidy but he had a toughness about him, except when he was with his wife and kids.

Oliver was groomed, not tough, still all male but a more polished version. He was gorgeous but, as far as Kat knew, he was used to Hollywood. In comparison, Dean was used to the outback, which was tough and rugged and, Kat imagined, just about as far from Hollywood as it was possible to get. Dean's life couldn't be more different from Oliver's.

'And what exactly does that entail?' Dean asked.

'It's exciting. I'll tell you about it over dinner,' Saskia said as she tucked her arm into Dean's elbow and prepared to lead him through the bar and into the restaurant.

Kat had told Saskia about the job offer. Saskia and Dean had been together since high school and Saskia was like a sister to Kat. As an only child, she appreciated the relationship she had with her cousin's wife. She was slightly envious of her cousins' marriages; they had what she wished for. They had found their 'one'.

Once upon a time, Kat had had that too. She had thought she was going to get her own happily-ever-after, but things hadn't turned out how she'd expected and now she was starting to wonder if she was ever going to find her soulmate. She was pretty sure she wasn't going to find him in Coober Pedy—the town was dwindling; people were leaving. Would she have to leave too?

'I would jump at the chance to take on that job if I didn't have you and the kids and work to worry about,' Saskia said, bringing Kat back to the present, 'if I was single and free, like Kat,' she added, directing her less than subtle remark to Oliver.

Kat needed to move them on before Saskia said something that would embarrass her. She hugged them both and said, 'Enjoy your dinner,' as she put some gentle pressure against the small of Saskia's back, encouraging her to leave and take Dean with her.

But Saskia wasn't done yet. 'Will we see you on Sunday or are you working?'

'I'll be there.'

'What's happening on Sunday?' Oliver asked when they were alone again.

'Family dinner.' It was a weekly occurrence and there was an expectation that everyone would attend, but Kat didn't mind. She adored her family. Kat had moved back in with her father after her mother passed away, and her extended family—her aunt Rosa, Dean and Saskia, Roger and his wife, Maya, and their children—had dinner together every Sunday.

'Family?'

Kat nodded. 'Dean is my cousin.'

'Your cousin! Do you have other family here?'

'Yes, of course. My whole family is here. This is where I grew up.'

'Here?'

'Yes. I told you that.'

'No. You never said you grew up here. You told me you lived here. Those are two different things.'

'I know what you're thinking,' Kat said.

'How can you know what I'm thinking?'

'Because it's what everyone who's not from here thinks. You

assumed I moved here for work because why would someone *choose* to live here?'

'I guess I did think it was for your job,' Oliver agreed. 'But that's partly because everyone I know moves where their job takes them.'

'I've lived here my entire life, just about.' Give or take a few years in Adelaide, but she tried not to think too much about those years. 'I choose to live here because my family is here. And because I miss it when I'm not here.'

'What do you miss?'

'The community. The people. The beauty.' She could see from his expression that he didn't believe her. 'I'll show you. There's more to the outback than dust and flies.'

'It's a date,' Oliver said, smiling again, and Kat realised, just a fraction too late, that he'd played her and got just what he wanted.

'It's not a date,' she protested.

'You can call it whatever you like,' he said with a smile, 'but I'm going to call it a date.'

He reached towards her and Kat thought he was going to pick up her empty glass, but his fingers reached for her hand. His thumb stroked the side of her wrist before he turned her hand over and ran his thumb over the sensitive skin on the underside. Kat's insides turned liquid, she felt as though her bones were melting, and it took all her energy not to close her eyes and give in to the heat that flooded through her.

She needed to leave. To get out from under the spell he was casting over her. She was feeling vulnerable and she knew she was in danger of falling for his charm. He created an energy around him, around her.

'I should go,' she said as she pulled her hand away, breaking the spell before she made a complete fool of herself.

'I guess I'd better get to the gym,' he said as he stood, 'but I'll walk you to your car first.'

He kept a slight distance between them as they walked outside but even so she was aware of a field of attraction and desire surrounding them. Or at least surrounding her.

She turned towards him as they stopped at her car.

'I'll see you at work,' he said as he opened the door that she'd once again left unlocked. 'And I'm looking forward to our date,' he added, 'but until then...' he said as he bent his head and leant towards her.

Kat didn't intend to but she lifted her face, angling it up to him.

Was he going to kiss her?

Her eyelids drifted down, half-closed.

She could feel his breath on her cheek and then his lips pressed against her cheek, just in front of her ear, briefly touching her. Too briefly.

She opened her eyes.

He'd kissed her but not how she'd expected him to. Not how she wanted him to.

He was watching her and she knew he could read her mind. She'd wanted him to kiss her properly. She knew it and he knew it.

She needed to get a grip, she thought as she slid into her car. She was sure he had the same effect on dozens, hundreds, of women. Just because she felt something didn't mean he did. He probably didn't notice it. It was probably something he did out of habit. George had warned her but she couldn't ignore or deny the feelings he evoked in her. She shouldn't be so fascinated but she hadn't met anyone like him. Ever. It was as if he was from a different world.

He scared her. Not in a frightening sense but in a sense that he would have seen far more than she ever had; she had no doubt he would have had his share of beautiful women around the world and she wasn't worldly enough to compete. She didn't *want* to compete. Not unless she knew she could win. And she suspected there would only be one winner if she let Oliver Harding get his way.

She was certain he was not the man for her. Just as she knew she wasn't the woman for him. She wasn't going to be anyone's conquest. But she couldn't deny he was attractive. Charming. And sexy.

She knew it would be almost impossible to deny her desire if he kept up his charm offensive, so she suspected the question wasn't *could* she resist him, but rather how long could she resist him for?

'Good morning! How was your date?'

Kat jumped, spilling her coffee over the kitchen bench as Saskia's voice interrupted her morning routine. 'Jesus, Sas, you scared the life out of me.'

'Daydreaming about a cute actor, were you?'

'No,' Kat fibbed. 'And it wasn't a date.'

'Looked like one to me.'

'I was just there to meet some of the cast and crew,' she said as she mopped up the spilt coffee. But she couldn't help the blush she could feel creeping across her cheeks as Saskia's comment reminded her that she had promised Oliver a date. At least, in his words she had.

Saskia raised one eyebrow but didn't comment. She leant on the kitchen bench and sipped from her own mug that she'd brought in with her. Kat knew it would still be hot; Saskia hadn't come far. She and Dean lived next door.

Saskia and Dean, Roger and Maya, plus Kat's aunt and uncle all lived in the same street, with their underground houses dug into the same hill. As their family had expanded they had simply dug more rooms and added new entrances so they all had their own front door. Kat's own parents had dug a house in the same hill and she had moved back in with her father when she returned to Coober Pedy from Adelaide. She didn't mind living close to her family—she enjoyed the feeling of belonging—but sometimes the proximity could be disconcerting.

If the houses were viewed from outside, all that was obvious were the front doors and some windows. Gardens, or what passed for gardens in the arid country, were at the front, complete with barbecues or pizza ovens and outdoor seating areas used on the warm nights. The houses themselves extended back into the hill. Internally her father's house had white, lime-washed walls, which gave a welcome break from the perpetual sight of red earth. A few skylights and air vents protruded from the surface, but there was no way of telling how large the houses were from outside, and some were very large.

'When do you start work on the movie?' Saskia asked as she sat down at the kitchen table.

'I'm going out to the set this morning, but only to get a feel for filming. There are no stunts today.'

Saskia looked Kat up and down. 'Is that what you're wearing?'

Kat was wearing black three-quarter-length trousers and a loose camisole top. The clothes were comfortable and cool, perfect for the late autumn heatwave they were experiencing, but she could tell by Saskia's tone that she didn't approve. 'What's wrong with this?'

'Nothing, if you don't mind Oliver seeing you dressed like a homeless person.'

'I'm not dressing for him,' she said, even as she began to rethink her outfit.

'You're right. It probably doesn't matter. He probably doesn't care what you're wearing—he's only interested in getting you out of your clothes.'

'Saskia!'

'How about you?' Saskia continued, ignoring Kat's exclamation. 'Are you interested? You'd have to be comatose not to be.'

'He's not my type.'

'What? Drop-dead gorgeous isn't your type?'

Kat smiled but shook her head at the same time. 'He could have his pick of women—what would he want with a country girl like me? Even if he did set his sights on me, I'm not going to fall for him just because his pickings are limited out here.' How did she explain to Saskia that he made her nervous and that it was a mixture of excitement and uncertainty? She suspected he was far too experienced for her, and she didn't want Saskia to laugh at her by telling her so.

'I'm pretty sure he's already set his sights on you, and it wouldn't matter where you were, Kat, you'd get noticed. But if you think you can't handle him…' Saskia paused, waiting for a response, but when nothing was forthcoming she continued '…then you might as well go dressed as you are, or I could find you something else to wear?'

Kat checked her make-up in her rear vision mirror. She wasn't wearing much as it was too hot and most of it would just slide off her face, but she touched up her signature red lipstick, telling herself she didn't want to look like a country cousin in comparison to the actors on set but not admitting that she was really driven by a desire to look good for Oliver. She felt a little silly that she'd let Saskia talk her into changing her outfit but she had to admit she did look more presentable, and that boosted her confidence. The white fitted top clung to her and showed just a few centimetres of tanned, toned midriff, and the black and white vertical-striped loose trousers hugged her hips before flaring out over the pair of low wedge sandals she'd added. She was only on set as an observer today—it was a chance to get a feel for how things worked before her attendance was officially required and, because there were no stunts scheduled for today, she didn't need to be in clothes that would have to withstand an emergency.

She was met by George's assistant, Erica, who escorted her to the make-up trailer.

Oliver winked at her as she stepped inside and Kat's nervousness about being on set was replaced by the nervous excitement that she felt every time she saw him. It had been a long time since anyone had paid her some attention and she couldn't deny she found it extremely flattering.

In Coober Pedy all the locals knew her and she didn't really interact with the tourists, except when they needed her medical expertise. She preferred to be at home when she wasn't at work, but that habit wasn't conducive to meeting people. She couldn't remember the last time someone had asked her out.

'All done.' The make-up artist removed the disposable collar that protected Oliver's costume and he stood up. He was wearing a space suit, dirty and torn, and his make-up made him look as though he'd been through an ordeal, lost on an alien planet. He hadn't shaved, and Kat assumed he was supposed to look dishevelled, thirsty, and possibly in pain, but, to her eyes, he looked unbelievably good. The fake dirt and dust made his eyes even more noticeable, a more vivid blue.

'What are you filming today?'

'Do you know the plot?'

'Not really. George gave me a little overview but not a script. I know it's a science fiction movie but I have to admit that's not really my thing. I like romantic comedies.'

'I'll have to remember that. OK, the plot in a nutshell: Earth has set up a space station, an air force base in the sky, the first line of defence against alien attack. One space station has been badly damaged and we are supposed to be evacuating and returning to Earth, but my "ship" is hit and crash-lands on another, previously undiscovered, planet. I have a dozen crew on board. Mechanics, scientists, astronauts, physicists, defence. I'm the commander, the most senior defence person on the ship. The planet has an atmosphere but it's thin. Low oxygen—a bit like high altitude. There are no trees, nothing green, it's a barren place, but gas readings indicate moisture and we think there could be water somewhere. I've gone off to scout.

'I crash my vehicle and damage the windshield, so I'm affected by exposure to the heat and by altitude sickness. I lose consciousness and when I wake up I find myself in a cave. We're going to use the caves you showed George—it's been added to the schedule. I don't remember crawling into the cave but I see drag marks in the dirt. It looks like someone dragged me in, and then I notice cave drawings—signs of alien life. The cave goes deeper into the earth and I go as far as I can without any light, and I'm sure I can smell water.

'The scene we're filming this morning is a few days later; I'm feeling better and I've managed to fix the all-terrain vehicle. I still haven't seen any other life forms but in the film the audience knows I'm being watched by something, although they haven't seen anything yet either. I return to the spaceship, where I'm greeted very warmly by the leading lady, who thought I must have died.'

Oliver was smiling and Kat could imagine how that reunion scene was going to play out.

'That's Julia?'

'Yep,' he said as they reached the set. 'Grab a seat here,' he told her, indicating a chair next to George and handing her a pair of headphones so she could listen to the dialogue.

Filming began with Oliver arriving back at the spaceship. Julia's character saw the ATV approaching and came out of the spaceship to investigate.

The scene moved inside and Kat repositioned herself so that she could continue to watch on a screen.

Julia was playing a space soldier, Oliver's second-in-command. She had some medical training and had to attend to his injuries. She insisted that Oliver be quarantined and undergo a medical check-up. They were alone in the scene and Kat could feel herself blushing as Oliver's character stripped down to his underwear.

There were several screens in front of Kat, each showing a different angle. There was a wide shot and then close-ups of Julia and Oliver. Kat focused on the screen showing Oliver. She couldn't keep her eyes off him. He drew her in...the incredible colour of his eyes, the intense look on his face. She felt as if he was looking directly at her, even though she knew he wasn't. She could see why he was such a star. He was gorgeous, charismatic.

The scene intensified. Julia's character leant towards Oliver and then they were kissing. Kat felt hot and flustered, unsure where to look. It felt voyeuristic but she couldn't look away. She wondered what it would be like to be Julia.

The scene had taken most of the morning to film and in between takes Oliver chatted to the cast and crew. Kat could see why women fell for him: he was nice to everyone. Finally, they broke for lunch and Oliver came and sat beside her. He had stripped off his costume and was wearing a pair of shorts and a T-shirt now, his character's persona discarded with his clothes.

'Are you OK? You're not bored?' he asked.

'Not at all. I'm used to sitting around, waiting. As a paramedic it's part of my job description; we're happy when things are quiet. And this is a far more interesting way to pass the time.' It was exciting. The whole experience was a novelty. She wasn't bored, far from it, although she was a little bit jealous. 'Julia seems to have recovered from her crisis of the other night,' she said.

'For now. Let's hope things have calmed down on that front, although I doubt it.'

'What happened?'

'Her husband had an affair. Julia didn't want to work on this movie, she didn't want to leave him alone, but she was contractually obligated, so she's not happy that she has to be here, so far away from home. I think George has promised to fly her husband out here but it remains to be seen if he'll turn up. This movie could save my reputation and end her marriage, so I understand why she's upset, but the less drama we have, the quicker filming is wrapped here and the sooner she can get home to the States.'

'She didn't look like she was missing her husband during those scenes.'

Oliver laughed. 'That's the idea. She's a good actress.'

'Are you sure that's all it is?'

'Are you jealous?'

'No,' she lied.

'Believe me, it's all acting. I may have a reputation of romancing my leading ladies but not the married ones, and I'm really trying to clean up my image. I don't need any rumours circulating. If she wants revenge I'm not the one who's going to oblige. I don't want to get into any arguments with irate husbands. I do have empathy for her, though; I've been cheated on before and it's not a good position to be in. It's bad enough going through something like that in private, but when your disastrous love-life gets splashed across the tabloids it makes you wary. I feel for her but I can't afford to make her problems mine—I've got enough of my own.'

Oliver picked up their plates and took them back to the serving counter, leaving Kat to wonder who cheated on him and why. Had it made him more careful about his affairs?

It didn't seem so if the tabloids were to be believed, but there were always two sides to a story. Maybe his romances were just casual, or for publicity. That would be one way to protect yourself from heartache. She wondered what it would be like not knowing who you could trust.

'Are you staying a bit longer?' he asked when he returned. 'Do you want to watch more filming? The next scene involves some of the other characters, while I'm missing, presumed dead.'

'Do you always film out of sequence?' Kat asked; she hadn't imagined it happening like that.

'More often than not, I guess we do, but it depends on a lot of things.'

'Like what?'

'Weather and location mostly. Or sometimes if an actor has

to lose or gain weight or change their hairstyle through the movie…that will affect the order. It also might depend on who is required for the scene, if we need a lot of extras, things like that; they might be brought in for a few days to do all their scenes. Then, of course, there are always retakes, which can be difficult to manage, particularly if we've got other filming commitments for other projects. Would you like to watch? Otherwise we could hang out in my trailer?'

'I thought you didn't want any rumours.'

'Rumours with you I don't have an issue with—you're single and over the age of eighteen,' he said with a smile.

'With protective relations who spend their days blowing things up for fun. Are you sure you want to take them on?'

'They blow things up for fun?'

'Yes, but it's legitimate. They're opal miners.'

'And they mine using explosives?'

'Sometimes.'

'OK, forewarned is forearmed, I guess. If you like I can show you the reels from the other day; you can see what the stunts look like and why the first-aid officer quit. No ulterior motive, I promise. I'll even leave the door open if it makes you feel more comfortable.'

'I can't believe you walked away without a scratch,' she said when she'd finished watching the footage. She had forced herself to concentrate but it had been difficult. They were sitting side by side on the couch, as it had the best view of the screen, but, while Oliver appeared relaxed, Kat was a bundle of nerves. She was super-aware of him beside her. She could feel him breathing, and every time he moved she braced herself in case he touched her. Each time he did her heart raced, her mouth went dry and her skin tingled.

'I had a few bruises and a headache but I'm fine.'

'Why on earth would you do your own stunts?'

'Because it's fun.'

'Don't you worry about getting hurt?'

'I've always loved testing my limits. My brother and I grew up in a house with very strict rules, thanks to our father, and I always enjoyed breaking them. I guess I thought of them more as recommendations.'

'What happened when you got caught?'

'We were punished, so I learnt the hard way to balance risk and reward. If I thought the risk wasn't worth the punishment I learnt to rein in my wild side. Stunts are calculated risks, mostly. The buzz I get from doing them outweighs the risk that something might go wrong. It's Chris's job, and yours, to keep me safe.'

'If Chris does his job right then you shouldn't need me,' she retorted. 'There's only so much I can do.'

Kat liked to follow the rules. She'd seen too many times the things that could go wrong when rules were broken.

There was a knock on the door and Oliver was summoned back to Make-Up and Wardrobe.

'We're filming a love scene this afternoon, so the set is closed,' he told her, 'but if you're free later, why don't you come back for dinner? I'm helping out on the grill.'

'I have an ambulance shift tonight.' She could have left it at that—he didn't know how things worked around here—but she found herself elaborating. 'But I can be on call. I'll let Dave know where I am and he can call me in if he needs me.'

'Are you sure? I don't want to be held responsible if you're needed.'

'Positive. As long as I'm contactable it's fine.'

She had intended to heed George's warning and resist Oliver's charms, but it was harder than she'd anticipated. It was one thing to tell herself that she could resist him when she was home alone, but quite another when he greeted her with a big smile and laughter in his blue eyes. He was charming and irresistible and she suspected it was only a matter of time before he would win her over.

CHAPTER THREE

KAT PUSHED OPEN the door to the police station and squeezed herself inside. It looked as if the whole town had come running when the cry for help had gone out, and the small station was bursting at the seams. She'd been getting ready to go back to the film set for dinner when she'd received a call telling her that a missing person report had come in. She had called Oliver with her apologies and headed for the station. Unfortunately, a missing backpacker trumped her other plans. She searched the crowd for her cousins, knowing they would be in the thick of the action, as she wondered if she'd get another dinner date. No, not a date, she reminded herself, an invitation.

She'd just spotted her cousins when she heard someone calling her name. She turned around to find Oliver coming through the door behind her.

'Oliver! What are you doing here?'

'Well, I thought your excuse was either the best rejection I'd ever received, or if it was true we figured you could use some help.'

'We?'

Kat looked at the men filing in behind him and saw that Oliver had brought Chris and some of the crew with him.

'Someone has gone missing?' he asked.

'Pietro Riccardo, an Italian backpacker, has been reported missing by his girlfriend. He went noodling—fossicking for opal,' Kat clarified when she saw several confused expressions, 'on his own. The girlfriend didn't go with him because she had a headache, and Pietro hasn't come back. There's a public noodling area in the centre of town but he's not there. The police have called the hotels, bars, pubs and clubs, thinking he might have just stopped for a drink, but he's not at any of those either. We have to start spreading the search.'

'Is there something we can do? Can we help?'

'If you'd like to, thank you. I'll see if I can get you assigned to my search party.'

'You're searching? You're not taking the ambulance?'

Kat shook her head. 'The crew who were already on shift will stay at the station. We don't know which way Pietro's gone, so there's no point sending the ambulance off in one direction, only for them to have to turn around and head a different way. We'll split up into search parties, and the search will be coordinated by the Coober Pedy mine rescue team.'

'You're telling me this happens often enough that you have an official search and rescue unit?'

'Yes. There are enough accidents on the mines with both miners and locals that we are needed fairly often.' Kat and her cousins were all members of the team. 'We're assuming the missing backpacker is injured, which is why he hasn't returned of his own accord, but there's also a high possibility that he's fallen down a disused mine shaft.'

'Are there really exposed mine shafts around here?'

'Of course. There are thousands of them. You've seen the warning signs, haven't you?'

'The signs that say "Don't Run", "Deep Shafts", "Don't Walk Backwards"?'

'Yes.'

'Those signs are serious? They're not just for the tourists to take selfies with?'

'They're definitely serious. We're not on a movie set; this is real.'

Oliver frowned. 'And just how often do people fall down mine shafts?'

'More often than you'd think and far more often than we'd like. You were told to watch where you walk around town, weren't you?'

'Yes. But I didn't really think about why.'

'Luckily for you most of the shafts in town have been covered over. It's just once you get out of town you need to be careful. People have gone missing and never been found. It's presumed they're down a hole somewhere. It's a perfect way to get away with murder.'

'You're kidding.'

'I'm not actually, but don't worry, that doesn't happen as much now. It's not the wild west it once was out here. People are a little more law-abiding.'

'OK, let me get this straight. We're going to be wandering around, in the dark, looking down old mine shafts.'

'He could be anywhere, and he might not be down a mine shaft, but if you're worried, no one will mind if you back out.'

'I'm not backing out. I offered to help and unless I'm going to be in the way I'm happy to be another pair of eyes.'

'The more people we have searching the better. Pietro didn't take his car, which is good and bad. Bad because we can't search for the car, which would be easier to find, good because it means he needs to be within walking distance of town, but bad again because we don't know in which direction he's gone and his mobile phone either isn't on, is flat or is out of service range.' She broke off as she was approached. 'Hey, Dave. Oliver, this is Dave Reed, another paramedic. Dave, this is Oliver Harding; he and some of the cast and crew from the movie have offered to help search.'

'Good to meet you; appreciate the help.' Dave was his normal, relaxed self; good in a crisis, he was one of Kat's favourite colleagues. They had been rostered on together for the night shift until the missing-person report changed their plans. Dave and Oliver shook hands as the crowd was silenced so instructions could be given.

They were spilt into search parties to head out of town in all directions. Kat took Oliver with her and they joined Dean and Roger. She was glad to be in the same search party as her cousins, not only because of their search and rescue skills but also because they were experienced miners who were fit and strong, but she was a little concerned about whether they would see Oliver as a valuable asset or as a liability. She'd been aware of them watching her as she'd spoken with Oliver and she hoped they didn't make him uncomfortable. As far as she was concerned, he was welcome to join them, and she didn't need her cousins to run interference on her behalf.

They collected their torches and Dave also handed Kat a backpack full of supplies that he had collected from the ambulance station on his way.

'What about tracker dogs?' Oliver asked after he'd offered to carry Kat's backpack and hoisted it onto his shoulders.

'The police force doesn't have tracker dogs, and the Aboriginal trackers we do have said the ground is too dry and there are too many prints in town to follow. If they knew which direction Pietro went in then maybe they'd have a chance, but,' she shrugged, 'we'll just have to walk and hope.'

Their group headed south, walking in a long line, side by side. They were supposed to spread out, swinging their lights in an arc several metres to either side of them, but Oliver kept bunching up, walking nearer to Kat, staying close to her. She wasn't sure if it was deliberate or if he wasn't aware that he was doing it, but she was very aware. He was quiet, there were no jokes, no banter, so he appeared to be taking this seriously, but she was still super-conscious of him.

The desert night was quiet and still, the air clear and cold. The sun had long since set, taking the heat of the day with it.

The search party continued their slow and steady pace, taking it in turns to call Pietro's name.

'Are you sure his girlfriend was at the hostel?' Oliver asked after several minutes of silence. 'They didn't have an argument and she saw an opportunity to get rid of him?'

Kat laughed. 'I don't think she's a suspect and I think you've got an overactive imagination!'

'Maybe I've read too many movie scripts, but there's always a twist in the tale.'

They were into the second hour of the search, when Pietro was finally located, injured but alive, at the bottom of a disused mine shaft.

Oliver sat on a rock in a desert in the middle of South Australia and listened to the experienced rescuers plan Pietro's extraction from the mine shaft. There were literally thousands of mine shafts, as Kat had told him, and he'd thought it was an impossible task to find someone who could have fallen into one, so had been amazed when Pietro had actually been tracked down. The whole situation was surreal.

He listened to Pietro's apologies echoing up from the shaft. Oliver felt for the guy. He sounded embarrassed. It turned out he was a doctor, in Australia on a three-month holiday before he was due to return to Italy to start his surgical residency. He was mortified that he had sustained an injury and needed rescuing, but Oliver thought he should be grateful that he'd been found, that the people of Coober Pedy knew what to do.

But even Oliver couldn't believe what he heard next. What those same people were planning on doing. Or, more to the point, who was going to be doing it. He stood up and approached Kat, forgetting in his consternation that he probably should stay out of the way and that this retrieval had nothing to do with him.

'What are you doing?' he asked. 'You're not going down there?' The shaft was pitch black, the opening narrow, maybe only three feet wide, but the drop to the bottom was deep. When they had shone their torches down hundreds of these while looking for Pietro, Oliver had got the impression that this was what the mines looked like until Kat had explained that a lot of these narrow shafts were from exploratory drilling. If opal traces, or anything that had potential, was found the miners would excavate further. They might go down the hole for a look but most of the mines were now open cut using big machines. But it seemed as though Kat was about to descend into this darkness.

'Of course I am,' Kat replied. 'Someone has to. That shaft is over thirty feet deep. He says he's broken his ankle but he could have sustained more serious injuries. He needs to be assessed and then he needs to be brought up to the surface, which means he needs a harness. Someone has to attach that to him. There's not much room, and I'm the only one with the right experience who will fit.'

'Is it safe? It won't collapse?'

'It's sandstone. The same rock we build our houses with. It's safe enough. You don't need to worry—I've done this before. It's no more dangerous than when you do your own stunt work. Probably safer. You're not worried because I'm a woman, are you?'

'No, of course not. I work with stunt women all the time, and I know they're as capable as men.' But he was worried because it was Kat.

'I'm trained for this. I'll be fine,' she told him as she stepped into a harness.

Oliver watched, his heart in his mouth, as Kat's cousin Roger checked the harness. He had to trust that Kat knew what she was doing but that didn't mean he had to like it. He didn't want anything to happen to her before he got a chance to know her better. He had never met anyone like her and the more time they spent together the more fascinating he found her. She looked like a supermodel but seemed completely unaware of how stunning she was. She was smart and sexy but with an unusual air of innocence. He knew he had to be careful. She didn't seem as wise in the ways of the world as the women he normally mixed with, and he'd seen how her cousins kept one eye on her at all times—which meant they had one eye on him too tonight, which, he had to admit, made him a little uncomfortable, but he was respectful, and despite what the tabloids said about him that had always been his way.

A winch on the front of the four-by-four police vehicle lowered Kat into the hole. Oliver didn't think he breathed once until, after what seemed like a lifetime, she finally emerged again. With Pietro strapped to her.

Oliver wanted to rush over to her to make sure she was OK but this was not about the two of them and this time he forced himself to wait in the background as Kat, Dave and the other paramedics, who had arrived with the ambulance, attended to their patient. He felt like a teenage schoolboy longing to be noticed, but he was prepared to wait.

Eventually, as Pietro was being loaded into the ambulance, Kat came over to him. 'I'm sorry, I have to go. Pietro's English is good but his Italian is better. I speak Italian,' she said with a shrug, 'so I've offered to go with him to the hospital.'

'Of course.' Oliver didn't have any expectations that they'd get time together tonight; he realised that her job came first. Much like his. He couldn't object to that.

'Thank you for your help. I'm sorry I couldn't make it to dinner.'

'That's OK. I've got tomorrow off. If you're free we could reschedule till then.'

She hesitated and he prepared himself for the brush-off, but she surprised him when she said, 'I'd like that. But, assuming the rest of my shift is quiet, why don't I pick you up in the morning? I have a place I'd like you to see. Can you be ready early? Say, eight o'clock?'

Saskia was ready and waiting when the ambulance pulled up at the hospital.

'This is Pietro Riccardo...'

Kat pushed the stretcher through the emergency doors as she listened to Dave's summary of Pietro's suspected injuries, most of which Saskia knew from the phone call they'd made en route, and then the summary of treatment so far.

'Put him in the first cubicle. Damien is already here; we'll get him sorted,' Saskia told them, before turning her attention to the patient. 'Hello, Pietro, my name is Saskia.'

'Italian is his first language,' Kat told her before translating for Pietro. 'Saskia is a nurse and this is our doctor, Damien,' Kat continued the introductions as they wheeled Pietro into a treatment bay. 'They're going to do a more thorough assessment and I'll stay to translate if you need me to, OK?'

'Grazie.'

'Are you in pain?'

Pietro was still clutching the little green Penthrax whistle but he shook his head.

Despite the pain relief he seemed quite capable of following the proceedings and understanding what Damien and Saskia were saying—perhaps due to his medical training the English words didn't sound too unfamiliar—but Kat stayed with him until he was taken for X-rays.

He was lucky. He had a fracture dislocation of his left ankle which needed surgery and a suspected ligament tear in his right shoulder, but he'd escaped more serious injury.

'I want him to have some detailed scans of his lower back, head and right shoulder, but I think he's been relatively fortunate,' Damien said as he reviewed the plain X-rays, which was all they were equipped to take at the Coober Pedy hospital. 'We'll need to call the flying doctor and get him transferred to Adelaide. Is he travelling with someone?'

'His girlfriend,' Kat said. 'She should be here—someone was going to collect her from the backpackers' hostel.'

Kat explained what was happening to Pietro while Saskia got him comfortable, and then she and Kat left him dozing while they waited for the retrieval team.

'So, I hear Oliver helped with the search,' Saskia said as she made them coffee.

'How did—?' Kat began to ask before realising she already knew the answer. 'Dean told you.'

Saskia just grinned in reply.

'What else did he say?'

'Nothing much.'

Kat knew that wouldn't be true. 'C'mon, Sas, Dean always has an opinion about any man in my life.'

She knew she'd made a mistake as soon as she'd finished the sentence and if she'd hoped Saskia had missed it she was out of luck.

Saskia almost spat out her coffee. 'I knew it! You like him. Not that anyone could blame you—there's a reason Oliver Harding has been voted the world's sexiest man. Twice.'

'I said *any* man.'

'You say tomato…' Saskia was still grinning. 'Dean said that Oliver couldn't keep his eyes off you.'

'He said that?' Kat felt a warm glow.

'Mmm-hmm.' Saskia considered her. 'So, you like him.' It wasn't a question.

'I do. But—'

'No buts—'

'But you know how people talk in this town.'

'You worry too much about what people think. Besides, you're twenty-seven, you're a grown woman, you're your own boss.'

'That's not exactly true. You know what it's like when you've grown up here—everyone has an opinion on how you live your life.'

'Well, all I'm saying is that he seems keen and it would be a shame to let this opportunity go to waste. If it's not you spending time with him, it will be someone else. Is that what you want?'

No. She didn't want that.

'You don't have to marry the guy,' Saskia continued. 'Don't

overthink things, just have some fun. Oliver looks like he knows how to have fun. How long is he here for?'

'Only a few weeks.'

'If you're worried about what people think I'm sure you could manage to be discreet for that long. Treat it like a holiday romance.'

'I'm not looking for a holiday romance. I'm looking for the person I'm going to spend the rest of my life with. What's the point of starting something that can go nowhere?'

'Are you kidding? The point is there's a man in town who has literally been voted the sexiest man alive and who seems to have taken a fancy to you. You've been bemoaning the lack of men here for months. Are you seriously telling me you'd pass up this opportunity? With a man who looks like he does? You must be crazy.'

She wasn't crazy but she was scared. Scared she wouldn't be able to control things. He had awakened her senses, he was making her feel things she hadn't felt in a long time. He made her laugh. He made her nervous. Excited. Happy. She liked him, really liked him, but she was worried things would get complicated. Coober Pedy was a small town. How could she expect to have fun without everyone else knowing her business? Could she keep him separate from her everyday life? She didn't need to be the centre of town gossip or to have any interference from her family.

Had she made a mistake by asking him to spend the day with her tomorrow?

Maybe she had, but she didn't want to change her mind. She had planned to take him away from town; she wanted to show him the wildness and beauty of her world. She could still do that. She had the perfect spot in mind. A place where she doubted they would see another soul.

Oliver was waiting in front of the hotel when Kat turned off the main street and climbed out of her dusty four-by-four. She was wearing a T-shirt and a pair of very short denim cut-offs. She looked amazing, but that wasn't enough to keep his attention. He was completely distracted by the canoe that was strapped to the roof of her car.

'Now I think I've seen everything,' he said as he kissed her cheek. She smelt of soap and sunshine. 'What on earth have you got planned for us? I thought we only had a few hours.'

'We do.'

'So the canoe is just for show?'

'You'll have to wait and see. Did you get my message?' she said as she looked him over. 'Did you bring something to swim in?'

'I did. But you have me intrigued. A canoe and a bathing suit. I flew into Coober Pedy and I don't remember seeing any water for about four hundred miles.'

'You weren't looking in the right places,' she said as they got into the car and slammed the doors. 'The name Coober Pedy means boys' waterhole.'

'Does it? I was told it meant white man in a hole.'

'That's sort of true. In the local Aboriginal culture a boy is a male who hasn't been through an initiation ceremony. There was a waterhole for those boys near here. The Pitjantjatjara word for white man is the same as for boy, as neither of them have been initiated, so some people translated it as "white man's waterhole" as opposed to "boy's water hole", and somewhere along the line it became "white man in a hole".'

They headed east out of town, past the never-ending mullock heaps that dotted the landscape—piles of dirt that had been dug out of the earth in the quest for opal—past numerous damaged, abandoned cars and dead animals that were decaying on the side of the road.

'The two often go hand in hand,' Kat said when Oliver commented on the roadside carnage. 'People don't drive according to the conditions. You shouldn't really drive at night out here if it can be avoided. Cattle, emus, kangaroos, even wombats can do a lot of damage to your car if you hit one of them, particularly at speed. We have a high number of fatal accidents.'

'But why don't the cars get towed?'

'Most do eventually,' she said as they drove past a utility vehicle that was crumpled, bonnet compacted, windscreen smashed. Black skid marks could be seen across the road. 'That one was recent. Just a couple of weeks ago. The teenage driver swerved to avoid a cow, lost control and rolled the car.'

'Were you here?'

She nodded. 'Dave and I were on shift.'

'Was everyone all right?' he asked as he kept his eyes on the wreck.

'No. There was a fatality. A boy had been riding in the tray of the ute—he was thrown out and died at the scene. Another was in a critical condition and was evacuated by the flying doctor, and two more were taken to the local hospital.'

'I can't imagine doing your job. It must be tough. How do you cope with it?'

'It's a rewarding job. I like feeling as though I'm making a difference. Even with that accident, the fatality was dreadful, a terrible waste of a young life, but Dave and I managed to keep the other boy alive until the flying doctor got here. I've seen so many accidents like this, so you take the good with the bad, but it's why I like to follow the rules, not break them. Life isn't something that should be taken for granted.'

He remembered her comment about him doing his own stunts and wondered if she would accuse him of taking life for granted. He didn't take it for granted but he did think that life was for living and he wasn't going to sit around and watch other people living their lives. He wanted to be a participant.

Kat slowed her car and turned off the road onto a smaller dirt track. The faded signpost read *Lake Cadibarrawirracanna*.

'There's a lake out here?'

Kat nodded. 'A salt lake.'

'Does the name have a meaning?'

'It does. It means *stars dancing on the water.*'

'It sounds beautiful,' he said, although he didn't think it actually would be. He couldn't picture a lake in this barren landscape. Not even his active imagination could envision that.

'It is. I wanted you to see the beauty in the desert. You just need fresh eyes.'

'Wow.' They crested a small rise and Oliver was stunned at the sight of a vast lake, shimmering silver in the sun, before them. It stretched for miles across the flat landscape, a few trees clinging to its edges. A flock of birds rose off the water and took to the sky, startled by the sound of the engine, but other than that there was nothing else but land, water and sky. Now that the birds had flown he couldn't see another living thing except for him and Kat.

Kat parked in the shade of a stand of trees and he helped her lift the two-man canoe from the roof of the car.

'Do you want to take the canoe out on the lake?' she asked as she passed him a blanket and some cushions from the back of the car.

Oliver spread the blanket on the sand. He didn't want to paddle just now. He wanted to just sit and take in the view. And Kat.

'Later, I think. I can't remember the last time I sat and did nothing. I'm usually doing a movie, learning lines for a movie, doing publicity, interviews, going to red carpet events.'

'Or going to parties.'

Something in her tone put him on alert. 'Have you been reading about me?'

'A little,' she admitted.

'Don't believe everything you read.'

'George told me the same thing. That's why I thought I'd ask you; you can tell me what was and wasn't true.'

'Such as?' he asked, although he was pretty sure he knew what she would have read and what subject she would be interested in.

'Did a girl overdose and die at a party at your house? Is that true?'

'Yes.' He wasn't surprised by her question, that story was currently the first thing that popped up if someone did an internet search on his name.

'What happened?'

'I'm not one hundred per cent sure. I was away; I was in New Orleans working on a film and had friends staying in my house. They held a party. From what the police told me the girl who overdosed allegedly brought the drugs with her, something went wrong and she died.'

'You weren't there?'

'No, but it was my house, so I was linked by association. My publicist and agent thought it would be a good idea to keep me out of Hollywood for a bit longer while it was investigated so they sent me here. I thought it was probably a good idea too but this time I haven't left any friends staying there. I used to host a lot of parties, but I'm rethinking that scene now. I'm going to make some changes to my lifestyle when I get home. This trip down under will give me a chance to reset.' He stood up; he didn't want to talk about his old life any longer, and he was telling the truth when he said he was thinking about making changes. It was time to start behaving more responsibly. He was thirty-two years old; he couldn't continue his partying ways for ever. 'How about that paddle now?'

They worked up an appetite taking the canoe out on the lake, but Kat had anticipated that and had packed a picnic.

'Where did you get all of this on a Sunday morning?' Oliver asked as she unpacked cold meats and fruit from an ice box.

'I raided the pantry. My family is Italian. Someone is always in the kitchen making something or preserving something. I have my father's salami, my aunt Rosa's sun-dried tomatoes, my cousin's wife's bread,' she said as she handed him a loaf of bread.

'This bread smells fresh—surely that wasn't in the pantry?'

'No, Maya, that's Roger's wife, made it this morning. She lives next door.'

'Next door?'

'Yes. My whole family lives in the same street. In the same hill.'

'That sounds a bit close for comfort.'

Kat shrugged. 'It's how it's always been.'

'I'd love to see inside an underground house.'

She was tempted to invite him to hers but there was bound to be someone around. If not her father, it would be her aunt or cousins. 'It's not so different to your hotel. We have front doors, front windows, electricity, running water. It's just on a smaller scale than the hotel.'

'What happens if you're claustrophobic?'

'I don't know. It doesn't bother me. The rooms are light and ventilated. We have skylights and air vents. You must have noticed all the metal shafts poking up out of the hills in town. Those are ventilation shafts. They're wrapped with wire to stop the snakes entering through them.'

'And it's safe? The houses don't collapse?'

'The rock around here is sandstone, and it's very stable—we can excavate large spaces without needing structural support. We've got some enormous underground spaces in town. The Serbian church and a couple of the museums are massive. If you want to see a house, Faye's is open to tourists.'

'You're not going to invite me over?'

'It's not my house. It's my father's.'

'You still live with your parents?'

She felt the familiar pang at the mention of parents. 'I live with my father,' she clarified. 'My mother died a few years ago.'

'I'm sorry, Kat. How old were you?'

'Twenty-two. She was killed in a car accident.'

'Out here?'

She nodded. The memories were still painful. Her feelings

of guilt still high. 'A bus had been sitting behind a truck, trying to overtake, the driver got impatient and pulled out over double white lines to have a look, and my mother was driving in the opposite direction. He smashed into my mother's car. It was his fault, he didn't obey the road rules, but he survived, while my mother died at the scene.

'I came back here after she died to be with my dad. And I'm still here. I am the single daughter of an Italian father. We don't move out until we get married.' Her family owned a lot of land and the only thing that would change when she married was that her father and uncle and cousins would dig her a house next to the rest of them, but Oliver had sounded so shocked she didn't think he needed to hear that too.

'How old were you when you left home?' she asked. Oliver was watching her closely and she wondered if he was going to let her change the subject. She hoped so; she didn't want to talk about her mother, she didn't want to be sad. She breathed a sigh of relief as Oliver followed her lead.

'I went to college in California when I was seventeen. My parents were in Japan.'

'You went to college? To study acting?'

'Actually, no. I went to law school. Acting wasn't considered a career and one of my father's sons was always expected to go into the defence force. My brother refused, so that left me. I had no intention of joining the force either so I enrolled in law school under the pretence that I could join the armed forces that way. But once I got to college, I realised I had visions of myself as a lawyer standing in front of a court room arguing cases. Performing, I suppose. Much like what you see in the movies. *That's* what I wanted to do. So I joined the drama clubs and I found I had a talent for it, so then I started auditioning for movie roles and when I got my first one I dropped out of law school. My father has barely spoken to me since.'

'Because you didn't join the army?'

'Because I am a disappointment and he disapproves of my career choice. Because I chose acting over fighting.'

'And what about your mother? What did she think?'

'My mother is the daughter of an army general and now a wife of an army general. She followed orders.'

'What?'

'Orders *might* be the wrong word,' Oliver said, but to Kat's ears it sounded as if it was exactly what he meant, 'but she certainly never questioned Dad's decisions. Never argued. I can't say that I blame her. Isaac and I learnt that lesson early on too. The moment we were old enough we left home. It was the only way we could do what we wanted. Our mother didn't have that option.'

'How often do you see your parents?'

'I don't visit. I speak to my mother when my father's not around. She believes her loyalty is to her husband, but I think she's happy if I'm happy.'

'And are you happy?' Kat couldn't imagine being happy without her family.

'Yes. I get to experience all kinds of things; I travel the world pretending to be other people and giving people an escape from their everyday lives, from the world. I'm having fun.'

'So, what's next for you, after this movie?'

'I would love to have a role in a musical. I've done comedy, action, romantic leads, but I'd love an opportunity to try something new. I'd be the next Hugh Jackman if I could. You know, he started on the stage in musicals.'

'Can you sing?'

'Not well.'

'Dance?'

'Not as well as I sing,' he laughed. 'But dancing I can learn. Growing up, I wasn't allowed to have dancing lessons. It wasn't something boys did. Of course the more I was told I couldn't do something the more I wanted to. Would you like to come dancing with me?'

'In Coober Pedy? There aren't a lot of places to dance around here.'

'All you need is some music and a willing partner. Actually, music is optional. We could dance right now if you wanted to.'

Kat had learnt by now that Oliver didn't take anything seriously. His life was all about fun. In comparison, she took *everything* seriously.

He was making her nervous. Not in a bad way, but she was worried that he was going to convince her to dance and she didn't think she'd be able to handle that. She knew being in his arms would be her undoing.

She stood up.

'Are we going to dance?' he asked.

She shook her head and reached for the ice box. 'No, we need to get going. I've got to get back—I'm going to my cousin's for dinner.' She tidied up the remains of their picnic, picked up their glasses and packed them away.

'The one who lives next door?'

'Yes.'

'You're having dinner together again?'

'It's kind of a weekly ritual.'

'Really? Wouldn't you rather stay here with me?' He was standing now too. He lifted her hair and tucked it over her shoulder. His fingers skimmed her flesh, making it hum where he touched her. He was standing close and his eyes were mesmerising. He was engaging, funny, charming and incredibly good-looking, and Kat was tempted but she didn't give in.

'I'm expected there.'

'And do you always do what's expected?'

'Pretty much.' Following the rules and doing what was expected was part of her personality, but circumstances had also influenced her behaviour. She'd seen death and disaster first hand, and growing up in such a harsh environment had tainted her perceptions of what she could get away with.

'That's a pity. We could have fun.'

She'd forgotten what it was like to have fun. To have dreams.

'You're blushing,' he said. 'Do you think I'm flirting with you?

Kat didn't reply. She couldn't. Oliver was standing so close, with his hand on her arm, and his proximity stripped her of the capability of speech.

'You should,' he added. 'I am.' He grinned, his slow smile stretching from one corner of his gorgeous mouth to the other.

'Why on earth would you want to flirt with me?'

'Because you are incredibly beautiful.'

She laughed. She wanted to believe him but she couldn't. 'You must have met hundreds of women who are more beautiful than me.'

'I can honestly say I haven't met one as beautiful as you who hasn't had any help. So either you have an amazing surgeon and I am a blind fool or you are naturally stunning.'

'I am ordinary.'

'I disagree. You are beautiful and interesting. A little mysterious. It's like finding a pearl or a diamond out of place. A thing of beauty in a hostile environment.'

'I think I'm more like an opal. Tough and at home in the outback.'

'Perhaps, but that definitely makes you unique, which makes you more interesting. At least to me. My father moved us around the world when I was growing up and for the past twelve years I've continued to travel in the world of showbiz, but I don't get to meet many people like you. You fascinate me. Your background, the career you've chosen, the fact that you look so unexpected out here and yet you seem so comfortable. Content. Everyone I meet is competing for something—the next part, the next girl, the next dollar. You're refreshing.'

'And you are a flatterer.'

'Is it working?'

Yes, she thought, but that's not what she said. 'Not yet. You'll have to try a bit harder. I'm not that sort of girl.'

She suspected that, where Oliver was concerned, she might be exactly that type of girl, but she would make him work just a little bit harder. It wouldn't do him any harm.

He bent his head, brushing his lips over her ear, and she almost gave in then and there. Could he feel it? she wondered. Could he feel her self-control slipping?

'Well, I'm not going to give up and, to be fair, I have warned you, the more I'm told I can't have something, the more I want it.'

He was teasing her, testing her, and she knew she would eventually give in. She didn't have a hope in hell of resisting him for ever.

CHAPTER FOUR

KAT WAS ON set early for her first official day of duty. The sun was still rising in the east and the morning light streaked the sky with pink and gold and turned the earth a muted red. The landscape looked as though it had been touched up by an artist's brush using all the colours of an Aboriginal painting—ochre, gold, crimson, scarlet and the pink of a galah's feathers. The view was incredible and Kat hoped the colours would be captured on screen.

She sat on a chair behind George. She could see Oliver on two different screens over the director's shoulder but, looking across the flat planes of the earth, she could also see him standing on top of the hill, waiting for his cue.

Her mind drifted as she waited for filming to begin. Once again, she found her thoughts returning to the day they'd spent together at the lake. She had been pleasantly surprised about what a good time she'd had. They had flirted and laughed but, more importantly, they had talked and talked. She had shared things with him that she hadn't talked about in a long time, things she had never talked to anyone except Saskia about. And Oliver had listened.

Kat was beginning to think that maybe they could have a relationship that had some substance to it. There was definitely an attraction between them and they shared a sense of humour, but was that enough to overcome the differences she also knew they had? He was worldly, charming, independent and liked to push the boundaries. She was sheltered, sensible, a nurturer and a rule-follower. He might think she was refreshing but she suspected he might soon be bored. She suspected that, in reality, she was too vanilla for him.

'Action.'

The command came through the headset she was wearing and jolted her back to the present.

She saw Oliver start walking. The land was dry, the earth hard-packed, but Oliver's feet were sinking into sand. She knew George wanted the effect of soft ground making it arduous going for Oliver's character, and the prop crew had added a deep layer of fine red sand to the hill, reminding Kat that, in Oliver's world, nothing was really as it seemed.

The camera zoomed in and Kat switched her attention to the screen. She couldn't look away as the camera focused in on Oliver's face. His blue eyes were electric against the rose gold of the sky.

He continued to trudge across the ground and she could see him scanning the horizon and then, suddenly, he disappeared from the screen.

Kat heard her sharp intake of breath and flicked her gaze back to the hill. Oliver was tumbling down, head first.

She knew this was a stunt but it looked so real. She saw Oliver bouncing off the ground and wondered if, or hoped, he was wearing protective padding. It looked dangerous. And painful. She didn't want to watch but she couldn't look away.

Her whole body was tense. Her hands were clenched into tight fists and she couldn't breathe. The whole stunt probably lasted twenty seconds but it felt like a lifetime before Oliver finally hit the bottom of the hill, landing with a thud. Kat imagined she could feel the air being forced out of his lungs.

She waited, still holding her breath, for him to get up. For him to move.

The set was quiet.

No one moved. No one spoke.

What were they waiting for?

Kat didn't know but one thing she did know was that Oliver still hadn't moved. Surely he should be up by now?

He must be hurt.

Winded. Injured. Unconscious.

He could be any of those things.

Her instincts kicked in. She leapt off her chair and dropped the headset onto the seat. She grabbed her backpack, which was at her feet, and took off across the red sand, sprinting as fast as she could over the stony ground, hoping someone would think to grab her heavier, second bag of equipment.

'Cut!'

She was halfway across the site when she heard George's direction. Were they still filming? Had she just ruined the scene? Was this all part of the action?

She didn't break stride. It was too bad if she'd ruined it. She didn't care. It would be much worse if their star was injured and she left him lying on the ground. She was going to do her job and she wasn't going to let anyone stop her.

She reached Oliver's side.

He still hadn't moved.

His eyes were closed but she could see his chest rising and falling. As she dropped her backpack in the dust and knelt beside him, he opened his eyes.

She looked into his piercing blue eyes. Was one pupil slightly more dilated than the other?

She placed one hand on his chest. 'Don't move.'

Kat's face swam into focus.

The first thing he noticed were her red lips. The rest of her was a little fuzzy around the edges. Maybe he was hurt worse than he thought.

'Are they still filming?' he asked.

'What?'

'Are they still filming? I'm supposed to get up and keep moving.' At least, that was what he thought he was supposed to do. His mind was a little hazy.

'They're not filming but you're not getting up until I've checked you out. You've just fallen down a hill and got the wind knocked out of you.'

'I was supposed to fall down the hill. It's called acting.'

He could see George and some of the crew approaching. He felt bruised and sore but there was no way he was going to lie meekly on the ground. It was time to get up. Kat's hand was on his chest, keeping him on the ground. He could stand if he wanted to—she wasn't putting any pressure on him, just a warning hold.

He lifted his head and felt the earth spin a little. There was a sharp, stabbing pain in his left side as he sat up and he struggled not to wince, hoping Kat didn't notice.

'Oliver! You're obviously hurt—lie down and let me check you out. What am I doing here if you're not going to listen to me?' It seemed she hadn't missed the grimace.

She insisted that he stay down while she examined him. She was obviously annoyed with him; he thought she was poking and prodding him a bit harder than was necessary. She made him breathe deeply, move his limbs and head this way and that. He managed to do everything she asked, albeit with some discomfort, but he was sure he wasn't badly injured.

Kat seemed to have a different opinion. 'I think you might have cracked a rib. You should go to the hospital for precautionary X-rays.'

'Is that really necessary, Kat?' George asked. 'Isn't there something you could do for him here? We're behind on filming already.'

'He's not in any condition to film any stunts until he gets checked,' Kat argued.

'What if I shuffle scenes so there is no more stunt work today? You can stay and supervise. If you think we're putting his health at risk I'll let you take him off for X-rays. But if he's managing he can have X-rays at the end of the day.'

'There's no crepitus, just tenderness and pain on inhalation.'

'I have no idea what that means.'

'I'm thinking out loud,' Kat said. 'It means that with strapping, some pain relief and anti-inflammatory medication he might be OK. Give me twenty minutes now—that's enough time for oral pain relief to kick in—and then we'll reassess.'

Oliver was able to strip his costume off with some assistance. His ribs were painful but he was determined not to give Kat any reason to cart him off to hospital. Once again he was semi-naked and being attended to, but this time it was Kat, not Julia, assessing his injuries. Unfortunately they were in a tent in the middle of the desert, surrounded by dozens of crew, and his injuries were real, which put a bit of a dampener on things.

Kat strapped his ribs and he managed to work through the rest of the day. He was stiff and sore as the day wore on but he didn't quit. Kat had watched him like a hawk and the moment they wrapped for the day she bundled him off to the hospital.

'Hello again, Oliver. This is a pleasant surprise.'

He recognised Saskia as he and Kat stepped through the doors into Emergency. 'I didn't realise you were a nurse,' he said, his hopes that he could talk his way out of an examination evaporating. He knew he wouldn't be able to convince both Kat and Saskia that he was fine.

He suffered through more tests with the doctor before he was sent for X-rays.

'You have a mild concussion,' he was informed. That made two this week, Oliver thought, but he kept that information to himself. 'But there's no apparent fracture,' Damien said when the X-rays were developed. 'That doesn't mean you can't have a small crack somewhere that's just not showing up, but there's no major skeletal damage. Just soft tissue—a sprain, some swelling and bruising. Ice packs, some pain relief and some anti-inflammatory meds should do the trick. Rest tonight and then movement as comfortable.'

'I can go back to work?'

Damien nodded.

'What about monitoring the concussion? He's staying at the Cave Hotel,' Saskia asked before looking knowingly at Kat and adding, 'Alone. Shouldn't he have some supervision?'

'You haven't got any nausea? Haven't vomited?' Damien asked.

'No,' Oliver replied. He wasn't going to consent to supervision or to being admitted to hospital. He had a dull headache but he wasn't going to jeopardise the movie or his career by appearing incapacitated. Besides, his vision had cleared.

'I'm not sure we can justify a bed,' Damien said, 'But if you feel unwell either come back in or call 000. That's the emergency number.'

'000 will just call Kat,' Saskia told him as Damien left them. 'That doesn't sound like a bad compromise.'

'No, it won't get me,' Kat said. 'I'm not working tonight.'

'Even better,' Saskia replied. 'Why don't you take Oliver with you now, Kat? You don't have anything else to do, do you? And that way you can keep an eye on him. Make sure he's OK.'

That sounded good to Oliver. 'I'll buy you dinner,' he offered.

'This isn't a date.'

'OK, but one day we'll have a proper date.'

He figured she could call it whatever she liked but he would treat it like a date.

It had been a long time since he'd asked a woman on a date because he'd wanted to get to know her. He'd been burnt once and had since shied away from dating except when he needed to do it for publicity. It kept things simple. There were no expectations if it was purely a business arrangement. There was no chance of disappointment on either side if the 'date' was mutually beneficial, and if the night ended with the two of them between the sheets it had always been mutually agreed upon with no suggestion that it made the evening into anything more than what it had been.

But he was well aware that he needed to curtail his brief encounters, he needed to clean up his reputation and make an effort to redeem himself from a party-going playboy to a serious, eligible, respectable man. He needed to commit some time to getting to know someone on a deeper level, to having a conversation that was about more than what cocktail he could buy them or what they'd like for breakfast, and he could do much worse than spend that time with Kat. He had no problem with getting to know her better. And, at some point in the near future, he would get her to agree to go on a proper date with him, but for now he'd be happy with whatever time she would give him.

In the end Kat agreed to dinner. Her only other option was to take Oliver home with her to feed him, and she was *not* going to introduce him to her father. Introducing someone she was dating was difficult enough, let alone someone for whom she had no label.

She knew she was being silly. If he was just a friend she wouldn't hesitate. But how would she explain Oliver? A work colleague? A movie star? Someone from out of town? Any of those descriptions would do but they wouldn't hide the fact that she was attracted to him and she hated to think what her dad would do or say if he noticed. He always seemed to be of the opinion that no one was good enough for his daughter and it would be humiliating if he gave Oliver the third degree. Oliver had made his intentions clear; he was pursuing her, but he had no more serious intentions than that. If he got her into bed she was certain that would be the end of it. She definitely didn't need to introduce him to her father.

She'd dropped Oliver at his hotel to shower and change before she raced home to do the same, cursing Saskia and her meddling ways all the while. Although she couldn't be too cross. There was a lot to be said about spending an evening with Oliver Harding. Even the anticipation was exciting.

She'd thrown a few supplies into the back of her four-by-four before picking him up again and driving him a few hundred metres to the petrol station.

'Do you want me to fill up the tank for you?' he offered as she turned off the road.

'No, thank you. I'm good,' she replied as she parked the car in a space out the front. 'This is where we're having dinner.'

'A roadhouse?' He sounded offended. 'I offered to buy you dinner. I can afford something fancier than a roadhouse diner.'

'Trust me, it's good. It's owned by Dean's best friend and there's a private room out the back.'

'Do you have a connection to everyone in this town?'

'Pretty much.'

Oliver held the door for her as they entered the roadhouse. They were warmly welcomed and ushered out the back, where they had the space to themselves. He pulled her chair out for her as she sat. She liked the attention. They ordered pizzas and talked about the places Oliver had lived in and travelled to. Kat had been to Adelaide to study and she'd been to Sydney once. Her life experiences were totally different to his but he didn't make her feel inexperienced. He was an entertaining storyteller, even for an audience of one, and Kat enjoyed listening to his tales. He questioned her about her childhood, what it was like growing up in Coober Pedy, and got her to divulge her most interesting work stories. She felt as if they could talk all night.

He picked up the bill when it was delivered to their table but it seemed he wasn't ready to say goodnight just yet. 'It's only early. Don't you think you need to keep an eye on me a little longer? Shall we have coffee? Dessert?'

'We can have dessert at the next stop.' Kat was pleased that he didn't seem keen for the night to end. She had other plans for them.

'There's more than one thing to do in town on a Saturday night?'

She bristled. 'There's plenty. I'm just not sure how much you'll appreciate.'

'Relax. I'm kidding.'

She unlocked her car and climbed in as Oliver held the door for her. She reached into the back seat and handed him a baseball cap.

'What's this for?'

'Protection.'

He raised an eyebrow and smiled. 'For you or me?'

'You.'

'You sure do things differently out here,' he said as Kat pulled onto the main street and drove back through town, turning right at the far end and onto a dirt road. She drove past a chain link fence. On the other side was a large screen.

'We're going to the movies?' Oliver asked.

Kat nodded. 'Outback style.'

She handed over cash at the gate before driving in to the outdoor theatre and reversing into a spot.

To their left was a small building housing the projection unit which also doubled as the kiosk. A couple of long benches were bolted into the ground in front of the kiosk for any patrons who hadn't driven, but these had been ignored in favour of a few, more comfortable, deckchairs. The whole set-up was very basic. Money had recently been spent on a new screen but funds were desperately needed to upgrade the rest of the facilities.

Kat tuned the radio and opened her door.

'Are you sweet or savoury?' she asked.

'Sorry?'

'The dessert I promised you. I'll get us something from the shop.'

'My buy.'

'No—' she started to argue, but he cut her off.

'I was buying dinner. If this is dessert then technically it's still part of dinner.'

She looked at him. Even with the baseball cap he was recognisable. His clothes were too city. He was too neat and tidy, too well-groomed.

'Thanks, but let's call it movie snacks, not dessert, and let me go.'

'Why?'

'Because I think it's better if you stay out of sight.' He frowned and she could see she'd confused him. She couldn't blame him. He had no idea what movie they'd come to see. 'I don't want you to be hassled.'

'No one has bothered me since I got to Coober Pedy. I don't think anyone could care less that I'm in town.'

Kat believed him. The locals were, by and large, unfazed by anything that happened outside of their world. Coober Pedy was a popular filming location for everything from documentaries to local horror flicks to Hollywood blockbusters and the locals couldn't care less. The ones who made a living from the tourists might be the exception but, while they liked the additional revenue that a film crew and any associated publicity might bring, even they wouldn't make a nuisance of themselves by hassling the stars. The locals were focused on making money, making a living, surviving. Movies being made in town was a good drawcard for tourists, which made the town money. That was all the locals worried about, so she wasn't surprised that they were leaving the movie contingent alone, but the tourists in town might be a different story.

'Most of the town, probably not. But the people who are here tonight might. The first movie is one of yours.'

'One of mine? Which one?'

'*This Is War.*' She waited to see if he was going to object. 'Do you mind watching one of your own? We're a bit limited for choice out here. There's a different double feature every Saturday night and tonight it's one of yours, but we could come back later for the second movie if it's a problem.'

Oliver glanced over his shoulder at the mound of pillows in the back of the car. 'If we stay, do I get to lie in the back with you and fool around?'

'Yes, to the first—'

'I know how this movie ends,' he interrupted with one of his slow smiles; 'you can afford to miss it—I can catch you up later.'

Kat laughed. 'My point *was*, that I will get the snacks because you're bound to be recognised here and I don't think it will make for a relaxing experience.'

'Relaxing in the back of your car with you was exactly the experience I had in mind.'

Kat raised her eyebrow and gave an exaggerated sigh. 'Sweet or savoury?'

'Surprise me.'

'Make yourself comfortable,' she said as she hopped out.

She returned with an armload of sweets and some cans of soft drink, passing everything to Oliver before climbing into the back. 'Take your pick. I have popcorn or FruChocs.'

'Fruit chocs?'

'FruChocs—chocolate-covered apricot balls. You have to try one. I've got beer too,' Kat said as she popped open a can, 'but you should probably steer clear of that if you've got a headache.'

'My headache seems to have gone,' he grinned. 'I'm feeling much better.'

The opening credits started to roll and Kat settled back. She was looking forward to the movie; it was a romantic comedy, which was much more her style than science fiction, but she knew she'd be happy to see anything that Oliver was in and was more than happy to be curled up in the dark with him. He had rearranged the pillows, making more of a semi-circle, encouraging the two of them into the middle of the car, like a little nest. She had to sit close, their shoulders and thighs touching. She didn't mind that at all.

She enjoyed the movie. At some point she felt Oliver's arm wrap around her shoulder. She was tucked against his side in the dark. Despite the fact they were surrounded by other cars, it had felt secluded and private and the nervous tension she usually felt when she was around him had dissipated. Maybe it was because she couldn't see him, but she was still aware of him. The nervous tension had been replaced by a heightened awareness. She had felt every movement he'd made, every breath he'd taken.

She'd felt his fingers twirling the ends of her hair and making tiny patterns on her bare shoulders. Her skin had come alive under his touch and she felt as if she could have stayed there for ever, cocooned with him in a world of their own.

'What did you think?' he asked as the final credits started to roll.

The film had made her cry. And laugh. And, not that she'd admit it, she'd got a little turned on in the sex scenes. 'I thought you were great,' she said, grateful for the darkness as it hid the fact she was blushing.

'You don't have to be nice. It's OK if you thought it was terrible.' He was looking at her, his blue-eyed gaze bright even in the dim light. He was smiling. She wondered if he was always happy.

'No, really, it was fun, but do you find it weird watching yourself on screen?' She had wondered if he'd enjoy it or find it uncomfortable.

'A bit. I tend to focus on everyone else's characters. Especially in the sex scenes.'

'About those. Were you sleeping with the lead actress in real life?' Her imagination had run away with her during those scenes. Lying in Oliver's embrace, it was all too easy to imagine that she was watching him make love to her.

'She was engaged.'

'That doesn't change my question.'

'You don't think much of my acting.'

'On the contrary. Those kisses looked pretty authentic. I just wondered if you really are *that* good.'

'At kissing or acting?'

She noticed he still hadn't answered her original question but she was prepared to let it go for now. She had other things on her mind. She wanted to know how it would feel to be kissed the way he'd kissed the heroine. She wanted to know what it would be like to be kissed by Oliver.

'Kissing,' she replied.

'Those kisses were nothing. It's just part of acting.'

'Is it true there are acting classes to teach people how to kiss?'

'Yes. But I'm not going to admit to having to learn how to kiss a girl properly.'

'So, you've never done one of those classes.'

'No. I've never needed to.'

She would bet he hadn't. She was sure he knew exactly what to do in the bedroom, exactly how to get a girl into bed with him and what to do with her when she got there. He would have had plenty of experience. All he'd have to do was look into her eyes and then smile. Say a few charming words. Kat knew that if she spent enough time with him and he kept up his charm offensive it would only be a matter of time before she succumbed. She was horny just watching him on screen, let alone having his arm around her, his thigh resting against hers. She could still feel his breath on her cheek, his fingers in her hair. Her heart was pounding and she wondered if he could hear it. Her hands were sweaty, her underwear damp.

'Don't confuse real life with acting. In a movie you have to think about everything except the act itself. That's scripted. In a movie you have to get the angles right. You don't want hands in the wrong places, noses getting in the way, too much tongue, too much saliva. It's *usually* all make-believe. And there are lots of different kisses.'

'What do you mean?'

'Think about the way you kiss your dad or your cousins and then think about the way you kissed your first boyfriend.'

She cringed at the thought. 'I'd rather not think about that.'

'Why not?'

'I was fifteen and it was a disaster.'

'Your second boyfriend, then.'

'That was a bit better.'

'How many boyfriends have you had?'

'A few. The choices are a bit limited out here, and you said it yourself—everyone is connected somehow. We all went to school together or are related.'

'I've learned that's not completely true. Plenty of people seem to have moved here from somewhere else. Surely there's an opportunity there. And what about when you were in Adelaide?'

'Yes, there were definitely more options then.' With the added bonus that they didn't have to be introduced to any of her over-protective family. But the only serious relationship she'd ever had had ended when she came back to Coober Pedy. She'd hoped he might follow her, but what was there here for him? She couldn't blame her ex for not wanting to live here. She had never intended to still be here at the age of twenty-seven. She had wanted to see the world but she felt duty bound to stay in Coober Pedy. She was waging a constant battle between her own desires and her beliefs as a daughter. 'What about you?'

'No boyfriends,' he smiled.

'Girlfriends?'

'Not as many as you might think. Now, where were we?' He reached towards her and ran his hand from her shoulder down her arm as he redirected the subject. Kat's skin tingled and her body sprang to life. He flipped her hand over and his thumb made slow circles over the sensitive skin of her wrist. She could scarcely remember her own name, let alone what they'd been talking about. 'We were talking about kisses, I think.'

Kat took a deep breath, closed her eyes briefly and then

forced herself to refocus as she opened them. 'What's next after the first kiss?'

'Technically, the second. But in reality, there are always more first kisses.'

'How do you figure that?'

'Every new person is a new kiss. Another first kiss.'

'Until you find *the* person,' she argued. 'The one you want to spend the rest of your life with.'

'Let's forget about numbering the kisses and just think about the way you want to kiss me.'

'I never said I wanted to kiss you.'

'Are you sure?' he teased and she nearly gave in. But she wanted him to make the first move. 'Anyway,' he said when she stayed silent, 'there are plenty more types of kisses.'

'Like what?'

'The kiss between two friends.'

He leant in close and kissed her on the cheek. His hands were on her elbows. The kiss was chaste.

The light from the movie screen played across his face, illuminating his eyes. He was looking at her closely and she was spell bound. He lifted his hand and ran his thumb across her cheek, stopping just in front of her ear. His fingers slid under her hair, gently caressing her neck.

Her eyes were locked with his. Her lips parted.

He brought his face close to hers and said, 'And then there's this one.'

CHAPTER FIVE

He pressed his lips close to her ear. She felt them on her earlobe as he ran his fingers down the back of her arm. The hairs on her arms were tingling. She'd never known the back of her arm could be an erogenous zone. Her whole body was tingling, desperate for his touch.

His other hand was behind her neck, his fingers splayed along the bones of her spine. His head dipped towards hers as her eyes drifted closed.

His lips pressed softly against hers.

She sighed and parted her lips on a breath.

Oliver's touch grew firmer and Kat opened her mouth further. His tongue was inside her, touching her, tasting her. He tasted like chocolate.

She melted into his embrace as the kiss deepened.

Their first kiss.

'I've wanted to do that since I first saw you,' he said when they finally came up for air.

'Was it worth waiting for?'

'You tell me.'

She nodded. It had been everything she'd hoped for. And more.

'Now do you believe me? My acting kisses are very different. That was me. All me. There's a big difference to kissing someone when you're surrounded by cameras, and when you're alone under the stars.'

'We're hardly alone.'

'You've been on set. You've seen how crowded it gets. This is as much privacy as I need when I'm kissing someone.'

'Can I have that one again?'

He shook his head. She was disappointed; it had been a pretty amazing kiss.

'We only get one first kiss,' he said. 'That's why it had to be perfect.'

'What comes next?'

'This one.'

He rolled her over, resting her back on the pile of pillows, trapping her under his weight. He pressed his lips to the side of her face, in front of her ear, before moving lower, dropping kisses along her jaw. His mouth moved lower still as he dropped feather-light kisses down her neck and along her collarbone.

He flicked the strap of her sundress off her shoulder and his fingers grazed her breast. Her nipple peaked as his lips pressed against the swell of her breast.

She put her index finger under his chin and lifted his head, bringing his lips back to hers. She slid her arms around his neck as she pressed herself against him.

His tongue explored her mouth. Tasting. Teasing, deeper and harder this time. There was an urgency to their movements now.

His mouth moved back to her jaw line, her neck. He pushed the fabric of her dress aside and cupped her breast with his hand as his thumb deliberately stroked across her nipple. He pushed the lace of her bra to one side, exposing her breast to the caress of his lips. He ran his tongue over her nipple and Kat dissolved.

She felt his hand trace over the curve of her hip, the thin cotton of her dress no protection against the heat of his hand. His mouth was still at her breast, his fingers were on her bare knee. Now his fingers were on the inside of her thigh.

Her skin was on fire. A waterfall of heat and desire started in her belly, overflowed and ran through her like a river.

His fingers moved higher until they came to rest just below the junction of her thighs. It took all her willpower not to spread her legs for him and beg him not to stop. She needed to remember where they were. Who she was. But it was almost impossible. He was sending her crazy.

He seemed to sense just when enough was enough. His movements stilled, pausing right at the last moment, the moment before they wouldn't be able to rein in their desires.

Kat was panting. Dizzy. 'What was that one called?'

'That was called "Your place or mine?".' His lips were on her neck again. She could feel her pulse under the gentle caress of his mouth. He lifted his head and looked into her eyes. 'Would you like to come and spend the night with me?'

She wasn't surprised to find herself giving his suggestion serious consideration. She wasn't ready to say goodnight.

'I think my concussion still needs monitoring,' he added.

'You told me your headache had gone.'

He grinned. 'It has. I seem to have made a remarkable recovery.'

'Did you even have a headache?'

Oliver lifted his hands in surrender. 'I swear I did. But it *has* gone, and it's fun to wind you up.'

'And you're all about fun, aren't you?'

'Yes. I am. That's not a crime. Fun can be very satisfying. You've had fun tonight, haven't you?'

She nodded.

'And the fun doesn't need to stop now. I've seen this movie.' Kat hadn't even noticed that the second feature had started. 'What do you say, shall we blow this joint?'

Kat didn't hesitate. She didn't think about her answer, she just went with her feelings. She knew her night wasn't over yet. She nodded again. Decision made.

'Are you sure?' Oliver checked. 'You promised George you'd stay away from me.'

She grinned. 'We both knew that was never going to happen.'

Her capitulation had not so much been a matter of time as a matter of timing. Of opportunity. And she knew this was her opportunity. She couldn't spend the whole night with him but they had a few more hours.

There was nothing that made her think this was a bad idea. Which wasn't to say it was a good idea. It probably wasn't one of her best, but there had been so many experiences she had missed out on in life because she worried about what other people might think.

She knew that never bothered Oliver. He had publicists and agents to worry for him.

There was no one here to see what she was up to.

There were so many reasons why this wasn't a great idea. They were complete opposites. She was all about family and helping people. He was about himself. He wasn't staying and she wasn't planning on leaving. But that was exactly why it could work. It could only ever be a fling. She was under no illusions that they could have a proper relationship and she assumed he was of the same opinion.

There were so many reasons why this wasn't a great idea but she didn't care. They were both consenting adults. No one was going to get hurt, she thought as she started the car and left the drive-in.

'Wow.' Kat collapsed onto the bed. Despite the fact that she was in Oliver's underground hotel room, where the temperature was a constant twenty-five degrees, a thin veil of sweat coated her body, testament to their energetic lovemaking.

'You can thank Lotte,' Oliver said.

'Lotte?'

'A German girl who took my virginity when I was fifteen and introduced me to the wonderful delights of women.'

'If I ever meet Lotte I will remember to thank her,' Kat smiled.

'You're not shocked that I was fifteen?'

Kat laughed. 'I might have only been having my first proper kiss, if you could call it that, at fifteen, but most of my friends skipped that bit. They went straight to getting married and having babies, sometimes not in that order. How old was Lotte?'

'Nineteen.'

'Now, *that's* a bit shocking. Is that even legal?'

'I have no idea. Possibly not. But I didn't care.' He shrugged and grinned. 'Show me a randy fifteen-year-old boy who is going to say no to a gorgeous, experienced older woman.'

'Where does a fifteen-year-old go to meet a nineteen-year-old Mata Hari?'

'My father was stationed in Germany at the time. I had one of my brother's IDs. We looked enough alike that the bars and clubs didn't really care. Isaac had just left home—Dad kicked him out when he announced he was gay. That really started my rebellious years. I was sick of following the rules. What did it get us? I realised it was always going to be my father's way or the highway, so I started exploring the highway. Sneaking off, lying. I couldn't wait to get out of home. I was miserable and I missed Isaac.'

'Where did he go?'

'He got a scholarship to university. He's an architect now. Living in Spain.'

'Do you see him very often?'

'Not often. Our lives are very different. He's married now, to his long-term partner.'

'Do you like his partner?'

'I do. But we don't have a lot in common any more. Our careers are different, our lifestyles too. I don't mean because he's gay, but he's very settled, nine-to-five work days, four weeks' holiday, vacations in Europe and Africa. He's happy.'

'And what about you? Are you happy?'

'I am now. Leaving home was the best thing I ever did. Our father was constantly disappointed in us. Nothing we did was ever good enough. I stopped trying to please him. Leaving home was the only way I was going to be able to find out who I was. And what about you? When are you going to leave home?'

'I went to Adelaide to study when I was eighteen but I came back when my mum died.'

'That was a while ago now; you said your friends are married with kids, but not you? You've escaped all that? Or do you have an ex-husband hiding in a mine, waiting for the chance to hunt me down?'

'You've been in too many movies. I don't have an ex-husband. I want to find someone who will give me what my parents had. My parents were married for thirty-two years and they adored each other. I am looking for my soulmate.' She rolled onto her side and tucked her leg over Oliver's, craning her head to kiss him firmly on his mouth. 'And now I need to go.'

'You're not staying?'

She shook her head. 'My father will expect me home. He always leaves a light on and he'll look for my car in the morning. If he doesn't see it, he'll worry.'

'Why don't you call him?'

'And tell him what? That I'm staying out all night to have wild sex with a gorgeous man?'

'I'm flattered. But perhaps your father doesn't need to hear all the details.'

'You do remember what he does for a living?'

'So, it's not an ex-husband but a father I have to worry about.'

'Remember, he warned me against men like you.'

Oliver burst out laughing. 'Men like me? What does that even mean?'

'Charmers. Heartbreakers. Men who are only after one thing.'

'I told you, don't believe everything you read. I've dated a lot of women—it keeps me in the headlines and is good for my career—but I certainly haven't slept with them all. I will admit, though, that I am after you.'

'And now that you've had me, is that it?'

'No. Stay here and I'll prove it to you.' His fingers found her naked breast and he brushed lightly over her nipple, sending waves of desire through her.

She placed her hand over his and lifted it from her body before she capitulated. 'I can't, I have to go. I need to get some sleep.'

'You can sleep here in a minute,' he said as he lowered his head and took her nipple in his mouth.

Kat arched her back as his tongue circled her breast. She almost gave in. 'I have to go to work early tomorrow.' He sucked on her nipple as his hand slid from her waist over her hip. 'But why don't you come over for dinner tomorrow night?'

She hadn't intended to invite him but the invitation was out there now and she couldn't take it back. She would blame her hormones. She couldn't think clearly while his mouth and hands worked their magic.

She wriggled out from underneath him and sat up. She needed to go before she said anything else she didn't really mean. Her mouth was working independently of her brain, or maybe her brain just wasn't working at all; maybe it was too overloaded by her other senses.

'I can't. We're filming tomorrow.'

'At night?'

Oliver wouldn't meet her eyes and she knew he wasn't telling her everything. She should just let it go. She should be relieved that he said no but she knew he was lying to her about something and she couldn't leave it alone.

'No,' he admitted.

'So, you have got what you wanted and now you'll walk away?'

'I'm not walking away but I don't do family.'

What the hell did that mean? She was desperate to know but she let it slide. She knew from his tone he wasn't going to discuss it further and she didn't need to know.

She bit her tongue as she got dressed. She didn't want to end the night on a fight. She didn't need to push the point. She shouldn't have invited him in the first place.

Oliver had been tempted to accept Kat's dinner invitation for this evening before common sense prevailed. Going on a few dates and fixing his reputation was one thing. Meeting her family was another thing altogether. It wasn't something he needed to do. It wasn't something he was prepared to do.

He was only in town for a few weeks, long enough to have some fun but not long enough for anything serious, and that suited him fine. Besides, he didn't have a great track record with families, his own included. And even if hers were wonderful, what would be the point of meeting them? He liked Kat but he wasn't going to get involved in her life. He knew he couldn't give her the things she wanted.

She'd told him she wanted to find her soulmate, and that wasn't him. He didn't believe in soulmates. His brother was the one exception. He though Isaac and his partner were a perfect match.

Oliver had never let himself fall in love. He'd had one relationship that he'd thought had the potential to become something serious but it had ended badly. His girlfriend had cheated on him, blamed him for not paying her enough attention. He knew he'd failed, he'd been focused on establishing his career, and he'd disappointed her.

He didn't want to be in a position again where he could disappoint someone, so he chose to keep his distance from people. He didn't date seriously and he didn't see his family. It was better not to get involved. That way people didn't develop expectations and he wouldn't disappoint.

His family was fractured.

He was a disappointment.

He avoided families for those very reasons.

But he couldn't get Kat out of his mind. He spent the afternoon filming a scene with Julia but it was Kat's face he was picturing. Her dark eyes, her smooth, lithe body. Her full red lips that did, amazingly, taste like summer cherries.

Jesus, he was hard again even now.

And, even though he knew he wouldn't go to dinner, it didn't stop him from thinking about Kat, from imagining what she was doing right at that moment, from thinking about what he was missing.

He knew that Kat's family had shaped her into the person she was. Into the compassionate, generous and open-hearted woman he was enjoying getting to know. He knew they were close and assumed they weren't as broken or as complicated as his own, but that still didn't mean he needed to meet them. He didn't want to risk disappointing Kat. Or her family. He knew he wasn't the man she was looking for. There was no need for him to meet her family.

It wasn't family he was missing. Kat's or his own. He was simply missing Kat.

Kat was glad she was rostered on to work; it gave her something to keep her mind occupied for the day. She might as well be at work, seeing as Oliver had blown her off. Being busy would stop her from thinking about him. Well, that had been her reasoning. She'd thought it would keep her busy but the shift had been quiet. Usually she was happy about that but today she needed the distraction. Just a minor vehicle accident or a suspected heart attack that turned out to be indigestion would have been enough. But she'd had far too much time on her hands and she spent it vacillating between reliving last night and wondering why Oliver wouldn't come to dinner. Was it really that he just didn't like being around other people's families, or did it mean he'd got what he wanted and she wouldn't see him again?

She'd been kidding herself to think they could have something meaningful. Family was everything to her and she couldn't imagine being with someone who didn't understand that.

She'd checked the filming schedule—Sunday was supposed to be a rest day—and she'd seen that nothing was listed. She hated that she was checking up on him but she couldn't stop herself. He'd said it was a closed set. Was it a love scene? Was he lying? Her thoughts went backwards and forwards…there were a thousand possibilities and she knew she could go crazy trying to work out what it all meant. Maybe it meant nothing.

She was relieved when the phone finally rang.

'Ambulance. What's your emergency?'

'I've got a fifty-eight-year-old man with severe stomach pains.'

'Oliver? Is that you?' she asked before her initial excitement at hearing his voice gave way to the realisation that he'd called 000, not her specifically.

'Kat? Yes, it's me. I'm with George. He's in a lot of pain and I don't know what to do.'

'Where is his pain?'

'Right side. Under his ribs. Could he be having a heart attack?'

'Tell me what other symptoms he has,' she said, trying to keep him calm. 'Any shortness of breath?' She could hear Oliver relaying her questions to George.

'No,' came the reply.

'Oliver, can you put the phone on speaker? George can hear my questions—he'll only have to nod yes or no and you can then pass the information on to me.' She paused briefly and then continued, 'Chest pain?'

'Yes,' came Oliver's reply.

'Back pain?'

'No.'

'Arm pain?'

'No.'

'Has he vomited?'

'Yes.'

'But he's not having difficulty breathing?'

'No.'

Kat scribbled a note to Dave while she spoke to Oliver.

Chest pain?

Abdominal pain?

Dave began a quick check of their supplies before lifting the keys for the ambulance off their hook.

'I don't think I can get him in the car to take him to the hospital,' Oliver told her.

'It's all right. We'll come to you. Where are you?'

'Still on set. We're in George's trailer.'

Kat was mollified. Oliver hadn't been lying to her about having to work. 'We're on the way.'

Kat and Dave arrived on set to find a restless George; he was unable to find a comfortable position.

The air-conditioning was working overtime but he still felt hot to the touch. Kat took his temperature and observed his colour. He had a tinge of yellow about him.

Kat removed the thermometer from his ear and relayed the elevated reading to Dave. She lifted George's shirt to palpate his stomach.

'Where is the pain?'

George indicated his right side.

'When did the pain start?'

'After lunch, maybe a couple of hours ago,' he said.

There was a small, faded scar in the right lower quadrant. 'Have you had your appendix removed?' Kat asked.

George nodded as Kat continued to feel his abdomen.

Dave was busy attaching ECG leads to George's chest. Kat clipped an oximeter onto his finger and listened to his respiration rate. His oxygen saturation was slightly low, heart rate was elevated, respiration rate rapid, temperature high, but the ECG trace was normal.

'Take a deep breath for me, George,' Kat instructed as she pushed her fingers into the upper right quadrant of his abdomen. George gasped with pain, holding his breath until Kat released the pressure on his gallbladder.

'OK, George, good news—it's not a heart attack and it's not appendicitis.'

'What's the bad news?' Oliver asked.

'I think it's probably a blocked bile duct.'

'What causes that?'

'Gallstones. I'm not surprised you're feeling terrible, George—it is a very painful condition, but easily remedied. You'll need further testing though.'

'Here?' Oliver asked.

Dave drew up a dose of analgesia to start controlling George's pain.

'No,' Kat replied. 'We'll take him to the hospital for pain relief but he'll need to go to Port Augusta or Adelaide for further tests.'

'And then what?'

'If it's gallstones he'll probably need surgery.' Kat was almost certain that her diagnosis was correct and with acute cholecystitis surgery was almost always required. 'It's not emergency surgery but it should be done some time in the next three days. The flying doctor will transfer him if necessary.'

CHAPTER SIX

KAT EMERGED FROM the water and Oliver's brain froze. Droplets of water clung to her body and her skin glistened. She wore a black bikini; he'd seen a thousand different women wearing black bikinis before—he had a house on Malibu Beach and gorgeous women were everywhere—but none of them had affected him the way Kat did.

He couldn't believe she'd accepted his invitation to come to Adelaide with him.

George had been transferred to Adelaide for surgery, so filming had been put on hold, giving Oliver, and the rest of the cast and crew, a few days off. Oliver had offered to fly down to Adelaide as well. George didn't need him—he had his assistant, Erica—but Oliver used it as an excuse to invite Kat to go too. And here she was.

They would have at least three days in the city. Three days that had the potential to be so much better than any date he had imagined. He'd booked them into the only five-star hotel at Glenelg Beach and as he watched the sway of her hips as she came towards him he wondered about his chances of getting her back to their suite and ravishing her before dinner.

No, he'd show her that there was more to him than the persona that the tabloids loved to write about. His womanising ways were, as he'd told her, mostly fabricated for publicity and he wasn't searching for publicity today. He had a corporate credit card and he'd used his alias when he'd booked the hotel room. The next couple of days were about him and Kat. He hadn't asked what she'd told her father—he didn't care; it wasn't any of his business.

Her olive skin was tanned and golden and Oliver feasted his eyes on her as she came out of the ocean. Her dark hair was slick and wet and he watched as she lifted her arms and gathered her hair in one handful and squeezed the salt water from it. Her breasts rose with the movement, two perfect golden orbs, and Oliver struggled to keep his eyes up.

Jesus, she made him feel like a horny teenager. He was in a constant state of arousal when she was near him, and her being almost naked was not helping. He couldn't remember the last time a woman had driven him to distraction the way Kat did and it made it difficult to remember that he was trying to be on his best behaviour. But try he would.

He couldn't, however, resist just one kiss.

He stepped towards her and met her in the shallows. He slid his arm around her waist. Her skin was damp and cool and smooth. He bent his head and kissed her.

He needed to keep it brief; he was only wearing a pair of swim shorts—there wasn't much to keep him decent.

'Are you worried someone will see you?' she asked as his lips left hers.

He noticed she didn't say 'us' and he knew she was thinking of him being stalked by the paparazzi, but he really didn't care. Not today. Not now.

'No one knows we're here,' he told her, including her with him. 'No one is expecting to see me.' He was wearing a baseball cap, more out of habit than for a disguise, but it had the added advantage that it shaded his eyes. He knew they were his most identifying feature. He had booked into the hotel under an alias and as far as he knew no one had been tipped off. He supposed the airline staff could have said something if they'd recognised him, but their plane tickets had been booked using the same corporate card and the plane had been tiny—twenty seats at most—and no one knew where they were headed once it had landed in Adelaide. He was confident they could go undetected. He had to admit, while he courted the paparazzi in LA, as it was important to keep them on side, it was refreshing to be incognito. It was a novelty to be able to pretend he had a normal life even if he suspected he'd grow tired and bored of normal after a while. But, for the moment, if it meant he could hold Kat in his arms on a public beach and be left alone he was all for that.

He kissed her again for good measure before taking her hand. He picked up one of their towels from the warm sand and wrapped it around her shoulders, hugging her close as he dried her back. The sun was low over the horizon now, turning the sky pink and gold, and he had plans to sip champagne on their balcony as they watched it set.

He took her hand and walked along the beach, leaving footprints in the soft sand by the water's edge. The tide was on its way out, the moats around the sandcastles were emptying and the beach was starting to empty too as families thought about getting home to feed their kids. There was still a group of teenagers jumping off the jetty into the sea. They stopped temporarily if the lifeguards or police turned up before they were at it again. Oliver thought it looked like fun and it was exactly the sort of thing he would have done in his youth too, but he didn't tell Kat that. He knew she liked to abide by the rules.

They walked into the shade underneath the jetty and as they emerged from the other side he heard a woman screaming. Her English was heavily accented and her distress was making her hard to understand, but when he looked in the direction she was pointing, into the distance, into the waves, out past a rocky outcrop, he thought he could see a head bobbing in the water and being taken out to sea with the outgoing tide.

The lifeguard station was empty, unmanned at this time of day, although the surf lifesaving club was still open. But, even so, he and Kat were the closest people.

Oliver didn't hesitate. He knocked his baseball cap from his head, let go of Kat's hand and ran into the shallows, ignoring Kat's cry of, 'What are you doing?'

He splashed through the water until it was knee-deep and running became difficult. He dived into the sea and struck out around the rocks. He was a strong swimmer. He was used to the Pacific Ocean and, in comparison, the calm waters of the gulf didn't look too difficult, although he knew it was one thing to swim in calm waters and another to try to rescue a frightened, drowning man. Maybe he should have waited for the lifeguards but that extra minute or two could be the difference between a good outcome and a bad; between life and death.

He was getting closer. He saw the man's head disappear under the water. Oliver put his head down and kicked harder, willing himself to reach the man before it was too late.

The man was sinking.

Oliver dived down, searching underwater for the man.

He found him. He was fully clothed and wearing shoes. His eyes were closed.

Oliver came up behind him and got an arm around his chest. He was a dead weight as Oliver kicked to the surface. He hoped the man was only unconscious—surely he couldn't have drowned that quickly?

He knew he had to keep the man on his back, facing away from him, in order to keep control of the situation. If he regained consciousness and panicked, he'd most likely drag them both under.

It seemed to take for ever to reach the surface, and Oliver was breathing heavily as he broke through the waves. It was hard work. He fitted his fingers around the man's chin, keeping his head above water as he kicked in a side-stroke action and headed for the shore, recalling the lessons learned a lifetime ago in his summer swimming lessons as a schoolboy.

Two lifeguards appeared beside him on a board. One took the unconscious man from Oliver and dragged him onto his belly across the board.

'He's not breathing,' Oliver panted.

'Do you need a hand?' The second lifeguard held out a hand to Oliver as the first began paddling back to the beach. They were only fifty metres from the sand. Oliver was tired but now that he wasn't towing a ninety-kilogram dead weight he knew he'd make it. 'I'm OK, thanks,' he said. His pride wouldn't let him be rescued. 'I can swim in.'

His feet hit the sand and he stood, aware that his legs were shaky with fatigue and adrenalin, but he knew he'd be fine as long as he kept moving.

Kat was waiting on the shore. He wrapped one arm around her shoulders, careful not to lean on her, even though it was tempting.

The lifeguards had started performing CPR on the rescued man and he could tell Kat was itching to help, but it wasn't her beat.

As they reached the lifeguards the man's chest started to move. The lifeguards quickly rolled him into the recovery position as he retched, sea water gushing from his mouth.

Bystanders had gathered, hovering around as the lifeguards called for an ambulance. Oliver was always amazed by people's curious fascination with disaster. He understood being curious—as an actor he'd made a habit of people-watching—but sticky-beaking at a potential tragedy was a whole different level in his opinion.

The lifeguards came over and thanked him for his assistance, even though he was sure some of them would have liked to berate him for diving in without thinking.

'You look like that actor,' said one.

'Oliver Harding,' said another.

'I get that a lot,' Oliver replied, not giving anything away. 'Name's Frank.' He stuck out his hand and shook theirs.

'Well, we appreciate your help, mate.'

'No worries,' he replied in his best Australian accent.

He could feel Kat looking sideways at him. She handed him his baseball cap and said, 'We need to get going, *Frank*.'

She waited until they were out of earshot from all the bystanders before she stopped walking and turned to Oliver.

'What was that all about?'

To his credit he didn't pretend not to know what she was asking. 'Frank is one of my aliases.'

'One of?' She raised an eyebrow. 'Is Oliver your real name?'

'Yes. Oliver James Harding, at your service,' he said with a mock bow.

'And when did you start speaking in an Aussie accent?'

'That's my job. Most of the movie crew are Aussies, and I've been paying attention on set. It's the best way to make people believe I am just a doppelgänger.'

'Why do you need a fake name?'

'I usually use it for checking into hotels, restaurants, that sort of thing. I don't expect special treatment, so I don't need to broadcast my movements. There's no need to give everyone a heads up about where I'm going to be and when. The paparazzi pay people to divulge that sort of information. If I want them to know my whereabouts there are ways of getting that information out to them, but if I want some privacy I need some measures to protect it. Mostly I'm happy to sign autographs or pose for photos, but I didn't think the lifeguards needed to deal with that palaver as well. I'm not saying that all of those bystanders would have wanted selfies or whatever, but in my experience at least some of them would and that can become a bit of a circus. It wasn't necessary and, besides, for the next couple of days I want it to just be us.'

She was more than happy for it to be just the two of them as well. She found it liberating being able to walk down the street and hold Oliver's hand and not worry about what people might say or think. If she found it liberating, she could just imagine how Oliver must feel. He was used to his every move being scrutinised and potentially splashed across the cover of a magazine, so she could understand the appeal of hiding his true identity.

They reached the hotel and Kat stepped inside as the doorman held the door. She felt as though she should apologise as they left sandy footprints on the spotless tiled floor. She smiled to herself as she wondered what the staff in this five-star hotel thought. She wondered if they could tell that she wasn't used to this level of luxury and attention. That she had never before stayed in a five-star, or even a four-star, hotel, had never been picked up from the airport by a chauffeur, had never slept with a Hollywood star.

'What name did you use to book the hotel?' She wondered if the hotel staff knew who he was.

'The same alias—Frank Foster.'

'How do you come up with the names? Is there a list somewhere of the top ten aliases?'

Oliver laughed. 'No. It was the name of one of my characters, one of my favourite parts.'

'That was the character in the movie we saw at the drive-in!'

'It was,' he said as he swiped the room card and held the door for her as she entered the penthouse suite. 'Would you like first shower before dinner?'

She smiled and reached one hand behind her back. She was looking forward to the next few days, and nights, in Adelaide. She was looking forward to spending time with Oliver, just the two of them without interruptions, with no work, no family. She hadn't hesitated when he'd asked her to come with him; she had three rostered days off and she was eager to spend more time exploring their attraction. One night in Coober Pedy hadn't been enough and she was prepared to forget that he 'didn't do family'. If he was keen to spend time with her alone she was happy with that.

Her fingers found the tie for her bikini top. 'I thought we could share,' she said as she tugged at the string. His mouth fell open as her top fell to the floor. She walked away from him but he caught up to her before she reached the bathroom. She stretched one hand out and turned the tap for the shower. He stretched one arm out and put his hand on her waist. He slid it up her belly until he was cupping her breast.

She turned towards him and pulled him under the water.

'What do you fancy for dinner?' Kat asked.

She was wrapped in the thick towelling robe from the hotel and he knew she was naked underneath. They'd only just stepped out of the shower but he debated about ordering Room Service and staying in. But he'd promised himself he would take her out and show her some fun. They'd be back in their room soon enough.

'Your choice,' he said. He couldn't care less what they ate. He wasn't thinking about food.

'I usually choose seafood when I come to the city. Fresh seafood isn't something we get a lot of in Coober Pedy.' She slipped the robe off as she walked into the walk-in wardrobe and Oliver wondered if it was too soon to take her to bed again.

No. He could wait. Sometimes letting the anticipation build was worth it. 'Can you guarantee me that no one will choke on a fish bone?'

'What do you mean?' She emerged from the wardrobe carrying a pair of high heels and dressed in a simple black halterneck dress that highlighted her shoulders.

'We keep running into people who need saving. I need a rest from all that. No more blocked bile ducts, drowning men or pulling men out of mine shafts. In fact, we should just steer clear of all men for the next two days.'

Kat laughed as she sat on the edge of the bed and slipped her sandals on. She lifted one foot and rested it on her opposite knee, sliding her sandal on and fastening the strap around her slender ankle. Her dress rode up to reveal the inside of her thigh. Her legs were long and smooth and tanned. He never knew watching a woman get dressed could be as sexy as watching one undress.

'We need to visit George tomorrow.'

Oliver swallowed and tried to focus on what she was saying as he reminded himself to behave. He didn't want her to think that sex was all he had on his mind and that he wasn't interested in spending time with her if she had her clothes on. 'OK, apart from George. No more emergencies, just us.'

'OK.'

Kat stood and leant towards the mirror that hung over the dressing table beside the bed. Her dress clung to her hips as she bent forwards. Oliver's gaze travelled up, over the curve of her buttocks. He watched as she applied her red lipstick and it took all of his self-control to let her finish, take her hand and lead her out of their suite.

He held her hand as they walked along Jetty Road. A signboard outside a hotel caught his eye. 'What about here? They have karaoke.'

'Karaoke? I thought we were looking for somewhere to eat?'

'We can do both.'

'I don't think karaoke places are renowned for their food,' Kat said.

Oliver pointed to an announcement painted on the pub window. 'It says they won "Best Pub Restaurant" last year.'

'You really want to go to a karaoke restaurant? I thought you said you couldn't sing.'

'I said I wished I was a better singer. And I never said I intended to sing tonight.'

'Well, I certainly won't be singing,' Kat laughed.

'Let's have a look at the menu and then decide. It'll be fun.'

She knew he was all about fun and, looking at his expression, she didn't think she could refuse him. 'OK,' she said as he held the door for her and they stepped inside.

'Have a seat,' he said as he pulled a chair out for her, 'and I'll get some menus.'

He returned with menus, a glass of wine for her and a beer for him. 'Is wine OK? I can get you something else if you prefer?'

'This is fine, thanks.'

'What do you think?' Oliver asked as she perused the menu.

The pub looked newly refurbished, the crowd was well-dressed and the menu looked good. Kat watched as a waitress delivered plates of food to an adjacent table. 'The food looks good,' she admitted, 'I think I can maybe overlook the fact that I'll have to listen to some karaoke.'

Oliver smiled. She could overlook anything at all if she got to sit opposite him for the evening, she decided.

'Where did you learn to swim?' she asked after they had ordered. He had been amazing today, jumping in without hesitation to rescue that man.

'I live on the beach in LA. At Malibu. The swell today was nothing compared to the Pacific Ocean. I've always lived near water. I was born in Italy, lived in Turkey, Hawaii and Germany. All the army bases had swimming pools and we spent summer holidays around the Mediterranean. I spent a lot of my spare time in the water. What about you?'

'I can swim but there's no way I'd be confident enough to jump in like you did. You've seen where I grew up. The town has a pool, and you've seen the lake, but I'm not used to waves. I didn't go out of my depth in the sea today.'

'Can I ask you something? The lifeguards revived the man, so why did he have to go off to hospital?'

'There is a latent risk after people take water into their lungs,' Kat explained. 'There's something called post-immersion syndrome, where your throat can spasm due to irritation of the vocal cords, which makes breathing difficult—that's more common in children—and there's also secondary drowning. If water gets into the lungs it can irritate them and cause pulmonary oedema, which is a build-up of fluid in the tiny air sacs that makes breathing difficult. He needs to be monitored, especially given his lack of English. The hospital will organise an interpreter to explain the risks and he may be discharged if they think he and his girlfriend understand what to watch for.'

'Will he be OK?'

'I would think so. He survived the drowning, and deaths from secondary drownings are extremely rare. At worst he might be unwell.' Kat reached across the table and held Oliver's hand. 'You saved his life.'

'A good day, then.'

'A very good day,' she said with a smile.

The karaoke began as they were finishing their meal, making conversation more difficult. Some of the singers were good, some were woeful, but because there was a prize at the end of the night there were plenty of participants. The winner would be decided by an audience vote.

'Some of these people should definitely save their singing for the shower,' Kat commented.

'You sure you don't want to have a go?'

'I'm positive,' she laughed.

'Can you excuse me?' Oliver said. 'I need to use the bathroom. Will you be all right on your own for a minute?'

'Of course, I'll be fine.' She loved the attention he paid her.

There was a scattered round of applause as another singer finished their song.

'And now, one final karaoke contestant. Give it up for… Frank!'

Kat looked at the stage. Was the MC introducing Oliver? He hadn't returned to their table yet but the stage was empty.

Then she heard a voice through the speakers. A male voice. Unaccompanied.

There was still no one on stage but he obviously had a microphone and, whoever it was, he could sing.

Kat looked around the bar.

Oliver was walking towards her. His blue eyes pinned her to the seat and the spotlight followed him as he sang.

A second spotlight fell on Kat and she hurriedly hid her face behind her hands as Oliver continued to sing about how he couldn't keep his eyes off her. She could feel herself blushing, and part of her wanted to slide under the table, but another part of her couldn't look away. She peeked through her fingers in time to see Oliver stop just before he reached her and step up onto the stage. He was poised and confident.

The music started up in accompaniment, just loud enough to be heard but still letting Oliver's voice shine. Kat was mesmerised. Oliver was born to be on stage.

The second spotlight dimmed, putting her back into the shadows.

The focus was all on Oliver. He didn't seem to mind. Kat knew he loved an audience but she also knew he was singing to her.

The crowd had fallen silent as soon as he'd started singing. They were expecting something special, nothing had been anywhere near as good as what they were hearing now.

He reached the chorus and invited everyone in the restaurant to sing with him. They didn't need to be asked twice. They didn't need to know the words; it was a simple repeat.

Oliver jumped down from the stage and offered his hand to Kat as the audience sang and clapped.

She knew he wanted to get her out of her seat but she hesitated for a fraction of a second, reluctant to dance in front of strangers. She was so used to worrying about what people would think, but then she realised that no one here knew her and no one would care about what she did—they were all too focused on Oliver.

He had the room eating out of his hand as he performed, so she could probably do naked cartwheels across the stage and still no one would give her a second glance.

She let him pull her to her feet.

He twirled her around, spinning her out and away from him as the crowd accompanied them vocally before pulling her in close, her back tucked into his side as he sang the next verse. She swayed with him as they moved in time to the music, oblivious now to the audience.

Thunderous applause surrounded them as he kissed her at the end of the song and returned her to her seat. He took a bow before he was unanimously declared the winner.

He graciously accepted his prize before quickly settling their tab so they could sneak away.

'Well, I don't know about you but that Frank Foster sure can sing,' Kat laughed as Oliver took her hand as they walked back to the hotel.

'Did you have fun?'

'I did.' It was the most fun she'd had in a long time; perhaps she should care less about what people might think and just let her hair down more often.

Kat felt as if she were floating. She was relaxed, sexually satisfied. Happy.

She and Oliver had gone for an early-morning swim, followed by a room service breakfast, followed by more lovemaking, and then they'd wandered through the shops. She was carrying several shopping bags, filled with clothes that would probably never see the light of day in Coober Pedy but which Oliver had insisted on buying for her as well as some gifts for her family.

'I could use a drink after that retail therapy,' Oliver said as he offloaded their purchases to the concierge. 'Would you like to grab a drink in the bar or…?' He paused, his train of thought interrupted, his attention caught by something else.

Kat turned and saw a woman walking towards them. She was short, blonde, extremely thin and expertly put together. Her hair, make-up and clothing were all immaculate. She looked just the type of person who would be in the lobby of a five-star hotel, and Kat's curiosity was piqued.

'Philippa! What are you doing here?' Oliver greeted her.

The woman looked over at Kat, not trying to hide her curiosity. 'Who is this?' she asked as she looked Kat up and down.

Kat frowned. She was wondering the same thing.

'This is Kat Angelis; she's an emergency paramedic, and she's overseeing my stunt work.'

'You're not working right now, though. George is in hospital,' the woman stated, clearly implying that she thought Kat shouldn't be there.

'Kat, this is Philippa Corcoran, my publicist.' Oliver introduced her, choosing to ignore the woman's implication.

Philippa nodded in Kat's direction before turning back to Oliver. 'I need to speak to you, Oliver. In private.'

Kat waited for Oliver to tell her that this wasn't a good time, but Philippa hadn't finished.

'We have a problem,' she added before Oliver could speak.

CHAPTER SEVEN

PHILIPPA WAS BEING rude and Oliver thought about arguing, but something in Philippa's demeanour stopped him from dismissing his publicist.

'How did you find me?'

'You checked in with your credit card. I see the statements.'

She had tracked him down and then flown halfway across the world to see him. Her news must be bad. Too bad for her to deliver over the phone, and he didn't want her to tell him what it was in front of Kat. Who knew what Philippa had to say? He didn't want Kat to hear anything sordid about him. Not without his knowing first what was going on.

'I'm really sorry, Kat, but could you give us a minute?'

'I'll get a coffee in the lounge,' she said.

He could tell from her expression that she wasn't happy, but she didn't argue. He'd make it up to her later.

Kat headed for the lounge and Oliver swiped his card and called the lift for the penthouse suite.

The penthouse door had scarcely closed behind them before Philippa pulled a folder out of her designer bag and handed it to Oliver.

He took it reluctantly. 'What is this?'

'You're being sued.'

'Sued? By whom?'

'The parents of Natalie Hanson, the girl who overdosed at your house.'

'What? That's ridiculous. I wasn't even there.'

'Unfortunately that doesn't matter. She died on your property.'

'And that gives them grounds to sue me?' Oliver stood in the middle of the living room and rifled through the folder. There was a legal document, he assumed the lawsuit, and photos of a young girl. He knew it was Natalie. She was beautiful, happy, smiling, looking as if she didn't have a care in the world. He felt for her parents, they didn't deserve this, but that didn't make it his fault.

Philippa took a seat on the sofa. 'They're saying you had a duty of care. They're saying their daughter didn't have a drug problem. That she must have got the drugs at your house.'

'The police thought she brought the drugs with her,' he said as he dropped the folder onto the coffee table.

'They haven't been able to prove that. There's a copy of the police report in that file.'

'Well, I definitely didn't supply them!' This could ruin his reputation. He'd been working hard to clean up his image, but stories about the number of celebrities he'd dated would seem trivial in comparison to an alleged drug problem. 'In all the thousands of stories I've had printed about me there's never been anything to suggest I'm into illegal drugs.'

'I know that,' Philippa said calmly. 'I know most of what they print about you isn't true, but you know the saying—throw enough mud and some of it will stick. We've worked hard to get you back in the good books, to keep you employed. The movie studios are jumpy. They don't want bad publicity. We need to manage this.'

Oliver sank into a chair. He didn't care what people thought about him but he did care about his career. 'How bad is it?' he asked.

'They're not suing you as a dealer. They're suing you as the landlord. Their argument is that you are liable because it's your property. We need to make sure your name is cleared.'

He had been sent to Australia to make a film in the middle of nowhere as a way of supposedly keeping him out of trouble, but that plan obviously hadn't worked and he knew this lawsuit could be a big problem.

How was he going to explain this to Kat? He really didn't want her to think trouble followed him. Thank God she'd agreed to give him and Philippa some privacy. He hated to think of her hearing this.

Philippa was talking and he forced his mind off Kat and back to what she was saying.

'This is serious. I've spoken to your lawyers already but we need to do some damage control and we also need some positive publicity to counteract any negative stories that come your way.'

'What do you suggest?' He couldn't think straight. All he could think about was Kat's reaction. She was so black and white; she thrived on following the rules. What would she make of this latest scandal? What would she think of him?

'I think you should get engaged.'

'What?'

'You need to show that you've reformed your partying, playboy ways. I know you don't have a drug-taking history, but drugs and partying are a marriage made in heaven for the media, and it only takes a few tabloids to make some suggestions and you have an even bigger PR problem.'

'But that playboy persona was just an image. You know that's not really me. You helped create it!'

'Again, *I* know that, but it's an image you've—we've—spent years selling. Now it's about how we manage it. An engagement is a perfect solution. You need a fiancée, someone who will stand by you and support you while you sort out these allegations. It will give you some positive publicity.'

'And who will agree to be a fake fiancée? Where do you suggest I find someone to play that role?'

Philippa didn't miss a beat.

'Someone trustworthy,' she said. 'An actress. We need someone who is wholesome, which will give you credibility. Someone the public can trust. A fan favourite. Someone they will believe is with you for all the right reasons and therefore you couldn't possibly have done the things you've been accused of because otherwise how would you have got her to fall in love with you?' She reached into her bag and pulled a stack of glossy A4 pages from it. Each page had a photo on it and Oliver could see they were actor bios. She handed him the sheaf of photos. 'I have a short list of actresses who I think would be perfect. I'm pleased you're out of America. That will work in our favour. We'll get you back to Coober Pedy asap, where the paparazzi and the media can't find you. You choose someone from those bios and I will organise a media announcement. I will control it all.'

'Is that why you're here, in person?'

Knowing that he, once again, needed someone to clean up his image was upsetting. Particularly as he was in this situation through no fault of his own.

Philippa was nodding. 'I needed to find you and speak to you before the paparazzi did. I needed you to see that my idea makes sense.'

'No.' Oliver threw the pile of photos onto the table. 'None of this makes sense. It's ridiculous. I had nothing to do with that girl's death and I will fight the lawsuit. Why do I have to create fake news about myself? I thought we were trying to clean up my reputation; I thought part of that was to stay out of the media spotlight. Isn't that one of the reasons I'm down under?'

'Yes. But the story is already out. Natalie's parents have gone to the media. We have to do something. We really do need to counter-attack with something positive. We can't have the media linking your name to a lawsuit and a lawsuit only. We need to give them something else, something good. I think it's our, *your*, best option.'

'I'm not interested.'

'I think you should consider it. Maybe read the stories that have been printed so far. You might agree you don't really have much choice.'

Philippa passed him a third stack of paper, this time printed copies of tabloid magazine articles. He took a cursory glance—he didn't need more than that to see they were all saying the same thing—this actress had died in his house. His name was being linked by association and her parents were suing him. It didn't matter that the tabloids weren't actually mentioning that he hadn't been in the house, that he'd been on location, filming. Fans would put two and two together and get whatever the hell number they pleased; he knew how this business worked. A few photos, a few quotes taken out of context, a few interviews with 'close friends' and there was a story. Suddenly he was into illegal drugs and a girl had died because of it. It was all that was needed to sell the magazines.

'Think of it as a job,' Philippa said. 'A role. You can play the part of the law-abiding, conscientious, clean-living, loved-up fiancé.'

He sat quietly while he thought. He knew he would have to do something. He was at a disadvantage, on the other side of the world, away from the publicity juggernaut that was Hollywood. He'd have to go on the attack. His father, the military general, would be pleased, he thought wryly.

'All right, I'll go along with this but I have one condition.'

Philippa nodded.

'I get to choose my fiancée…'

'Of course.' Philippa started to gather up the sheaf of actress biographies that Oliver had discarded but he shook his head.

'…But not from those.' He knew what he wanted. Whom he wanted. 'I want it to be Kat.'

'The girl downstairs?'

'Yes. It will be far more believable to think I've fallen in love with someone in Australia rather than with a Hollywood actress who I've absolutely no history with.'

'Give me some credit,' Philippa argued. 'If you have a look through those bios you'll see several women in there with whom you have been romantically linked in the past.' She shrugged. 'I'll say you rekindled an old flame.'

'No,' Oliver insisted. 'It will be better if she's not a celebrity. There's no dirt to dig up.'

'Are you sure?'

He wasn't sure at all. Not about Philippa's plan and not about getting Kat to agree—but admitting that would get him nowhere. 'Yes. Trust me. I can do this.'

'Yes, I don't doubt that. But can she?'

Would she? was actually the question. 'There's only one way to find out,' he said as he stood up. 'I'll go and get her.'

Oliver closed his eyes and rested his head on the wall of the lift as it descended to the lobby. How did he tell Kat about this? What if she believed that he was to blame for Natalie's death? What if she believed he had a history of drug use? He knew she wouldn't abide that. He knew she'd be disappointed in him and that was the last thing he wanted.

She was sitting at a table by the window, flicking through a magazine. He sat opposite her and reached for her hands, an apology ready. 'Kat, I'm sorry about that.'

'Is everything OK?'

'Not really. Can you come upstairs? I'll explain then.'

Kat followed without question and Oliver let himself breathe again. Maybe it would be OK.

He opened the door to their suite and held it for her. 'Philippa is still here,' he warned, 'and there's something I need to ask you.'

Kat looked wary. 'What's going on?' She was looking from him to Philippa and back to him again.

'Oliver needs a fake fiancée for a fake engagement—'

'Philippa! Please.' Oliver held up a hand. 'I'll handle this.'

Kat's wary expression changed to one of confusion. 'Handle what exactly?'

Oliver still had hold of her hand. He led her to the sofa in the sitting room. He sat on the edge of the coffee table, his knees touching hers. 'Apparently I'm in the headlines again. You remember we spoke about the girl who died of a drug overdose at my house?'

Kat nodded.

'Her parents are suing me. They're saying their daughter didn't have a drug problem and that as the owner of the property I am partly responsible for her death.'

'Are you?'

'No. I told you I wasn't there.'

'Where did the drugs come from?'

'I have no idea. Not from me. I have never touched illegal drugs.'

He saw her glance down at the coffee table. The photo of Natalie's smiling face was poking out from under the pile of papers, touching his thigh.

She picked up the photo. 'Is this her?'

Oliver nodded.

'Do you think they have a case against you?'

'I don't know.'

'Oliver's lawyer will have something to say,' Philippa said.

Kat looked at Oliver enquiringly.

'I have to argue this. I can't stay silent. I am innocent.'

Kat was quiet. Oliver waited anxiously, his heart lodged in his throat, to see if she was going to believe him.

'What if they win? What happens then? It doesn't bring their daughter back,' she said.

'They want money,' Philippa replied. 'If they won there would be a financial settlement, but that's not really the problem. If they win it could ruin Oliver's career.'

'What are you going to do?' Kat looked at Oliver.

'We're in damage control,' Philippa interjected. 'Oliver will refute the charges but he also needs something to boost his image, to maintain his appeal. Something to counteract any negative publicity. He needs something to make him look like a saint, not a sinner.'

'And what does this have to do with me?' Kat looked at Oliver.

'I want you to marry me.'

'Marry you?'

He hadn't just said that, had he? That wasn't what he'd meant to say. He was *sure* that wasn't what he'd meant to say.

'You don't have to actually get married,' Philippa responded. 'Just agree to be engaged.'

'And that would entail what exactly?' Kat's tone was frosty.

'Pose for some photos together. Maybe give a couple of joint interviews.'

'Why me?'

'It makes sense,' Oliver told her. 'We can have a whirlwind romance.' It wouldn't be difficult at all to pretend to be in love with Kat. She was gorgeous, kind, smart, and he liked who he was when he was around her. She made him a much better version of himself. He wanted her to think highly of him, he wanted her to respect him.

He didn't want this lawsuit to paint him in a bad light, not to his fans but especially not to Kat. She was becoming important to him. Asking her to be his fake fiancée did make sense, but that wasn't his primary motivator. He couldn't imagine asking anyone else. But he was hesitant to tell her his real reasons. He wasn't sure if he could handle hearing her thoughts. What if she thought he was a disappointment?

'That's a good idea,' Philippa finally agreed. 'You can say you fell head over heels, madly in love the moment you met. It was love at first sight. The fans will lap that up. At least the ones who didn't dream of marrying you themselves. They'll be hoping it all falls through.'

Oliver looked at Kat. She didn't look impressed. 'I don't think you're helping, Philippa,' he said before doing his best to get Kat on board. He really didn't want to pretend to be engaged to anyone but her. 'Kat, it'll be fine. When we get back to Coober Pedy we'll be tucked away in the middle of the desert, so you don't have to worry about crazy fans—I don't think even my craziest fans would find us there.'

'You actually have fans who stalk you?'

'On occasion. But I'll look after you. And this is only temporary. Please?'

'That's right,' Philippa spoke up again, 'it's only temporary. Just continue with the story until this gets sorted. I'll organise everything for your public engagements, your wardrobe, hair, make-up et cetera for any interviews and photo shoots, and you'll be financially compensated for your time and inconvenience.'

'You're going to pay me?'

'Of course. Think of your assistance as being a service for hire, if you will.'

Kat wished Philippa would stop talking. The more she spoke, the more incensed Kat became. She couldn't believe Oliver's publicist thought this was a good idea.

She turned to Oliver to give him a piece of her mind, but he looked devastated. With the exception of when he was acting, she'd only ever seen him in a good mood. Seeing him so despondent gave her pause for thought. 'Is this the best idea you could come up with?'

'Yes,' Philippa answered, even though Kat's question had been directed at Oliver.

She kept her gaze focused on him.

'I'm not sure. It would work,' he paused, 'but whether it's the only option or the best one, I don't know.'

'Why would you choose me?'

'Because I think it's the most believable scenario. I wasn't in a serious relationship when I left the States, so for me to suddenly become engaged it needs to be to someone I've met in Australia. I know you better than anyone else here. But you need to be comfortable with the idea.'

'Can I have some time to think about it?'

Oliver looked at Philippa, reminding Kat again that the whole exercise was staged. Like Oliver's life, everything was manipulated for publicity, for the media, for the fans. Her life was so simple and straightforward by comparison. Would she be able to pull this off? Did she want to?

'We have a little bit of time,' Philippa said. 'It's the middle of the night back home. Your lawyer will make a start on getting character statements about you and he'll look into Natalie's past as well. Can I leave it with you to discuss and let me know tomorrow? I've booked into this hotel too.'

Oliver nodded and showed Philippa out of the suite.

Kat remained on the couch. Stunned. She wasn't sure what to think and even less certain about what to do.

'Are you OK?'

'I'm not sure I understand what just happened.'

'I need your help.'

'That bit I understand, but I need some time to get my head around it.'

Oliver's phone pinged with a text message, distracting them both. She was relieved; she didn't want to talk about the situation right now.

Oliver took his phone from his pocket and looked at the screen. 'It's George; he's out of Recovery and ready for visitors. Did you still want to come or would you rather stay here?'

She didn't want to stay behind. Going to the hospital would give her something to do, something else to think about. 'I'll come with you.'

'I don't want to mention this lawsuit to George. Not yet. He's got enough to worry about.'

Kat nodded. That suited her. She didn't know how they would explain the situation they were in.

She was pleased to find George in good spirits after his laparoscopic surgery to remove his gall bladder. He was alert and his pain seemed to be under control.

'What's the story, George?' Oliver asked. 'How long before we're back filming?'

'Apparently I can be discharged once my pain is under control and I can move about comfortably. I think I should be back on deck at the end of the week.'

'Did you tell the doctor you'll be going back to Coober Pedy?' Kat asked.

'I said "on location". And that I need to fly. The airline will need a letter from her giving me permission to fly and I need to have someone accompany me.'

'We can do that, can't we, Kat?' Oliver asked. 'We've got to fly back at some point.'

Kat wasn't sure they should rush it. She turned to George. 'It's one thing being comfortable in hospital in the city, George, but it's another thing being in the desert, five hundred kilometres from town.'

'Days off are costing the studio money,' he replied. 'I promise I'll follow medical advice. I'll sit in a chair and direct. You can keep an eye on me.'

'I can't be there twenty-four-seven,' Kat said as she refilled George's glass from the water jug on his bedside table.

George gestured at the jug as Kat emptied it. 'Oliver, could you please find a nurse and see if I can have my water jug refilled?' He waited until Oliver had left the room before turning back to Kat. 'What did he mean, "We've got to fly back at some point"? What's this "we" business? Why are you here? I meant it when I told you to stay away from him, Kat. I don't want you getting hurt.'

'It's OK, George. I can handle it. I'm not going to get my heart broken.'

Thank God they hadn't mentioned the latest development and Oliver's proposal. She hated to think what George would have to say about that. Agreeing to Oliver's request would be the antithesis of staying away from him. A holiday fling was one thing; pretending to be his fiancée was another. The more she thought about it, the more she thought she couldn't do it. She'd have to tell Oliver.

'Oliver and I have decided we've had enough drama,' she continued as Oliver came back into the room; she didn't want him to think they'd been discussing him behind his back, 'so if you promise you will take it easy and can stay out of hospital, I'll agree to be responsible for your health.'

'I know you think I have a chequered medical history but I am normally, fit and healthy.'

'So it's just when I'm around, then?'

'Seems to be.'

'You never did tell me how you two met,' Oliver said as he looked from one of them to the other.

'I was scouting some bush locations in the Adelaide Hills years ago. I twisted my knee and tore some ligaments and had to be carried out. Poor Kat was one of the paramedics at the scene. We got talking about where I'd filmed, what I was looking for. Kat told me about several films that had been shot in Coober Pedy. I'd heard of it, of course, but had never been. I was keen to film there, so when this movie got off the ground I got in touch with Kat to see what connections she had.'

'I told him I'd moved back to town.'

'And the rest is history.'

Their third day in Adelaide began just as perfectly as the others. Oliver hadn't pressed her for her answer yet. He'd planned a day's outing for them and was keen to get on the road. Kat didn't argue. She didn't want to tell him her decision, not yet;

she didn't want to disappoint him and potentially taint their last day in the city.

Oliver had organised a car and a driver through the hotel and Kat was enjoying being chauffeured around the Fleurieu Peninsula. Oliver had wanted to get out into the country and see something green, so they had visited a couple of wineries in McLaren Vale, played tourist at the weird and wonderful d'Arenberg Cube, before stopping for lunch at a clifftop restaurant recommended by the hotel concierge that overlooked the beach at Port Willunga.

They were seated on the veranda of the restaurant looking over the water. Oliver had his sunglasses on, hiding his distinctive blue eyes. Kat knew he wanted the anonymity today and the sun was high in the sky, reflecting brightly off the water, making sunglasses kind of mandatory, but she wished he'd take them off. She loved being able to look into his eyes.

Kat couldn't believe people actually lived like this—chauffeured cars, five-star hotels, sipping champagne on an oceanside cliff-top. Oliver's future, legitimate fiancée would be a lucky woman.

She knew she couldn't avoid the topic any longer. He had been patient but she suspected Philippa would be less so. She knew she'd be expecting an answer the moment they arrived back at the hotel.

She'd spent many hours last night imagining what it would be like to be engaged to him. It was all too easy to imagine and that was when she knew she really couldn't agree to his proposal.

'We need to talk about your request,' she said.

'Have you made a decision?'

She nodded. 'I don't think I can do it.'

'Why not?'

She knew her feelings for him were all too real and she was terrified he'd see that. She couldn't act, and if she played her part convincingly he might figure out that she had fallen for him. She couldn't allow that to happen. They were too different.

They had no future and it was best if she didn't get any more involved. She was starting to worry that she wouldn't get out with her heart intact, and playing the part of his fiancée would only make things harder. But she needed a reason that she could give him. 'What if I'm not convincing enough? If people see through me that won't help your case. It'll make us both look ridiculous. If I don't do it, will you be able to find someone else?'

'Yes. Philippa had some ideas. She'll pick someone. I told you it was totally your decision.'

She'd half hoped he'd try to talk her round. But she knew he'd only do that if this was real, not make-believe. She knew she was replaceable. She knew Philippa had several other possible candidates to put in front of Oliver. He'd said he wanted her, but that didn't mean he needed her. He just needed someone. He was smart enough to know there was no point in coercing a fake fiancée into playing the role. That would never work.

He accepted her decision without argument and Kat tried to hide her disappointment. It had been her choice after all.

The waitress had cleared their plates that now showed no traces of the freshly caught King George whiting they'd devoured. Oliver ordered coffee as Kat's mobile vibrated on the table. She glanced at it without intending to pick it up. It was Saskia. She'd call her back.

The phone stopped ringing but buzzed almost immediately with a text message.

Call me—urgent.

Her heart plummeted as icy fingers gripped it and tugged it lower in her chest. Waves of cold fear ran through her. Saskia knew where she was, she'd encouraged her to go with Oliver, and Kat knew she wouldn't interrupt without good reason.

'It's Saskia,' she said as she picked up her phone and showed Oliver the text message. 'I have to call her.'

Oliver nodded.

Kat took her phone outside. She was aware that Oliver stood as she did but he didn't follow her.

She pressed redial and stood on the cliffs at Port Willunga, facing the ocean but not seeing it as she waited for the call to connect and Saskia to answer. It was a glorious day but Kat couldn't focus on anything, her thoughts scrambling in her head as she tried to guess what was wrong. She was desperate for her call to be answered.

'Sas? What is it? Is it Papa?' she said the moment the call connected.

'He's OK.' Saskia immediately tried to quell Kat's rising panic. 'He's on his way to Port Augusta with the flying doctor.'

'What happened?'

'He had a heart attack.'

'What? When?'

'This morning.'

Oh, God. Why had she agreed to come away with Oliver? What was she doing in Adelaide? Her father needed her.

'How is he?' What if he didn't make it? What if she lost him too? Her family was everything to her.

'He's stable. But we'll know more when he gets to Port Augusta. I thought you might want to meet him there.'

'Of course I do. I'll go to the airport now. Has someone gone with him?'

'Rosa has.'

'Can you message Zia Rosa, tell her I'm on my way?'

'OK. Call me later. I love you.'

'Love you too…thanks, Sas.'

'On your way where? What's happened?' Oliver was beside her. She hadn't noticed him come out of the restaurant.

'It's my dad. He's had a heart attack.' Her voice caught on a sob. 'He's being flown to Port Augusta. I need to get there.'

The driver pulled up beside them as Kat finished speaking. Oliver held the car door open for her. 'Hop in. I've paid the bill—we can go straight to the airport.'

She didn't ask how he knew what needed to be done; she was incapable of thinking logically. She was just grateful that he was there and was willing and able to sort things out. Someone needed to take control and her muddled brain wasn't capable of thinking of anything but getting to Port Augusta. The actual logistics of the trip were beyond her.

'Can you look up flights to Port Augusta for me? I have no idea when the next one will be.'

'I'll call the hotel. They can organise it for us.'

Oliver had his mobile phone in his hand. 'It's Frank Foster,' he said.

Kat was only half listening. She heard something about a plane and bags.

She kept her eyes locked onto her phone, waiting in vain for an update from someone. Anyone.

'How long does it take the flying doctor to reach Port Augusta?' Oliver asked her.

'An hour.'

'So, they're unlikely to be there yet,' he said gently, taking her phone and turning it face down in her lap. 'I'm sure your aunt will call you as soon as she can.'

'What if I don't get there in time?'

'I'll make sure you do. I have a plan. I'm sure everything will be all right.'

'But what if it's not?' Her voice wobbled. 'I was in Adelaide when my mum passed away. I can't go through that again.'

'Kat.' Oliver turned in his seat to face her. He picked up her hands and his touch calmed her, reassured her. 'Saskia said he was stable. He's in the hands of the flying doctors on his way to specialist care. You have to trust them to do their job and trust me to get you there. Do you?' He continued when she nodded. 'And is there anything else you could have done for him if you'd been there? Other than what is happening now?'

'No.' She shook her head.

'So, take a breath. I'll get you there as soon as I can.'

She took his advice and tried her best to relax. She was glad Oliver was with her. When she'd been in this position last time, when she'd received the phone call with the news that her mum had been in a car accident, she'd been alone. This was better.

The car called past the hotel where the concierge was waiting with Kat's bags, as Oliver had arranged, before continuing on to the airport. Kat grew more edgy as they approached the airport. She hoped there wouldn't be any delays with the flight to Port Augusta, no late passengers, no mechanical or security issues. Every minute counted.

The driver pulled to a stop well before the main terminal. Oliver had the door open almost before the wheels had finished turning.

'Why are we getting out here?' Kat asked. The entrance to the terminal was still several hundred metres ahead of them.

'I've booked us a private plane. We can go straight onto the apron. It's waiting for us. It'll take off as soon as we get there.'

'A private plane?'

'It's the fastest way of getting us there. Call your aunt—let her know you're on the way.'

Oliver took Kat's luggage from the driver as she nodded and brought her aunt's number up on the phone. She walked as she talked, disconnecting as Oliver introduced himself to the pilot and they walked out onto the tarmac.

'How is he?' Oliver asked as the pilot stowed Kat's luggage.

'Stable. My aunt will text any updates while I'm in the air.'

'Good news. Let's get going.'

'You're coming with me?' Kat asked as Oliver stepped onto the stairs behind her.

He nodded. 'I didn't think you were in any state to be sent off alone. You don't mind, do you? I didn't think you'd want to be alone with all your thoughts. I won't interfere at the hospital, I'll just see you safely there.'

Of course he wouldn't interfere at the hospital—he didn't do family.

'No, I don't mind. I'd love some company.'

'Good. I'll come back to Adelaide later, once I know you're OK, so that I'm back to accompany George when he's discharged, as promised.'

'I don't know how to thank you,' she said as she collapsed into the seat and felt the plane immediately begin to taxi.

Oliver handed her a bottle of water from the fridge. 'You don't need to thank me. I'm pleased I could do this for you.'

The leather seats were large and comfortable, the air-conditioning was just the right temperature and the bottled water refreshing. Oliver sat beside her and wrapped his arm around her shoulder, holding her close. Kat closed her eyes and finally let herself relax. She was on the way. Oliver had got her this far; there was nothing more she could do right now.

Kat hesitated at the entrance to the hospital emergency department. She could see her aunt Rosa in the waiting area. She didn't want to introduce her to Oliver. Not now. She didn't want to explain who he was and why she was with him. She didn't want distractions.

She turned to Oliver. 'Thank you for all your help. That's my aunt Rosa over there. I can manage from here.'

'You'll be OK?'

Oliver couldn't hide the look of disappointment on his face. She felt terrible for brushing him off but she couldn't deal with any introductions at the moment. He'd told her he didn't do family. He couldn't expect to meet any more of hers. Not now. Not today.

She nodded. She couldn't worry if she'd upset him. She didn't have room in her head to worry about his feelings.

Oliver's breath was coming in short, sharp bursts, keeping time with his fists as he punched into the boxing pads Chris held in front of him. Thwack, thwack, grunt, breathe.

'Take it easy, buddy, you've got to look after that strained rib muscle.'

Oliver could feel the muscle complain every time he landed a punch, but he welcomed the pain. It kept him focused on the exercise, it kept his mind off Kat. A solid session in the gym was the only way to exhaust him. It meant he could collapse into bed at the end of the day and hopefully get some sleep.

'I reckon that will do for today,' Chris said, allowing Oliver one more punch. 'You can cool down on the bike.'

Oliver wasn't ready to call it quits. Not on the session and not on Kat. He picked up his towel and wiped the sweat from his face and neck. He'd go for a run on the treadmill and then cool off.

He cranked the treadmill up, jogging at a pace to keep his heart rate elevated, but the exercise didn't require his full concentration and his mind, inevitably, turned to Kat. He hadn't seen her for three days. She was still in Port Augusta, with her father, who was recovering after heart surgery. She hadn't told Oliver when she'd be back. He hadn't asked.

They'd communicated via text message. He hadn't known what was expected of him. She'd refused to be his fake fiancée but he wasn't really sure why. He could only assume she didn't want to be associated with him and any rumours. He could only assume she was disappointed in him and the situations he found himself in.

She said she believed him, but what if she didn't? Her opinion was important to him. *She* was important to him but he didn't know what to do about that. She had shut him out and he knew he couldn't go after her. He had to move on. With a fake fiancée.

He'd offered to help get Kat to Port Augusta because he could and because he wanted to. He wanted to help her and he also wanted to prove to her that he was capable of thinking about someone other than himself. Something other than his career. But he knew his offer hadn't been completely altruistic. He had hoped it might help her to see past some of his mistakes. Had hoped it might help her to change her mind about him.

But it hadn't helped. She'd sent him away. She hadn't wanted to introduce him to her aunt or her father. He understood it was a stressful time for her but he'd mistakenly, stupidly, thought that he could help ease that stress. That his presence would provide some comfort.

He'd told her he understood her decision not to be his fake fiancée, but it had stung.

She had rejected him.

And now he had to choose someone else to 'propose' to but it was a decision he'd been delaying. Not only because he didn't want it to be someone else but also because it would mean the end of his time with Kat. Once he had a fiancée in the eyes of the world his time spent with Kat would be over. It would have to be.

Philippa had been hounding him to make a decision and he'd promised her an answer tomorrow, but he still couldn't see past Kat. If he needed a fiancée, he still wanted it to be her. It didn't matter how many times he told himself that he'd manage, that he could live without her, he couldn't get her out of his head.

He missed her.

He decreased the speed on the treadmill, slowing it to a walk. He'd go back to his room, shower and have another look at those photos from Philippa. He'd choose someone else and try to forget about Kat. He obviously had stronger feelings for her than she did for him.

He'd made a mistake.

He'd focus on the movie. On his career. Just as he'd always done. Only he knew he'd lost some of the enjoyment that he usually got from work. It was no longer enough to keep him satisfied. He needed Kat.

Kat looked out of the window of the plane at the ochre earth and pale mullock heaps that dotted the landscape. She was relieved to be coming home and relieved that her father was recovering well following surgery to insert a stent into his blocked artery. She had a lot to be grateful for.

Normally she'd be pleased to see the familiar landscape but she had other things on her mind today. She was eager for the plane to land, eager to be home, but more eager to see Oliver. She'd missed his company over the past few days and she intended to head straight to the film set once she'd picked up her car. She needed an Oliver fix and she had something to tell him.

He'd texted her asking after her dad but hadn't intruded. She hadn't asked if he was keeping his distance deliberately or whether a text message was the level of communication he was happy with when it came to discussing her family. She'd been pleased to hear from him but appreciated that he hadn't pushed her. She'd wanted to be able to concentrate on her father without distractions. But now she was keen to see him. Her father was being transferred by ambulance home to Coober Pedy and was going to make a full recovery; she didn't need to feel guilty about spending time with Oliver.

She thanked God for Oliver and his calm, unflappable personality when she'd needed to get to her father's side quickly. For someone who knew how to have a good time it was reassuring to see that it wasn't all about red carpets, private jets and five-star luxury. She'd known he had a good work ethic, she'd seen plenty of evidence of that, but to see such a compassionate side was something special. And it had made her rethink what he'd asked of her.

He had been there for her when she needed him. It was her turn to do the same for him.

She was excited to see him. She'd missed how he made her feel—beautiful, special and fun. He'd shown her there was more to life than working and living here. She didn't want to be disappointed by her life but she wondered how she would go back to normal once he'd left. There'd be no more five-star hotels, no more karaoke serenades, private jets or amazing sex. She suspected he would move on without a backward glance but she doubted she'd be able to do the same. She imagined things would never be quite the same for her again.

She drove out to the film set, the cluster of dusty trailers, marquees and huts in the desert a familiar sight to her now. She parked and headed straight to his trailer. If he wasn't there she'd search elsewhere.

She knocked on his door and was relieved when it opened, and her heart leapt in her chest when she saw him standing there. She'd almost forgotten how gorgeous he was.

'Kat! You're back!' He stepped towards her and she expected him to greet her with a kiss but he stopped in his tracks, stepped back and held the door open wider. 'Come in.'

She stepped inside and saw Philippa sitting on the couch. Was that why he'd held himself back?

'We're just in the middle of something.'

'Actually, I needed to see both of you.' She'd wanted to see Oliver first but her news did involve them both. She might as well tell them together.

Philippa was shuffling through some papers on the coffee table, her movements drawing Kat's eye. She could see pages of photos spread out on the table. Had he picked another fake fiancée? Of course he had.

'Have you chosen someone else?' she asked. She hadn't imagined this scenario. Why hadn't she? She should have known. She'd been stupid. He wouldn't need her now.

'Yes,' said Philippa.

'Why?' asked Oliver.

Oliver hadn't said yes. Maybe there was still a chance he needed her. 'I came to tell you I would do it.'

'Really?' Oliver was staring at her.

'If you still need me.'

'Yes! Definitely.' His smile stretched across his mouth, from one corner to the other, and Kat knew she'd made the right decision.

'I do have one condition,' she added. She waited for both Oliver and Philippa to nod, to show they were at least paying attention. 'I want you to donate any money that you were happy to pay me to the Coober Pedy drive-in, to go towards the upgrading of the facilities. It can be a donation on behalf of Oliver to the town.' She didn't want any remuneration but she had decided this was one thing she could do, one way she could make sure something else positive came out of this. It would be a win for the town and she could sell it as being a grand gesture on Oliver's part. Maybe it would get him some more positive publicity.

'Done.' Philippa didn't hesitate and Kat wondered if she should have named a price.

'And I want another donation to the flying doctor service too,' she said, hoping she hadn't overstepped the mark.

'No problem,' Philippa replied.

'Are you sure you're OK with this?' Oliver asked her. There was the smallest of creases between his blue eyes. He looked worried. She didn't think she'd seen him look worried before. He was normally so full of confidence, so carefree.

She wasn't sure she could pull it off but she knew she wanted to try. She wanted to help. 'Do you really think we can convince people to believe we're in love?'

'Oliver is an actor,' said Philippa. 'It's his job to make people believe.'

'But I'm *not* an actor—do you think I'll be able to do this?'

'I don't; you were Oliver's choice. If you think it's too much for you to handle then I have plenty of other potential fiancées for him.'

Kat was not about to let Philippa get the better of her. She remembered Oliver's words—he wasn't one to back down from a challenge. Neither was she. It wouldn't be hard to pretend to be in love with Oliver. Not too hard at all.

'I want it to be you, Kat.' Oliver reached for her and her

body came alive at his touch. 'We can do this.' His blue gaze locked her in place. Their hips were touching. He ran his hands down her upper arms and Kat breathed in deeply as her insides trembled. 'I don't want to do this without you. Are we good?'

She nodded, incapable of speech while his eyes held her attention and his hands held her elbows.

He bent his head and Kat closed her eyes as his lips touched hers. Softly, lightly, a gentle caress.

'Thank you,' he said as he lifted his head, leaving Kat to wonder which kiss that was. It didn't matter, it had been just what she'd wanted. Exactly what she needed.

'I'll take you to dinner tonight,' he said, 'just the two of us—we need some time to sort out how this is going to work—but now I have to get back on set. Can you meet me at the hotel at seven-thirty? I'll book a table in Mona's restaurant.'

She nodded. She could do this and she'd worry about the consequences later.

Kat dressed carefully, it wasn't every day she got engaged. Even if it was all a charade having dinner at Mona's was reason enough to dress up.

She stepped into the red trouser suit she'd bought in Adelaide. That Oliver had bought her. He'd seen it in a shop window on Jetty Road and had insisted she try it on. He'd said the colour red would always remind him of her. She'd protested that she had nowhere to wear it, it was far too smart for anywhere she went in Coober Pedy, *and* it was too expensive. Oliver had told her she looked beautiful and had bought it for her.

She zipped it up and looked in the mirror. She had to admit it fitted her well but if she hadn't been meeting Oliver she doubted she would have had the confidence to wear head-to-toe red. It was such a bold statement. But Oliver gave her confidence. She recalled the admiration in his eyes when he'd first seen her in this outfit and she crossed her fingers that he'd like it just as much tonight.

* * *

He was waiting for her in the hotel lobby. He smiled and took her hands, holding them wide apart as he looked at her. His eyes were bright as he said, 'You look sensational.'

He did too. He had also dressed up and wore pale cotton trousers, a pale blue dress shirt and a navy jacket. He had no tie and wore leather shoes, without socks. He looked as if he'd walked off the page of a fashion catalogue.

He stepped in close and let go of her hands. He put his fingers under her chin, tipping her face up to him and kissing her on the lips. Kat felt the now familiar flutters in her belly as the touch of his lips warmed her from the inside.

'Are you hungry?'

She nodded. He took her hand and she walked beside him towards the restaurant. It was only past the bar, further into the hotel, further underground, but it took them several minutes as several hotel guests requested selfies with Oliver. He asked Kat if she minded, which she didn't, before he posed happily with fans.

When they eventually made it into the restaurant he asked for the quietest table, away from curious ears but still within sight of other diners. He was acting as though he didn't have a care in the world.

'Aren't you worried about the lawsuit?' Kat asked after the waiter had taken their order.

Oliver shook his head. 'I feel sick when I think about what happened to Natalie; she shouldn't have died and I feel terrible that it happened in my house, but it wasn't my fault and I have confidence in my legal team. I admit I've had my fair share of headlines over the years and this is right up there in the scale of monumental disasters, but I know I did nothing wrong. I believe justice will be done. I can't imagine what it must be like for Natalie's parents and I feel for them, I really do, but I'm not going to be made the scapegoat.

'I am not going to let them ruin my reputation or my career.

It's one thing to have a reputation as a playboy, another one entirely to be implicated in an accidental death.'

'I know I agreed to be your fake fiancée until you're off the hook,' she said as the waiter brought their meal and Oliver ordered more drinks, 'but do you have any idea how long that might take?' Kat didn't know how successful she'd be in pulling off the role of a fake fiancée, or, more to the point, she was worried that the longer their plan lasted, the more difficulty she'd have separating fact from fiction.

'I'm hoping not long. I want to get it settled and out of the papers. I've spoken to my lawyer. He's got several statements and photographs of Natalie which seem to contradict her parents' claim that she never touched drugs. I feel bad that he has investigators trawling through her private life but her parents instigated this and my lawyer thinks he will have enough evidence soon to get Natalie's parents to drop the lawsuit. I can't thank you enough for what you're doing for me but it shouldn't be for too long. Is that OK?'

She nodded.

'Thank you. I owe you a favour. Two probably.'

'I'll let you pay for dinner.' She smiled, relieved to hear him being so positive about the situation.

'I was going to, and that only takes care of one favour.'

'I'll think of something else,' she said, knowing exactly what she would ask for.

'Good,' Oliver said just as the waiter appeared with a bottle of champagne. 'I want to propose a toast.'

'What are we toasting?' Kat asked as Oliver handed her the glass that had been poured.

'To a successful partnership.' He smiled and touched his glass to hers. 'I think we could make a good team,' he said as she sipped her champagne. 'Which brings me to another question for you.'

Before she could ask what it was Oliver had stood up from the table and dropped to one knee.

'What are you doing?' Kat almost choked on her champagne.

'Legitimising our agreement.'

Kat was aware of a lull in conversation as the other restaurant patrons all turned to watch them.

'From the moment I first saw you I was captivated but you have shown me so much more than your beauty. Not only are you beautiful, sexy and smart but you are also kind, generous, caring and loving and I need you in my life. I can only hope that you need me too and that I have some of the qualities you value in a partner. Kat, will you do me the honour of accepting my proposal of marriage?'

Kat's heart was racing and her hands were shaking but she still noticed that there was no declaration of love. There wasn't anything that could be construed any differently on her part than what it was—a fake proposal.

She knew the other patrons watching wouldn't notice. They'd only see Oliver, down on one knee, proposing. They wouldn't be listening to the words. They'd be caught up in the theatrics. After all, he was an actor. But no matter what they heard and how well Oliver played his role, she knew the engagement was fake and she needed to remember that was all it was. And she had a part to play.

CHAPTER EIGHT

OLIVER WAS STILL down on one knee, waiting. The restaurant was silent, the other patrons all waiting too.

Kat wasn't used to such a public display and the attention made her mind go blank. She had no idea what her lines were. She wasn't used to this at all. She felt tears in her eyes but, while they lent authenticity to the spectacle, she had no idea why she was crying.

Somehow, she managed to nod and suddenly applause rippled around them as Oliver sprang up from his knees and gathered her into his arms and kissed her. Despite her knowing his proposal was a sham, his kisses felt real and Kat took some comfort from that. Being kissed by Oliver was a memory no one could take away from her. That was something she could keep.

She was aware of a barrage of camera flashes as people recorded and photographed Oliver's proposal. She knew the pictures would be uploaded to social media, and perhaps it was all part of the plan—if not Oliver's then definitely Philippa's. She understood this was what she'd signed up for: Oliver needed the positive publicity.

The applause died down when they sat. Oliver topped up their champagne glasses before reaching behind him, into the pocket of his jacket. When he turned back to Kat he held a small velvet box in the palm of his hand. He flipped open the lid.

Nestled inside was a diamond ring. Teardrop-shaped, in a high claw setting, it was enormous, stunning but totally impractical in the rough and tumble outback and seemed even more so to Kat when she considered her job. She needed something that was tough, that could withstand getting knocked and wouldn't tear into the rubber gloves she was always pulling on for work. She would have chosen a bezel setting and would have preferred an opal.

'Where did this come from?'

'Philippa picked it out this afternoon.'

His proposal might have felt real but it didn't take much to shatter the illusion. Six little words.

Someone else had chosen the ring.

He picked up her left hand and slid the ring onto her fourth finger. It was a perfect fit. The deal was done.

A final burst of camera flashes lit up the room.

Kat looked around nervously. 'The news will be well and truly out before I make it home tonight—you'd better hope my father doesn't hear about this before I have a chance to explain.' She needed to tell her family what was going on. She realised, too late, she should have warned them already.

'I would like to be there when you tell him.'

'Why?'

'Because it's the right thing to do. It's courteous and one thing I've never been accused of is having poor manners. And it's important that I meet your father if we're going to manage to sell this story to the media.'

He was right. Her whole family needed to meet him and she could use his support when she told them of the arrangement. She wasn't sure how they would react to this news. 'You could come to dinner tomorrow.'

'Your weekly family dinner?' He sounded worried.

'It's at Dean and Saskia's…but if you don't think you can handle it…'

'I'll be fine.'

Saskia greeted them at the door and Oliver relaxed slightly. Saskia was a familiar face at least.

He didn't do family but he knew he had to make an exception in this case. Even though he and Kat were only posing as a newly engaged couple, he knew it was important that he meet Kat's father and make sure he got him on side.

But the warm greeting he'd hoped for wasn't forthcoming. Saskia barely acknowledged either of them and if she said 'hello' he must have missed it. She pulled Kat inside and whispered, rather loudly, 'I can't believe you didn't tell us, Kat. It's all over the internet.'

Saskia was brandishing her mobile phone and, without pausing, tapped it and held it up so they could see the screen. A video of Oliver's proposal, recorded by a restaurant patron last night and uploaded to the internet, was running.

Kat's face went pale. 'Does Papa know? Has he seen this?'

Saskia shook her head. 'No.'

'It's not what you think.'

'What does that mean?'

'I'll tell you after we've spoken to Papa.'

Saskia picked up Kat's left hand. 'Where's the ring?'

Her hand was bare.

'In my purse. I was worried about damaging it.'

Oliver knew she was thinking the ring had to be returned. He was finding he was attuned to her thoughts and often knew what she was going to say before she spoke. He was an experienced observer of people, their mannerisms, gaits and habits—it all helped when he was trying to build a character. He was a good mimic of accents too but, while he listened to *how* people spoke, he didn't always listen to what they said. It was different with Kat. *He* was different with Kat.

Kat was definitely upset, obviously worried about her father's reaction to their news, and Oliver's own nerves intensified. He hoped he could pull this off. And he hoped it wasn't a mistake to be meeting Kat's family en masse. To be breaking this news to them collectively.

He was tense as Saskia led them into the house and Kat introduced him to her father. Tony did not look impressed. Kat had warned him on several occasions about her protective father. Oliver just hoped he gave him a chance.

'Papa, this is Oliver Harding. Oliver, this is my father, Tony.'

Oliver extended his hand. 'It's a pleasure to meet you, sir.'

Tony's handshake was firm, his palm rough. He looked Oliver up and down, taking in his neatly pressed clothes, his soft leather shoes, his manicured nails. Oliver was certain he didn't approve and it bothered him. He wanted Kat's father to like him. He knew Kat would be influenced by her family's perceptions of him and he didn't want anything they said or thought to make Kat think less of him.

'You're an actor.'

It was a statement, delivered as though Tony felt actors were on a par with axe murderers.

'Yes, I am.' He wasn't going to apologise for his career choice. He was good at his craft and he made a very good living. He was successful.

'And American.'

'Papa!'

'Settle down, Katarina; an American is as welcome for dinner as the next person. What would you like to drink, Oliver? Will you have a beer?'

'That sounds good, thank you.'

Maybe the night would go better than expected, Oliver thought as he accepted a drink and was introduced to Roger's wife, Maya, as well as Kat's aunt Rosa. Despite doing his best over the years to avoid families—both his own and anyone else's—he found it was nice to be able to put faces to the names that he'd heard so often from Kat.

The family gathered in the spacious living room; although Kat had described their underground houses to him, he was still surprised by the size of the rooms and the height of the ceilings. The room was large and airy with one window that looked out into the front 'garden', which was really just more bare earth with a couple of native eucalyptus trees, an outdoor seating area and a barbecue. Along with the adults, there were several children who ran in and out of the room, interested only in the food that was laid out on the coffee table, but even when Saskia sent them off with their own bowls of crisps the conversational noise level was still high.

Until Kat said, 'Papa, we have some news.'

The noise level in the room dropped immediately, almost as if someone had flipped a switch or pulled a plug. Five pairs of eyes swivelled in their direction. Even though Kat had spoken, Oliver was aware that a lot of the attention was focused on him. Kat had said 'we' and it was obvious her family were keen to hear what was coming next, and Oliver knew they would be gunning for him if they didn't like what they heard.

'It's nothing to get excited about but we wanted to tell you before you heard anything on the grapevine. Oliver and I are engaged.'

'What?' Tony was looking from Kat to Oliver as if he couldn't believe what he was hearing. Oliver and Kat were sitting on the same couch, not touching, and there was a good several inches between them, but even so, Oliver got the impression that Kat's father would very much like to pick him up and put him on another chair, far away from Kat, in another room even.

Oliver was watching Tony but out of the corner of his eye he could see both Roger and Dean. He noticed that they both sat up a little straighter in their chairs, waiting for Tony's reaction, waiting to see if they needed to spring into action. Pick Oliver up and throw him out of the house, perhaps? Oliver didn't doubt that between the two of them they'd have no trouble managing that.

'You're going to marry a man I've never met, and you,' he turned to Oliver, staring him down, 'you didn't have the decency to come to see me first.'

Oliver wondered if he was joking. His expression suggested he wasn't. Did he really expect that a man would still ask his potential father-in-law for permission to marry his daughter? Did people still do that? Oliver prided himself on his manners but, he had to admit, he had no idea about proper proposal etiquette.

'Papa, calm down. We're not actually going to get married.'

'What on earth does that mean? People don't get engaged to *not* get married.'

'I'm doing this as a favour for Oliver. It's for publicity. It will help his career.'

Dean and Roger were still bristling but at least they'd stayed in their seats. Saskia had excused herself earlier and was busy in the kitchen, and the only person who seemed to be on their side, judging from the sympathetic looks she was sending Kat's way, was Maya. He wasn't sure about Aunt Rosa.

'Would you like to explain exactly *how* an engagement can help a career?' Tony was addressing Kat, completely ignoring Oliver.

'Oliver needs some positive publicity. The media have got hold of a story, a false accusation, and Oliver needs something to deflect attention, something to put a positive spin on things. His publicist thinks an engagement will do the trick. I've agreed to help, just until everything settles down again.'

'And what about you? What do you get out of this arrangement?'

'You know how the Cooper Pedy Residents' Association has been fundraising for improvements for the drive-in? Oliver is going to donate money towards the upgrades and also to the flying doctors. I'm doing this for the town.'

'That's all well and good but what about your reputation?

You'll have two broken engagements, Katarina. No man will marry you after that!'

Two? What was he talking about? Oliver's head was spinning as he tried to follow the rapid-fire conversation—perhaps he'd misheard. But before he had a chance to clarify just what had been said Kat was responding to her father.

'Papa, don't be ridiculous. No one even needs to know about this one.'

'Everyone *will* know about this one though, won't they?' Aunt Rosa commented. 'Isn't that the point?' Perhaps she wasn't on their side.

'Kat,' Saskia interrupted as she re-entered the room, 'have you got any balsamic vinegar at your place? I seem to have run out.'

'I'll go and have a look.'

'We'll talk about this when you get back,' Tony muttered as Kat stood up.

'Oliver, why don't you give Kat a hand?' Saskia instructed with a nod.

Oliver didn't hesitate. Saskia had given him an excuse to escape the heat and maybe both he and Tony needed a chance to rein in their tempers and digest information. Tony that his daughter was engaged, and Oliver the news that Kat was engaged *again*. He couldn't believe Kat hadn't said anything.

He followed Kat next door, the heat of the afternoon assaulting him as he left the coolness of the underground dwelling to step outside.

'You've been engaged before?' he asked as the front door closed behind him. He'd wanted a chance to see Kat's home, to be able to picture her there whenever he wanted to, but he was far too bewildered to take in his surroundings. There were other things occupying his thoughts.

'Yes.'

Oliver was astounded. He'd asked about an ex-husband,

so she could have mentioned an ex-fiancé…she'd had plenty of time.

But then again, why would she have? They didn't have to know everything about each other. Even if he wanted to.

'When?'

'Six years ago. When I was in Adelaide.'

Six years! She would have been so young.

'What happened?'

He wanted to know everything, even though he was aware it wasn't really any of his business. It shouldn't matter but he was surprised to find he felt jealous. He'd wanted to be the first one to propose to her.

He knew he was being ridiculous. His proposal wasn't real, but part of him liked pretending it was.

'Mum died.' Kat's voice wobbled and Oliver felt terrible for hounding her. She'd told him about losing her mother a few years earlier. He should have remembered that and put two and two together. 'And I left Adelaide and came back here.'

'And he didn't?'

Kat shook her head and Oliver could see tears gathering on her lashes. Was she crying for her mum or for someone else?

He moved towards her, wanting to take her in his arms and comfort her, but she held up a hand. 'I'm OK,' she said and her words felt like a slap in the face. 'Adam came back with me initially but our plan was never to stay permanently. He was a vet. Is a vet. But there's no work here. Dad had his first heart scare when Mum died. Shortness of breath, difficulty breathing. We thought it was a panic attack but it was cardiac complications, so I didn't feel that I could leave him to cope with losing Mum alone. Even though he's got family living next door I didn't think it was the right thing to do and, to be honest, I didn't want to leave him. I didn't want to leave at all. I needed to have my family around me too. Adam stayed for a while but he didn't like it here. He was bored. He went back to Adelaide. I stayed.'

'For the past five years?'

'Yes.' Kat turned her back and walked into the kitchen. Oliver followed. 'In the beginning there was a lot going on. I was upset with him for leaving. I felt he didn't support me. I was struggling after Mum died and that was our first hurdle, and I figured if we couldn't get through that together there wasn't much hope for our future. Life isn't smooth sailing. I needed to know I could depend on him.

'When I needed him he wasn't there for me. He expected to be the most important person in my life, which he was, mostly, but my family needed me more, and I needed them. Adam wasn't the man I thought he was. Family comes first and there was no room in his life for my family.'

'Kat, I'm sorry, I had no idea.'

'Of course you didn't.'

'Are you sure about doing the whole engagement thing again?' Was she really prepared to have another broken engagement just to help him out, because they couldn't possibly make this work, could they? They came from two completely different worlds and he didn't intend to get married, ever. She was looking for her soulmate.

'It's fine.'

He wished she sounded more convincing but she was no actress. He could imagine how upset she would have been. He knew she wanted to find 'the one' and live happily ever after.

'Are you sure?' He really needed her to stick with the plan and, despite worrying that he might be adversely affecting her life, he really hoped she meant it. 'The whole western world will know about this, Kat. That's the point.'

'Well, it won't cause much of a ripple in Coober Pedy. You said yourself that the tabloids will move on eventually. They'll find another story. A bigger one. They won't be concerned about you, or us, for ever. It will be fine. *I'll* be fine.'

'And your father?'

'Don't worry about my father. I can handle him.'

'You shouldn't have to handle him.' He felt responsible and

therefore obligated to help. Kat shouldn't have to handle her father. 'This is my fault. I've put you in an awkward position, and I need to fix it.' He was determined to win Tony over.

'He doesn't know you. I think it's just the shock. I probably should have told him in private; maybe I could have explained things better.'

'I don't want you to bear the brunt of this. That's not fair.'

'It'll be OK; my father can be a little protective of me but I'll get him on side. We should get back,' she said, holding up the bottle of vinegar, 'before they send out a search party.'

Kat's cousins and her father were in the front, and only, garden, standing around the barbecue. Oliver knew this was his opportunity to attempt to fix things.

He knew how important family was to Kat and, if he didn't, she'd just made it perfectly clear once again. Her family came first. Their opinion mattered to her. It mattered to him too but for different reasons. He wanted to make things easier for Kat but he also needed her family to support, at least publicly, this fake engagement.

Her father and cousins were polite, offering him another drink and making space for him at the grill, but it was clear it was going to have to be up to him to extend an olive branch. That wasn't a problem; he could do that.

'I can understand you have reservations,' he said, extending that branch, 'but I guarantee Kat won't be disadvantaged by helping me.' He wasn't expecting the barrage of questions that came flooding back to him.

'How can you be sure? You can't know her well.'

'You were obviously surprised to hear she'd been engaged before.'

'How do you expect to pull this off if you know nothing about her? How do you expect to convince everyone you're madly in love?'

'What's her favourite food? Her middle name? Her dream job?'

He was surprised to find he knew the answers. He had talked to Kat more than he'd ever talked to anyone. They'd shared plane journeys, car rides and dinners. They'd had hours alone together. She might have kept some secrets but he was convinced he knew the essence of her.

'Her favourite food is roast lamb but she will eat seafood any chance she gets, especially prawns. Her middle name is Maria, after her grandmother, and she always wanted to join the flying doctors but now, ultimately, she'd like to work with the air ambulance. Her favourite colour is red, her favourite movies are romantic comedies and her ex-fiancé's name is Adam.' They didn't need to know that he'd just learnt that but he'd give them what they want to hear even if it wasn't what they expected. 'She is kind and generous, warm-hearted, loving.'

Kat was all the things he'd never really experienced in one person before. The people he was normally surrounded by all had an agenda. Even if they were pleasant and honest they all needed something from him—a job, a favour, a photograph. He enjoyed Kat's company all the more because she seemed to enjoy his. She didn't expect things of him and she seemed to like him, the real him, not the movie star.

'I was raised to be hard-working and respectful. I like Kat and I respect her.' He avoided mentioning that he had nothing to do with his father and very little to do with his mother—he suspected that wouldn't win him any fans. In his opinion his family dynamics were irrelevant; he'd worked hard to become the man he was today, to have confidence in his abilities.

'I am a good person.' He wanted to be even better. He wanted to be someone she would be proud of. He wanted to be someone who deserved someone like Kat in his life.

It was obvious Kat's family didn't think he was that person. They didn't think he was good enough and that bothered him. He would have to prove himself. To them and to Kat.

He wished Kat hadn't told her father the engagement was fake—maybe he'd be less hostile if he thought Oliver's intentions were honourable, but then again, maybe not. Either way, he doubted that Tony would be going to give a glowing recommendation of his new son-in-law-to-be if asked either.

'Family is the most important thing in her life,' Oliver said. 'She told me you and her mother were married for thirty-two years, and she wants that too.'

'And what if your little stunt stops her from getting that?'

'It won't. I promise this won't harm her reputation. I'll make sure that she is the one who calls off the engagement, that she comes out of this with her reputation intact.'

'How can you be sure?' Tony demanded. 'You're playing with her feelings. Her life. You should think carefully about what you are asking of her. Think about what she needs.'

He knew Tony was right. He needed to consider Kat's needs before his own but he didn't think that the fake engagement and Kat's needs were incompatible. They were both getting something out of the arrangement and he was positive they could do this without any repercussions.

Dinner was far from the relaxed Sunday night meal Kat was used to. The atmosphere was tense, everyone was on edge, and she wondered if she'd made a mistake agreeing to Oliver's request.

It was important to her that her family liked Oliver. It shouldn't matter—they weren't going to have a future together—but still, she hadn't expected this level of disapproval.

She, Saskia and Maya tried hard to keep the conversation flowing but it was difficult and there were plenty of uncomfortable silences. When Roger's phone rang in the middle of dinner, Kat jumped, startled by the shrill sound.

Roger got up to take the call but everyone could hear his half of the conversation and the tension increased as they waited to hear what had happened. It was clear there was an emergency of some sort. Dean was out of his seat before Roger disconnected the call.

'That was Emilia,' Roger said. 'Jimmy was due home an hour ago and Emilia hasn't been able to get him on his cell phone.'

'What's going on?' Oliver asked Kat.

'Emilia's husband is a miner. Being late home and not answering his phone isn't unusual—phone reception can be dodgy out here—but he could have had an accident and she can't go and check on him because she doesn't know where he was working. That'll be why she called Roger. He knows where Jimmy's been working. He and Dean will go and take a look. Either Jimmy's phone has gone flat, is out of range, he's found opal or there's been a slide. An accident.'

'Is there anything I can do to help?'

'Not this time. The boys will raise the alarm if necessary. If there has been an accident the mine rescue team will be called in to help, and I need to be available. I'm going to have to take you back to the hotel, just in case.'

'Will you need your car?'

'No.'

'Why don't I borrow it? You don't need to drive me around. I can get myself home and that frees you up now. I will come back in the morning and pick you up—you're working on set tomorrow, right?'

Kat nodded. 'Are you sure?'

'Positive.'

'All right, I'll grab my keys.'

Kat waited while Oliver thanked Saskia and said goodbye to Rosa, Maya and her father. Her father was cool but at least he was acknowledging Oliver, although she was ashamed of the behaviour of the men in her family.

'I'm sorry about Papa—I didn't expect him to be quite so hostile,' she said as she and Oliver left the house.

'Don't worry about it. It doesn't matter if they don't like me as long as they don't make things difficult for you. Will you be OK?'

She nodded and stood outside the house and watched him drive away, wondering again if this would work out according to the plan.

She went inside to give Saskia and Maya a hand cleaning up.

'That went badly,' she said as she picked up a tea towel and started to dry the glasses.

'What did you expect?' Saskia asked.

'Why exactly did you agree to this?' asked Maya.

'He asked for my help.'

'And you couldn't refuse.'

'No, I couldn't. I owed him a favour. He got me back to Port Augusta after Papa's heart attack. He was amazing. So calm and in control. He did that for me and now I can do this for him.'

'What was so bad that he needed to create a good fake news story to deflect the bad news?'

Kat explained about the lawsuit. 'That's why I agreed to help him.'

'Your father will go ballistic if he hears about that.'

'That's why I'm not saying anything to Papa and the boys. Oliver is certain the lawsuit will be dropped and I believe him. They already don't trust him and I don't want to make things any worse.'

'You don't think they'll find out?'

'How? They never look at any entertainment news. They're only interested in three things—finding opal, the price of opal and the football.'

'And family,' Maya added as her phone beeped with a message. 'It's Roger,' she said. 'Jimmy's OK. He found a seam of opal and lost track of time.'

'Are you sure you're OK with this whole fake engagement?' Saskia asked; it was obvious she wasn't going to let this go. 'I know you like him. You don't feel like he's taking advantage of your generosity? Your feelings?'

'It's a business deal. It's not hurting anyone. I'm helping him. Just like he helped me and like he'll be helping the community with his donation to the drive-in and to the flying doctor.'

'It's one thing for him to help with a search or to donate money; it's another thing completely for him to get you involved in this publicity stunt. And what about going forwards? What's the plan then?'

'He'll win the lawsuit and then we'll call it off.'

'When will that be?'

'I'm not sure exactly.'

'And you're OK with that?'

Yes.' She'd have to be. It was the deal she'd made.

Kat scarcely had time to worry about her family's opinion of Oliver over the next week. Philippa had done her job and the video footage of Oliver's proposal had gone viral. The media had turned up in full force, clamouring for a story, and Kat's life had become a whirlwind of interviews and photo shoots interspersed between her work on and off set. It left barely any time for the two of them to be alone together and even less time for her to dwell on all the reasons her family disapproved of the 'engagement'.

She had explained Oliver's involvement in getting her to Port Augusta from Adelaide to see her father, and she thought that maybe her Papa was softening a little, but it didn't really matter. It wasn't a real relationship. Her family didn't have to like him. It wouldn't bother Oliver, he didn't do family, and she wouldn't let it bother her.

They had done a couple of interviews early in the week, all arranged by Philippa, for the Australian media. Kat had been super-nervous but the journalists had been gentle and Oliver had been beside her all the time. He was very relaxed in front of the camera and his experience and calmness helped to settle Kat. Those interviews would be syndicated around the world but today they were faced with several interviews on a much larger scale. These would be the last of their joint interviews and first up was a panel of print journalists from the States followed by an interview that would go to air on American television.

Philippa had organised hair and make-up for Kat and she'd flown in a selection of outfits for Kat to choose from. Kat had insisted on Australian designers but she'd never heard of half of the ones Philippa had chosen. To give her credit, all the outfits were gorgeous but that made it impossible to choose just one. In the end Kat had asked Oliver's advice and he'd chosen a sleeveless cobalt-blue trouser suit with a halter neckline. The colour of the outfit reminded her of Oliver's eyes.

She felt overdressed, and over-made-up, for the middle of the morning but Oliver had reminded her that the television interview would be screened in the evening and she would look perfect.

He had held her hand and led her to the couch for the interview. He'd insisted that they be seated on a couch, not two separate chairs, and Kat had been grateful for that; she'd needed him close.

The interview began with all the questions Kat had become used to. How they had met. What Kat did for a job. How she had found growing up in Coober Pedy.

Oliver was very attentive: he was constantly touching her, his hand on her thigh, around her shoulders or holding her hand. He made her feel beautiful and she almost believed his answers when he talked about how they'd met, what he had thought when he first saw her and how they'd fallen in love. He almost had her convinced that he had real feelings for her but then she remembered that he did this all the time—put on a show for the media. He would give them what they wanted to keep himself in the headlines. It was all just an act. Even when he held her hand, a move that appeared so relaxed and natural, she noticed that he made sure her engagement ring was on show.

She forced herself to concentrate. This was their last interview and she had a part to play.

'Have you set a date for your wedding?'

'Not yet.' Oliver fielded most of the questions but he looked at her before answering, giving the impression that they were a team.

'Where will you get married?'

'We haven't decided.' He squeezed her hand and smiled at her and Kat knew the audience would think they had decided but were keeping that information to themselves.

'Will it be a big celebrity wedding or something private?'

'I'd like a big wedding. I want to show Kat off to everyone but she hasn't met my friends yet. It might be a small wedding if she doesn't like them.' His blue eyes sparkled as he laughed.

'Will they like her?'

'They will love her.' He looked at Kat, holding her gaze, his expression now earnest.

'Have you met her family?'

'I have.'

'And what did they think of Oliver, Kat?'

'They found him charming.' That was true of Maya and Saskia at least. Kat didn't feel she needed to be any more specific—in fact, Oliver had coached her in what to say.

'What about this lawsuit? You're standing by your man while he fights these charges, Kat?'

'Of course.'

'Any comment, Oliver?'

'No comment. I have every faith in our justice system. I am extremely sorry for the Hanson family's loss but we are focusing on our own future.'

'And what does that future look like, Kat? Will you be starting a family?' The journalist moved quickly along. Kat knew from previous interviews that they had to ask the question but, as it was all based on supposition, they couldn't really continue with that line. 'Do you want children?'

'Of course,' she replied, keeping her gaze directed at the

journalist. 'Very much.' She couldn't look at Oliver; she was afraid he'd see the truth in her eyes.

'Oliver?'

'Definitely.'

He was looking at her and Kat's heart flipped in her chest. He looked as if he meant every word.

'The movie is about to wrap on location and filming will move back to the States. Are you going to be moving too, Kat?'

'Kat will join me later. It won't be much fun for her in the States, away from her friends and family, while I'm working.'

Oliver was giving answers they hadn't discussed but Kat knew it didn't matter. None of this was real and by the time 'later' came around the lawsuit would be over and Oliver wouldn't need her any more. The idea was upsetting but there was nothing she could do.

Kat's heart sat like lead in her chest. It was supposed to be a party—it *was* a party—but she was miserable. The movie had wrapped on location and Oliver was leaving tomorrow. Filming would finish in the studio in the States. She knew she would miss him, she knew her life would never be the same without him. But she would cope, she'd have to.

She was talking to Julia when she saw him crossing the room towards them. It was getting late and she knew, at best, they only had a few hours left. She pasted a smile on her face, although her heart was breaking.

'Kat, could I borrow you for a second?'

He could have her for a lifetime if he wanted.

She nodded.

'I have something I want to give you,' he said as he took her arm and led her to a quiet corner. He sat her down and handed her a pile of beautifully wrapped gifts. A stack of box-shaped presents, but none small enough to be jewellery. They looked like books.

Kat swallowed her disappointment and opened the first one.

It was a photograph. He'd made copies of some of the publicity photos they had taken together. He'd framed them for her and included her favourite one. It captured her sitting on his lap. She was smiling and he was laughing. His head was thrown back, and they weren't looking at each other—she was leaning forwards away from him—but his arms were wrapped tightly around her waist, as if he was afraid to let her go. She wished that were the case.

Even though it was all an act she couldn't deny the photos were gorgeous. She looked happy; she glowed. She looked like a woman in love.

She hoped he didn't notice.

'These are gorgeous. Thank you.'

She knew she would treasure the pictures. One day. She wasn't sure if she was ready to display them just yet. She might need some time before she was ready to see his face every day, before she was ready to see the reflection of her unrequited love.

She hadn't meant to fall in love with him. She'd thought she'd be able to come out of this with her heart intact but it seemed fate had other ideas in store for her. It was time to bring this all to an end before she crumbled completely.

'Oliver?' she said as she wrapped the frames up again. She would look at them later. Alone. 'There's something I wanted to speak to you about. You're leaving tomorrow and I'm not sure what you and Philippa want me to do or say about our "engagement" once you're gone.'

'I thought maybe I'd say you're coming to visit me in a few weeks. What do you think?'

She didn't want to visit. She wasn't interested in a holiday. This was her chance to find out if he had genuine feelings for her at all. She wanted him to offer her a future. A life together. She wanted him to propose to her for real. But it seemed a few more days was all she could have. It wasn't enough, not nearly, and she wouldn't settle for that. 'Is that necessary? Don't you think the lawsuit might be resolved by then?'

'That wouldn't matter. You could still visit me.'

She shook her head. She'd hoped she wouldn't be faced with this scenario, the one where Oliver didn't profess his undying love, but she'd thought this through, just in case. 'We have to call the engagement off eventually. It will make our break-up more authentic if we don't see each other again after you leave. I thought we could go with the story that I am staying here while my dad recovers. When the lawsuit is over your life will go back to normal. You won't need me any more. You'll forget all about me.'

She waited for him to say that wasn't what he wanted.

'You don't want to visit me?' he said, which wasn't the same thing at all.

'I wouldn't want to leave Papa.'

'Kat, he's fine. He's recovered well from his surgery. You could leave for a few weeks.'

She felt guilty using her father as her excuse but she wanted more than a few weeks. She wasn't going to settle for less even if it meant suffering a broken heart. She knew that if he loved her they would find a way to work things out. But it looked as if she wasn't going to get her wish. 'I have to stay.'

'If that's what you want.'

No. It wasn't what she wanted at all. She wanted him to say he loved her, that he couldn't live without her, that he would stay with her. But she knew that was impossible. 'I should go,' she said. She didn't belong here. In his world.

'Now?'

She nodded. She loved him but she didn't expect him to love her back. She needed to make a clean break. She couldn't stand the thought of saying goodbye but she knew she had to. And she had to do it quickly.

They didn't speak as he walked with her to her car. There was nothing left to say.

He took her in his arms and spun her to face him. 'You are wrong, by the way,' he said as he lifted her chin and looked into her eyes. 'I'll never forget you,' he said as his lips came down onto hers.

The kiss was gentle. Sad. Kat didn't know that was even possible.

She knew it was a goodbye kiss but she thought it might be better called the 'break my heart' kiss.

'You have an open invitation to visit me any time, so let me know if you change your mind,' he said as she made herself let go of him.

She nodded and got into her car. She could feel tears threatening to spill and she didn't want to cry in front of him. She didn't want him to see how her heart was breaking.

She wiped away her tears with the back of her hand as she drove away. She didn't look back. She knew she'd turn right around if she did.

He watched her drive away. He could scarcely breathe and his heart ached in his chest. He wasn't ready to say goodbye. He wanted to chase after her, to beg her to reconsider but he knew he'd be wasting his time. She wasn't going to leave her father. Her family came first. It was what she had always told him but he'd hoped that maybe he would be worth the sacrifice on her part. But if she wouldn't leave for a few weeks, how could he ask her to leave for ever?

And how did he expect it to work? What would they do going forwards? Where did he see them? Did they have a future? Could he expect her to leave everything she loved behind to travel with him? To live his nomadic existence…his lonely, nomadic existence? He couldn't ask her to leave with him. Everything she loved was here. Her family, her career, her world. She was surrounded by people who loved her. And she had chosen to stay with them. He'd known she would but he'd hoped differently.

He wanted her to love him, to choose him, but was that fair? Did he love her?

He didn't know. He'd never been in love before. All he knew was that, watching her drive away, he felt as if she was taking his heart with her.

He stood and watched until her tail lights disappeared. Leaving him alone again. As always.

CHAPTER NINE

'HOW ARE YOU? Have you heard from him?' Saskia asked as she sat on Kat's bed and watched her tidy her room.

'No.'

Oliver had been gone for a week. Kat had seen an interview he'd given at Sydney Airport as he left the country. He'd been asked about his fiancée and he had looked suitably upset when he'd replied that Kat was staying in Coober Pedy temporarily while her father was recovering from surgery but was planning to join him later.

She knew that wouldn't happen.

'You should have gone with him.'

'I can't leave Papa. I'm all he has.'

'It's not for ever, Kat. And that's not true. He has Rosa, me, the boys, Maya. We're all here. You could have gone.'

'What would be the point? It's not real, Sas. It's all make-believe.' Oliver had asked her to visit but Kat wanted more. She wanted for ever. She wanted true love.

Saskia picked up a framed photo. Kat's favourite. 'It looks pretty real.'

'It was all an act.' At least on his part. She wanted to believe they shared something real but she really wasn't sure. She'd fallen in love with him and their connection had felt real to her, but what if she'd fallen for Oliver because of a fantasy? Because she'd always dreamt of finding the one. What if he wasn't the one but was simply an option? 'He doesn't need me.'

'Are you sure? You could go and find out. What's the worst thing that could happen? You find it's not what you thought and you come home miserable. You're already miserable, so isn't it better to take a chance? What are you afraid of?'

She was afraid he wouldn't want her. That she wasn't sophisticated enough and wouldn't have anything in common with his life. His friends. His world. That she wouldn't belong. That she'd look out of place and he'd see she wasn't right for him.

She was afraid that their differences were bigger than their similarities because, after all, what did they really have in common? They had talked and laughed and loved. They had shared secrets and dreams, but those secrets and dreams were so different.

She felt as if she knew him but she was scared to take a chance. It was easier to stay than to take a risk. She liked to play it safe. She liked to follow rules. She liked routine. He was a rule-breaker, independent. She needed her family and friends. He was a loner. She could get past all those differences with the exception of family. She wasn't sure if she could be with someone who didn't value family.

'We are too different.'

'Don't be ridiculous.' Saskia wasn't holding back with her opinion. 'Since when do you think that every couple has to be exactly alike? Why should they think alike, act alike? Imagine how boring that would be. Think about how he makes you feel.'

He made her feel special. He made her feel beautiful. He made her happy. And now he'd made her miserable. She was lonely. She missed him.

'If you're not going to go to him maybe you just need to get away from here for a while. Away from the memories. We should have a girls' trip. Maya and I could leave the kids with our husbands and go with you. What do you think?'

'Maybe,' she said, but what she thought was, what if she was away and something else went wrong? Or, even worse, what if Oliver came back for her but she wasn't here?

She knew that was a ridiculous notion but she could admit, if only to herself, that it was what she was dreaming of.

She'd fallen in love with him but there was nothing she could do.

He was gone. It was over.

Kat looked at the clock. Fifteen minutes until the end of her shift.

Her life had been dragging on painfully slowly for the past four weeks since Oliver had left. Every morning she woke up hoping to feel better. Hoping she wouldn't feel as though part of her was missing. When would it end?

'Do you think it's safe to get changed now?' she asked Dave. 'Saskia and Maya are going to collect me from here.'

She was going out to dinner with her cousins' wives to celebrate Maya's birthday. The other crew would be here to take over shortly and she wanted to be ready to go, but she knew how often a last-minute emergency would derail any plans for an on-time knock-off.

'Sure. It's been—'

'Don't say it!' Kat held up her hand in warning. She was superstitious enough to stop Dave from uttering the word. The minute you said a shift had been quiet, chaos would descend.

Dave laughed. 'Go and get changed. I'll hold the fort.'

Kat barely had time to get her boots off before Dave was knocking at the door. 'Kat, we've got a call-out. Are you still dressed?'

She sighed and stuffed her feet back into her boots, leaving her bag with her change of clothes behind.

'Take your bag with us,' Dave said. 'I might be able to drop you straight to dinner.'

She doubted that—it seemed as though everything that could

go wrong did. Her life was a mess. 'Where are we going?' she asked as they climbed into the ambulance.

'Out towards Crocodile Harry's place,' he said as he handed her the GPS coordinates so she could punch them into the sat-nav as he drove. 'A couple of tourists; one's had a fall, a suspected fractured leg.'

Crocodile Harry's was only ten minutes out of town. It was where George had filmed the cave scenes and the mention of it made Kat immediately think of Oliver.

'Do we know what we're looking for?' Kat asked.

'A white Toyota Landcruiser.'

Lucky, then, they had the GPS details. Those vehicles were a dime a dozen out here.

Dave drove west into the setting sun. Kat flipped the sun visor down, the sun was low in the sky making visibility difficult, and her sunglasses weren't providing enough resistance against the glare as she searched the horizon.

'I see a car.' She pointed to their left, to where a four-by-four sat on top of a hill. It was approximately in the right position according to the satnav.

Dave turned off the main road and bumped his way over the rough terrain. As they approached Kat could see a table and chairs set up beside the vehicle. It looked as if someone had gone to a lot of trouble to set up a picnic to watch the sunset. Four tall posts had been erected and fairy lights were strung between them. Solar powered, they were just beginning to shine in the dusk. The table and two chairs sat beneath the lights.

Kat jumped out of the ambulance, swung open the back door and grabbed her kit. She headed for the vehicle.

A man appeared from below the crest of the hill. The way he moved reminded her of Oliver and she felt a pang of loss as she blocked that thought. She had been thinking of him on the drive out here and now her imagination was playing tricks on her.

The man came closer. He looked just like Oliver.

She held her hand up to shield her face from the setting sun. Surely it couldn't be him?

'Hello, Kat.'

It was him. The sound of his voice set her heart racing. He smiled his familiar smile; it started at one corner of his mouth, spreading across his lips and lighting up his eyes. Kat couldn't breathe. She felt dizzy and was afraid her legs would buckle.

'Oliver? What are you doing here?'

'Waiting for you.'

She looked around in confusion. 'Where's the patient?'

'There isn't one.'

She turned around to question Dave, unable to work out what was going on. Dave stood behind her holding the bag that contained her change of clothes. Clothes she had packed to wear to dinner with Saskia and Maya. He passed the bag to her, swapping it for the medical kit, and walked off without a word.

'I don't understand,' she said, turning back to Oliver. 'I'm supposed to be having dinner with Saskia.'

He was shaking his head. 'You don't have any other plans. Dave, Saskia, Maya—they're all part of this.'

'Part of what?'

'Come and sit down.' He took her hand and Kat clung to him, not sure she was going to be able to walk without help. Her brain had frozen. Nothing made sense.

Oliver pulled out a chair for her at the table and she almost collapsed into the seat. The table had been covered with a white tablecloth, and two champagne glasses, an ice bucket with a bottle of champagne and a vase of flowers had been laid out on top. She stared at the tableau.

'Did you do this?'

He nodded. 'I did it for you. There's something I need to discuss with you. It's about our engagement. There's something I need.'

'I'm sorry, I should have thought,' she said as she started to tug at her engagement ring. Her hands were hot and clammy, the ring tight on her finger. It wouldn't budge.

She wasn't sure why she was still wearing it. It was totally impractical in her job but she hadn't been able to make herself take it off. She pretended she was worried she might lose it but that wasn't true. She wore it because it was a reminder of him. She'd been surprised that he had never asked for it back, but then they'd never officially called off the engagement. She supposed this was it.

But that didn't explain the champagne, the flowers, the table under the lights. She was totally confused.

'What are you doing?' he asked her as she continued her futile attempt to remove the ring.

'Of course, you need this back.' She reached into the ice bucket and grabbed some ice cubes to cool down her finger.

'What? No! That's not what I came for. You can keep it.'

'I don't want it,' she said as she finally tugged it free. 'You need to give it back to Philippa.'

'I suppose I should,' he said as he took it and slipped it into his pocket. 'You never liked it anyway.'

He was right, she hadn't, not only because it was impractical but also because it had no meaning. It hadn't been given with love.

'It's a beautiful ring,' she said, 'but it was never mine to keep. I know we need to end our engagement but you didn't need to come all the way back here.' Oliver had been in touch a week ago to tell her the lawsuit had been dropped. She'd known then that he didn't need her any more. 'I could have sent the ring back to you.'

'I'm not here for the ring, Kat. I'm here for you.'

'For me?'

He nodded. 'I never should have left. I should have fought for you. For us. I should have told you I love you.'

'You love me?'

'I do.'

It was exactly what she'd wanted to hear but she couldn't understand why he hadn't told her this before. What had changed? What was going on? 'Why didn't you tell me this before?'

'I was scared.'

'Of what?'

'I didn't think I deserved you. I didn't think you would choose me. I thought you would choose your family. I know how important they are to you and I didn't know how I could compete with them, but then I realised I don't want it to be a competition. I don't want you to choose them or me. I want you to choose me as well. I want to be your family too. I just hope I'm not too late.

'I want to be the man you deserve, the man you love. I want you to be proud of me. You have given me a sense of purpose—you have made me want to be a better version of myself. A better person, a better son, a better man. But I had to work out who I was. Who I wanted to be.'

'I don't understand.'

'Let me explain.' He reached across the table and held her hand. 'I don't think I have ever really felt comfortable in my skin. I have never truly felt a part of something; I've always felt as though I'm a disappointment. I think that's why I love acting—it's a chance to escape from myself, from reality. It's a chance to be someone different, someone who isn't real, someone who won't disappoint real people. For years I've been searching, trying to find my place in the world, trying to work out what my purpose is, but it's been a lonely existence. But since I met you I can see myself as part of a bigger picture. Part of something special.

'I want to be part of something real. You exist in the real world and you've shared your world with me, you've shown me what is out there. I'm tired of make-believe—I want to be part of your world. Of your life. I love you and I want to marry you.'

'You want to marry me?'

'I do. I love you and I want to spend my life with you. Until

I met you I didn't believe that there could be one person who was the right fit for me, or that I would be the right person for somebody either. I thought that sounded clichéd, boring, that there would be nothing left to look forward to, but you have shown me that with the right person I can have all of that and more. I can have someone to share that with. Something to look forward to together. I want to be part of something bigger than myself. I want to be part of us. Everything about you has made me change my mind. I'm a changed man. Trite maybe, clichéd certainly, but that doesn't mean it isn't true. I want to be the man you want to spend the rest of your life with. I need you.'

The sun had set now. It was nearing winter and the end of the day came quickly in the desert. The temperature was dropping as darkness fell. The sky was dark and clear and the fairy lights merged together with the stars.

'I wanted to bring you out here so it was just you and me this time. This is about us. Just us. I want you to know this is real. There's no performance. No agenda. I know you think we are very different but there is one thing we have in common: we both want to be loved. I love you and I hope that, just maybe, you love me too.'

He stood and knelt in the red earth beside Kat. 'Katarina Maria Angelis, I love you, I adore you, I need you. I want to spend the rest of my life with you, as your husband. Please will you make my life complete? Will you marry me?'

'Yes,' she said as she pulled him to his feet. 'I do love you and I do adore you. I need you too and yes, I will marry you.'

She wound her arms around his neck and kissed him deeply, pouring all her emotions into the kiss, letting him know that she loved him, adored him and needed him.

'There's one more thing,' he said as he pulled a ring box from his pocket. He held it in the palm of his hand and flipped the lid open. A round black opal was nestled inside. Even in the semi-darkness it flashed with vibrant colours—red, blue and green. It was in a bezel setting, surrounded by diamonds. Kat didn't recognise the setting but she was sure she recognised the stone. Black opals were extremely rare.

'Is that my mother's opal?'

Oliver nodded. 'Your father said you've always loved it. He gave it to me and I got it reset today.'

'My father gave this to you?'

'Yes. Along with his blessing. I went to see him, to explain my intentions. I wanted him to believe that I deserve you. I wanted him to trust that I am worthy of marrying his daughter. That I will take care of you. That I love you.'

He slipped the ring onto her finger. It was perfect.

He was perfect.

And, as he kissed her again, Kat knew they would be perfect together.

* * * * *

Outback Heiress, Surprise Proposal

Margaret Way

Welcome to the intensely emotional world of

MARGARET WAY

Where rugged, brooding bachelors meet their match in the burning heart of Australia....

Praise for the author:

"Margaret Way delivers...
vividly written, dramatic stories."
—*Romantic Times BOOKreviews*

'With climactic scenes, dramatic imagery and bold characters, Margaret Way makes the Outback come alive."
—*Romantic Times BOOKreviews*

Margaret Way, a definite Leo, was born and raised in the subtropical River City of Brisbane, capital of the Sunshine State of Queensland. A Conservatorium-trained pianist, teacher, accompanist and vocal coach, she found her musical career came to an unexpected end when she took up writing, initially as a fun thing to do. She currently lives in a harborside apartment at beautiful Raby Bay, a thirty-minute drive from the state capital. She loves dining *al fresco* on her plant-filled balcony, overlooking a translucent green marina filled with all manner of pleasure crafts, from motor cruisers costing millions of dollars and big, graceful yachts with carved masts standing tall against the cloudless blue sky, to little bay runabouts. No one and nothing is in a mad rush, and she finds the laid-back village atmosphere very conducive to her writing. With well over a hundred books to her credit, she still believes her best is yet to come.

PROLOGUE

IT HAPPENED VERY unexpectedly—as an extraordinary number of things tend to do. An unusually tense meeting of the board of the giant mining company Titan was in progress. Sir Francis Forsyth, Chairman and CEO of the company, and patriarch of the largest land-owning family in the country, was seen to be becoming increasingly angered by some concerns being voiced by his middle-aged son and heir, Charles.

The still strikingly handsome septuagenarian, piercing blue eyes narrowed, addressed his hapless son in a tone of voice that sent a shiver of pity through the other board members who found this belittling of Charles very much like a public caning. The general feeling was that Charles, admittedly not the brightest chip off the block, endured a lot of punishment from his dynamo of a father, who looked on him with a ferocious disappointment he rarely bothered to hide.

Like now.

'Charles, when are you going to face the fact you're becoming a bloody liability around here?' Sir Francis gritted, removing his glasses. 'Because that's what you are. You are not the man to find solutions to problems. You have to look to *me* as your source of guidance. Not fire off these pie-in-the-sky suggestions. You do realise as a businessman *profit* is the name of the game? That and keeping our shareholders happy. Yet you continue to—' He broke off abruptly as another voice, vibrantly attractive, completely self-assured, spoke up in defence of the now ashen-faced Charles.

'What is it, Bryn?' Sir Francis turned his handsome head with exaggerated patience to the young man on his right.

Bryn Macallan was the brilliant grandson of his late partner, Sir Theodore Macallan, co-founder of Titan. Everyone on the board shared that opinion. Sir Francis, too, greatly admired him, yet paradoxically also feared him. Bryn Macallan, who had already gained an impressive reputation at an early age, was the real thing. An actual chip off the old block. On top of everything else, he was making it increasingly difficult for Sir Francis to retain the control he had settled into since Theo had died some years back. Bryn Macallan, no bones about it, was after the top job sooner rather than later—and there didn't seem a damned thing Francis Forsyth could do about it.

Could it perhaps be divine retribution?

'I'm drawn to at least some of Charles's suggestions,' Bryn was saying, completely unfazed by the chairman's mood and attitude. 'We *do* have a duty of care to our workers. We have the expert's safety report on Mount Garnet. We've all had time to read it.' He glanced around the table to receive confirmation. 'I'd like to raise a few concerns of my own, as well as making some additional suggestions as to how we can best go about implementing necessary changes. We have the eyes of the nation on us. We carry a great responsibility. I know we're all aware of that.'

'Hear, hear!' Several of the other board members—the most powerful and influential, it had to be noted—nodded.

Bryn Macallan, though barely thirty, was held in very high regard around the table. The way he looked, the way he spoke, and his formidable brain power brought vividly to mind his late, deeply lamented grandfather. Bryn Macallan was the up-and-coming man. He far outstripped poor Charles, or indeed any other contender for the top job. Such was his aura. An aura given to few people.

Francis Forsyth more than anyone else was acutely aware of it. 'We are indeed, Bryn,' he countered smoothly, knowing Bryn's recommendations would be positive, but less harmful to Titan. He needed to be heeded. 'I'm equally sure we're all eager to listen to what you have to say. But not to Charles's blathering. He sounds like a man on some sort of guilt trip.'

Charles sat frozen in place. 'Why do you do this to me, Dad?' he asked with a bizarrely child-like hurt in his voice. 'Never a word of encouragement.'

Maddened, Sir Francis jabbed the air with a forceful finger. It made not only his son flinch. 'The last thing *you* need is encouragement,' he told his heir blisteringly. 'You can't seem to understand—' He stopped to draw more breath into his lungs. The breath appeared to fail. Instead, it turned into a violent paroxysm of coughing.

Bryn Macallan, predictably, was the first to react.

'Get the paramedics here *now!*' he shouted, rising swiftly from his chair. He was sure all at once that this was something very serious. Alarmingly so. But before he could get to Sir Francis, the chairman slumped sideways, then toppled to the floor, his face taking on the colour of a wax sculpture.

The life of arguably the richest and certainly one of the most powerful men in the country was all but over.

Bryn began CPR—he had to if there was any chance of saving Sir Francis. He was thankful he had spent time perfecting the procedure.

The paramedics, urgently despatched, arrived in under six minutes. They took over from Bryn Macallan, but it was evident to them all that the nation's 'Iron Man' was dead.

Charles Forsyth was so shocked by the violence and suddenness of the event he sat in the grip of paralysis, unable to stand, let alone speak. The truth was he had thought his father was going to live for ever.

It was left to Bryn Macallan to take charge. Bryn, though he experienced the collective shock, felt no great grief. Sir Frank Forsyth had lived and died a ruthless man—brilliant, but guilty of many sins. Wearing the deep camouflage of long friendship he had done terrible things to the Macallan family in business since the death of his grandfather.

'Frank has always had the potential to be an out-and-out scoundrel,' Bryn's grandmother had warned him after his grandfather's funeral. 'It was Theo, as honourable a man as Frank is amoral, who kept that potential for ruthlessness in check. Now Frank holds the reins. Mark my words, Bryn, darling. It's time now for the Macallans to look out!'

Her prediction had been spot-on. Since then bitter rivalries and deep resentments had run like subterranean rivers through everything the Forsyths and the Macallans did. But the two families were tied together through Titan.

The Forsyths had their vision. Bryn Macallan had his.

It was Frank Forsyth and Theo Macallan, geologists, friends through university, who had started up Titan in the late 1960s. They had discovered, along with part-aboriginal tracker Gulla Nolan, a fabulous iron-ore deposit at Mount Gloriana, in the remote North-West of the vast state of Western Australia—a state which took up one-third of the huge island continent. Today this company, Titan, was a mighty colossus.

Within minutes the death of the nation's 'Iron Man' was part of breaking news on television, radio and the internet. The extended family was informed immediately. The only family member not present in the state capital, Perth, was Francesca Forsyth. She was the daughter of Sir Frank's second son, Lionel, who had been killed along with his wife and their pilot in a light plane crash en route from Darwin to Alice Springs. Francesca had been orphaned at age five.

It had been left to her uncle Charles and his wife Elizabeth to take on the job of raising her. Indeed, Elizabeth had taken the bereaved little girl to her heart, although she and Charles had a daughter of their own—Carina, their only child, some three years older than her cousin. Carina had grown up to be the acknowledged Forsyth heiress; Francesca who shunned the limelight was 'the spare'.

What was not known by society and the general public alike was that Carina Forsyth, for most of her privileged life, had harboured a deep, irrational jealousy of her young cousin—though she did her best to hide it. Over the years she had almost perfected the blurring of the boundaries between her true nature and the role of older, wiser cousin she presented to the world. But sadly Carina was on a quest to destroy any chance of happiness her cousin might have in life. She had convinced herself from childhood that Francesca had stolen her mother's love. And the melancholy truth was that, although Elizabeth Forsyth loved her daughter, and went to great lengths to demonstrate it, the beautiful little girl, 'child of light' Francesca, through the sweetness of her nature *had* gained a large portion of her aunt's heart.

Francesca, acutely intelligent and possessed of a sensitive, intuitive nature, had not been unaware of her cousin's largely hidden malevolence. Consequently she had learned very early not to draw her cousin's fire, and was equally careful not to attract undue attention. *Carina Forsyth* was the Forsyth heiress. What Carina did not appreciate was that Francesca had never found any difficulty with that. Enormous wealth could be a great blessing or a curse, depending on one's point of view. Being an heiress was not part of Francesca's ethos.

Even the cousins' looks were polarised. Both young women were beautiful. Not just an accolade bestowed on them by a fawning press. A simple statement of fact. Carina was a stunner: tall, curvy, a blue-eyed blonde with skin like thick cream, and supremely self-assured as only those *born* rich could be. Francesca, by contrast, was raven-haired, olive-skinned, and with eyes that were neither grey nor green but took colour from what she was wearing. Seen together at the big functions their grandfather had expected both young women to attend, they made startling foils: one so golden, secure in her own perfection, with the eye-catching presence of—some said cattishly behind her back—a showgirl, and the other with an air of refinement that held more than a touch of mystery. Carina went all out to play up her numerous physical assets. Francesca had chosen to downplay her beauty, for obvious reasons.

The greatest potential for danger lay in the fact that both young women were in love with the same man. Bryn Macallan. Carina's feelings for him were very much on show. Indeed, she treated Bryn with astonishing possessiveness, managing to convey to all that a deep intimacy existed between them. Francesca had always been devastated by the knowledge. Indeed, she had to live with constant heartache. Bryn preferred Carina to her. There was nothing else to do but accept it—even if it involved labouring not to show her true feelings. She knew exactly what might happen if she allowed her emotions to surface, however briefly. There could be only one outcome.

What Carina wanted, Carina got.

While the heiress was at the family mansion to receive the news, Francesca was at Daramba, the flagship of the Forsyth pastoral empire, in Queensland's Channel Country. Francesca, a gifted artist herself, since leaving university—albeit with a first-class law degree—had involved herself in raising the profile of Aboriginal artists and acting as agent and advisor in the sale of their works. For one so young—she was only twenty-three—she had been remarkably successful.

Unlike her glamorous high society cousin, Francesca Forsyth felt the burden of great wealth. She wanted to give back. It was the driving force that paved the way to her strong commitment to the less fortunate in the broad community.

Francesca, it was agreed, needed to be told face to face of her grandfather's sudden death and brought home. Bryn Macallan elected to do it. An experienced pilot, he would fly the corporation's latest Beech King Air. He was considered by everyone to be the best man for the job. Though everyone knew the late Sir Frank had dearly wished for a match between Bryn and his elder granddaughter Carina, the fulfilment of that wish had always eluded him. The two rival families were also keenly aware that Bryn and Francesca shared a special *bond,* which was not to be broken for all the families' tensions. Bryn Macallan was, therefore, the man to bring Francesca home.

CHAPTER ONE

LOOKING DOWN ON the ancient Dreamtime landscape, Bryn experienced such a feeling of elation it lifted the twin burdens of ambition and family responsibility from his shoulders—if only for a time. He loved this place—Daramba. He and his family had visited countless times over the years, when his much-loved grandfather had been alive. These days his mother and his grandmother didn't come. For them the close association had ended on the death of Sir Theo, when Francis Forsyth—mega-maniac, call him what you will—got into full stride. It had been left to Bryn to bridge the gap. It was part of his strategy. His womenfolk knew what he was about. They were one hundred per cent behind him. But in spite of everything—even the way his family had been stripped of so much power by stealth—he found Daramba miraculous.

The name in aboriginal, with the accent on the second syllable, meant waterlily—the native symbol of fertility. One of nature's most exquisite flowers, the waterlily was the totemic Dreamtime ancestor of the Darambal tribe. The vast cattle station, one of the largest in the land of the cattle kings, was set in the Channel Country's riverine desert. That meant it boasted numerous lagoons in which waterlilies abounded. This was the year the long drought had broken over many parts of the

Queensland Outback, giving tremendous relief to the Inland. Daramba's countless waterways, which snaked across the station, the secret swamps where the pelicans made their nests, and the beautiful lagoons would be floating a magnificent display. Even so, there was nothing more thrilling than to see the mighty landscape, its fiery red soil contrasting so brilliantly with the opal-blue sky, cloaked by a glorious mantle of wildflowers that shimmered away to the horizon.

It was a breathtaking display, almost too beautiful to bear—as if the gates of heaven had been opened for a short time to man. All those who were privileged to see the uncompromising desert turned into the greatest floral display on earth—and there weren't all that many—even those who knew the desert intimately, still went in awe of this phenomenal rebirth that flowed over the land in a great tide. Then, when the waters subsided, came the all too brief period of utter magic when the wildflowers had their dazzling days in the sun: the stiff paper daisies, the everlastings that didn't wilt when plucked, white, bright yellow and pink, the crimson Sturt Peas, the Parrot peas, the native hibiscus, the Spider lilies and the Morgan flowers, the poppies and the Firebushes, the pure white Carpet of Snow, the exquisite little cleomes that were tucked away in the hills, the lilac Lambs' Tails and the green Pussy Tails that waved back and forth on the wind. One would have to have a heart of stone not to be moved by such a spectacle.

Bryn was vividly reminded of how in her childhood Francesca had revelled in the time of the flowers. All those miles upon miles of flowers and perfume. It had been her own childhood fantasy, her dreamworld, one of her ways of surviving the tragic loss of her parents. He remembered her as a little girl, running off excitedly into an ocean of white paper daisies, her silvery laughter filling the air, while she set about making a chain of the wildflowers to wear as a diadem atop her long hair. Beautiful hair, with the polished gloss of a magpie's wing. Usually Carina had ruined things, by eventually tugging the garland off her younger cousin's head and throwing it away, claiming the paper daisies might be harbouring bugs. The truth of it was Carina had been sending out a message that demanded to be heard. Francesca was meant to live in her shadow. And she never let her forget it.

'There's no telling where this might end!' his grandmother, Lady Macallan, had once confided, a furrow of worry between her brows. 'Carina deeply resents our little Francey. And it will only grow worse.'

It *had*. Though a lot of people didn't see it, Carina was very cunning—but Francey wouldn't hear a word against her. That was the essential sweetness of her nature. Francey was no fool—Bryn was certain she privately admitted to herself that Carina was as devious and manipulative as that old devil Sir Frank, and he knew he, himself, was a bit of an erotic obsession with Carina. It was naked in her eyes, every time she looked at him. And he had to admit to a brief, hectic affair with her when the two of them were younger. Carina was a beautiful young woman, but, as he had come to discover, there was something twisted in her soul. He supposed he could live with it as long as no harm came to Francey—who, in her way, was as big an obsession with Carina as he was. Carina's mother, Elizabeth, had doted on the angelic bereaved child that had been Francesca. She had taken Francey to her heart. That was when it had all started. He was sure of it.

The Beech King Air B100, their latest acquisition, was flying like a bird. It differed from Titan's other King Airs, its model easy to distinguish on the ground, with different engine exhausts, and the propellers in flat pitch at rest. Bryn loved flying. He found it enormously relaxing. He had already commenced his descent. The roof of the giant hangar was glinting like molten silver, almost dazzling his shielded eyes. He fancied he could smell the scents of the wild bush. There was no other smell like it. Dry, aromatic, redolent of vast open spaces and flower-filled plains.

* * *

Station kids on their lunchbreak ran at him the instant he stopped the station Jeep. He patted heads and shoulders while distributing a small hoard of sweets, asking how they were doing and telling a few kid-oriented jokes that were greeted with merry peals of laughter. Rosie Williams, the young school-teacher, stood on the porch, smiling a bright welcome.

'Good to see you, Mr Macallan.'

'Good to see you too, Rosie.' He sketched a brief salute. No matter how many times he told her to call him Bryn, she couldn't get round to it. 'Hope these kids aren't giving you any trouble?' He ruffled the glossy curls of a little aboriginal child standing next to him, confidently holding his hand.

'No, no—everything's fine. We're making a lot of progress.'

'Great to hear it.'

More giggles. Sunlight falling on glowing young faces.

A few minutes later he was back in the Jeep, waving a friendly hand. He hoped to find Francesca at the homestead, but that was all it was—*hope.* He'd probably have to go looking for her. The remote station had not yet been contacted with news of Sir Frank's death. Best the news came from him. Face to face.

Five minutes more and he came into full view of the home-stead. After Frank Forsyth had acquired the valuable property in the late 1970s he'd lost little time knocking down the once proud old colonial mansion that had stood on the spot for well over one hundred years, erecting a huge contemporary structure more in keeping with his tastes. Eventually he'd even got rid of the beautiful old stone fountain that had graced the front court, which had used to send sparks of silver water out onto the paved driveway. Bryn remembered the three wonderful winged horses that had held up the basins.

His grandfather, when he had first seen the new homestead, had breathed, *'Dear God!'*

Bryn remembered it as though it were yesterday. Sir Francis had come tearing out of the house when he'd heard their arrival, shouting a full-throated greeting, demanding to know what his friend thought.

'It's very *you,* Frank,' his grandfather had said.

Even as a boy he had heard the irony Sir Frank had missed.

'Fantastic, Sir Francis!' Bryn had added his own comment weakly, not wanting to offend the great Sir Francis Forsyth, his grandad's lifelong friend and partner. Anyway the new homestead *was* fantastic—like a super-modern research station.

It faced him now. A massive one-storey building of steel, poured concrete and glass, four times as big as the original homestead, its only nod to tradition the broad covered verandahs that surrounded the structure on three sides. No use calling it a house or a home. It was a *structure.* Another monument to Sir Frank. The right kind of landscaping might have helped to soften the severity of the façade, but the approach was kept scrupulously clear. One was obviously entering a New Age Outback homestead.

Jili Dawson, the housekeeper, a strikingly attractive woman in her early fifties, greeted him with a dazzling smile and a light punch in the arm.

'Long time, no see!'

'Been busy, Jili.' He smiled into liquid black eyes that were alight with affection. Jili's eyes clearly showed her aboriginal blood, which came from her mother's side. Her father had been a white stockman, but Jili identified far more with her mother's family. Her skin was completely unlined, a polished amber, and her soft voice carried the familiar lullaby rhythms of her mother's people. 'I don't suppose I'm lucky enough to find Francey at home?' he asked, casting a glance into an entrance hall as big as a car park.

'No way!' Jili gave an open-handed expansive wave that took in the horizon. 'She with the group, paintin' out near Wungulla way. Hasn't bin home for coupla days. She's okay, though. Francey knows her way around. Besides, all our people look after her.'

'Wasn't that always the way, Jili?' he said, thinking how close contact with the tribal people had enriched his own and Francey's childhood. Carina had never been a part of any of that, holding herself aloof. 'Listen, Jili, I've come with serious news. We didn't let you know yesterday because I was coming to fetch Francey and tell her in person.'

'The man's dead.' Jili spoke very calmly, as though the event had already cast its shadow—or as if it was written on his forehead.

'Who told you?' He frowned. 'Did one of the other stations contact you?' News got around, even in the remote Inland. On the other hand Jili had the uncanny occult gift of tribal people in foretelling the future.

Jili rocked back and forth slowly. 'Just knew what you were gunna say before you said it. That was one helluva man. Good and evil. Plagued by devils, but devils of his own makin'. We know that, both of us. I honoured your fine, wise grandad, and your dear dad. A great tragedy when he bin killed in that rock fall. But they're with their ancestors now. They look down from the stars that shine on us at night. I have strong feelings for your family. You bin very kind to me. Treat me right. Lot rests on *your* shoulders, Bryn, now Humpty Dumpty has gone and fallen off the wall. What I want to know is this—is it gunna change things for Jacob and me? Are we gunna lose our jobs?'

Jacob Dawson, Jili's husband, also part aboriginal, was a long-time leading hand on the station—one of the best. In Bryn's opinion Daramba couldn't do without either of them. And Jacob would make a far better overseer than the present one, Roy Forster, who relied far too heavily on Jacob and his diverse skills.

'It all has to be decided, Jili,' he said, with a heartfelt sigh. 'Charles will inherit. I can't speak for him. He can't even speak for himself at the moment. He's in deep shock.'

Jili looked away, unseeing. 'Thought his dad was gunna live for ever,' she grunted. 'Seems he was as human as the rest of us. How have the rest of 'em reacted?' She turned to stare into Bryn's brilliant dark eyes. They were almost as black as her own, yet different because of their diamond glitter.

'Some are in shock,' he said. 'Some are in surprisingly good cheer,' he added dryly.

'Well, wait on the will,' Jili advised. 'See if he try to put things to rights. There's an accounting, ya know.'

Bryn didn't answer. In any case, it was much too late now. His grandfather and his father were gone. He came to stand beside her, both of them looking out at the quicksilver mirage. They both knew it was the end of something. The end of an era, certainly. But the fight was still on.

Jili was watching him. She thought of Bryn Macallan as a prince, grave and beautiful; a prince who acknowledged *all* his subjects. A prince who was ready to come into his rightful inheritance. She laid a gentle, respectful hand on his shoulder. 'I promise you it be right in the end, Bryn. But a warning you must heed. There's a bad spell ahead. Mind Francey. That cousin of hers is just waitin' to swoop like a hawk on a little fairy wren. Bad blood there.'

Wasn't that his own fear?

He changed up a gear as he came on a great sweep of tall grasses that covered the flat, fiery red earth. Their tips were like golden feathers blowing in the wind. It put him in mind of the open savannahs of the tropical North. That was the effect of all the miraculous rain. The four-wheel drive cut its way through the towering grasses like a bulldozer, flattening them and creating a path before they sprang up again, full of sap and resilience. A lone emu ducked away on long grey legs. It had all but been hidden in its luxuriant camouflage as it fed on shoots and seeds. The beautiful ghost gums, regarded by most as the quintessential eucalypt but not a eucalypt at all, stood sentinel to the silky blue sky, glittering grasses at their feet. It was their opal-white boles that made them instantly recognisable.

A string of billabongs lay to his right. He caught the glorious flashy wings of parrots diving in and out of the Red River gums. Australia—the land of parrots! Such a brilliant range of colours: scarlet, turquoise, emerald, violet, an intense orange and a bright yellow. Francey, when six, had nearly drowned in one of those lagoons—the middle one, Koopali. It was the deepest and the longest, with permanent water even in drought. In that year the station had been blessed with good spring rains, so Koopali, which could in flood become a raging monster, had been running a bumper. On that day it had been Carina who had stood by, a terrified witness, unable to move to go to her cousin's assistance, as though all strength had been drained out of her nine-year-old body.

It was a miracle Bryn had come upon them so quickly. Magic was as good an answer as any. A sobbing, inconsolable Carina had told them much later on that they had wandered away from the main group and, despite her warnings, Francey had insisted on getting too close to the deep lagoon. With its heavy load of waterlilies a child could get enmeshed in the root system of all the aquatic plants and be sucked under. Both girls could swim, but Francey at that time had been very vulnerable, being only a beginner and scarcely a year orphaned.

Could she really have disobeyed her older cousin's warnings? Francey as a child had never been known to be naughty.

When it had been realised the two girls had wandered off, the party had split up in a panic. He had never seen people move so fast. Danger went hand in hand with the savage grandeur of the Outback. He had run and run, his heartbeats almost jammed with fear, heading for Koopali. Why had he done that? Because that was where one of the itinerant aboriginal women, frail and of a great age, had pointed with her message stick. He had acted immediately on her mysterious command. Yet how could she have known? She'd been almost blind.

'Koopali,' she had muttered, nodding and gesturing, marking the word with an emphatic down beat of her stick.

To this day he didn't know why he had put such trust in her. But he had, arriving in time to launch himself into the dark green waters just as Francey's small head had disappeared for probably the last time. That was when Carina had started screaming blue murder…

So there it was: he had saved Francey's life, which meant to the aboriginal people that he owned part of her soul. Afterwards Carina had been so distraught no one had accused her of not looking after her little cousin properly. Carina, after all, had been only nine. But she could swim and swim well. She'd said fright had frozen her in place, making her incapable of jumping into the water after her cousin.

It had taken Bryn to do that.

'Thank God for you, Bryn! I'll never forget this. Never!' A weeping Elizabeth Forsyth had looked deep into his eyes, cradling Francey's small body in her arms as though Francey was the only child she had.

Carina had been standing nearby. He had already calmed Francey, who had clung to him like a little monkey, coughing up water, trying so hard to be brave. That was when the main party had arrived, alerted by his long, carrying *co-ee,* the traditional cry for help in the bush. All of them had huddled prayerfully around them. Catastrophe had been averted.

'How did you know they were here, Bryn?' Elizabeth had asked in wonder. 'We all thought they'd gone back to the main camp.' That was where a large tent had been erected.

'The old woman spoke and I listened.' It had been an odd thing to say, but no one had laughed.

Aborigines had an uncanny sense of danger. More so of approaching death. The old woman had even sent a strong wind at his back, though such a wind blew in no other place in the area. When everyone returned to the campsite to thank the old woman she'd been nowhere to be found. Even afterwards the aboriginal people who criss-crossed the station on walkabout claimed to know nothing of her or her whereabouts.

The wind blew her in. The wind blew her out.

'Coulda been a ghost!' Eddie Emu, one of the stockmen, had told them without a smile. 'Ghosts take all forms, ya know!'

Magic and the everyday were interconnected with aboriginal people. One had to understand that. Eddie claimed to have seen the spirit of his dead wife many times in an owl. That was why the owl took its rest by day and never slept at night. Owls hovered while men slept. Owls gave off signals, messages.

All in all it had been an extraordinary day. Little trembling Francey had whispered something into his ear that day. Something that had always remained with him.

'Carrie walked into the water. I did too.'

So what in God's name had really happened? Simply a child's terrible mistake? His mind had shut down on any other explanation. Carina had not been sufficiently aware of the danger and had later told fibs to exonerate herself from blame. It was a natural enough instinct.

Bryn came on them exactly where Jili had told him: Wungulla Lagoon, where the great corroborees had once been held. He seriously doubted whether a corroboree would be held to mark Sir Frank's passing. Francis Forsyth had not been loved, nor respected in the purest sense. Feared, most certainly. It hadn't taken the station people half a minute to become aware of Sir Frank's dark streak. Everyone had obeyed him. No one had trusted him. Who could blame them? He himself had not trusted Francis Forsyth for many years now.

He parked the Jeep a short distance off, approaching on foot and dodging the great mushrooming mounds of spinifex, bright green instead of the usual burnt gold. Francey was in the middle of a group of women, five in all, all busy at their painting. They looked totally involved, perfectly in harmony with their desert home.

Francey might have nearly drowned in Koopali Lagoon at age six, but at twenty-three she was a bush warrior. She could swim like a fish. She was fearless in an uncompromising environment that could and did take lives. She could handle the swiftest and strongest horse on the station. She could ride bareback if she had to, and find her way in the wilderness. She could shoot and hunt if it became necessary. In fact she was a crack shot, with an excellent eye. She knew all about bush tucker—how to make good bread from very finely ground small grass seeds, where to find the wild limes and figs, the bush tomatoes and a whole supermarket of wild berries and native fruits. Francey knew how to survive. She had made friends with the aboriginal people from her earliest childhood. In turn they had taught her a great deal about their own culture, without compromising the secrets forbidden to white people. They had taught her to see *their* landscape with her own eyes. And now she had a highly recognisable painting style that was bringing in excellent reviews.

Over the past few years since she had left university as one of the top three graduates in law for her year—Francey had thought it necessary to know her way around big business and the administration of her own sizeable trust fund—she had begun to capture the fantasy of aboriginal mythology with her own acutely imaginative vision. Her paintings—Bryn loved them, and owned quite a few—were a deeply sensitive and sympathetic mix of both cultures. She'd already had one sell-out showing, stressing to press and collectors alike the great debt she owed to her aboriginal mentors. As it happened all of them were women, who were now commanding quite a following thanks to their own talent and Francesca's endeavours. Aboriginal art *was* extraordinarily powerful.

She rose to her feet the moment the Jeep came into view. She was walking towards him, as graceful as a gazelle. She had the Forsyth height—tall for a woman—and willow-slender beautiful limbs. Her face was protected by an attractive wide-brimmed hat made of woven grasses, probably fashioned for her by one of the women. Her long shiny river of hair, that when loose fell into deep lustrous waves, was caught back into a thick rope that trailed down her back. A single silky skein lay across her throat like a ribbon. She wore the simplest of gear: a pale blue cotton shirt streaked with paint, beige shorts, dusty trainers on her feet.

'Bryn!' she called.

Her voice, one of her great attractions, was like some lovely musical instrument.

'Hi there, Francey!'

Just the sight of her set up a curious ache deep inside him. He knew what it meant. Of course he did. But how did he turn things around? They stood facing each other. Their eyes met. Instant communication. And they both *knew* it—however hard she tried to disguise it. She lifted her face to him and kissed his cheek.

The cool satin touch of her flesh! He could see the flush of blood beneath her smooth golden skin before the familiar dissembling began. Both of them seemed to be stuck in roles imposed on them from childhood. That would change now.

'It has to be something serious to bring you here, Bryn.' She held her tapering long-fingered hands in front of her in an instinctive gesture of defensiveness. 'It's Grandfather, isn't it?' She turned her head abruptly, as if responding to a signal. The women were still sitting in their painting circle, but they had all left off work. Now they lifted their hands high in unison, palms facing upwards to the sky.

Now we have moved to an end.

Bryn recognised and wasn't greatly surprised by the ceremonial gesture. These people were extraordinary. 'Yes, Francey, it is,' he confirmed gravely. 'Your grandfather died of a massive heart attack yesterday afternoon. I came as quickly as I could. I'm very sorry for your pain. I know you can only be thinking of what might have been.'

'I wasn't *there,* Bryn.' Her voice splintered in her throat. 'I knew the moment I saw you what you were going to tell me.'

'I'm sorry, Francey,' he repeated. 'You're getting so close to these people you're acquiring their powers. How do *they* know? It's not guesswork. They *know.*'

'Uncanny, isn't it?' She flung another glance over her shoulder. The women had resumed their painting. 'But then they're the oldest living culture on earth. They've lived right *here* on this spot for over forty thousand years. They can scent death.'

He nodded. He had seen it happen many times. His eyes remained locked on her. She had lost colour at his news, but she was pushing away the tears. She wore no make-up that he could see, beyond lipgloss to protect her mouth. Her skin was flawless, poreless—like a baby's. Her large almond-shaped eyes, heavily and blackly lashed, dazzled like silver coins in the sunlight.

'He didn't want to see me?' It came out on a wave of sadness and deep regret.

Bryn found himself, as ever, protective. He hastened to explain. 'It wasn't a case of his wanting to see anyone, Francey.' He knew the hurt and pain of exclusion she had carried for most of her life. 'It happened at a board meeting, not at the house. None of us had the slightest idea he was feeling unwell. One moment he was shouting Charles down—a bit of an argument had started up, nothing really, but you know how he detests… detested…any other view but his own—and that was it. It was very quick. I doubt he felt more than a moment's pain. We didn't contact you right away because I wanted to tell you in person. I have to bring you home. He's being given a State funeral.'

'I suppose he would be!' A deep sigh escaped her. 'What great wealth and politics can do! As for home…' Sudden tears made her eyes shimmer like foil. 'That word should mean *everything.* It's meaningless to me. I don't have a home. I never had a home since I lost my parents.' She cast him a despairing look. 'I spent my childhood trying to find a way through grief. I had to focus on what my father once said to me when I was little and a wasp stung me. "Be brave, Francey, darling. Be brave."'

'You *are* brave, Francey,' Bryn said, knowing that for all the Forsyth wealth she had had a difficult life.

Her beautiful eyes glistened with blinked-back tears. 'Well, I try. Some of the worst things happen to us in childhood. Sadly I haven't left mine entirely behind. Carina used to tell me all the time I should be grateful.'

'Well, that's Carina!' he said, unable to keep the harsh edge from his voice.

Francesca was vaguely shocked. Bryn *never* criticised Carina. Not to date. 'I don't think she was trying to upset me, Bryn,' she pointed out loyally. 'She meant me to buck up. But enough of that.' She made a dismissive gesture with her hand. 'I don't often feel sorry for myself. But Grandfather's death has come as a shock. He lived like he truly believed he was going to go on for ever. Well into his nineties at any rate. I'm very grateful you've come, Bryn.'

He shook his uncovered dark head, sunlight striking bronze highlights. 'No need for gratitude, Francey. I wanted to come.'

She gave a broken laugh that ended on a sob. 'You and your family grew much closer to me than my own. Isn't that incredible? I'm so grateful you were there for me.'

He heard the affection and sincerity in her voice. His mother and grandmother always had been strongly but subtly protective of Francesca, careful not to show their resentments of the Forsyths. Now an opportunity had opened up and he had to take it.

'We've never spoken about this, Francey, and you probably don't want to hear it from me now, but Carina isn't quite the friend you think she is.'

She didn't look at all shocked by his comment. She looked ineffably sad.

'Why *is* that, Bryn?' she asked in a pained voice. 'I've never done anything—never would do anything—to hurt Carina. I've been extremely careful to stay in the background. I don't compete in any way. *She* is the Forsyth heiress, not me. And I don't want to be. I try to live my own life. Whenever we have to attend functions together I never draw attention to myself. I always dress down.'

'You should stop that,' he said, more bluntly than he'd intended.

Now she did look shocked. 'You think so?' She sounded hurt.

'I do,' he told her more gently. 'No one could fail to see how beautiful you are, Francey, even in that bush shirt and shorts. You shouldn't be driven into playing down your looks or your own unique style.'

She blushed at the *beautiful*. Better maybe that he hadn't said it.

'It seemed to make good sense to me,' she confessed, rather bleakly.

'Yes, I know.' He studied her downbent face. 'You had your reasons. But I don't believe it would make a difference anyway.' He decided to turn up the heat one more degree. Jili's warnings were still resounding in his ears. 'Carina believes you stole her mother's love from her. That's at the heart of it all.'

Her luminous gaze swept his face. 'But that's a terrible burden to lay on me. I was a child. Five years of age. I was a victim. I never wanted my parents to die. It was the great tragedy of my life. Losing my grandfather here and now, painful and sudden as it is, in no way compares. The worst thing that can happen to you only happens *once.* I'm sorry for the way that sounds, but I can't be hypocritical about it. Grandfather never loved me. He never wanted *my* love. He never showed me any real affection. The only time I got treated as a granddaughter was when we were all on show. Just a piece of play-acting, a side-show. I was his granddaughter by chance. I'm not blonde and blue-eyed like the Forsyths. I'm my mother's child. And I lost her. *Still* Carina can resent me?'

Hate you, more like it. 'I'm afraid so. Carina's resentments are not of your making, Francey, so don't look so upset. It's her nature. She's inherited the Forsyth dark side.'

'But surely that must be a cause of grief to her?' she said, her voice full of pity for her cousin.

'I don't think she sees it like that,' he responded tersely, alarmed that Francesca's innate sense of compassion should work against her. 'One has to have an insight into one's own behaviour. I don't think Carina has that. I'm glad this is out in the open, Francey, because we both know there will be tough times ahead. It's best to prepare for them.'

'She must be terribly upset.' She fixed her eyes on him. 'Carrie idolised Grandfather.'

'She's coping,' he said.

'That's good. Carrie is very strong. And she has you. She loves *you,*' Francesca added softly, as though offering the best possible reason for Carina to be strong.

Why did people think Carina Forsyth was the fixed star in Bryn's firmament? Francesca thought it the most. 'She only *thinks* she loves me, Francey.' His retort was crisp. He didn't say love wasn't in Carina's heart or soul. Carina wanted what she couldn't have. It was a psychological problem.

'It's not as simple as that, Bryn,' Francesca contradicted him gently. 'You're very close. She told me you were lovers.' Her voice was low, but her light-sparked eyes were steady.

'Okay.' He shrugged, his voice perfectly calm. 'So we were. Things happen. But that was a few years back.'

'She says *not.*' It wasn't like Bryn to lie. Francesca had long since made the judgment that Bryn had no time for lies.

He couldn't suppress the sudden flare of anger. It showed in his brilliant dark eyes. 'And of course you believe her?'

Her lovely face flamed. 'You're saying it's *not* the truth?' Momentarily she came out from behind her habitual screen.

For answer he flashed a smile that lit up his stunning, lean-featured face. It was a face that could in repose look somewhat severe—even at times as hard and formidable as Francis Forsyth himself. 'Francey, I'm a free man. I like it that way.'

'You might not always feel the same, and Carina will be waiting for you.' She pulled her sunglasses out of her pocket and hid behind the dark lenses. 'Do you want to say hello to the group?'

'Of course. I wouldn't think of bypassing them.'

He moved alongside her as they made their way back to the artists at work. Their only protection from the brassy glare of the sun was a magnificent overhanging desert oak. In cities nature was controlled. In the Outback it manifested its tremendous intensity and power.

'I see Nellie is here today,' he commented. Nellie Napirri, a tribal woman of indeterminate age—anywhere between seventy and ninety—generally focused on the flora and fauna of the riverine desert. The great Monet himself might have been interested in seeing her huge canvases of waterlilies, Bryn thought. As well as using traditional earth pigments, the familiar ochres, she used vibrant acrylics to express her Dreaming.

'I thought we might have seen the last of her,' Francesca confided. 'Nellie is a real nomad. But she came back. She'd been on a very long walkabout that took her up into the Territory. Imagine walking all that way. And at her age! Goodness knows how old she is. She's been around for as long as anyone can remember. It's unbelievable.'

Bryn's mind was swept back to the day when Francesca had almost drowned, but for miraculous intervention. He vividly remembered the old woman—the way she had vanished from the face of the earth but had in all probability gone walkabout. For him that day had amounted to a religious experience. He could still see Carina's small straight back, her long blonde hair cascading over her shoulders. She had been facing Koopali, fixed to the ground. He would never forget the way she had started screaming…

The little group of painters, gracious and well-mannered, came to their feet, exchanging handshakes with Bryn. Four pairs of eyes fixed themselves on him.

'Big fella bin gone,' Nellie announced in a deep quiet voice. Her curly head was snow-white, her eyes remarkably clear and sharp for so old a woman. It was obvious she had been appointed spokeswoman.

Bryn inclined his dark head in salute. 'Yesterday, Nellie. A massive heart attack. I'm here to take Francesca back with me.'

Nellie reached out and touched his arm. 'Better here,' she said, frowning darkly, as though seriously concerned for Francesca's welfare. She searched Bryn's face so carefully she might have been seeing him for the first time. Or was she trying to see into his soul? 'Your job look after her, *byamee.*'

'Don't worry, Nellie, I will,' he answered gravely. He knew *byamee* was a term of respect—a name given to someone of high degree. He only hoped he would be worthy of that honour. He recalled with a sharp pang of grief that the tribal people had called his grandfather *byamee.* He had never in all the long years heard it applied to Sir Frank.

A look of relief settled on Nellie's wise old face. 'You remember now. I bin telling ya. *Not over.*' All of a sudden her breath began to labour.

Francesca reacted at once. 'Nellie, dear, you mustn't worry. Everything is going to be fine.' She drew the tiny bent frame beneath her arm. 'Now, why don't we show Bryn what we've been doing?' she suggested bracingly. 'You know how much he loves and appreciates indigenous art.'

It sprang to Bryn's mind how Carina had once passed off her young cousin's desire to promote the work of indigenous artists as 'trying to exorcise the fact she's an heiress by working among the aborigines.'

Carina wasn't only callous, she could be remarkably blind—especially when it came to perceiving what was *good.* She was no judge of Francesca's work. Francesca Forsyth was a multigifted young woman. His mind ran back to the many times he and Francey had got into discussions, not only about Titan, but about the various projects handled—or mishandled might be a better word—by the Forsyth Foundation. Francey had a seriously good brain. When he was in a position to do so, he would endeavour to get her elected to the board, no matter her youth. Hell, he was still considered very young himself, though youth wasn't the issue it once was. It was more about ability. And Francey was ready for it. She had inherited her father Lionel's formidable head for business. His grandmother had confirmed that with an ironic smile.

'When it comes right down to it Francey, not Carina, would make the greatest contribution. Only as fate would have it Carina is the apple of Frank's eye. He never was much of a judge of character.'

It was as they were taking their leave that Nellie found a moment to speak to Bryn alone. She raised her snowy white head a long way, trying to look him squarely in the eye. 'You bin her family now,' she said, as though impressing on him his responsibility. 'Others gunna do all in their power to destroy her.'

'Nellie—'

She cut him off. 'You know that well as me. She sees good in everyone. Even those who will turn against her.'

He already knew that. 'They will seek to destroy me too, Nellie.' He spoke as if she were not a nomadic tribal woman but a trusted business ally. Moreover he saw nothing incongruous about it. These people had many gifts. Prescience was a part of them.

'Won't happen,' she told him, her weathered face creasing with scorn. 'You strong. You bin ready. This time you get justice.'

She might have been delivering a speech, and it was one he heard loud and clear.

They were in the station Jeep, speeding back to the homestead, with the silver-shot mirage pulsing all around them. The native drums had started up, reverberating across the plains to the ancient eroded hills glowing fiery red in the heat. Other drums were joining in, taking up the beat—*tharum, tharum*—a deeply primitive sound that was extraordinarily thrilling. They were calling back and forth to each other, seemingly from miles away. The sound came from the North, the North-West.

It was a signal, Bryn and Francesca realised. Now that Bryn's coming had made it official, the message was being sent out over the vast station and the untameable land.

Francis Forsyth's spirit had passed. Consequences would follow.

'Nellie fears for me,' Francesca said. 'It looked like she was handing on lots of warnings to you?' Her tone pressed him for information.

'Your well-being is important to her and her friends.' Bryn glanced back at her. She had taken off her straw hat, throwing it onto the back seat. Now he could fully appreciate her beautiful fine-boned face, which always seemed to him radiant with sensitivity. She was far more beautiful than her cousin. Her looks were on a different scale. The thick shiny rope of her hair was held by a coloured elastic band at the end and a blue and purple silk scarf at the top. Incredibly, her eyes had taken on a wash of violet. 'You've been wonderfully helpful to them as a patron, and best of all your motives are entirely pure.'

'Of course they are.' She dismissed that important point as if it went without saying. 'It looked like matters of grave importance?'

'Isn't your welfare just that?' he parried.

'Who is likely to hurt me?' she appealed to him. 'I'm not important in anyone's eyes—least of all poor Grandfather. God rest his troubled soul. I do know he had his bad times.'

Why wouldn't he? Bryn inwardly raged, but let it go. 'You're a Forsyth, Francey,' he reminded her gravely. 'It's to be expected you'll receive a substantial fortune in your grandfather's will. It's not as though there isn't plenty to go around. He was a billionaire many times over.'

'A huge responsibility!' There was a weight of feeling in her voice. 'Too much money is a curse. Men who build up great fortunes make it extremely difficult for their heirs.'

She was thinking of her uncle Charles. So was Bryn. 'I think there's an old proverb, either Chinese or Persian, that says: "The larger a man's roof, the more snow it collects." Charles, God help him, has had a bad time of it. I can almost feel sorry for him. Frank treated him very unkindly from his earliest days. Charles never could measure up to his father's standards of perfection.'

'Such destructive behaviour,' Francesca sighed, thinking that at least her uncle treated Carina, his only child, like a princess.

'I agree. It was *your* father who inherited the brains and refused point-blank to toe the line. It took a lot of guts to do that. Charles has worked very hard, but sadly for him he doesn't have what it takes to be the man at the top. Charles is just valued for his *name*.'

Unfortunately that was true. 'Our name engenders a lot of hostility.' She had felt that hostility herself. 'It's not *all* envy. The Macallan name, on the other hand, is greatly admired. Sir Theo was revered.'

'A great philanthropist,' Bryn said quietly, immensely proud of his grandfather.

'And a great *man*. He had no black cloud hanging over him. I've never fully understood what my grandfather did to your family after Sir Theo died. No one speaks of it.'

'And I'm not going to speak of it now, Francey,' he said, severity back on him. 'It's a bad day for it anyway.'

'I know. I know,' she apologised. 'But you haven't put it behind you?'

'Far from it.' He suddenly turned his smooth dark head, so elegantly shaped. '*You* could be the enemy.'

She looked out of the window at the desert landscape that had come so wondrously alive. 'You know I'm not.' She loved him without limit. Always would.

He laughed briefly. 'You're certainly not typical of the Forsyths.' She was the improbable angel in their midst.

Her next words were hard for her to say. 'You hate us?' It

was very possible. She knew Lady Macallan had despised her grandfather with a passion. There had to be a story there.

A shadow moved across his handsome face. 'I can't hate *you,* Francey. How could you even think it?'

She sighed. 'Besides, how could you hate me when you own half my soul?' She spoke with intensity. But then, wasn't that the way it always felt when she was with Bryn? The heightened perceptions, every nerve ending wired?

'Do you believe it?' He turned his dark head again to meet her eyes.

'I wouldn't be here without *you,* Bryn,' she said, on a soft expelled breath. 'I like to think we're…friends.'

'Well, we are,' he replied, somewhat sardonically. 'I want you to promise me something, Francey.'

Something in his tone alarmed her. 'If I can,' she answered warily.

'You *must,*' he clipped out, abruptly steering away from a red-glowing boulder that crouched like some mythical animal in the jungle of green gilt-tipped grasses. 'If you're worried or unsure about something, or if you need someone to talk to, I want you to contact me. Will you do that?' There was a note of urgency in his voice.

'I promise.'

He shot her a brilliant glance that affected her powerfully. 'You mean that?'

'Absolutely. I never break a promise. A promise is like a vow.'

'So let's shake on it.' He hit the brake and brought the vehicle to a stop in the shade of a stand of bauhinias, the branches lavishly decorated with flowers of purest white and lime-green. 'Give me your hand.'

On the instant her heart began fluttering wildly, as if a small bird was trapped in her chest. She was crazily off guard. She only hoped her face wasn't betraying the turmoil within her. 'Okay,' she managed at last. She gave him her hand. Skin on skin. She had to fight hard to compose herself. Beneath her reserved façade she went in trepidation of Bryn Macallan and his power over her. So much so she feared to be alone with him, even though she spent countless hours wishing she were.

But how did one stop longing for what one so desperately longed for?

Bryn's hand was gripping hers—not gently, but tightly. It was as though he wanted her to understand what her promise might mean in the days ahead.

To Francesca the intimacy was breathtaking. The heat in her blood wrapped her body like a shawl. Her limbs were melting, as though her body might collapse like a concertina. For glittering moments she accepted her deepest longings and desires. She was irrevocably in love with Bryn Macallan. She couldn't remember a time she hadn't been. It was the most important thing in her life. She was off her head, really. And it was *so* humiliating. Carina was the woman in Bryn's life. She had to clamp down on the torment.

'Where will it finally end, Francey?' Bryn was asking quietly, not relinquishing her hand as she'd thought he would. 'You know I mean to take over Titan?'

He waited in silence for her response. 'I'm aware of your burning ambitions, Bryn,' she said. 'I know you want to put things *right.* I don't know your secrets, and you won't tell me, but I do know you would probably have the numbers to oust Uncle Charles.'

'Without a doubt!' Not the slightest flare of arrogance, just plain fact, though the muscles along his jaw clenched.

'Grandfather's dearest wish was for you and Carina to marry.' She turned to look him squarely in the face. 'To unite the two dynasties.'

'I'm well aware of that,' he answered, his tone suggesting her grandfather's dearest wish didn't come into it.

Or so she interpreted it. Was she wrong? 'And it will happen?'

If for whatever reason the longed-for alliance didn't eventuate, he knew Carina would become his enemy. He laughed, but there was little humour in it. 'Why don't you leave all that to me, Francey? My main concern at the moment is *you.*'

Heat started up in her veins. 'Me?' She was unable to find another word.

'Yes, you. Don't sound so surprised. I don't see much of you. Certainly not as much as I'd like,' Bryn continued as she remained silent. He firmed up his hold on her trembling hand, then—shockingly—raised it to his lips.

'*"Thus with a kiss I die."*' he quoted lightly, but Francesca's heart flipped in her breast.

It was easy to identify Romeo's final line. What was Bryn thinking, saying that? It bewildered her. So did his darkly enigmatic gaze. Didn't he know how difficult it was for her, loving him and knowing he was with Carina? But then, how *could* he know? She did everything possible to hide her true feelings.

'Break out of your shell, Francesca,' he abruptly urged. 'You've been over-long inside it.'

She felt a rush of humiliation at the criticism. Doubly so because he was right. 'I thought it was for my own protection.'

'I understand all that.'

There was a high, humming sound in her ears. 'May I have my hand back?'

'Of course.' He released her hand on the instant, leaning forward to switch on the ignition. 'We should get back anyway,' he added briskly. 'I want to leave as soon as possible.'

'I'm ready.'

It wasn't a good feeling.

She could feel her heart sink.

The Jeep bounded across the vast sun-drenched plain accompanied by a great flight of budgerigars—the phenomenon of the Outback that had materialised again. Francesca gazed up at them, wondering if and when she would see Daramba again. She was certain her uncle would inherit the pastoral chain, but Charles had never much cared for Daramba.

Like all inhabitants of the great island continent, in particular of remote Western Australia, he was used to vast open spaces, to incredible *emptiness,* but on his own admission something about Daramba spooked him. It was there, after all, that Gulla Nolan had mysteriously disappeared. The verdict after an intensive search at the time was that Gulla had been drunk and had slipped into one of the maze of waterholes, billabongs, lagoons and swamps that criss-crossed the station. Everyone knew Gulla had had a great liking for the booze. Gulla Nolan had been the famous tracker Sir Theodore Macallan and her own grandfather had taken along with them on their expeditions. Gulla had been with them when they had discovered Mount Gloriana.

To this day no one knew Gulla's fate—although it was Sir Theo who had set up a trust fund which had grown very substantially over the years, for Gulla and his descendants. One of them was a well-known political activist—a university graduate, educated through the Gulla Nolan Trust and—ironically—a sworn enemy of the Forsyths. It was quite possible, then, that her uncle would sell Daramba, if not the whole chain.

CHAPTER TWO

THE FUNERAL OF Sir Francis Forsyth was unique in one respect. No one cried. Though it should be said there was no easy way to shed a tear for a man more often described as 'a ruthless bastard' than a jewel in the giant State of Western Australia's crown. Nevertheless, the Anglican Cathedral St George's—Victorian Gothic Revival in style, and relatively modest compared to the huge Catholic Cathedral, St Mary's, built on the site that had actually been set aside by the Founding Fathers for St George's—was packed by 'mourners'. This covered anyone who was anyone in the public eye: a federal senator, representative of the Prime Minister, the State Premier, the State Governor, who had once privately called Sir Francis 'an appalling old villain', various dignitaries, representatives of the pastoral, business and the legal world. All seated behind the Forsyth family on the right, the Macallan family to the left.

The truly ironic thing was that Sir Theodore Macallan, co-founder with Sir Francis of Titan, had been universally loved and admired. But then, Sir Theo had been a great man, with that much-to-be-desired accolade of being a true *gentleman* bestowed on him. That meant a gentleman at *heart* as well as in the graciousness of his manner. It had helped that he had been a huge benefactor to the state as well. Sir Frank, on the other hand, had always kept his philanthropy in line with tax avoidance schemes—all legal, naturally. He had long been known to proclaim he paid his taxes along with everyone else, of course. One didn't get to be a billionaire and not have an army of lawyers whose whole lives were devoted to protecting the Forsyth business empire against all comers—including the government.

The Forsyth heiress, Carina, looked *wonderful,* they all agreed. Everyone craned their heads for a look, even though footage of the celebrity funeral would appear on national television.

The whole funeral scene had been revolutionised over recent years: the style of eulogies, the music that would never have been allowed in the old days, the kind of people given the opportunity to speak, even the things they got away with saying. The entire ritual had been rewritten. And today most of the mourners, some of whom had expressed behind-the-scenes opinions that the world was a better place without the deceased, had dressed up as much as they would have if they'd been going to a huge social function like the Melbourne Cup. There was even the odd whiff of excitement in the air. Many, on meeting up with old friends, had to concentrate hard on not breaking into laughter, though some light laughter would be allowed during the eulogies.

Carina Forsyth attracted the most attention. She always wore the most glamorous clothes and jewels—even to her grandfather's funeral. Everyone looked at the size of her South Sea pearls, a steal at $100,000 a strand! The state had always been famous for its pearling industry. No one was about to bring up a fairly recent scandal when a society wife—present on this sad day—had accused the heiress of having an affair with her businessman husband and labelled her 'a tramp.' Well, not today anyway. Not before, during or after the service. Possibly over drinks that evening.

The 'spare' Forsyth heiress, as Francesca had long been dubbed by the press, by comparison was very plainly attired.

A simple black suit, modest jewellery, no big glamorous hat, and her long hair arranged in a low coil at her nape, held with a stylised black grosgrain ribbon. She even wore sunglasses in church—a sure sign she wanted to hide. Not that the 'spare' needed to hide. Francesca Forsyth had already established herself in the general community's good books. As a Forsyth, like her cousin, it wouldn't have been necessary for her ever to lift a finger, but Francesca was creating a real niche for herself in public-spirited good works—like the aunt who had reared her, the much admired Elizabeth Forsyth, who—oddly—was seated with the Macallans. Then again, everyone knew about the split in the Forsyth family ranks.

While Carina was feted, and treated with a near sickening degree of deference—at least to her face—her cousin was winning for herself a considerable degree of affection and admiration of which she was unaware.

What everyone needed to know now was this: what were the contents of Sir Francis Forsyth's will? It was taken for granted that his only son Charles Forsyth would be the main beneficiary, though Charles had always been judged by the business community as 'dead wood'. There were all sorts of interlocking trusts in place to provide income for various members of the extended family, but the bulk of the Forsyth fortune would pass by tradition to his eldest son—Sir Francis's younger son, Lionel, with whom he had fallen out anyway, being deceased.

The entire business world could clearly see Charles Forsyth's clear and present danger. He was sitting in the front pew on the left.

Tall, stunningly handsome, powerfully lean and sombre of expression, Bryn sat between his aristocratic grandmother, Lady Antonia Macallan, and his beautiful mother, Annette Macallan, who had never remarried despite the many offers that had followed in the wake of the tragic death of her husband. Bryn Macallan was firmly entrenched as a power player. It was said he had handled without effort everything the late Sir Francis had thrown at him—and Sir Francis had done a lot of throwing. Considered one of the biggest catches in the country, he was not yet married. Everyone in the state knew Sir Francis had worked for an alliance—a business merger—between Macallan and his granddaughter Carina, but so far nothing had eventuated. It was generally held that it was only a question of *when.*

The mining giant Titan was too big to be owned by any one family—indeed, any one person—but Macallan, through his family history, his prodigious intellect and business acumen, looked very much as if he could at some stage become the man in control. Surely that was reason enough for him and Carina Forsyth to finally tie the knot? Both of them had 'star quality'.

Hundreds of people flocked back to the Forsyth mansion, a geometric modern-day fortress, wandering all over the huge reception rooms and the library as if it was open house and the property would soon be up for auction. Very few of them had ever been invited inside, so most faces were stamped with expressions of wonderment, amazement and occasionally dismay—but huge curiosity none the less.

Although the day was quite hot, Charles Forsyth stood in front of a gigantic stone fireplace—one might wonder from whence it had been acquired…from one of the Medici clan, probably—looking chilled to the bone. The aperture, filled on that day with a stupendous arrangement of white lilies and fanning greenery, was so vast a fully grown man could have been roasted standing up.

'Buck up, Dad, for God's sake!' Carina uttered a wrathful warning into her father's ear. Though she loved her father, sometimes his manner simply enraged her. She quite understood how it had enraged her grandfather.

'The devil with that!' her father replied. 'I've seen the will.'

'So?' Carina drew back, as if a particularly virulent wasp, hidden away in the lilies, had chosen that moment to sting her. 'It's what we expected, isn't it?'

'No, it isn't,' Charles Forsyth admitted, his face abruptly turning red.

Carina turned her back to the huge crowded living room, squarely facing her father. Her eyes had turned a chilling iceberg blue. 'So *when* were you going to tell *me*?'

Her tone was so trenchant, so much like his father's, that for a moment Charles Forsyth looked terrified. 'You'll know soon enough. I wish you weren't so much like him, Carrie. It frightens me sometimes. You're right. I should buck up and circulate. Most of them have only come to goggle and giggle anyway. This place *is* in appalling taste. Forget any notion Dad was revered, or even liked. Even the Archbishop was hard-pressed to come up with the odd kind word. My father has the rankest outside chance of getting into heaven.'

Carina gritted her perfect white teeth. 'Get a grip, Dad! There *is* no heaven.'

He laughed sadly. 'You may be right. But there is, God help us, a hell. There's no glory in *inheriting* a great fortune, Carina. Whatever you believe. You've no idea of normal life because you've been so pampered. Nothing has been expected of you except to look glamorous. The job of stepping into your grandfather's shoes is bigger than you and I can possibly imagine. I'll be the first to admit I don't have the intellect. And I'm far from tough. Everyone knows my bark is worse than my bite. We need someone as tough as he was, even when he *was* slowing down. He knew it himself. He was coming to rely more and more on Macallan's judgment, and the good will that goes with the Macallan name. Sir Theo *wasn't* a scoundrel.'

It took all of Carina's self-control not to lash out in anger. She had adored her grandfather. She *adored* strength and ruthlessness in a man. They were assets, not mortal sins. 'I'm not going to listen to this!' she said, her eyes turning hard and cold as stones. 'Gramps was a great man.'

'That's your view, certainly,' her father answered wearily. 'But you won't find many to agree with you.' For a minute

Charles Forsyth was almost tempted to tell his daughter just a few of her grandfather's venial sins, even if he left out the mortal ones. But what purpose would that serve? 'We owe our great success in the main to Sir Theo,' he told his daughter patiently. 'We owe him many times over. What we need now is a *fighter!* You must be aware Orion is awaiting its opportunity to move in on us? I'm not a fighter. I'm a coward. Your mother told me that at the end, before the divorce. I have no guts. She was right. She was always right.'

'Leave Mum out of this,' Carina said furiously. 'She betrayed us both when she left you. See the way she was sitting with the Macallans? Hiding behind that black veil? She hated Gramps.'

'And she despised *me* while she was at it,' Charles Forsyth said sadly. 'I don't blame her. Every time Dad bawled me out I crumpled like a soggy sponge. I spent a lifetime being despised by my father. I was so in awe of him, so desperate to please him, I never got a chance to develop my own character. Can I help it if with his passing it seems like an intolerable burden has been lifted from my shoulders—?' He broke off, as if exhausted. 'The best thing you can possibly do, Carrie, for yourself and for the rest of us is get Macallan to marry you. That would solve *all* our problems. He's a man who could handle the Forsyth Foundation as well. But Macallan doesn't seem to be in any rush to ask you.'

That touched an agonisingly raw nerve. 'Keep out of it, Dad,' Carina warned, staring at her father with something approaching ferocity. 'I'll handle this in my own way.'

'No doubt!' Charles shot a troubled glance across the room, to where Bryn Macallan was standing in quiet conversation with his niece, Francesca. Macallan's height and his superb athletic build made Francesca, who was tall for a woman, look as fragile as a lily on a stalk. Beautiful girl, Francesca. Totally different style from his daughter. Far more elegant, he suddenly realised. And so much more to her. Already at twenty-three she was making quite a name for herself as an artist. Not that any of that mattered any more…

Carina's gaze had followed her father's, because she always followed Bryn and Francey's whereabouts. 'Just like Gramps didn't tell you everything, neither do I. Sometimes it's best *not* to know. Francey's no threat, if that thought has ever crossed your mind. It's *me* Bryn wants, but he needs to bring me to heel. I rather like that.' She gave her father a vixen's smile. It was more chilling than her glare.

For some years now it had been Charles Forsyth's worst nightmare that his daughter would morph into his father. It was happening right in front of his eyes.

'There is a bond between them, you know.' Unwisely he found himself pointing it out. 'Bryn did save Francey's life all those years ago.'

Carina's eyes flashed blue lightning. 'Bryn—always the hero! Dear little Francey had taken Mum over even *then*.'

Charles Forsyth was shocked by her tone. 'Nothing deliberate, Carrie. Francesca was such a *lovely* child.'

'And *I* wasn't?' Carina asked fiercely, her creamy flushed cheeks only heightening her knock-out beauty.

'Of course you were. You were perfect. You *are* perfect,' her father lied desperately. Often as a child Carina had been truly horrible. Once she had even ransacked her mother's study. *Horrible!* 'Poor little Francey was an orphan,' he said, in an effort to win his niece some sympathy. 'She was in desperate need of tender loving care, which your mother gave her. You were *never* neglected, Carrie. Not for one moment. Why do you blame your cousin so? She was the innocent victim.'

'Actually, *I* was the victim,' Carina said, never more serious in her life. 'Though you and Mum never noticed. Francey was no innocent. She might have started out that way, but as time went on she and Mum were always in league in a conspiracy against me.'

Charles Forsyth was torn two ways. Between love for his

daughter and a growing fear that he didn't really know or possibly even *like* her. 'That's not right, Carrie! You should speak to someone about this. What you have is a phobia, and it seems to be growing worse.'

Carina laughed. 'Sorry, Dad, but I'm spot-on. Mum lived for Francey. Think of it! My own mother loves my cousin far more than she loves me, her only child.'

'Maybe you wouldn't let her love you?' her father countered.

'How could I, when she was always turning to Francey?' Carina answered, as though the explanation was obvious. She put up a hand to pat her father's cheek. Oddly, it caused him to jump as if she had administered an electric shock. 'Look, Dad, I love Francey. I admire her essential *goodness.* We're not only first cousins, we're the closest of friends. She often comes to me for advice, and I'm delighted to give it. I can't help it if occasionally I have a little growl about Mum's affection for her. I'm no saint.'

No, you're not, God help us! Charles Forsyth felt a blindingly sharp pain in his right temple. Lord knew what might happen if Macallan suddenly switched his attentions from Carina to Francesca. With all he now knew, it *could* happen. There were all sorts of surprises in life. A huge one was about to hit them like a tidal wave. And there would be hell to pay if ever Carina's plans were thwarted. Carina had a formidable array of weapons—not the least of them his father's legendary ruthlessness. *He* wouldn't want to be in the shoes of any woman who tried to oust Carina in Macallan's affections.

Now more than ever early retirement seemed a welcome option for Charles Forsyth. He was ready to quit the stage. He hadn't really needed to be shoved.

The reading of the will was set for an hour after the last mourner had left. Francesca thought she might faint away from distress and fatigue by then.

'Are you okay?' Bryn found her sitting quietly in a corner,

partially obscured by a tall and luxuriant indoor palm. He drew up a chair beside her.

'Sort of,' she said, enormously grateful for his company. 'Death is very sobering, isn't it? What I profoundly regret is the fact I wasn't able to make a real connection with Grandfather and now I never will. But Carina was his great favourite, after all.'

'She was so like him,' Bryn offered by way of explanation.

Francesca smiled faintly. 'Yes. I always understood it was *my* job to keep quiet and out of the way. Lord knows how I would have turned out if not for Elizabeth and the innumerable kindnesses shown to me by your family. In a way—' she looked about them at the daunting opulence of the room '—I still feel like I'm in enemy territory in this great terrible house.'

'It is a bit of a monstrosity,' Bryn quietly agreed. He'd thought that the first time he had walked into the mansion all those years ago.

'I used to hope and pray Carrie and I might become inseparable,' Francesca confided poignantly. 'The two Forsyth girls.'

'It never happened.' A simple statement of fact.

'No. Our relationship, nevertheless, is close and binding. But somehow, underneath it all, I felt unsettled and confused. I'm much happier now living my own life, standing on my own two feet, looking to the future.'

'The future is what matters, Francey,' he told her, continuing to watch her closely. She was very pale, and far more genuinely upset than Carina. 'You have to let everything else—the bad things—recede into the past. Something inside tells me you're fated to be a powerful force for good.'

His comment made her heart topple. 'Oh, Bryn!' She waved an agitated hand, as if dismissing the very idea.

'No, I mean it,' he said. 'You have a light around you, Francey. You did from your childhood. That light drew me to you.'

She was starting to feel really dizzy. 'You mean the day I nearly drowned?' What was going on inside his head? His heart? She couldn't be mistaken. There was a lot of feeling somewhere there.

'Then, and now,' he said.

She gave an involuntary shiver as memories crowded in. 'I often revisit that day in my dreams. The sense of danger is still with me.'

'Danger?' His black brows drew together in a frown. 'You've never spoken of it before.'

'So much I haven't put into words.' She sighed, feeling the weight of her suspicions. Carina, her own flesh and blood, a threat to her? Nothing good could possibly come out of saying that to Bryn. She knew better than anyone the relationship between Carina and him was too close. Her subconscious might grapple with her clouded memories, but she had to keep them under lock and key. Who would believe her anyway? She had often heard Carina describe her as 'nerve-ridden', all the while managing to sound deeply concerned. One thing was certain: exposing Carina could only bring heartbreak.

And trouble.

There was always that nagging thought. Crossing people like Carina, who thought what *she* wanted should be the law of the land, could develop into a life-threatening matter.

'No point in keeping it locked up inside you.' Bryn's frown darkened his handsome face. 'Better to speak to someone you trust about these things. I've told you I'm always ready to listen.'

'And I appreciate that, Bryn.' She made no attempt to conceal it. 'Life can be a lot tougher when you're rich.' She gave a little laugh, but the sound was very tense. She didn't want to be around for the will reading. She wanted to be well away.

Bryn briefly touched her hand, giving her his beautiful magnetic smile. 'Isn't that the truth? Look, you sit here quietly. I have to have a word with Frank's elder sister and her husband. But I'll be back.'

'Don't worry about me,' she said, realising her head was lolling slightly forward. 'I'll be fine.'

'I'll be back,' he repeated, looking every inch the hero.

Hang in there, Francey, she urged herself as Bryn walked away to join the Forsyths. *Everything passes.*

A moment later, Carina zoomed across the room to chide her. 'Don't droop, Francey. We have a duty to support one another.' Her eyes flicked over Francesca's slender figure. 'And couldn't you have done better than that suit? It's okay, I guess, but you try much too hard to pretend you don't have money when the whole damned country knows you have.'

'Perhaps you're right. Anyway, *you* look a billion dollars.'

'That's my job. Gramps took such pleasure in how I looked. It's no easy task to look this good every day—especially when one has to attend the funeral of the person who loved me most in this world.'

Francesca realised that just might be true. 'I'm sorry, Carrie,' she murmured. 'Truly sorry. Grandfather did love you. He adored you.'

'And he would have loved you too, only there was always something *difficult* about you, Francey. You didn't fit in, and you never gave Gramps the reverence he deserved. He was a great man, yet that seemed to mean nothing to you.'

It took an effort, but Francesca had to deny the charge. 'That's not true. I gave Grandfather all the respect in the world. I couldn't rise to reverence. I associate reverence with saintly people—fallen war heroes, great humanitarians and the like. And, let's face it, I didn't have your wonderful self-assurance and I didn't have the Forsyth blonde, blue-eyed good-looks.'

'No, you missed out there. But you're attractive enough,' Carina told her, quite objectively. 'The pity of it is you don't do much for yourself.'

'Well, I intend to make a start,' Francesca said, making a visible effort to straighten her shoulders. 'Maybe tomorrow. I apologise if I'm looking a bit fraught. I haven't had much sleep.'

'And I have?' Carina cast her large blue eyes towards the ceiling. 'You do have dark circles under your eyes. No wonder you were hiding behind those sunglasses. Perhaps I should give you a good shake?' She glanced at Francesca sidelong. 'Remember how I used to shake you awake when we were kids? You used to keep me awake with your night terrors. Mum had fixed you up with a nightlight too. Sconces were left burning along the corridor, and if that weren't enough, I was in the next room. No one seemed to care much if *I* didn't like all that light shining in on me.'

'Poor, poor Carina. I do remember.' Francesca reached out a hand for the high back of a chair that really should have been in a museum to steady herself.

'You were always having such terrible dreams. What were they about? Nightmares about drowning?'

Why did Carina always bring that subject up? Was she constantly checking to see if Francesca's memory of the near tragedy remained dim?

'They were the worst.' Francesca gave a shudder. *Pitching or being pushed headlong into the dark green lagoon.* Even when she woke up she had felt bruised.

'Needless to say Mum always had to get up to comfort you. You weren't happy with little me. Mum had to come to pet you and soothe you back to sleep. Pathetic, really. Sometimes I used to think Mum loved you more than me.' She smiled into Francesca's eyes as if asking a question: what sort of mother would do that?

'Have a heart.' Francesca shook her aching head. 'I was only a little lost kid, Carrie. Your mother was just looking out for me.'

'Something she's doing to this day.' Carina only just succeeded in covering her intense resentment. 'Dad and I were terribly upset she sat with the Macallans. We could see that as a betrayal.'

'Perhaps Elizabeth wasn't prepared to be hypocritical?' Francesca suggested, loyal to the woman who had reared her from the age of five. 'She didn't have a good relationship with our grandfather, did she? His fault, not hers.'

'Hey, hey—be fair now!' Carina was looking more taken aback by the minute. 'I suppose it was *Dad's* fault she couldn't get far enough away from him?' she asked heatedly.

Francesca could see Carina was as upset in her way as she was in hers. 'Look, don't upset yourself, Carrie. It's just that your mother didn't believe it possible to remain locked in a marriage that wasn't working.'

'How can *you* be sure of that?' Carina's matt cheeks were hot with blood. 'You have no insight into relationships. God, you haven't even *had* a real one, have you? You can't count Greg Norbett…or Harry Osbourne,' she added contemptuously.

'Certainly not after you made a play for him.' Francesca surprised herself by making the charge. 'Why did you *do* that? You weren't interested in Harry.'

Carina backed off a notch, touching Francesca's cheek very gently. 'I only did it to make you see what he really was. I didn't want you to get hurt. I've never wanted to see you suffer, Francey. You're still my little lost cousin. I have to look out for you. Harry Osbourne was no good for you.'

'Harry was okay,' Francesca said. 'He was never as close to me as you thought. We weren't lovers. Nothing like that.'

Carina made no effort to conceal her amusement. 'Gosh, are you still a little virgin? I bet you are!' She trilled with laughter that caused heads to turn.

'Maybe, as a Forsyth, I don't fancy the idea of my affairs getting around.'

That appeared to hit the bullseye. 'What does *that* mean?'

Francesca shrugged. 'Nothing, really.' What sense was there in baiting Carina? 'Sadly, not all married couples live happily ever after.'

'Well, *I* plan to.' Carina stared fiercely at her cousin, like a fencing opponent determined on slicing her through. 'I love Bryn. I've always loved him. I was *meant* to have him and I'm going to make certain I do. So don't ever be fool enough to get in my way, cousin.'

Threat came off Carina in waves.

Francesca was all too familiar with the look. Just so had their grandfather looked when he was laying down the law. 'When have I ever done that, Carrie?' she asked quietly. 'We could have been good friends if you'd only given me a chance.'

'Given you a chance?' Carina couldn't have looked more taken aback. 'I've no idea what you're talking about. To my mind we're the best and closest of friends.'

'Surely it's time to face the truth? We're not, Carrie. We might as well stop the pretence.'

Carina was holding her hands so tightly together she might be fearing she would lash out. 'I don't believe this. And on this day of days!'

'Maybe that's the reason. It's the end of an era; the end of the old life. I *wanted* to belong. I wanted us to be more like sisters than cousins. But sadly we were never that.'

Carina's anger suddenly disappeared like a puff of smoke. 'I hate to hear you talk like this, Francey,' she said. 'It makes me feel quite wounded. You obviously have no memory of all the fondness I showed you. What you're saying sounds quite neurotic. I can't help knowing all these years that you've been sick with envy. Don't worry. I forgive you. It's natural enough. But I've always tried to be there for you. I've always tried to protect you from unpleasantness. I shielded you from Gramps. You made him angry, always looking at him with those big tragic eyes. Anyone would think you were accusing him of something.'

Francesca shook her head. 'Nonsense!'

'Not nonsense at all. If I were you, I'd count myself lucky.'

'A lot of the time I do,' Francesca freely admitted. 'Look, Bryn's coming over.'

'He's coming to *me!*' Carina pointed out very sharply, her possessive blue eyes following his progress. 'I dearly need his support.'

'Of course you do.'

The life force that was in Bryn Macallan made him fairly blaze. Both young women felt it. Both were electrified by it.

Francesca made her escape as swiftly as she could. She mightn't know the *whole* truth of Bryn's relationship with her cousin, but she knew enough not to interfere.

If only... If only...

She made the mistake of glancing back, and any tiny hope she might have nourished withered and died. Bryn held an anguished-looking Carrie against his breast, his raven head bent over hers, a shining blonde against the funereal black of his jacket.

Who said unrequited love wasn't hell?

CHAPTER THREE

WHEN FRANCESCA FINALLY made it to the relative sanctuary of her old suite of rooms, she found Dami, the maid, putting a pile of fluffy fresh towels in the *en suite* bathroom, which was almost as big as the living room in Francesca's apartment.

'Is there anything else I can do for you, Ms Forsyth?' Dami asked. She had already unpacked Francesca's things and put them away. 'Would you like tea?'

Francesca glanced out of the window. It was still brilliantly light. 'That would be lovely. Thank you, Dami.' There had been any amount of food and drink downstairs, but she hadn't felt able to touch a thing. The 'mourners', however, standing in groups holding plates and glasses aloft, had availed themselves of the sumptuous spread. It might have been a wedding, not a wake. 'Are you settling in well?' she checked with the maid, who was a fairly recent addition to the staff.

Dami looked shocked to be asked. 'Yes, thank you, miss.' She gave a little nervous bob. 'What kind of tea, please?' Eagerness was visible in every line of her slight body. She began to sound off a list.

It was Francesca's turn to smile. 'Darjeeling will be fine, Dami. Perhaps you could find a sandwich to go with it?' It struck her all of a sudden that she had better have something to keep up her strength.

'Of course, miss,' Dami said, preparing to withdraw. 'Shall I draw a bath for you later?' It was her job to look after Francesca's every need, and she was obviously taking it very seriously.

Francesca shook her head, marvelling that, after a lifetime of it, she still couldn't get used to the Forsyth lifestyle of being waited on hand and foot. Even her grandfather's morning papers had had to be pressed with a warm iron before they were brought to him. 'I'm not sure of my plans, Dami,' she said gently. 'In any case, I can manage, thank you.'

'Yes, miss.' Dami gave another little cork-like bob, then vanished to carry out Francesca's wishes.

After Dami had gone Francesca slipped out of the offending black two-piece suit to which Carina had given the thumbs-down. There was absolutely nothing wrong with it. In fact it was quite elegant. But Carina, she knew, didn't go for the understated. She hung the suit away, then pulled a pair of narrow black linen trousers off the hanger. She had brought a silk blouse to wear with it, silver-grey in colour. Her head was aching so badly she pulled the pins out of the confining knot and then shook her hair free. Immediately she experienced a sense of lightness that seemed to lessen the throbbing pain in her temples. It might be a good idea to wait for Dami to return with her tea before taking any medication. She wasn't used to it. Not that there was a problem with a couple of painkillers.

A few minutes later there was a tap on her door and she went to it, fully expecting to see Dami standing there, either carrying a tray or pushing a trolley. At least she wouldn't have had to come any distance. There was a service elevator, as there had to be in such a mausoleum. Only in the end it wasn't Dami.

Bryn's brilliant black eyes studied her. 'Hi!'

'Hi!' Her heart rose like a bird's. How did one repudiate love? Even when one knew it was paramount to do so?

She yearned for him to lean down and kiss her. Not her cheek, as was their custom, but her mouth. Wasn't that her most exquisite dream? Only she knew it wasn't good or wise.

'What are you doing here?' She hoped her naked self wasn't there for him to see in her eyes. 'I thought you'd be with Carrie?'

He answered question with question. 'May I come in?'

'Of course.' She stood back to admit him. 'I'll leave the door open. I asked Dami to get me a cup of tea. Would you like one?'

'Dear God, no,' he moaned, walking to the window and looking out over the vast lawn. 'I wanted to see *you*.' He turned around to regard her, catching her in the act of trying to fashion her long lustrous hair into yet another knot. 'Leave it,' he said, his tone more clipped than he'd intended. 'I like seeing your hair down instead of always dragged back.'

Her hands stilled at his command. For that was what it was. A command. 'Gosh, it's not that bad, is it?' she asked wryly.

'Of course not. I'm sorry. I tend to feel a bit strongly about it.'

'Really?' She couldn't have been more surprised. 'So I'll leave it loose, then?'

'Damn it, *yes*. It suits you.' Loose her hair was the very opposite to the sleekness she achieved with her various coils. It sprang away from her face, full of volume. Swirls of hair cascaded sinuously over her shoulders and down her back to her shoulderblades. Yet she obviously considered wearing her hair loose hugely inappropriate on the day of her grandfather's funeral.

'Okay. I get the message. I must remember you don't like my hair pulled back. It's just that I don't like to go down to the will-reading—'

'What has leaving your hair down got to do with the will-reading?' he interrupted. 'It's beautiful hair.'

'I thought you preferred blonde?' It just flew out. She hadn't meant to say it at all. Now she was embarrassed.

'Blonde hair is lovely,' he agreed. 'But it doesn't get the *shine* on it sable hair does.'

'Don't tell Carrie that.'

He gave a half smile. 'Carrie thinks she has the best head of hair in the entire world.'

'Well, she'd have to come close.' Francesca leant over to realign an ornament. There was the sound of tinkling from the corridor. Silver against china. In the next instant Dami appeared in the open doorway, carrying an elaborate silver tray normally associated with very tall butlers and banquets.

Bryn crossed the room to take the tray from her. 'I'll take that, Dami. It looks too heavy for you.'

'I think maybe a little bit,' Dami admitted, and blushed. 'Shall I fetch another cup?' She looked anxiously from Francesca to Bryn.

'No, that's fine, Dami,' Francesca smiled. 'Mr Macallan doesn't want tea.'

'I can only drink so many cups,' Bryn groaned.

'You would like something else?' the maid asked.

'Nothing, Dami. Thank you.' Francesca shook her head. Even Dami was staring at her flowing mane with what appeared to be outright admiration.

By the time she had closed the door Bryn had poured a cup of tea for her from the silver pot. She had seen it countless times before. It was part of a valuable five-piece Georgian service. The matching lidded sugar bowl was there, and beside it a silver dish with lemon slices. The bone china tea cup and saucer had an exquisite *bleu celeste* border and a gold rim, as did the matching plate, holding an array of delicate triple-layer sandwich fingers, all very elegantly presented.

'Come along,' Bryn said, as though it was his duty to get her to eat. 'I notice you didn't touch a thing downstairs when everyone else was most enthusiastic. You'd think the whole country was going to be hit by famine in a matter of days.' He glanced back at her. 'Leave your hair alone.'

'Goodness, you're bossy!' she breathed.

'I have to be. I know you grew up thinking your hair had to be tied back in plaits. It was Carrie's golden mane that was always on display. Even Elizabeth knew better than to present you as a foil for her daughter.'

'Oh, hold on!'

'It's true.'

'Okay, it's true. No secrets from you,' she said with a helpless shrug. 'Elizabeth spent a lot of time brushing my hair as a child and telling me how beautiful it was. *"Just like your mother's!"* She always said that, smiling quietly, before hugging me to her with tears in her eyes. She and my mother had become the closest of friends, she said. Growing up in this strange house only Elizabeth affirmed my value. Then she had to make her own escape.'

'Well, the Forsyths tend to stomp on people,' Bryn said, very dryly. 'It took a tremendous amount of guts for your father to get out. He was never forgiven, of course.'

'I used to think *I* bore the brunt of that. The father's sins visited on the daughter?' She hesitated for a moment. 'It's always puzzled me why Elizabeth married Uncle Charles. All right, I know he would have been very handsome—he still is—and a Forsyth with all that money. But he's so…shallow.' She gave a little shamed sob. 'No, I'll take that back. I'm sorry. *Not* shallow. But not a lot to him. Or not a lot that shows.'

Bryn shrugged. 'You know why. Your grandfather drained the life out of him. There's a word for your grandfather, but I can't use it on this particular day. He made his own son feel forever anxious and insecure. He made him feel he would never be good enough to take over the running of the Forsyth Foundation, let alone Titan. Oddly enough, Charles is now acting as though a huge load has been lifted from his shoulders and dropped onto someone else's. Did you notice?' He shot her a laser-like glance. 'He even tried chatting up Elizabeth. He sounded as though he was actually *aching* for her company.'

'I can't think she can be aching for his,' Francesca said sharply, then winced. 'Oh, what would I know? Maybe Uncle Charles knows something the rest of us don't?' She finished off one of the sandwiches, then used the edge of a linen and lace napkin to brush away a crumb.

'He could know the contents of the will,' Bryn mused aloud. 'But it's inconceivable he might be bypassed. Or *is* it?' He spoke as though the thought had just occurred to him.

'What are you saying?' Francesca stared back. 'By tradition Uncle Charles will take over from Grandfather, won't he?'

'Well, we'll soon know.' Bryn deflected her question briskly, an edge of mockery in his tone.

'We?' There was a flicker in her eyes. 'You mean you're staying?' She had thought now that he had brought her home he had come to say goodbye.

'It appears I'm a beneficiary.' He gave a brief laugh that was quite without humour.

'Good Lord! Aren't you wondering what it is?'

Bryn held up a hand. 'A set of golf clubs? He borrowed my grandfather's and never gave them back. Come here, Francey.' He watched her rise gracefully from her chair and walk towards him. 'People do the damnedest thing when it comes to making wills. We all might be in for a few shocks. Even the wicked, like Frank, aren't absolutely sure they won't have to face up to a higher authority. Give an accounting. Face the music. Listen while a long list of sins are read out.'

Her father had been sinned against, Francesca thought. His share of the family fortune had been slashed right back. 'Well, Carrie was very anxious you should stay.' She lifted her eyes to his, aware she was trembling. 'She needs your support.'

'Carrie is well able to look after herself,' he replied, without expression.

'Yes, but we all need a shoulder to cry on from time to time. I couldn't help seeing the two of you together. The way you gathered her to you.' The kind of intimacy she imagined herself and Bryn might share!

'So? What would you have had me do?' he countered, raising a black brow. 'Carrie was looking for comfort. I gave it. All three of us have been locked together since we were kids.'

'I've never felt it was a *triangle,*' Francesca said slowly, hardly able to sustain his concentrated glance. *Until now.*

'Sure about that?' Very gently he lifted a finger and began to twine a silky lock of her hair around it.

The slightest contact; a wild adrenalin rush. 'What are you doing, Bryn?' Her voice quavered, soft and intense. By now he had drawn her face closer, his filled with mesmerising intent.

'Looking at you,' he answered, mildly enough. 'What else? You must be used to it by now. You're very beautiful, Francey, though I see it torments you.' She would have dreaded upstaging Carrie, he knew. Something she could easily have done.

'I'm unsure *why* you're looking at me,' she questioned. 'And with such concentration.'

'Should that make you feel threatened?' He drew back a little, to stare down into her eyes, putting her further off-balance.

Oh, my God... Oh, my God... Oh, my God...

The breath caught in her throat. 'I've never felt *more* threatened.' Her head was beginning to swim.

'Does that happen when I touch you?' A kind of agony was deep in his voice.

Such a change in pace! Such a tremendous build-up in pressure. What was he *doing*? Her heart seemed to be pumping at the base of her throat. Her will giving way under the force of his. 'You are *not* to kiss me, Bryn,' she warned, aware she sounded pathetically frantic. 'If that's what you're planning.' She had been exposed to such a look many times before—desire—but *never* from Bryn. Yet there seemed no way out. As if it was something he fully intended to do.

Her whole body was locked rigid. All the breath was sucked out of her. How could she resist him? It would take every ounce of her will and self discipline. She knew in her heart of hearts she didn't have enough.

'How do you know I haven't been planning to kiss you for

some time?' he challenged her, a burning intensity in his eyes. His hands closed slowly and gently around her throat, a warm, living rope binding her to him.

'Bryn, it makes no sense to experiment.' She tried to free herself to no avail. 'You have no reason to hurt me.'

That appeared to make him angry. '*Hurt you?* Would kissing you do that?' He maintained his hold on her, the air thrumming with electricity.

'You need to consider that possibility.' Even as she argued her position, hot blood was thrashing through her veins. 'It could hardly be worth it.'

'Now, that's where you're wrong,' he said very crisply, his dynamic face all taut planes and angles, his eyes glittering with such dark radiance Francesca was forced to close hers.

Pretend it's make-believe.

How could she, when every nerve was screaming *reality*? Francesca found herself standing perfectly still while his hands slipped over the curve of her shoulders, then he locked a steely arm around her quiescent body.

Sensation was so overwhelming she gasped aloud. She knew she would remember these moments all her life: what it meant to be swept away. But if she allowed herself to go with it, this would be a life-changing moment. An emotional disaster, even. She wasn't equipped to handle disaster.

But what use to fight the tyranny of the senses? His dominant face was bent over her. What could seem absolutely wrong, could also seem absolutely *right.*

He kissed her—not once, but repeatedly, the pleasure blotting out all resistance.

Each kiss was deeper, more seductive, than the last. She could taste the salt of her own tears. 'Bryn, you *mustn't.*' Yet she was going with the moment. It might only happen once. Rapture was flooding her heart and her mind and her body. Filling up every little bit of her, swirling into the deepest recesses. The masks were off!

It was an agony to think of it, but if she didn't stop him soon, she would be totally consumed. She *had* to end it. There would be no way back. She would never have the life she'd once had again. She *had* to stop him.

She didn't.

Why? She could die for this. Die for it day after day after day…

'Some shall be pardoned, and some punished.'

Who was that? Shakespeare, of course. *Romeo and Juliet* again. Tears ran down her face.

Bryn took them blindly into his mouth, savouring them like nectar. 'Francey, I'm sorry. Don't cry. Please don't cry!' he begged, but the instant he said it his mouth closed on hers again like an all-powerful compulsion. Desire was thundering, smashing through Bryn's defences. Her parted lips bloomed, opened like petals to him.

Just this once. Just this once, Francesca prayed. She couldn't hold back the inexpressibly aching yearning. She couldn't turn away from the sheer splendour. She was truly *alive,* made feverish by the exploration of his tongue, stunned by her own high-spiralling sensuality. The illumination was blinding. She felt ready to give him everything he desired. Thereby flouting every rule by which she had lived.

This is Bryn Macallan.

The warning voice in her head suddenly tolled loudly, gathering strength as if to deafen her. *Loving him is a danger.*

Hadn't it been drummed into her right from the beginning? He and Carina had been lovers. Could still be, for all she knew. Carina would never give up on Bryn even if Bryn was prepared to. There was a huge difference between her and Carina. *Try to remember it.* Carina was the Forsyth heiress. The perfect partner for Bryn Macallan. Besides, it would break Carina's proud spirit if she were to lose him.

Bryn, sensing her inner turmoil, drew back a moment, looking down at her beautiful face, still in thrall. Her eyes were closed, her long black lashes lying like crescents on her pale golden skin. Slowly he slipped a hand across her face, tracing the fine bone structure.

'I couldn't fight it any more,' he said, an edge to his voice as though his own nerves were jangled. 'The moment was bound to come.'

Her eyes flew open. 'Then we must forget it!' she cried passionately.

His admission had done nothing to calm her troubled heart. The way forward was fraught with dangerous snares. She had revealed herself when she had fought so diligently not to. No other man could affect her like this. No other man could even come close. She had spent so long hiding her true feelings that now she was aghast at what she had done. They had given in to an involuntary urge. That was it. In the stress of the day, they had given way to a passing desire. But did that excuse her? She *knew* how Carrie felt about Bryn. This was *treason.*

'Francey, don't go into a panic.' His voice rasped. He placed his two hands on her delicate shoulders, looking down on her bent head.

'How can I not?' She dared him to doubt it. She had never experienced anything remotely like this. She had never been so aware of the softness of her woman's body against the hardness of a man's, so aware of the expanse of a man's chest, his strong arms enfolding her, his superb fitness, his superior height. It was *thrilling!* But that wasn't all there was to her feeling for Bryn. She had enormous respect for him. She didn't want that to change. She had always turned to him for support. As a child; as an adult. Still she was afraid. If Bryn wanted her even for a brief moment there was much to be afraid of. In the heat of the moment both of them had taken a great step into the unknown.

'Francey, I'm sorry. I've obviously upset you.' He could see her anguish.

'There's no future in this, Bryn,' she pleaded. 'You know that. More likely there will be consequences.'

'Don't be ridiculous!' He cut her off more harshly than he knew. 'You sound like you might never be seen again.'

'Like Gulla Nolan?' The name tumbled from her lips. What mysterious force had prompted her to mention *him*? And why now?

A darkness descended on Bryn's face. 'Whatever made you bring up Gulla Nolan?'

'God knows.' She found the strength to break away. 'I can't pretend *I* do. His name just came into my mind.' Her eyes were shimmering like silver lakes. 'The last thing I want, Bryn, is to threaten our friendship. It means everything to me.'

His handsome features tightened. 'Francey, I'm much *more* than your friend.'

She rounded on him. 'So don't break my heart. Don't break Carrie's heart. I'm speaking for both of us.'

His reply carried swift condemnation. 'I guess that means you don't want to break out of your safe little hidey-hole?'

She reacted as if he had slapped her. Her cheeks flushed. 'You might say that. I have to forget what's happened here, Bryn. I'm sure you will too. It's an odd day all round. There's so much at stake.'

'Like what?' he asked sharply, staring at her with what she thought was a lick of contempt.

She reacted by throwing up helpless hands. 'You know the answer to that. What *is* it you want from me? *Really?*' Tears gathered again behind her eyes. 'I'll never forgive you if you tell me those kisses meant nothing.' Could romantic dreams possibly become romantic nightmares?

The answer was yes.

'I wasn't the only one who lost my head, Francey,' he told her bluntly. 'If that's what you're convinced it was. I always knew there was a lot of passion behind the Madonna façade.'

'Well, I'm not proud of myself,' she uttered emotionally. 'You're a very sensual man, Bryn. I admit I lost my head. But it's not as though you intend to make a practice of it.' What she had most ardently desired was now worrying the life out of her. But such was her perilous world. The world of the Forsyths and the Macallans. Enough money and power to act any way they liked. Great wealth created impregnable cocoons. Carina would not be mocked.

'I'll be fighting not to for a while,' he told her, bitterly sardonic. 'But let's leave it there, shall we?' He turned purposefully towards the door, tall and commanding. 'This conversation is going nowhere.'

'Because it *can't.*'

His black eyes were full of scorn. 'So you're *still* the little girl afraid to step out of her cousin's shadow?'

She reacted with spirit, even though she could see the smouldering anger in his eyes. 'That's a brutal thing to say, Bryn.'

His laugh cut into her deeply. 'The truth often is. But I won't press it further. Not today, anyway. But it's high time you took up a full life and started slaying your dragons, Francey. You're the best and the brightest of the Forsyths. Wake up to it.'

It was a pep talk he obviously thought she was badly in need of. She wrapped her arms around herself protectively. 'I'm sorry, Bryn. I'm sorry we got into this.'

'It didn't feel like you were sorry when you were in my arms,' he pointed out, so cuttingly she flushed. 'Anyway, forget it. What's done *is* done.'

'I'm sorry,' she repeated. She couldn't bear to see him walk away in anger. She made a huge effort to change the subject before he left. 'Can you tell me something before you go? Please? Something I've always wondered about. That old story of Gulla Nolan…the way he disappeared without trace.'

Bryn froze in his tracks. Hadn't he mulled over the old mystery for years? How strange Francey should bring it up now. But then that sort of thing often happened with Francey. Over the years she had said many things to catch him off guard and cause him to re-think. 'What is there to tell? No one knows anything. A thorough investigation was carried out. The tribal people on and around the station were questioned.'

'Maybe they did know something but feared to speak out.' She looked back at him, huge-eyed. 'Who would have believed them anyway? Things being what they were—still are—an aboriginal's word against the findings of Sir Francis Forsyth? Unthinkable! They hated him with a passion. Maybe they even put a curse on him and his family. My family. My parents—' She broke off, knowing she was deeply overwrought.

He retraced his steps. 'No, Francey, *no!*' He made no further attempt to touch her. 'Don't even go there,' he warned. 'My grandfather had Gulla's disappearance investigated. He shared a real bond with Gulla. But in the end no one knew anything. Gulla went on extended binges. That in itself was a danger. His disappearance is just another bush legend.'

'You don't really believe that,' she said. 'I can hear it in your voice. You're just saying it to make me feel better. Even if he had died out there and the dingoes had taken his body the bones would have been found, traces of his clothing.'

Resolutely he turned on his heel, ignoring the dull roaring in his ears. 'We should go downstairs.'

'You mean before Carina comes up?' Her voice shook.

'Neither of us should put it past her.' His tone was openly ironic. 'Look, Francey, I don't want you walking around in a state of dread. I won't even look sideways at you if you don't want it.'

'Don't look at me *at all* might be better.'

He gave a hard, impatient laugh. 'I can't go so far as to promise that. So don't expect it. Let's just take it one day at a time, shall we? And do try to remember I'm *not* a married man. Not engaged either, last time I checked.'

Douglas McFadden, distinguished senior partner of McFadden, Mallory & Crawford, the Forsyth family solicitors, was seated behind the late Sir Francis Forsyth's massive, rather bizarre mahogany desk in the study. The desk was lavishly decorated with ormolu mounts and lions' feet, the gilded claws extended. Francesca had been truly frightened of those claws as a small child.

Like the rest of the mansion, the ballroom-sized study was hugely over the top. A life-size portrait of Sir Francis in his prime—some seven feet tall and almost as wide, its colours enriched by the overhead light—hung centre stage on the wall behind the desk. It said a great deal for her grandfather—undeniably a strikingly handsome man, if not with the look of distinction the Macallans had in abundance—that the portrait was able to dominate such an impressive room. The artist was quite famous, and he had captured her grandfather's *innerness,* Francesca thought. The man behind the mask. Francesca found herself looking away from those piercing, somehow *gloating* blue eyes.

The beneficiaries, some fourteen in all, looked suitably sober. With the exception of Bryn they were all Forsyths, like herself: some the offspring of her grandfather's two younger sisters, Ruth and Regina, who wisely lived very private lives, well out of their brother's orbit. Four of the grandsons, however, worked for Titan. Sir Francis himself had recruited them, as some sort of gesture towards 'family'. They did their best—they were clever, highly educated—but they could never hope to measure up to Bryn Macallan in any department. At least one of them—James Forsyth-Somerville—knew it. Bryn Macallan was his hero.

Bryn, the outsider, sat as calm and relaxed as though they were all attending a lecture to be given by some university don. Possible topic: was Shakespeare the real author of his plays? Or was it much more likely to have been the brilliant and aristocratic Francis Bacon, or even Edward De Vere? Anyway, it was a talk Bryn appeared to be looking forward to. He sat wedged—the delectable filling in a sandwich—between herself and Carina. The two Forsyth heiresses. She had to recognise she was that. Much as she had sought to remain in the background, she *was* an heiress—a Forsyth, like it or not.

'I don't care where the hell you sit, as long as Bryn is with me!' Carina had snapped at her as they had entered the study, lined with a million beautifully bound books her grandfather had never read.

Bryn, however, had taken his place on Francesca's right. 'Okay, I hope?' he'd asked with faint mockery, causing Carina, who had seated herself dead centre, directly in front of the desk, and had patted the seat beside her, indicating for Bryn to take it, to jump up and grab the other chair, pure venom in her eyes.

In the end everyone was arranged in a two-tiered semicircle in front of the huge mahogany desk. It was difficult to believe Sir Francis was dead. One of the great-nephews, Stephen, kept looking behind him, as though expecting Sir Francis's ghost to walk right through the heavy closed door.

Francesca had noticed her uncle Charles had poured himself a stiff whisky before positioning himself to one side, as though instead of being her grandfather's only surviving son and heir he didn't think he would figure much in the will. How very odd!

A quick glance at Bryn confirmed it. 'Could be a rocky ride!' he murmured, just beneath his breath. He looked tremendously switched on. Ready for the performance to begin.

The elder of Sir Frank's two sisters, Ruth, choked off a little sob, probably thinking there was still time to show a little grief. She hadn't been able to manage it up to date. Carina, however, wasn't impressed by the display. She swung about to frown at her great-aunt. 'For God's sake, not *now!*'

Ruth leaned towards her, murmuring a falsehood. 'But I'm missing him so!'

'Rubbish! You haven't so much as spoken to him for months,' Carina flashed back, before turning to address the always dapper solicitor, with his full head of snow-white hair of which he was justifiably proud. 'Well, what are we waiting for, Douglas? Read it out.'

Bryn leaned in towards Francesca, his voice low. 'A command—and a very terse one at that! Frank couldn't have done better.'

Francesca prayed fervently there wouldn't be more outbursts from Carina. If their grandfather had been a tiger, Carina was a tigress in the making.

As though in agreement, Charles Forsyth sank back heavily in his chair. The room stank of danger! Ruth gave another hastily muffled moan. She too was unnerved by the fact that her great-niece had turned into what looked very much like the female version of her late brother. Frank might have come back from wherever he had gone.

Francesca stole another glance at Bryn, thinking that in some strange way they were acting very much like a pair of conspirators. Bryn reacted by raising his brows slightly, his smile laced with black humour. He was inoculated against Carina's outbursts.

Francesca sat quiet as a nun, pale as an ivory rose, her elegant long legs to one side, and her head, with her hair in a sort of Gibson Girl loose arrangement, inclined to the other, showing off her swan's neck and the delicate strength of her clean jawline. She might have been the subject of a painting herself, Bryn thought. A study of a beautiful, *isolated* young woman. He vowed to himself that state of affairs wasn't going to continue. The sleeping princess had to wake up.

Douglas McFadden responded impassively to Carina's rudeness. He had had half a lifetime of it from Sir Francis. 'Very well, Carina,' he said obligingly, picking up his gold-rimmed glasses. He did, however, take his time to settle them on his beak of a nose. Once done, he appeared to take a deep breath, then launched into the reading of the last will and testament of Sir Francis Gerard Oswald Forsyth…

Already Francesca had begun to panic. She desperately wanted it all over. Great wealth ruined people. She had seen it with her own eyes. But none of them, with the exception of Charles Forsyth, was prepared for what was to come.

* * *

It was Carina who tempestuously brought proceedings to a halt.

'It *can't* be true!' She catapulted out of her chair, sending it crashing to the floor. Her blonde hair flew around her visibly blanched face. Her furious blue eyes lashed the solicitor. 'What kind of bloody lunacy is this?' she shouted, her voice loud enough to shock the profoundly deaf. Her arms flailed wildly in the air, causing her copious eighteen carat gold bracelets to out-jangle a brass band.

'Carrie… Carrie.' Charles Forsyth very belatedly tried his hand at remonstrating with his headstrong daughter, while the great-aunts moved their chairs closer together, in case things got so bad they might have to cling to each other for support. Their menfolk stared steadily at the Persian rug, their faces varying shades of red.

Bryn moved smoothly to pick up Carina's chair, setting it right. 'Why don't you sit down again, Carrie?' He placed a kindly restraining hand on her shoulder. He didn't appear at all shocked by Carina's outburst, Francesca noticed. Indeed, he was looking about him, as though deciding on the next object Carina might send toppling.

'You're supposed to be here to support me, Bryn!' she protested, not sparing a glance in her father's direction. She ignored him. As she would from that day forward. Nothing her father said from now on would hold much value for her.

'Please. Sit down,' Bryn advised, bringing his powerful influence to bear.

Carina obeyed. 'Just *when* did Gramps make such a will?' she cried out the moment she was seated. 'I *know* what was in his will—the real will—and it surely wasn't this! This stinks to high heaven of conspiracy.'

Douglas McFadden pursed his lips and looked profoundly displeased. 'I beg your pardon, Carina.'

'Carrie… Carrie,' Charles Forsyth bleated. His fair handsome face was ruddy with distress. 'It's all in order, I assure you.'

Carina's blazing blue eyes narrowed to slits. 'You *knew* about this, Dad? What kind of a fool *are* you? You're the great *loser!* You've been cut out, and you look like you're accepting it. Gramps has publicly dismissed and humiliated you. *You* are the rightful heir. *You* administer the Forsyth Foundation. You *have* to fight this. By my reckoning you'll win.'

'Don't bet on that.' Bryn sent her a lancing glance.

'But… But…' Carina actually sputtered, looked fearfully taken aback.

'I'm not fighting anything, Carina,' Charles Forsyth told her quietly, but with surprising finality. 'I'm very happy with my lot.'

'Which is a lot *indeed,*' Bryn murmured. Maybe Charles would become a better man, a more self-confident man, without his father forever glowering over his shoulder, stripping him of any hope of self-esteem.

Carina glared her contempt for her father. 'Why would you be happy?' she cried, turning into the daughter from hell right in front of his glazed eyes. 'Gramps was right about you. You don't fire on all cylinders. Don't you *understand* what's happened here? You don't even look upset. You've been treated disgracefully. *I've* been treated disgracefully.'

'You've been left a great fortune, Carrie,' Bryn pointed out. 'Give yourself a moment to let that sink in.'

She blushed hotly. 'Do you *mind*? We've been passed over.'

'Not really, Carrie. What *more* do you want?' her father added, grateful for Bryn's intervention.

'A damned sight more than you seem to think.' Carina swung her blonde head back to face the solicitor. 'You ought to be disbarred, McFadden. You're as big a fool as Dad.'

The great-aunts gasped. They had never heard anything so nasty. And to dear Douglas!

'I really don't have to listen to this, Carina.' Douglas McFadden, veteran of countless highly volatile will-readings, spoke in a perfectly even tone. 'I have carried out your late grandfather's instruction to the letter. It was his wish that his granddaughter, Francesca Elizabeth Mary Forsyth, should control the Forsyth Foundation. I would remind you, as Bryn has tried to do, that your late grandfather knew *exactly* what he was doing.'

'He couldn't have!' Carina was just barely resisting the violent urge to scream. 'Gramps had no great love for Francesca. Hell, most of the time he ignored her.'

'Perhaps he knew things about *you,* Carrie, that made him act like that?' Charles Forsyth suggested, in a voice that bore overtones of guilt.

'That's the trouble with you, Dad—'

Once again Bryn put out a restraining hand. 'There's more to be read, Carrie. Why don't you let Douglas get on with it?'

'I'd like to,' Douglas McFadden said, peering over the top of his spectacles. 'I really would. As Sir Francis has clearly stated, he deeply regretted falling out with his late son Lionel, Francesca's father. He may not have shown the depth of his regret, but he spoke to me many times about it. It was very much on his mind. He trusted me as his friend and adviser—especially after the loss of his closest lifelong friend Sir Theo.' The solicitor inclined his head respectfully in Bryn's direction. 'Sir Theo's much loved grandson is here today, and is also a beneficiary. I would like to point out that Francesca was at the very top of the law graduates of her year—no mean feat—though she has chosen art as her career. A *successful* career, I might add.'

Again Carina projected her naturally loud voice, as though the solicitor was in desperate need of a hearing aid. 'Since when were *you* an authority on the kind of things Francesca does, Douglas?' she challenged him. 'All that Dreamtime stuff.'

Bryn turned on her eyes that had grown daunting, with a downward cast to his beautifully curved lips. 'If I were you I'd be a little bit worried about heaping ridicule on the Dreamtime, Carrie. There could be some danger in that. And actually, Douglas is a recognised art connoisseur, with a fine collection.'

'That Gramps paid for,' Carina bit off. 'But not Francey's own stuff. I think it's pitiful.'

'Then we can all rest assured that it's good,' Bryn returned suavely, forcing Carina to swallow hard.

Oh, my Lord! Francesca furtively pressed Bryn's jacketed arm, trying to signal him to stop. It was abundantly clear that Carrie was bitterly resenting Bryn's defence of her.

Douglas McFadden judged it time to intervene. 'What conversations Sir Francis and others *have* had with Francesca—who *was* named after her grandfather—led him to believe she has a very fine mind. Her viewpoint *counted,* in his opinion. He was convinced she had inherited *his* and her own father's head for business.'

'And you expect us to *believe* this?' Carina ground out the words with difficulty, her jaw was so locked on its hinges. 'Francesca has a fine mind and *I* don't?'

'Of course you do, Carina.' Douglas McFadden gave her a deeply conciliatory look. 'But, well…you never did take much interest… I mean…' Unusually for him, he began to stammer, but Carina Forsyth in full flight was not a pretty sight. She had broken through all normal control. Which didn't really surprise him after all.

To prove it, Carina's voice rose meteorically. 'Gramps wasn't happy about women in business, Douglas. You know that. Tell him, Bryn.' She appealed to the still seated Bryn. He was unmoving, yet he still exuded energy and a blazing intensity. 'Don't just bloody sit there mocking us all. Gramps was very proud of me the way I am. I'm the most photographed woman in the country, and certainly the best-looking and the best dressed. Now *this!* Why should *one* person have control? And Francesca, at that! She has absolutely no *right.*' She flashed her cousin a look of furious anger and betrayal, as though Francesca had spent years working on their grandfather behind the scenes.

'She *is* a Forsyth,' Bryn pointed out provocatively.

It caught Carina blindside. 'Oh, *Bryn!*' She would devour the woman who took Bryn away from her.

'It has come as a shock to you, Carina. I can see that.' Douglas McFadden spoke with empathy in his voice. 'But Sir Francis gave long and careful thought to this. As your father and Bryn have pointed out, you have been left a great fortune. You were considered at one time…but your grandfather had to make a final decision. Charles had indicated he feared the heavy responsibilities. Isn't that so, Charles? Your grandfather took note. *You,* as of now, are one of the richest women in the country, Carina—free to do anything you want for as long as you want. But in the end Sir Francis came to believe Francesca was the best person in the family to head up the Foundation. She's clever. She gets on well with people from all walks of life. She is highly principled. She knows what duty is all about, and the burden of responsibilities that come with great wealth. She is her father's daughter, and she will have her advisers around her. Her grandfather firmly believed she would have the wisdom to *listen* to what they have to say and take it on board. He believed she has the capacity to properly evaluate the thousands of requests the Forsyth Foundation receives annually. Furthermore, he believed she would carry out his wishes to the letter. He may not have been the greatest of philanthropists during his lifetime—'

Many would have said *miserly,* Bryn thought.

'—as was his closest friend and partner Sir Theo, but he wished for things to be different in the future. He was, in fact, very proud of the way Francesca has set about making something of herself. The way she's using her own money to fund the promotion of aboriginal art. Very proud indeed. Francesca is a compassionate young woman. Compassion is what the Foundation needs when it comes to prioritising future grants.'

Not everyone agreed. 'Francey? But she's only a baby. This sounds like a disaster!' A scandalised Ruth whispered to her shellshocked sister behind her hand. 'What will people think?'

'Yes, what *will* people think?' Carina, who had the hearing of a nocturnal bat, swung her blonde head over her shoulder to stare down her flustered great-aunts. 'God knows what you two will get. That's if anything is left.'

Bryn, every nerve-ending in his body sensitised to Francesca's reactions, extended the hand that had been hanging loosely at his side. Francesca grasped it for dear life. It couldn't have been more obvious that she was stunned by all she had heard. Perhaps most of all the fact her grandfather had been *proud* of her.

To confirm it, Francesca took a deep, shaky breath. Her grandfather had always acted as if she barely existed for him. Now *this!* This was a whole new dynamic. Couldn't he have said just *once* he was proud of her? Given her a clue? She would only have needed him to say it *once*.

Francesca, I'm proud of you!

She could have lived on it for years.

Carina, so intent on conveying to her great-aunts the shocking injustice of it all, missed the significant linking of hands. Instead she gave a whooping hysterical laugh. 'Gramps must have been off his rocker!' she hooted, turning back to the solicitor. 'Whoever made that will wasn't the real Gramps at all. More like some pathetic old guy whose mind was starting to wander. What does he want her to do, anyway? *Give* it all away? I warn you right now, Francesca will do that—*big-time!* There'll be no fortune left. She's a genuine bleeding heart!' She was alight with self-righteous rage. 'I don't want to hear another word of this. Gramps *adored* me, yet he has given Francey the whip hand over me. Forget Dad. He's gutless. He only wants *out!*'

Francesca's beautiful skin flushed with dismay. 'Uncle Charles—Carrie—I'm not happy about any of this,' she said, appealing to each one in turn. 'I'm as shocked as you are.'

'Believe that and you'll believe anything!' Carina was laughing full-on, with scathing cynicism.

'But, Carrie, it's *true*. I'd be happy to give it all back to you.'

She was conscious that Bryn had pressed her hand hard, no doubt telling her to shut up.

'And we'll be happy to take it,' Carina snapped back. 'You little *Judas!*'

Bryn's resonant voice suddenly boomed, stopping even Carina in her tracks. 'Carrie, that's enough. Francey has no need to explain herself or make any apology to anyone,' he said in a hard, disgusted tone. 'You can see how shocked she is. She had no idea. I suggest we allow Douglas to finish the reading. You can carry on *after* that, if you like. The rest of us can beat a retreat.'

'You mean you're taking Francey's side over mine?' For a moment Carina looked utterly confused. 'You really think I'm going to shut up and take this, Bryn? What the hell—?' She broke off, finally registering the linked hands—one so darkly tanned, the other the smoothest pale gold. 'Well, well, well,' she snarled, now in a white-hot rage. 'What have we got here?'

'You've got *me* offering *Francey* support,' Bryn replied without a moment's hesitation.

This put Carina into an ecstasy of jealousy and hate. 'Let go of the conniving little bitch's hand.'

It was obvious Bryn wasn't going to let that slide. His expression turned so daunting the very air in the room froze. 'I think you've reached the point where you'd do best to shut up, Carrie,' he warned, brilliant eyes aglitter.

But Carina was too far gone. 'Can I trust you, Bryn. *Can* I?' Her blue eyes raked his dynamic face. 'You haven't hatched a little plan or anything?'

'You want someone to trust, Carrie, you'd better find a puppy,' he returned with biting humour.

The battle lines had been drawn. The enemy was in plain view.

It was a total nightmare, Francesca thought. The worst possible disaster. Yet through it all Bryn continued to keep hold of her hand.

'Going to turn our attention to Francey now, are we?' Carina challenged him with great bitterness. 'You'd do anything to get control of Titan. We all know that. You'd even take up with Francey and abandon me. You swore you loved me. You swore when the time was right we'd get married.'

Bryn uttered a single word. 'Delusional.'

How easy it is to sow the seeds of doubt, Francesca thought. She thought of those long passionate kisses Bryn had given her. How could Bryn, of all people, do a thing like that when he had made a promise to Carina? It *wasn't* Bryn. It didn't fit anything she knew about him. Nevertheless, she very quietly withdrew her hand from his, before Carina took it into her head to spring at her like a jungle cat. Could it be possible Bryn was deliberately provoking Carina?

A charged atmosphere surrounded them both. Carina, mercifully, stayed in place, while Bryn rose to his impressive height, as though standing guard over the more vulnerable Francesca.

'Am I?' Carina cried. 'Delusional? Why would I be? You *know* what we talked about.' She transferred her burning blue gaze to her cousin. 'Don't let him fool you. Or has he started to already? He's as devious as they come. The master manipulator. Gramps always said that. He warned me we always had to be on our guard around Bryn. I know he was talking to you in your room, Francesca. The maid told me.'

'Poor thing!' Bryn cut in derisively. 'I bet it was more like an interrogation.'

'Carrie, please stop,' Charles Forsyth said with surprising authority. 'You too, Bryn. We really don't need all these personal matters to be aired here. Douglas needs to proceed.'

'Of course he does!' Carina hissed. 'But I'll have my say if I want. This *is* my home.'

'*My* home,' her father corrected her, in a voice no one had ever heard him use with her before. This was his princess. Or at least she had been, until she had started making it very plain she thought her father thoroughly deserved to be overthrown.

Oddly, Carina looked tremendously shocked. She blinked. 'So you want me out?' She clenched her hands in front of her breast, as though at any moment her father might have one of the servants pitch her out onto the street. She realised in a rare moment of self-evaluation that any one of them would be pleased to.

'Don't be absurd, Carina,' her father answered, torn between parental loyalty and pity. 'Of course this is your home.'

'I should damned well think so.' Carina returned fire; she was nothing if not resilient. 'So what does *he* get out of it?' She resumed her seat, pointing an accusing finger at Bryn, who was now sitting in an elegant slouch, his expression quite unreadable. 'Let's hear it. More shares in Titan? The Macallans already own twenty-three percent of the company.' The Forsyths had the majority shareholding in the multi-billion-dollar corporation; something that had happened only after Sir Francis had succeeded the late Sir Theo Macallan and became Chairman and CEO.

'I'll continue now to read out Sir Francis's wishes.' The solicitor consulted the impressive-looking legal document. 'Ah, y-e-e-s,' he said slowly. 'Bryn Barrington Theodore Macallan, in recognition of his own outstanding abilities and his valuable contributions to the ever-escalating success of Titan, and in memory of my great affection and admiration for his late grandfather, my lifelong friend, Sir Theodore Macallan—'

'Get on with it, Douglas,' Carina barked, in a frenzy of impatience.

Douglas McFadden's pale grey eyes narrowed, but he spoke at the same measured pace. 'Bryn Macallan inherits a fifty percent share in Sir Francis's pastoral empire, its flagship being Daramba. Francesca inherits the other fifty percent on the understanding that Bryn is in sole charge of the business end of the enterprise. Evidently Sir Francis believed Francesca would be fully occupied elsewhere, whilst Bryn was the best man to handle an extra job. Charles had already indicated to his father he had little interest in the pastoral side of things. Rule number one with Sir Francis was always, Who is the best person to handle the job?'

Bryn, who after all these years among the Forsyths had thought himself impervious to shock, felt winded. It was as if he had received a violent blow to the solar plexus. He swallowed on the startled oath that was stuck somewhere in his throat. He had been way off the mark in expecting some token bequest. Maybe his grandfather's golf clubs back. This was astounding news—or maybe Frank's last-ditch attempt to get into heaven? He turned his head to gauge Francesca's reaction. She was trembling with emotion, as well she might be. Her eyes were huge with distress, the pearly grey of her blouse further brightening their silver lustre. In all probability she was retreating once more into her protective shell.

Carina had well and truly brought her fierce jealousy out into the open. Damn her lies! Marriage was a word he'd never mentioned. Let alone thought about. That went for the L word as well. What he and Carina had had for a short time was sex—which had turned out to be a terrible mistake. Not that he had taken advantage of an innocent young virgin. Carina had a head start on just about everyone in that department. A free spirit, or so she called herself—even in those days. But he knew as well as anyone: throw enough mud and some was bound to stick. The undermining would continue. He had to be prepared for it. Carina, like her grandfather before her, would never let up. As for his bequest? Given a moment or two to reflect, he knew what Francis Forsyth had ripped off from the Macallans over the years would pay for this share of Forsyth Pastoral Holdings many times over.

Francis Forsyth had evidently believed in a Supreme Being after all. Maybe even in meeting up with Sir Theo and old Gulla again. Highly unlikely. Their destinations would be poles apart.

CHAPTER FOUR

'ALL I'M SAYING IS, give yourself time for it to sink in,' Bryn advised. He had accompanied the stunned and visibly upset Francesca back to her apartment, where at least she thought she would be safe.

'This is a disaster, Bryn. You know it is.' She led the way into the living room, switching on lights as she went.

When she had left here this morning she had never dreamed what the day would bring: the massive upheavals, the responsibilities that were waiting to claim her. If she *wanted* them. She wasn't at all sure she needed a lifetime of being in the front line. Strangely enough, she thought she *could* make a better fist of handling the Foundation than either her grandfather or her uncle. But there were other huge responsibilities. She tried to calm herself with the thought that she would have first-class people around her to advise and guide her. She could afford to hire the best minds. Douglas McFadden had given her the definite impression he thought she was up to the task. And Bryn had appeared to welcome it. No one's opinion was more important to her than Bryn's.

Now he spoke in a clipped voice, a decided edginess about him. 'I know nothing of the kind, Francey. You're very young to take on so much, but age isn't an issue like it used to be.

Youth can be a big advantage. Fresh ideas. Seniority has gone by the board. It's a case of the best person for the job. You're it. Whatever else Frank was, he was no fool. He wanted to keep the Forsyth fortune intact, not frittered away.'

Such a clever, complex man was Bryn. Macallan to her Forsyth; Montague to Capulet. Warring families. Since the death of Bryn's grandfather hadn't that been the case? Even if the war had been largely waged underground? Bryn followed her, removing his beautifully tailored black jacket, finely pin-striped, before throwing it over the back of an armchair. Then he unbuttoned the collar of his white shirt and yanked down his black tie as if it were choking him. 'It's one hell of a shock, I know. But think about it. Charles wants out. No problem there. I thought he was very reasonable about the whole thing. He never wanted a career in business in the first place. He was forced into it. Now he's his own man, or near enough. There's no immutable law of nature that says great talent has to be passed down to the next generation. Charles has no head for business. Your father, though the younger brother, was the logical heir. Sir Frank, even if he did his level best not to show it, was shattered when your father was killed. It seems he had expected them to make up. A tragedy all round.'

Her own assessment. Francesca sank dazedly into the comfort of one of the custom-made sofas covered in cream silk. She'd had a whole range of silk cushions made—gold, orange, imperial yellow, bronze and a deep turquoise—to pick up the colours in the exquisite eighteenth-century six-panel lacquered screen mounted on the wall. The screen had belonged to her parents, as did so many pieces of the furniture, paintings and objets d'art, a mix of classical European and Asian, in the apartment. They had been in storage all these years from the old house. What she had done, in effect, was wrap herself around with her own family even if they had gone and left her.

'Yes,' she agreed soberly, 'a tragedy.'

'Are you okay?' He studied her intently. 'You've lost all colour.' In the space of a single day her willowy slenderness now bordered on the fragile. Francesca fascinated him. She had always seemed to him quite simply unique.

'I will be when my mind clears and my blood starts flowing again.' She rested her head back. 'I wish my father were still here.'

How well Bryn understood that, having been cruelly robbed of his own parent. 'Misfortune on both our houses,' he said grimly. '*Your* father could handle what was too difficult and too big for Charles. Not good for Charles's ego. Their mother was the only one who was kind to Charles.' He didn't mention Charles's mother, or all the women Sir Francis, confirmed widower, had had in his life since the demise of his wife without elevating a single one of them to the stature of second wife. Too canny to be caught with a huge settlement if a second marriage fell through.

'So in his way Uncle Charles has had a sad life.' She looked up at Bryn—the man who had brought her so throbbingly alive; the man her own grandfather had made partner in his pastoral empire. Her grandfather must have seen Bryn was far and away the best person to take over the running of the giant enterprise. Certain men—men like her grandfather and Bryn—could successfully juggle any number of companies without once dropping the ball or losing sight of their objectives. Bryn would probably transform Forsyth Pastoral Holdings, which she knew in recent years had suffered sharply reduced profits and too many changes in management.

'If we're going to be charitable, and I suppose we might find it in our hearts to be after what today has brought, he *has,*' Bryn replied wryly. 'If you ask me, Charles wants to get back with Elizabeth.'

The same bizarre thought had occurred to Francesca. 'Then he has his work cut out for him,' she said. 'Just as Grandfather bullied him, he tried to bully Aunt Elizabeth. Only Carrie was safe.'

'Safe?' One of Bryn's black brows shot up. 'Carrie was a little dictator from the day she was born.'

Another sharp comment from Bryn? 'Well, she must have changed a lot after I arrived.' Francesca looked back on the past. 'I remember her as being very *contained,* even secretive.'

'Oh, she's that!' Bryn agreed, then markedly changed the subject, impatient with more talk of Carina. 'God, I could knock back a Scotch!' He heaved a sigh.

'Please, help yourself.' She waved a listless arm. 'I don't seem able to get up.'

'Why would you? You're winded, like me. Can I get you something?' he asked, moving towards a drinks trolley that held an array of spirits in crystal decanters; whisky, brandy, bourbon, several colourful bottles of liqueur, all at the ready for Francesca's guests.

'Glass of white wine,' she said, not really caring one way or the other. 'There's a bottle of Sauvignon Blanc in the fridge. You'll have to open it.'

He was back within moments, handing her a glass. She took it, savouring the fresh, fruity bouquet before allowing herself a long sip. 'No point in saying cheers, though most people would think I had a great deal to cheer about. Little do they know!'

'We were both born into a world of privilege, Francey,' Bryn said, taking a good pull on the single malt and letting it slide down his throat. 'Responsibilities and obligations go along with that. For us, anyway.' He didn't join her on the sofa, but took a seat in a parcel-gilt walnut antique armchair that was covered in a splendid petit-point. The bright colours stood out in high relief against his darkness—the black eyes and the black hair, the skin darkly tanned from the time he spent sailing as much as his hectic schedule would allow. It comforted her to see him sitting there, like some medieval prince. The armchair was one of a pair her parents had bought in Paris on their very last trip there.

'Carina may not have got what she confidently expected, but

she's been left a very rich woman in her own right. Boy, wasn't she a shocker, telling poor old Douglas off? Once or twice she even made me laugh. All those war whoops she kept giving. When she was a kid her grandfather gave her full permission to disregard her mother's efforts to mould her. Your grandfather was very pleased she was showing some "spirit", as he thought of it. Showed she took after him and not her father. Whatever you remember, you must realise Carina was a very spoilt little girl? Now she's a spoilt young woman, determined on running amok. Did you notice Ruth's husband, a distinguished medical scientist? He spent the time trying to look like he wasn't there at all. And Regina's very agreeable husband—I like him—was afraid to speak in case he got told to stay out of it. I don't think any one of them smiled, even when they found out they were leaving considerably better off than when they'd arrived. None of them is going begging in the first place; in fact, there's quite a few hundred million between them.'

'They were all looking very warily at me, I noticed,' Francesca commented wryly. 'Even James—and I thought he liked me.'

'He more than *likes* you,' Bryn pointed out dryly, amused when she didn't appear to hear, or care if she did. Poor old James!

'No one had the faintest idea what Grandfather intended.'

'Charles knew,' Bryn said. 'He sat to one side, knowing he wouldn't be named as his father's heir as everyone expected. As for the rest of us! Nobody knows what tomorrow might bring.'

'Did *you* know?' she found herself asking, realising how desperately she needed that vital piece of information.

His dark head shot up, a flash of anger like summer lightning in his eyes. 'Francey, you *can't* be suggesting I knew in advance about the will and what your grandfather intended for you?'

'Just a question,' she said lamely, and then looked away, unable to sustain that concentrated gaze.

'Not *just a question* at all,' he fired back. 'Let me put it bluntly. Do you or do you not trust me?' He spoke as if her trust or lack of it was crucial to their friendship.

'I wonder you should ask,' she evaded, suddenly beset by myriad doubts.

'But *you* asked, and I want to know.' He wasn't letting her off the hook. 'Did you consider even for a single moment that I knew the contents of your grandfather's will and didn't tell you?'

She could feel her whole body going enormously weak. At that moment she lacked the capacity to deny it. 'I won't lie to you, Bryn. I don't want any lies or evasions between us. It did cross my mind, but for *less* than a moment. You *are* a Macallan.'

'Is that it?' he asked ironically. 'I'm a Macallan, and therefore not to be trusted?'

She paused before speaking. 'Bryn, I would trust you with my life. I *owe* you my life. But I also know of the conflicts that lie at your heart. You won't discuss them with me, even when I ask what's at the root of the enmity I've so easily divined. You, Lady Macallan and Annette, your mother, both of whom I love and respect, all considered my grandfather to have been a scoundrel.'

Bryn tossed back the rest of his drink, then moved back to the drinks trolley for a refill. 'God, what a day! *Most* people thought Frank a great rogue, Francey.' He expelled a long breath. 'For all the things he did to anyone who opposed him, and to competitors in business, be they so-called friends or colleagues. He could have been condemned a thousand times over.'

'But it's far more than that with you. It's deeply personal. I know you won't rest until you're CEO of Titan.'

He turned back to her, his whole persona on high alert. He had such a range of expressions, she thought. One minute daunting, the next the most beautiful smile in the world, and then, when he was engrossed in something he found interesting or beautiful, his striking face turned vividly expressive. At certain times too, like now, he had a look of what the French would call *hauteur.* It wasn't arrogance. Bryn wasn't arrogant—unless it was the unconscious arrogance of achievement.

'Well, now, that's up to the board, Francey,' he said. 'Naturally you will have to take *your* place there now. We'll be able to vote for one another,' he tacked on suavely.

She flushed. 'It's no joke, Bryn.' She waited until he had resumed his seat and did not tower over her. 'It would be a further whiplash in Carina's face not to offer her a place. I don't know if it will ever sink in that Grandfather chose *me* over her.'

Bryn groaned. 'That's an easy one to answer. You're one hell of a lot brighter than Carina. She was never academically minded. She had no use for further education. She preferred the Grand Tour—swanning around Europe. No, Francey. Carina's beauty might dazzle, but not her brain power.'

'Her beauty dazzles *you.*'

'It *did.* I've admitted that. But only for a while. I don't deny I've made my mistakes, Francey, but I managed not to get *too* carried away. I hate to say it, but there's something a bit off about Carina. The twists in her personality have notched up a few gears since we were together. You saw what she was like today.'

'She had every reason to be shocked,' Francesca said, programmed to be loyal. 'A massive disappointment was at the bottom of her grievances.' Despite the way Carina had acted, Francesca was still moved to defend her cousin. 'She felt betrayed—not only for herself, but for her father.'

'Oh, come off it, Francey.' Bryn spoke impatiently. 'Carina has a total disregard for others. She uses people. It's an inherited trait. You heard the way she went for her father—and in front of the rest of the family. He didn't deserve that, even if he has to take some responsibility for turning her into what she has become. Had *you* been her handsome, clever, *male* cousin, instead of another woman, she would have taken it a whole lot better. Don't you see the last thing Carina wants is to be burdened with heavy responsibilities? She wants to be perfectly free to enjoy herself, to live a life of endless self-indulgence. Frank knew that. Her father knows that. It's the way she was reared, after all. What you have to grasp is this: it's all about *you.* And *her.* Had it been up to Carina, she would have stripped you of your last penny.'

'And would that have been such a great disaster?' Francesca asked ironically. 'I don't want any of this. I can make my own way—and I am.'

Bryn came to sit again, not in the splendid walnut chair but close beside her, bringing with him his immense sexual aura. Oh, this man! What influence he had over her. And there didn't seem to be a thing she could do to lessen its effect. Rather, it was expanding with every passing moment.

'Listen, Francey,' he said, leaning close, so the fine cotton of his shirt brushed against the skin of her arm. 'I know you're a very private person. You like to live out of the limelight. And you've succeeded to an extent. But you're no more entitled to a normal life than I am. That's one of the burdens of being who we are. Privacy goes out the door. Carina revels in attention. She's fortunate in that way. She adores being chased by the paparazzi and being endlessly photographed. That's *her* life. It gives her enormous satisfaction, even if she does like to lodge the odd complaint. You're not like that. But you'll have to concentrate on the main game. You are now in a position to do a great deal for others. There's your saviour.

'There's so much the Foundation can do. Grants to medical science can play a much bigger part than they have in the past. Finding cures for killer diseases, saving lives. It all takes a colossal amount of money. There are so many projects that should have been taken up that the Foundation ignored. It came to the point where the Foundation was simply throwing money at organisations that should have been way down the list. You can change all that. Look what you've already achieved in the area of indigenous art. What about a museum, solely to house aboriginal art, bark paintings and other art forms? You could consider that down the track. Make it self-supporting through a series of initiatives. There are many programmes, crying out for funding. You know my own family's main interest is centred on saving children. You've been to the big charity dinners my grandmother regularly holds. She has carried on my grandfather's work.'

'And she's worshipped,' Francesca said, knowing that for a fact. 'I don't know that I can ever become another Lady Macallan.'

He leaned a little further towards her, surprising her by kissing her cheek. Just an affectionate gesture—one of countless she had received from him over the long years—yet it was more meaningful than the most ardent kiss any other man had ever given her.

'All it's going to take is a little time and experience. You've got everything else. And you've got my support. Any future ideas you might have that you want to discuss or thrash out you'll have my attention.'

'Thank you. I'm really going to need you.' She felt as if she had been launched upon a big, cold and demanding world where power was everything. And now it had been handed to her, an unwilling and unprepared recipient.

'We're going to need one another.' Bryn frowned at some passing thought.

'What if Carina wants to contest the will, as she threatened?' Francesca asked. 'Wouldn't she be justified? She *is* senior to me, and she's Uncle Charles's only child. Besides, she has always known how to get her father on side. The rest of the family will support her.'

Bryn gave a short laugh. 'No, they won't.'

'You sound so sure?' She turned her attention to examining his dynamic face. If only she could peel away all pretence, all the complex layers that lay between them.

'The rest of the family are cool-headed,' Bryn explained briskly. 'Whereas Carina is a hothead. None of them actually trust her. I don't even think they like her. They all know Charles is not right for the job. We've all known it for years. My grandfather spent a great deal of his time priming me. Ultimately for control. I won't deny it. Francis Forsyth didn't make Titan everything it is. My grandfather was the prime mover. Frank became something of an enforcer. Anyway, I knew what my grandfather wanted. *I* want it. Charles doesn't. Carina can't pretend she has the necessary qualifications—'

'That's why Grandfather wanted her to marry *you,*' Francesca broke in. 'The subject can't be avoided, Bryn. He planned it all. A marriage between you and Carrie would have united the two families. Ended the war. Carina would have been happy, and well suited to playing the role of beautiful high society wife.'

'It was a scheme thought up without considering me or my wishes,' Bryn told her with heavy bluntness.

'What *are* your wishes?' She was terribly confused. Carina had taken every opportunity to let her know Bryn belonged to her. And there was no getting away from the fact she and Bryn had sustained an intimate relationship, even if Bryn claimed it was over.

'Maybe *you* would suit me a whole lot better. What if I wanted to marry *you*?' he asked, sounding as if he might be serious. 'Let's face it. You're a very classy lady. Super-smart.' His eyes were brilliant with mockery, flattery—what? Was it possible that Bryn, the quintessential businessman, had simply vaulted to the best possible option now that *she* was the Forsyth heiress?

Though her heart was racing, it was high time she got herself together. 'I've never for a moment considered it,' she said, amazed she could sound so composed. She had been raised to accept Bryn was for Carina. It was like an alliance, a tradition drawn from the Middle Ages. The knowledge had hung over her head like a sword.

'I think you have, but you've covered it up.' There was real gravity in his voice.

'It's not as if you don't know *why.*' She felt driven to spring up, away from him. It wasn't easy to think when Bryn's power over her was so strong. Those wild moments between them had not only compounded his power a thousandfold, but made it irreversible. It wasn't easy living with a blazing obsession. It was the best and the worst kind of love. From childhood—hadn't she survived because of him?—she had felt so close to him he might have been a kind of twin; a twin she had created lacking a sibling to love. Even as a child she'd had a remarkable insight into Carina's nature. She had always known her cousin didn't love her, never would. She had also known Bryn would forever stand between them.

Bryn, who was desperate to push the issue, had to relent. 'You look played out.' He spoke quietly. 'Why don't I go? You need time on your own. Time to recover and absorb everything that has happened. It's been one long and gut-wrenching day. Death has its own contagion. I know you ached for your grandfather's love and didn't get it, but he must have loved you, Francey, in his own strange way. Take comfort from that. Perhaps he felt enormous guilt about his estrangement from your father? Especially in the light of what happened. Perhaps he thought you were judging him in some way? You were such a serious, *thinking* child, and you had a way of turning those beautiful light-filled eyes on one.'

She was taken aback. Hadn't Carrie said much the same thing? 'Did I? In what way?'

He gave her a faintly twisted smile. 'Oh, you always looked as though you were trying to read one's soul. Maybe Frank found that difficult to face. There were dark places in his soul he wouldn't have wanted you to see. Anyway, Douglas confirmed he was proud of you. That should mean something. He loved Carrie, but he even asked me from time to time why she wasn't getting out there and doing something. He would have liked Carrie to carve out some sort of a career—even getting into the world of fashion, opening boutiques or whatever. She lived for clothes. Neither of us has ever seen her in the same outfit twice.'

'You're not saying he was disappointed in her?' Francesca asked, trying to piece all this together. She'd had no idea.

Bryn shook his head. 'That's a difficult one to answer. It's hard, when you're possessed of a manic energy like Sir Frank was, to view pointless pursuits with a totally tolerant eye. I think he was always going to leave you Daramba.' Abruptly he changed the subject, his dark eyes steadily on her. 'Apart from anything else, he knew how much you loved it.'

'*He* didn't love it,' Francesca said, a catch in her voice. 'He wouldn't go there.'

'Perhaps he had a reason.' Bryn's answer sounded grim. 'He wasn't liked, either as the big boss or a man.' The tribal people had regarded Francis Forsyth as a trespasser on sacred ground. And perhaps a lot *more.* 'How do you feel about his leaving me a half-share?' He captured her gaze. 'I want you to tell me the truth. I can stand it.'

She gave a laugh that held the faintest sob. 'I want *you* more than anyone by my side, Bryn. You already know that. We both love Daramba.'

'That apart,' he said, brushing their mutual love for the great Outback station aside, 'what about my taking control of the business side of the entire operation?'

'You're welcome,' she said wryly.

'I'm going to want to make a lot of changes,' he said, trying to prepare her, reaching for his jacket, then shouldering into it.

How handsome he was. How masculine. She loved the breadth of his shoulders that made his clothes sit so well; the sharp taper that emphasised his lean, narrow waist and hips, and his long, athletic legs. 'Go for it,' she said, trying for lightness on this bleakest of days. 'I have a few ideas of my own you might be interested to hear.'

His brows knotted. 'Of course. I have no intention of going

ahead with anything without discussion. We're partners, Francey.'

She nodded, taking enormous comfort from that. 'Partners. I do have a good business head.'

'I know.' He moved towards her with the easy male grace that so characterised him. 'Clever girl! You'll have countless opportunities to bring your expertise to bear.'

'That's if I accept my inheritance,' she replied, her expression grave. 'I want time to think about it. My life would revolve around the Foundation. What time would there be for *me*? I'm serious about my art. I'm serious about helping other artists.' She paused, feeling a jolt of non-acceptance she had to stifle. 'But I fully expect to take my seat on the board of Titan.'

There was a glitter of admiration in his brilliant eyes. 'Sounds like you've already made up your mind.'

She stood there looking at him, in such an agony of need it made her press her hands to her sides. 'It's important for me to know how *you* think and feel.'

'But you *do* know, Francey.' He could read the huge uncertainties that were in her. It was so easy to understand. What she had been offered was almost too big to grasp. 'As far as I'm concerned, you have the brains, the guts and the nerve to carry this off. Do it for everyone's sake. You have the power to change lives for the good. I understand your fears and doubts. But don't get bogged down, thinking your grandfather's will was unfair to Charles and Carina. They've been very handsomely provided for. Your grandfather knew what he was doing.'

For once let Forsyth and Macallan be on the same side, he prayed. Only with Francesca at the helm was that possible. 'Now, I'm off,' he said briskly, before his control snapped and he pulled her into his arms. God knows he wanted to, but he knew what would happen next. Carina had convinced Francesca of her lies, and her bullying had made it nearly impossible for Francesca to accept that someone might want her instead of her cousin. Whatever she *said,* whatever barriers she threw up, he knew she was very vulnerable to him. His role, however, was to shield and protect her.

At his imminent departure Francesca knew a moment of pure panic. 'I don't want you to go.' Her need for him rose to overwhelm her.

'Yes, you do,' he said. 'I don't want you weighed down with emotion, Francey. Some things have to stay on hold.'

That sobered her. She made a huge effort to pull herself together, walking with him to the door. 'So much to do, Bryn,' she said, determined not to crumble under the weight of it all. 'So many meetings. So many people to get to know. So much information I'll have to read and try to absorb.'

'One day at a time, Francey,' he advised, moving further away. Her aura was more intense than he had ever known. 'Don't let it crowd you. All you have to do is remember you're not alone.' He didn't bend to kiss her cheek. He wasn't *that* much of a knight in shining armour. 'What do you say we fly out to Daramba the weekend after next?' he asked. 'Both of us will definitely be needing a break by then.'

Her face lit up from within, its illumination filling him with surging desire. 'That sounds wonderful!'

Resolutely he opened the door, keeping his hand fixed firmly to the handsome brass knob. 'Good. I'll arrange it. You can bring a chaperon if you want,' he added, only half in jest. 'Ring you tomorrow. I'm off now to see my girls.'

She knew he was referring to Lady Macallan and his mother, Annette, who shared the beautiful historic Macallan mansion. It was a far cry from the Forsyth mausoleum. After the tragic death of her husband, Annette Macallan had suffered a long period of depression that had ended in a breakdown. Sir Theo and Lady Macallan had looked after her like a beloved daughter.

'Give them my love,' she said. 'Tell them I'll speak to them soon. I need to speak to Elizabeth as well. Grandfather didn't find it in his heart to leave her even a small memento.'

'What heart?' Bryn asked with a brief, discordant laugh. If

Francis Forsyth had thought he would win the Macallans over by leaving him a half-share in the Forsyth pastoral empire he had thought wrong. Frank Forsyth's treachery had been like a knife in the back to his grandfather. Sir Theo had died knowing what a deadly serpent he'd had for a lifelong friend.

The days that followed gave Francesca her first real understanding of the power and far-reaching influence of great wealth. There was an endless list of concerns she had to address, and then, when she had given them her full attention, endeavour to prioritise.

She had a model to go on. The Macallan Foundation, among other things, funded medical research into childhood diseases. That was their main focus. The Macallan Foundation built research centres and hospitals, and awarded endowments and scholarships to educate doctors not only for the home front but for third world countries as well. The Macallan name was enormously respected. She wanted the same respect for the Forsyth Foundation. She wanted to be assured that the Forsyth Foundation would be doing the work it was meant to do, much in the way of the Macallan Foundation—which Bryn administered.

If she needed advice—and she desperately did—he was the best person to turn to. Lord knew he was approachable enough, for all the burden of responsibilities placed upon him. But even knowing this Francesca felt she had to spare him and bring her own perfectly good mind to bear on it all. She refused to be the figurehead her grandfather had been. She had to start building a new life for herself. Not one she had wanted, but one she realised offered her the greatest opportunity for doing good. She had to start learning from everyone who was in a position to help her. When she was ready she was going to make changes—she had all but decided already on a glaring few—but for now she needed a tremendous amount of help.

The paperwork alone was staggering. Her routine had entirely changed as her life had speeded up dramatically. She woke at five instead of seven. Leapt out of bed. She went to bed very late. Yet even with that timetable she felt *energised.* There was so much to be done. A big plus was that she met daily with people who were not only in a position to help her, but were going out of their way to do so, seemingly delighted to be called on. That gave her a great confidence boost. Bryn left messages for her constantly, to tell her to get in touch with this one or that. All whiz kids who could run things for her as she wanted and then report back. She had to learn early how to delegate or go under, he told her, speaking from experience and the benefit of his own heavy workload.

She needed secretaries—all kinds of secretaries. Even press secretaries to front for her. She had endured a very scary onslaught of attention from the media almost from the minute the news of her elevation within the Forsyth family had broken. She needed people around her she could trust. *Really* trust. Loyalty was top of her agenda. Valerie Scott, a senior foundation secretary, was working for her now.

Valerie was a very attractive, highly competent divorcee in her late forties, tall and svelte, with snapping dark eyes and improbably rich dark red hair. She dressed well, with discreet good jewellery and accessories. As a Hartford—her maiden name—she was a member of an old Establishment family that had not only fallen on bad times but gone bust. A string of dodgy investments had figured somewhere along the way, Francesca seemed to recall. After Valerie's marriage break-up from a successful stockbroker, who had left her for a look-alike twenty years younger, Sir Francis had given Valerie a job. Her 'office' was an open area right outside his door, with Valerie seated behind an antique desk of very fine rosewood with more of the ormolu, lions' masks and feet her grandfather had favoured.

It wouldn't have surprised Francesca in the least to learn that Valerie had become more than a secretary to her grandfather. He'd had countless affairs, yet still been a man incapable of true love. Still, Francesca found her new secretary courteous and obliging, with an air of having everything fully under control. Time would tell. At the moment Valerie was proving extremely useful. She had no mind to replace her. She certainly didn't want to put any woman out of a well-paid job—especially one who had to fend for herself. For the time being things could continue as they were. She didn't want to become a suspicious person—it wasn't her nature—but sadly she had entered a very suspicious world.

Bryn had taken time out to fully alert her to security threats. The offices and executive conference room were regularly swept for bugs. Telephones, cellular and cordless, were by their very nature a threat. If royalty could have their phones tapped, so could anyone. Some years back a small transmitter had been discovered to be concealed inside her Uncle Charles's phone. She knew her grandfather from that day on had upgraded security measures, making sure all telephones and audio visual equipment were removed from conference rooms where confidential matters were discussed. Even so, more and more sophisticated devices were coming on to the market. Trusting one's staff was extremely important. A strip search apart, who knew what anyone was hiding? Thank God it hadn't come to that.

It would have given Francesca the greatest pleasure and satisfaction to have been able to take Carina on board. A different Carina, who herself was open to change. But Carina continued to complain bitterly to anyone who would listen about how she and her father had been robbed. Court action, however, to overturn their grandfather's will did not eventuate. The view of the public was that the *right* heiress had been handed the job. The public was rarely wrong.

'Leopards don't change their spots,' Bryn remarked during a late-night telephone conversation. They both had such a packed agenda it was difficult to meet. 'You can't seriously believe Carina would involve herself in *any* kind of work?'

'It could make her feel better about herself. It could be the start of some sort of reconciliation between us.' Francesca spoke hopefully. 'I don't want this feud to continue, Bryn.'

'Dream on, Santa Francesca!' A theatrical groan travelled down the wires. 'Carina doesn't share your concern for the less fortunate. She thinks by looking gorgeous she's more than repaying her debt to society.'

Gradually Francesca was brought around to thinking she might ask Elizabeth to come on board. She still wanted people she could *trust.* If needs be, with her life. She no longer felt as safe as she once had. She was a sitting duck in so many ways. She had her allies, but she had to become a hard-headed realist. She had her enemies too. People who were lying low, waiting for her to fail. But Elizabeth was different. Elizabeth had raised her. Elizabeth had always been on the charity circuit, but Francesca thought she could do a great deal more if she were allowed to.

She spoke to Bryn about it, over a hastily arranged lunch date.

'An interesting idea—maybe a bit provocative, given the estrangement in the family.' He had taken his time to reply. 'You know that Lady Antonia and I have done everything we possibly could to get my mother involved in our foundation, but her heart doesn't seem to be in anything any more. Not since my father died. My mother is a one-man woman.' His sigh was full of a deep regret. 'But I have to say I understand it.'

'Do you think Annette would help me?' she stunned him by asking.

In the middle of taking a bite out of a bread roll he coughed, then quickly swallowed a mouthful of water. 'God, Francey!' he exclaimed, touching a lean hand to his scratched throat.

'I've shocked you?'

'You have. But shock on.'

She kept her eyes on him. 'Annette and I get on so well together. You know we do.'

He nodded. 'Okay, so you're very sensitive and intuitive. Both my grandmother and my mother have a soft spot for you. And it's *you* more than anyone outside myself that my mother confides in. She knows whatever she says to you you'll be certain to keep it between yourselves. My mother doesn't trust a lot of people. With good reason. But she trusts you.'

Francesca did something she had never dared to do before. His lean tanned hand was lying on the table. She reached across and closed her hand over it, interlocking their fingers. 'That goes both ways,' she assured him, feeling stronger for his touch. 'I trust Annette. I've told her a lot of things I haven't told anyone else.'

'Including me?' Did she know his senses were being heightened to a painful edge? He wanted to pick up her hand and carry it to his mouth. But he knew that would only scare her off.

'Yes, including you.' She blushed, rose mantling her beautiful skin. 'But just think of this for a moment. Lady Macallan is such an exceptional woman that Annette might consider herself unable to act on her level. But with me? She's known me since I was a baby. I'm the merest beginner.'

'Are you really? The merest beginner? You'd have fooled me.' Bryn's brilliant black eyes glittered, but in his way he was already tossing this extraordinary idea around in his head. 'You could ask her.'

'I have your permission?' There was a quick flare of joy in her eyes. 'You don't know how much I appreciate that. We both know people might question why Annette Macallan would choose to join the *Forsyth* Foundation in any capacity.'

'Count on it,' Bryn confirmed bluntly.

'Oddly enough, I think she might enjoy it. As much love as there is between Lady Macallan and Annette, Lady Macallan is a formidable woman—a true personage. It's in *that* sense your mother might feel overshadowed.'

Bryn gave her a fathomless stare. 'She told you that?'

'No, no, no!' Francesca shook her head. 'Your mother would never say such a thing. Lady Macallan is her second mother.

She adores her. It's just something I sense. Surely you've sensed it too?'

When he answered his tone was crisp enough to crackle. 'God, Francey, I'm confronted by this every day of my life,' he said. 'I'm very proud of my grandmother. What a woman! And I think I get some of my own strengths from her. But she and I have been waiting for years now for my mother to take back her life. She was only a girl when my father married her. Just nineteen. She had me less than two years later. Dad was her lord and master. He didn't aim to be that. It just happened. They were very much in love, right up until the end. We were all so damned happy. Too happy. One shouldn't ever tempt the gods. After Dad was killed much of my mother died too. Her own parents—my Barrington grandparents—didn't stand by her. Oh, they tried for a while, but gradually they became impatient with her. She was supposed to pull out of it after a certain period of mourning. She didn't. I'm sure she'll be saying my father's name with her last breath.'

'And who's to say he won't be waiting for her?' Francesca spoke gently to this man she loved, wanted to be with through eternity. 'Millions and millions of people believe in a resurrection, an afterlife.'

Bryn's sigh was jagged. 'Be that as it may, we have to get through what life we have *now.* Speak to my mother if you want. Anything that helps her helps me. But don't be disappointed if she gently rejects the idea.'

'That's fine. I won't press her. I understand her pain. I understand the way she felt nearly destroyed without your father. But she did live for you.'

A terrible frustration showed itself in Bryn's eyes. 'She can't continue to live for me, Francey. She has to live for herself. God, she's only just turned fifty. She's a beautiful woman. Yet she has locked herself away for years. Dad would never have wanted that. He loved her so much he would only want her to be happy.'

Francesca smiled in an effort to relieve his tension. 'Let me talk to her. In some ways I'm not in a good situation, am I? A lot of people are waiting for me to screw up. Carina is hoping one of these days I'll simply *disappear* into the desert and never come back. I need help. No one knows that more than you. I want a woman—women, as it happens, as Elizabeth is another—I can trust. I'll put it to Annette that way. I won't be asking a great deal of her. I'll do as you say. Take it day by day.'

Bryn gave a hollow laugh. 'If you can get my mother out of the house I'll worship at your feet for ever.' Though wasn't he already doing just that? 'Did I tell you, you look stunningly beautiful?'

'Yes, you did.' Colour mounted beneath her flawless skin. 'It's a new outfit. I didn't go shopping. No time. I asked Adele Bennett to pick me out a wardrobe, which she did, and then brought it all over.'

'You couldn't have asked for anyone better,' Bryn said, his eyes travelling over her. She wore a sleeveless navy silk dress that showed off the elegant set of her shoulders and her slender arms. The dress was very simple in design but striking in effect, with broad strokes of colour as if she, the artist, had taken to it with a brush: violet, yellow, and a marvellous splash of electric blue that put him in mind of a kingfisher's plumage. It looked wonderful on her. Adele Bennett he had met at various functions. She owned exclusive boutiques in several state capitals. She must have relished the job of outfitting Francesca, with her beauty, her height and her willowy figure.

'You like what you see?' she prompted gently, though she felt more as if she was being consumed by his brilliant black gaze.

'Francey, I have to say *yes.*' He threw up his dark head, then gave a swift glance at his watch. 'Shame we have to part, but there it is. I have a meeting at two-thirty.' He lifted a hand to signal the waiter, who came on the double. 'By the way, I thought we'd take *this* weekend off to visit Daramba.' He spoke as if he wouldn't brook any argument. 'I've cleared my schedule sufficiently to warrant it. I can't and won't wait another week.

It's absolutely essential to find time for relaxation. We've both been doing precious little of that. So see you keep the weekend free. Understood?' He lifted his eyes from the plate where he had placed his platinum credit card and smiled.

Such a smile! His whole face caught light.

'Understood,' she said calmly, when inside she felt wildly happy. She had held the thought of them being together at Daramba all these long days. The thought had sustained her—a wonderful weekend that was waiting for her. And she had no intention of taking along a chaperon. A chaperon was all very well for the old Francesca Forsyth. But the old Francesca had been forced out of her shell. She was now the Forsyth heiress, like it or not. She no longer lived her old life. She no longer lived like a normal person. She even felt emboldened enough to throw her own cap in the ring. Maybe Bryn had been right all along. He *was* a free man.

It was getting on towards four on the Friday afternoon prior to their trip to Daramba when Carina of all people burst through the door, bringing with her a whoosh of perfumed air.

'Carina!' Francesca rose from her desk, aware that Valerie Scott was hovering in the background, wringing her hands and looking extremely agitated. Obviously she had taken fright. 'It's all right, Valerie,' she said, a model of calm.

It was doubtful if anyone on the planet would be capable of stopping a Carina hell-bent on gaining entry to what after all was their late grandfather's resplendent office. Francesca had reduced the splendour considerably by stripping it of its more florid touches and personalising the space. She had taken down two of the blue chip colonial paintings that would fetch a small fortune and replaced them with one of her best paintings, which she had held back from sale, an Outback landscape, and one of Nellie Napirri's stunningly beautiful waterlily paintings. In a very short time they had proved to be excellent conversation starters, putting visitors at their ease.

'Yes, go back to work,' Carina instructed the woman in imperious tones. 'And never try to stop me from entering this office again.'

Scarlet in the face and mottled in the throat, Valerie made a valiant effort to defend herself. 'I wasn't trying to *stop* you, Ms Forsyth. I was merely trying to let Ms Forsyth know you were here.'

'It didn't look like that to me,' Carina said in her clipped, high-handed voice. 'You can shut the door.'

'Of course.' A deeply mortified Valerie was already attempting to do that very thing.

Inwardly churning—the cheek of her!—Francesca waved her cousin into a leather chair opposite. One of their grandfather's choices, it should swallow her up. 'Is there something you want, Carrie?'

Carina remained standing. 'What do you think I want?' she challenged, already falling into what could be a question-for-question session.

'I have no idea. Why don't you tell me?' Francesca invited, surprised her tone was so easy and natural, and giving a thought to her composed inner strength—which was growing by the day. As ever, Carina looked a million dollars. A goddess of glamour in a white linen suit cinched tightly at the waist by a wide gold metallic belt. There were strappy gold stilettos on her feet, and a very luxurious white and gold leather tote bag over her shoulder. No wonder she had tempted Bryn. Carina would make the blood run hot in an Eskimo's veins.

Carina frowned, carelessly plonking her very expensive bag on the carpeted floor before dipping into the plush seat, showing off almost the entire length of her very good legs. No neat ankle crosses for Carina. Her wonderful hair had been cut to clear the shoulder, side parted, full of natural volume.

'How are you, by the way?' She looked up to fix Francesca with a piercing blue gaze growing more and more like their grandfather's.

'I'm fine, thank you. And you?' What was this all about? Francesca thought. Was Carina's bad-girl side in remission? Dared she hope? The word *epiphany* sprung to mind. Maybe Carina had had one on the way over.

Carina flicked a frowning, all-encompassing glance around the vast room—the wall-to-wall bookcases crammed with weighty tomes, a magnificent pair of terrestrial and celestial globes on mahogany stands, the large paintings, memorabilia, dozens of silver-framed photographs of Sir Francis with famous people, trophies and awards—then said sarcastically, 'Made changes, I see. Like to show off you're such a clever chick.' Her eyes moved to the painting of the waterlily lagoon surrounded by aquatic plants. 'I don't like *that!* Too highly coloured. Aboriginal work, isn't it?'

'Nellie Napirri,' Francesca said. 'I love it. The colours are very true to our lily-filled billabongs. Surely you recognise that? You've seen enough of them. It's not a misty Monet, though I'm absolutely certain Monet would have loved it too. You mightn't be aware of it, Carrie, but Nellie's work is fetching big money these days.'

Carina made a face that signified complete uninterest. 'She'll only blow it on the rest of her tribe. That's the way they are. The place looks okay—more feminine, I guess—but you scarcely fit into Gramps's shoes.'

'Neither of us do, come to think of it,' Francesca answered evenly.

'Are you happy?' Carina shot at her.

Francesca pushed the file she had been reading to one side. 'Off hand, I'd give it an eight out of ten. But I've been much too busy to question my state of mind, Carina. Would you like to tell me what you're here for? Not that I'm not pleased to see you. I *am.* I don't want bad feeling between us. You're my cousin. We're family.'

'Some family, right?' For a moment Carina regarded the impressive array of gold gem-studded bracelets on her right arm—

emerald, ruby, amethyst, topaz, a couple more. On her left she wore a solid gold watch set with diamonds; a diamond-set gold hoop encircled the narrow wrist above it. Every mugger in the world would have thought her a dream target. 'Look, I'll come straight to the point. It's not easy for me, but I want to apologise for the way I've been acting. I've been a damned fool. It's just…'

'You were shocked.' Francesca hastened to help her cousin out, even though she knew she might never rate another apology in her life. 'You've been led to believe everything would be different. I felt the same way.'

'Ah, well…' Carina sighed, a recent convert to being philosophical. 'I think Gramps was way ahead of Dad and me.' She gave Francesca a wry smile. 'Dad is a lot happier these days. Bless him. Had Gramps left him in control he would surely have died of a heart attack before his time. As for me! Want the truth?'

'Yes, please.' Lord knew she didn't want more lies.

'Doing what I do makes me happy,' Carina confessed, as though Francesca had never for a moment known. 'I wouldn't want to be cooped up like you, trying to get your head around mind-boggling stuff. I know you're smart, but Gramps left too heavy a burden on those bony shoulders. You're too thin, you know that? Men don't like skin and bone. Anyway, very few people ever take women seriously in business. I expect you've already found that out?'

'I could name you any number of women being taken very seriously in business, Carrie,' she said. 'Maybe you're not as much in touch with the current scene as you thought. People have been very helpful, as a matter of fact. I have a great deal to learn, but I seem to be coping. I don't do things on my own. As I said, I have help.'

'Of course! The staff would probably be able to run the place without you,' Carina flashed back, a teeny crack showing in the *bonhomie*. 'First thing you want to do is get rid of the thumper outside the door.'

Francesca struggled with that for a moment. 'Thumper?' Her black eyebrows rose. 'I thought a thumper was a nightclub bouncer?' Carina, big on the nightclub scene, would know.

'Whatever!' Carina threw her head back so forcefully her hair bounced. 'I don't like her. She was having an affair with Gramps—did you know?'

'Well, I'm sure *Gramps* put the hard word on her.' Francesca spoke very dryly, to her own amazement. She had never called her grandfather Gramps in her entire life. 'Grandfather wasn't everything he should have been.'

'Oh, hold on!' Carina was about to take umbrage on their grandfather's behalf—took a short pause for reflection and thought better of it. 'Why *her*?'

'Being right outside the door might have helped, don't you think? But I've never much liked gossip, Carrie. Valerie is divorced. Grandfather was a widower—'

'With one helluva sex life!' Carina gave one of her little whoops. 'If there was a Nobel Prize awarded for a lifetime of having lovers it would have been given to Gramps. I suppose that's what did him in at the end. Thought he was God's gift to women, isn't that right? Maybe he had a premonition he was going to die. There *was* another will, you know.'

Francesca nodded. 'Yes, Douglas told me.'

'Still retaining that old fool?' Carina reacted with disgust.

Francesca remained calm and confident. Just a taste of power had given her a massive injection of those much needed qualities. 'I trust him, Carrie. He has a fine reputation. And he's gentlemanly.'

Carina's mouth down turned sceptically. 'At least that's what he likes to present to the world. I bet he can talk dirty just like the rest of us.'

'Now, that, Carrie, defies belief. I must lead a different life to you, as well. I've never talked dirty in my life.'

'No, you're a terminal Miss Goody Two-Shoes,' Carina said with affectionate contempt. 'You really ought to stop. Or maybe you intend to? Bryn tells me you're off to Daramba for the weekend?' Her tone made it clear she thought Francesca knew she and Bryn were back in touch and didn't give a hoot.

It took a tremendous effort for Francesca to keep the shock off her face. 'I didn't realise you were speaking to him these days?' She told herself Carina was a pathological liar. But that posed the question: who else knew? She hadn't said a word to anyone. She couldn't believe Bryn went about advertising his intentions. He operated on the basis that one could never be too careful. Then there was the fact he had never mentioned having contact with Carina, let alone a reconciliation.

'Oh, come off it, sweetie,' Carina mocked, as though she knew every thought that was running riot through Francesca's head. 'We've both known Bryn since we were kids. Do you honestly think Bryn and I would remain out of touch for long?' she jeered. 'Actually, it was Bryn who made the first move. Surely he told you? Maybe not. My intuition says he didn't. He plays his cards close to his chest. But that's half the reason I'm here. It was Bryn who suggested it. He really does think everything through. He says it's not wise for any of us to continue this feud in public or in private. Besides, the last people I want to quarrel with are you and Bryn. How can I put this?' Her stunning face took on an unfamiliar expression of earnestness, even soul-searching. 'I *need* you both. The people all around me I can't trust. I don't for one moment think they're for real. They're all over me to my face; treacherous behind my back. Envy, of course. You were never like that, Francey. Neither was Bryn. We're all just too bloody rich for most people. They hate it. Money has to stick with money. It's Them versus *Us!*'

'Sounds a bit like paranoia to me, Carrie,' Francesca said. 'Besides, we *do* get all the perks. I can't afford to see it your way. I'm now dealing with so many people from all walks of life. So, when did Bryn tell you we were off to Daramba?' She spoke as if it were of no great importance when inwardly she was feeling sick and vulnerable. It had only been over lunch on Wednesday that Bryn had suggested bringing forward their trip.

'Yesterday, I think,' Carina said, rolling her eyes upwards, as though yesterday's date was written on the ceiling. 'Yes, it had to be yesterday. I'd go with you, but Daramba has never held the same fascination for me as it has for you and Bryn. The break should do you good. I'm off to Sydney tomorrow myself. The Cartwrights are having another one of their gala parties. All the glitterati will be there. I have the most incredible dress! You'd love it! Not that you could pull it off. It's so darn sexy. Softly, softly does it with you, doesn't it, luvvy? I, on the other hand, like to shake people up.'

'No one better at it in the country,' Francesca assured her. 'Have you spoken to your mother?' She tacked that on as though it were an afterthought. In reality she was trying to divine whether her cousin was on the level. People expressed themselves in so many ways. Speech, of course, but also body language—the way they moved, their hands, eyes. Wasn't there a theory that the eyes moved left or right according to whether one was telling the truth or not? The trouble was she couldn't remember which side indicated the lie.

'Next one on my list,' Carina told her with a saddened little smile. 'It's taken me over-long to rebuild my bridges. What say we do lunch early next week? I think it would be good for the press to see us out and about together.'

'Next week is all pencilled in, I'm afraid, Carrie,' Francesca said. It was true enough. 'Maybe the following week?'

'I'll have to think. Let that secretary do some of your work,' Carina suggested crossly. 'It won't hurt her. What's her name again?'

'Valerie Scott. Surely you've met her any number of times before? You were always calling in on Grandfather.'

'Unlike you,' Carina abruptly fired up, fixing Francesca with a steely eye. 'I've met her, of course, but some people you just meet and forget. It's people like me that make a lifelong impact. That hair has to go, and she could lose some weight. No wonder she lost hubby. Did you see the size of her backside?'

'You're too figure-conscious, Carrie,' Francesca sighed. 'Valerie is a very attractive woman.'

'One can never be too figure-conscious.' Carina shuddered, retrieving her tote. 'I hate that matronly upholstered look. I'm almost tempted to tell her.'

'Please don't,' Francesca begged as Carina rose to her feet. 'Sure I can't offer you a cup of coffee?'

'No time!' Carina gave a clatter of her heavily weighted down arm. 'I'm having dinner tonight with someone you know.'

'Oh, who's that?' Francesca looked up casually, but her hands were gripping the edge of her desk hard, the knuckles showing white. If Carina said Bryn, their trip would be off.

'Greg Norbett.'

Francesca's fingers unlocked as the ferocious tension disappeared. 'Greg? Isn't he still married?' she asked, as calmly as she could. 'Gosh, it's only been a couple of years.' They had both attended Greg's wedding to a lovely girl.

'It's at the separation stage.' Carina spoke carelessly, as though it were only a hop, step and a jump to divorce. 'You need to be married at least a year before you get a divorce. Otherwise it's just tacky. What was it he saw in *you*?' she joshed, her blue eyes full of cousinly teasing.

'Why don't you ask him?' Francesca said. Greg Norbett had actually proposed to her after a fundraising party. A surprise because she'd never encouraged a relationship with him. What a good thing she hadn't been attempted to accept Greg's proposal, given his limited attention span. She felt very sad about his wife. It wasn't very sporting, Carina sleeping with other women's husbands. In some respects Carina rated a moral zero.

Francesca came around her desk to accompany her cousin to the door, though it was more like a flat-out sprint, keeping up with Carina's pace.

'Have a great weekend, Francey!' Carina turned to say. 'I

mean that!' She bent slightly—she was tall, especially in those stiletto heels—to give Francesca an air peck. 'Bryn likes to look out for you. He's been at it for most of your life.' It was said in a tone that in someone else would have been gentle amusement, but somehow from Carina sounded snide. 'Can I give you a word of advice?' She swept on before Francesca could say yay or nay. 'I'm much more savvy in the ways of the world than you are.'

'No argument there,' Francesca said.

'Enjoy yourself,' Carina told her magnanimously. 'But whatever you do, *don't trust Bryn.* He's a master manipulator.'

'I suppose we all are from time to time.'

Carina's brows rose. 'Be that as it may, Francesca, I trusted Bryn Macallan to my cost. He was the love of my life. He took my virginity.'

It *was* possible, but the new Francesca wasn't sure she believed her. 'Sure you hadn't abandoned it before that?'

Carina levelled her with an affronted frown. 'Have your little joke. I expected you to fly to Bryn's defence, but you know yourself, Francey, I'm a far better judge of character than you are. I know Bryn's a sizzlingly exciting man. Zillions of women can only get to dream about a guy like Bryn, but *I* had him for the longest possible time. *I* was the one to clock up the hours. And where did it get me? Absolutely nowhere. No engagement, no wedding, like I'd been promised. Worst of all, no damned respect. D'you know what I think?'

'Please tell me.' Francesca remained outwardly calm.

'He has turned his attention to *you.*' Carina whipped that out like a master stroke. 'Bryn doesn't need me any more. He doesn't need any more money. It's power he's after. That's what he's all about. That's what he *does.* Just like Gramps. We women are only pawns. It has never been any different, right down the centuries. We get *used.* I certainly was, and I don't want it to happen to you. I really do care about you, Francey. This is *family* now. You know what they say?'

'Blood's thicker than water?' Francesca hazarded a guess.

She already knew that wasn't always the case. 'So, what do you suggest I do?'

'Don't *ever* let him into your bed,' Carina warned her, regarding Francesca like a Mother Superior with a wavering novice. 'He'll try it, but don't worry. Just make sure it doesn't happen. He'll be everything you ever wanted or wished for, but there will be a price to pay. He'll have you, body and soul. God knows, I've had to fight hard to free myself of the madness.'

Francesca knew she wasn't exaggerating. 'Has the madness gone?' she asked gently. Tender at heart, she was profoundly sorry for her pain. Carina was her cousin, after all. They had spent much of their lives together.

Carina backed up to the door, looking disturbingly near tears, which further upset Francesca. Carina never cried. Not even at their grandfather's funeral, when one would have thought she could have squeezed out a few. 'It gets less and less every day,' she said, blinking her eyes valiantly. 'There are plenty of other distractions. Like poor Greg. He's such a bore! His poor little wife should sue him for causing her grievous mental distress. I'm twenty-six going on twenty-seven, Francey, and I've relinquished all faith in men.' The genuine unhappiness in Carina's brilliant blue eyes said more than a thousand words ever could.

'Oh, Carrie, I'm sorry.' Francesca reached out to take gentle hold of her cousin's arm. Love was the very devil! This had to be terrible for the proud Carina. 'Twenty-six is no age. You're so beautiful, so much admired. You have the world at your feet. There are plenty of good men out there.'

Carina gave a laugh to cover her distress. 'Not the ones I've encountered. As long as I can save *you.* That's all I care about. Don't take a gamble on Bryn, Francey. You'll *never* win.' She opened the heavy door, then stepped into the wide carpeted corridor, totally ignoring Valerie Scott, who sat at her desk, head bowed so close to her work she had to be going cross-eyed. 'I'll be in touch,' she promised with a big smile. 'Next time you take off I might come with you. Out there we can really bond.'

Francesca said nothing. Bonding wasn't an activity Carina had paid much attention to in the past. But there was always hope. Wasn't hope supposed to spring eternal? Could a leopard change its spots? The answer in nature was a resounding *no!* Applied to humans, the verdict wasn't so reliable. What *exactly* had Carina come to tell her? Was this another one of her strategies? Changed spots or not, she didn't fancy the idea of putting her head in a leopard's mouth.

After Carina had gone on her way, leaving a minefield of possibilities, Francesca withdrew to her office, closing the door. It wasn't her practice to do it all the time, but she did it now, directing a little sympathetic smile Valerie's way. Poor Valerie! Carina had been very rough on her. Then again, there was the possibility Carina was in the early stages of turning herself around. Who could deny there were great life-changing forces constantly at work?

One good thing about being the official Forsyth heiress. If she disappeared, even in the Outback, people would notice.

CHAPTER FIVE

THEY FLEW INTO Daramba well before noon. Once over the vast station Bryn brought the King Air down low, so they could get a closer look at the condition of the land. The endless miles of wildflowers had all but vanished, ready to reappear with the next Wet Season's good rains, but the ancient landscape—the infinite Inland Sea of pre-history—still frothed in blossom from the trees. Daramba was in prime condition, the fiery red earth thickly sown with thick Mitchell and Flinders grass, the ubiquitous spinifex, salt bush, hop bush and the succulent pink *parakeelya* cattle liked to feed on. There were clusters of billabongs, three or four linked, before a break of a few miles streaked away to the horizon, the iridescent blue of the sky holding a couple of white clouds, like giant cotton wool balls. No rain in them. No rain anywhere over a state more than twice the size of Texas.

The great system of water channels that ran like intricate lacework all over the Channel Country glittered in the sun, some silver, others dark green, with occasionally a cloudy opal-blue or lime-green, framed by the dark green fringing trees that grew along the sandy banks. It created a whole kaleidoscope of colour. And there was movement as well as colour. A mob of brumbies with a long-tailed bay at the front—tall and powerful for a wild horse—its harem behind, the half-grown foals alongside, suddenly shot into view from a thick screen of bauhinias, probably taking fright at the sound of the plane's engines. They were a marvellous sight in flight, and because of easy access to feed and water in glossy condition.

Stockmen on the ground looked up and waved their dusty hats as they made their passes over campsites and holding yards where fat cattle were penned almost bumper to bumper. In the middle distance a big mob was moving like the giant Rainbow Snake of aboriginal legend, twisting and turning as they made their way to one of the billabongs with a couple of stockmen riding back and forth among them, urging the beasts on and keeping them in an orderly formation. They didn't look as if they needed much urging, Francesca thought.

Away on the western border of the station, the midday heat was reflected off the ramparts of the Hill Country, with its turrets, minarets and crenellations, its secret caves with their well-guarded aboriginal rock paintings. At this time of day the eroded hills with their fantastic shapes glowed furnace-red. Early morning they were a soft light pink that deepened during the morning to rose, and then the fiery red of high noon. Late afternoon they changed to a haunting deep purple, incredible against the flaming backdrop of the sunset, then, as the sun dropped towards the horizon, faded to a misty lilac. Night fell abruptly in the Outback, like a vast black velvet curtain decorated with a billion desert stars. Now, in the noon fire, the whole area was bathed in the shimmery veil of mirage.

Francesca felt so thrilled to be back she was a little shaky with it. She knew she had to relax, but her whole body was zinging. Two days alone with Bryn! What ecstasy! She hadn't told him Carina had called in to the office to see her. By the same token, she hadn't questioned him in any way regarding Carina, much less mentioned how it had hurt her—hurt like the very devil—to hear he had told Carina about their planned weekend on the station they now jointly owned and that they were back in contact. She wasn't looking for conflict. In a way she was considering opting out of the whole business of Bryn, Carina and herself. The infamous love triangle. Carina wasn't cured any more than she was. They were both hopelessly in love with Bryn. But she wanted more than anything to cherish this time they would have together. Life being what it was, it might be all she was going to get.

'Homestead coming up now.' Bryn turned his head towards her. What was he really saying to her with that beautiful heart-wrenching smile?

She smiled back. She was a woman in love. She didn't even care if she wasn't disguising the fact all that well. Most probably she was giving herself away with the flush in her cheeks and the sparkle in her eyes. Every second she had with the man she loved was important. Love, the most powerful of all alchemies, made it very difficult to get and then keep one's bearings.

On the ground he caught her hand, walking her to the waiting station Jeep. Her faint trembling was conveying itself to him like a warm vibration. He had always felt immensely protective of Francesca when she was a child, then right through adolescence, and even now when she was all grown up. A woman.

'You're trembling, Francey. What's the matter?' He looked down at her, knowing he wanted her more than anything else in the world. Knowing too, he had reached the point where he was past pretending. But he had to tread carefully. The last thing he could afford to do was startle her like one could spook a nervous, high-strung filly. So he waited. It would be so much better for her to come to him.

The voice that he found so alluring was full of excitement. 'Nothing's the matter. I feel great. You know how I love this place.'

'Best place in the world!' he confirmed.

'You don't know how much joy it gives me to know we're of the same mind.'

She turned up her face to him so trustingly. It was a poetic face, he thought. Lyrical in style, the contours delicate where Carina's were bold and arresting. His mother always said Francesca reminded her of one of her favourite actresses, who had died in the mid 1960s: Vivien Leigh—Lady Olivier. One of the reasons he had bought the DVD of *Gone With the Wind* had been to see if Francesca was really as much like Vivien Leigh as his mother always claimed. She was. The resemblance lay in the high-arching black brows, the light eyes, the sensitive cut of the mouth, the curling cloud of dark hair, and again that delicate bone structure.

'Why are you staring at me like that?' She gave him a smile that tore at his heart. 'It's really me.'

'It is indeed.' How could a woman project such sensuality and an airy lightness of manner at one and the same time? He moved, rather abruptly, to open the passenger door for her.

Francesca followed, a little puzzled by his reaction. Today he wore a light blue and white checked open-necked shirt and blue jeans, the short sleeves of his shirt exposing the sleek muscles in his darkly tanned upper arms. He was a beautiful man. How many years now was it she had been sketching Bryn? She'd lost count. He was a marvellous subject, and one of her strengths was capturing the essence of her sitter, whether they were aware she was sketching them or not, which was often the case. Bryn actually owned dozens of her sketches; had grabbed them off her. Many he'd had framed in ebony and hung in groups. But he didn't possess a single sketch she had made of him. His mother had many. So did Lady Macallan. Both women had told her they treasured them.

'This *is* Bryn!' Annette always said, with motherly pride in her eyes.

As she went to get in the Jeep, Bryn laid his hand briefly on her shoulder. 'I've got something to tell you.'

At once she drew back, stifling a gasp. *No, no, Bryn! Don't spoil it.*

'It's not *that* bad.' He frowned, taken aback by the play of emotion across her face. Was it distress? What did she think he was going to say? 'I gave Jili and Jacob the weekend off to spend in the Alice,' he quickly explained. 'I think we can survive without them, don't you?'

'You did what?' Surprise filled her voice as enormous relief pumped in.

'You have some objection?'

'I thought we were equal partners?' She was struggling against the compulsion to simply fold herself against him, to surrender to the blazing force that was in him, let it *scorch* her. But she had to be careful. She had to think everything through. Wasn't it a woman's unattainability that made her so desirable? History certainly suggested it.

'We are. I hope we always will be.'

'You mean that?'

'Don't you?' He pinned her gaze, his own fathomless.

'Nothing is going to change me,' she answered briskly, thinking that was the way to go. 'And that's fine about Jili and Jacob. No problem!' How could she say that, when the piece of news had had a tremendous impact on her? They would be quite alone. And he had planned it that way.

'Then why are you looking so unnerved?' He tucked a stray raven lock behind her ear.

'Well, it *was* kind of a bolt from the blue, Bryn.' She turned to slide into the waiting vehicle. 'I wish I could tell you otherwise, but I'm not much of a cook,' she tacked on when he was behind the wheel.

His laugh came from deep in his throat. 'It was never your cooking skills, Francey, that attracted my attention.'

She belted herself in, and then smoothed back her long hair, giving herself time to settle. 'I didn't know I had.'

'That is just so untrue, Francey,' he mocked. 'Quite beneath you, in fact. We've always had a connection.' He turned on the ignition. 'God, it's good to be back. It's a magnificent day.'

'It is indeed!' The air was so pure, so dry, so bush aromatic—

and the space and the freedom! It was like no place else. And, let's face it, she was thrilled to the core to be sharing these precious days with him. Separate rooms? She could feel the yearning that was in her shooting off her like sparks.

'Jili will have left plenty of food for us,' he was saying. 'We'll have lunch. Go for a drive around the main areas. Check everything out. Catch up with the men. I'm not all that happy about Roy Forster staying on as overseer.' He cast her a questioning glance.

'Me either,' Francesca said. 'Forster was Grandfather's choice. A real yes-man. Jacob would be a better choice for the job. Roy pretty much relies on Jacob anyway. But how do we go about demoting Roy? I wouldn't want to sack him. He's competent enough—'

'But not the right man for the job,' Bryn finished off for her. 'What about if we shift him to one of the other stations, say Kurrawana in the Gulf?'

'You've thought about it?'

'Yes.'

'He mightn't want to go.'

'On the other hand he might jump at it. Let me handle it,' Bryn said.

'Yes, boss.' A little dryness escaped her, when in reality she was in awe of his many skills, all of which he had mastered. Everything Bryn did was done not only with the highest level of competence, but with considerable flair.

'You don't like that idea?' A black brow shot up.

She slanted him a smile. 'What? You calling the shots? Only teasing, Bryn—though you *do* give orders to the manner born. Grandfather wanted you to run the whole operation.'

'You'll be consulted all along the way. That's a promise. No decision will be made without your approval. I won't take anything on alone.'

'That's great to know. But I trust you, Bryn. I know you'll

be working hard to bring Daramba back to what it was. It has deteriorated a bit.'

'It will be a whole different story when Jacob takes over,' Bryn said.

The hours were passing far too swiftly for Francesca. It was a marvellous experience to be with Bryn. They both had quick, curious minds, both were keenly observant, so they were able to spend the afternoon in stimulating discussion. It was uncanny, really, the way they kept arriving at the same conclusions.

Francesca took great satisfaction from the fact that Bryn listened carefully to every suggestion she had to make. And most of them he seemed prepared to take on board. It occurred to her in hindsight that on those rare occasions when she had got into discussion with her grandfather he had listened too. How odd to think of that now. But, unlike her grandfather, Bryn's manner with the station staff was relaxed and friendly. She could see how well they responded to it, without ever overstepping the line. Never in all the years had any member of her family joined the men for their tea break, but she and Bryn did so now, enjoying the smoky billy tea and the freshly baked damper that the men had liberally smeared with home-made rosella jam or bush honey.

There was a new stockman in the team, Vance Bormann, a big man, bulky on top but by no means overweight, more like a prize fighter, with a swarthy face, weathered skin and a full, macho-looking moustache. He wore his battered black Akubra low over heavy-lidded dark eyes. Roy Forster had taken him on only a few weeks back. The general opinion was the man was good at his job. Francesca, on the other hand, was none too sure she liked the look of him—a woman's opinion? In fact she had a vague feeling she had seen him some place before. She couldn't for the life of her think where or when. Maybe he reminded her of some cowboy in the old Westerns? The guy who was always the baddie.

She found herself sitting in court, surrounded by station employees she had known for years, talking in particular to one of the stockmen she had favoured from childhood. Taree Newton—part aboriginal, his hair now a mass of pure white curls—was a man who could handle any animal on the station and fix any piece of machinery, and he could tell wonderful stories of the Dreamtime and 'other-world' matters, some of which as a child she had found deliciously scary.

'Catch up with me, little'un,' Taree used to call to her as she tagged after him. 'Catch up with me.' Taree, her guardian angel. He had always been on the move, with a string of jobs to do. 'Plenty a work, Missy Francey. Too much work.' But he had always found time for her, keeping the keenest eye on her. Aunt Elizabeth had used to call Taree 'Francey's nanny'.

She noticed Bryn had taken Roy Forster aside, no doubt to discuss Roy's future. There would always be a place for Roy within the pastoral chain, but unquestionably Jacob would fill the role of overseer here a good deal better. Jili would be thrilled! She glanced up to catch Vance Bormann staring at her. She had the impression he had been observing her long and hard. He was very much a stranger, for all her feeling that she had sighted him before. When he realised she was aware of his staring, he swiftly rose from where he had been sitting, going back through the trees as if he were ready to continue work. It wasn't unnatural for a man to stare at a woman. She had received plenty of attention from the male sex for years now. But this was the first time she had thought there was something sinister about it. Surely not? If she mentioned it to Bryn she knew the likely consequence would be the man would be out of a job. Maybe it was his rather unfortunate looks? But wasn't it unfair judging a book by its cover?

Late afternoon, as the heat of the blazing sun was abating, they took the horses out. She a glossy-flanked liver-chestnut mare called Jalilah; he a big black gelding, Cosmo, with a white blaze and white socks—both ex-racehorses, alert and very fast when underway.

Francesca's face shone with pleasure. She had so missed not being able to go for a ride. Now she revelled in the scent of horseflesh, the scent of leather, the scent of the still blossoming bush. Bryn rode close beside her, his hands easy on the reins. He was an experienced rider, as she was, though both of them knew he would always beat her in a race. Initially the horses were restless—Jalilah particularly skittish, having been cooped up for too long—so once away from the home compound and out onto the flats they gave the horses their heads.

Manes and tails streamed like pennants in the wind as they headed out to the first line of billabongs. Sunset wasn't that far off. Afterwards the world would swiftly turn from delicate mauve to pitch-black. They would need to be back within the compound by then.

Not far from their destination the mare, high-strung at the best of times, was spooked by a pair of wallabies that shot up out of nowhere and then bounded away. The mare reared, forelegs folded up under her, but Francesca, leg and thigh muscles working, got her quickly under control, to the point where the mare steadied, dancing nervily on the highly coloured red sand laced with water-storing pink *parakeelya,* and the bright green spinifex that would soon turn to a scorched gold.

The hills in the distance that had appeared so solid and so glowing a red at noon now appeared to be floating free of the ground, their bases disguised by the thick silver-grey mist formed by condensation from the many rock pools. Without so much as a word to the other, in silent communication they rode down on Kala-Guli Creek, the prettiest and most secluded spring-fed pool on the entire station. Unless one knew exactly where to find Kala-Guli, any visitor unfamiliar with the vast landscape could ride on unawares. Not all of these beautiful hidden pools, however, were safe. Many a poor beast had been sucked in and lost for ever in the quicksand that often lurked where there was plenty of underground water.

It had been suggested at one time that was the way Gulla Nolan had disappeared, but those who had known Gulla refused point-blank to go along with the theory. Gulla had known this country like the back of his hand. If Gulla had been sucked into quicksand he would have been dragged there, hands and feet tightly bound. At various times over the years Francesca had fancied she'd heard Gulla's cries of terror, amplified by the desert wind. But then, as Carina had frequently told her scornfully, she had way too much imagination.

White cockatoos appeared in magic droves, settling like winged angels in the trees. Bryn and Francesca dismounted, tethered their horses, stretched their limbs, then walked down towards the waterline, with bushy ferns and brittle ground cover grasses snagging the hems of their jeans. Butterflies of many colours, beautiful to the eye, drifted about like petals, luminous when slanting rays of sunlight caught their wings. Francesca trailed a hand over a native honeysuckle, a brilliant yellow with a honeysuckle's true perfume. The creek was several feet below the level of the plain throughout its course. Here the heated air off the grasslands turned balmy, perfumed with the scent of hundreds and hundreds of wild lilies, purple in colour, which grew in profusion along the banks of the long, narrow stream. It was enormously refreshing after the dazzling power of the sun.

'Man finds his true home in nature,' Bryn commented, lending a hand to her as they moved down a fairly steep and slippery slope.

'I suppose that's where we're closest to God.'

He gave her a half-smile, feeling a profound tenderness for her and her strong spiritual beliefs. 'Do you ever pray for me, Francey?' he asked.

Of course she prayed for him. He was so very special to her. 'What do you think?' she replied, eyes sparkling.

'I think I may be in need of it.' He tightened his hold on her as they moved further down the bank, where little wildflowers similar to pansies showed their velvety faces.

'Me too,' she said, and it wasn't banter.

And there were the moss-covered rocks of various shapes and sizes she so loved and had often sketched. Some, shelf-like, jutted out into the water, forming a natural sunbathing area. How they had used it when they were young! Only now the feathery acacias fanned right out over the creek from both sides, dipping in low arches like weeping willows, their branches cascading to within touching distance. Here too a white mist hung low, like a smoky haze over the stream for as far as they could see. By the time they stood on the golden stretch of dry sand a flock of finches had zoomed down over the water, drinking their fill, then rising in a whirr of tiny wings. It all added to the extraordinary fascination of the place.

'This is exquisite, isn't it?' she breathed quietly, letting the fresh coolness get to her and her heated skin. The creek was completely deserted, except for them and the colonies of birds. Brilliant little lorikeets, rising flashes of sapphire, ruby and emerald, darted and wheeled through the branches above them. 'It looks like it has been here since the beginning of time.'

For answer, Bryn began to unbutton his shirt. 'Let's take a quick dip,' he suggested. 'It looks so darn inviting.'

She drew in her breath sharply, her whole body tensing, the lower half of her body flooded with sexual heat like spiralling little flames. 'Are you serious?'

'Of course I'm serious,' he said, stripping off his shirt and regarding her with amusement. 'God, Francey, we've taken a dip here countless times over the years.'

'I'd need my swimsuit first.'

'Oh, come off it,' he mocked. 'Strip down to your bra and briefs. I bet they're more respectable than most bikinis on the beach.'

She watched him, dry-mouthed, unzip his jeans and then step out of them, very comfortable with it. All that was left to cover his superb male body was a pair of navy briefs that clung low on his hips. There wasn't a skerrick of excess flesh on him. She couldn't seem to tear her eyes away from his sculpted body, nor control her eyes' descent. She could feel her cheeks flush. She could hear the beat of her heart.

'I don't know that I want to take off my clothes,' she said, her voice trailing off uncertainly. She was just so modest. Maybe too modest—and no one made her feel more acutely conscious of her own body than Bryn.

'Excuse me,' he corrected, suddenly looking up at her, 'you *do.* It'll cool you down. Come on, girl! I'm not going to drown you, if that's what you're wondering.'

His mockery fired her up. 'Okay. Turn your back until I'm in the water.'

'Francey, you amaze me—but okay.' His voice was languid, lazy, taunting. He stood studying her for a moment longer, then stepped up onto a flat-topped rock that jutted out into the deep water and dived off it, surfacing a moment later, with water streaming off his jet-black hair, his face and wide shoulders, the hard muscle of his gleaming upper torso. 'The water's great. Come on!' He beckoned to her, much as he had done through all the years of her childhood. He only had to beckon and she followed.

Quickly she looked around her. Plenty of branches from which to hang her clothes—a sapphire-blue tank top and her jeans. She was already out of her riding boots. She turned away, hearing the sound of Bryn's splashing. Damn him! If she were Carrie she'd have had all her clothes off in less than a minute. Carrie was quite comfortable with nudity. She had a great body. Not that there was anything wrong with Francesca's own body. Nothing wrong with her underwear either. She liked good lingerie. Her bra was silk, with matching briefs, pale pink, patterned with violet and blue flowers and tiny red hearts. All quite respectable. Maybe he wouldn't notice the hearts.

Just as she reached the water, dipping in an exploratory toe, he shocked her by surfacing in the middle of the pool, treading water while he stared at her with open delight.

'You look exquisite!' he called out. 'If I were gifted, like you, I'd depict you as a mythical water nymph—say, Ondine. But naked, of course. Nakedness absolutely obligatory. Either emerging from the depths of the pool, or perhaps lying stretched out on that rock shelf over there, with flowers in your long hair. Either one would work.'

She saw his eyes linger on her small, high breasts, then slowly and deliberately move down her body to her legs. 'Sounds pretty erotic!' She was panicked, but felt a strange desire to stay exactly where she was, with his eyes on her.

'Eros should be your middle name!'

'Now, that's bizarre!' she protested. He couldn't be serious. Just having a bit of fun. She had never seen herself as an erotic being, unaware that many people described her as intensely alluring. 'Carrie is the exhibitionist,' she said, for once accurately nailing her cousin. 'But you already know that.'

'Well, actually I *do!* But that's an entirely different thing.'

What wouldn't he know about Carrie after their affair? And according to Carrie the sexual intrigue continued. She didn't want to believe that. Bryn had denied it. But the niggling thought remained that Carrie would always be there before her.

'Stand there a moment longer, can't you?' he called 'You know your body is perfectly proportioned, like the ideal dancer's? Neck to waist, to hip, to knee, to ankle.'

'Got a tape measure, have you?' She made very slow progress into the emerald-green pool waters, some part of her revelling in his frank stare.

'I have a really good eye.'

'I know that.' She felt as if he was slowly peeling what little she still wore off her. It was like being held in golden chains. Bound to him. More like a wildly shy adolescent than a grown woman, she plunged in, striking out without hesitation. The water was surprisingly cold at first, but all the more energising for that. She was a good swimmer, fast over short distances. Naturally he was stronger. He caught her in the middle of the pool, though she pretended to duck away.

It didn't make one scrap of difference. He had her.

Bryn experienced the searing realisation that his hands had taken on a life of their own. He pushed the straps of her bra down over her shoulders, revealing the tender upper curves of her breasts and the half-hidden rosebud nipples.

It was an enormous shock and an enormous excitation. Francesca's heart worked its way into her throat.

'You know what you are?' His voice was intense.

'Show me.'

She couldn't control it. Yearning burst from her, sweeping her away. Within seconds it had demolished the dam of loneliness that had been built up over the years, leaving in its wake a great curling wave of emotion. She felt transcendent, ready for his kiss, which came the instant he had her locked in his arms.

'Francey!' He took the sweet mouth that opened to him. Took it hungrily. His tongue reached into the moist cavern, its tip teasing her. It was glorious, the press of flesh against flesh. A delirium of pleasure. The softness of her now naked breasts against the taut plain of his torso. Heart of one thudding into the other.

They went under, neither of them drawing back, bobbed up against each other, gasping, then slowly sinking, their mouths locked, her long, slender legs hooked around his. She wasn't going to lose this one chance. She would show him she was a woman. Not the hesitant and fearful girl he had watched growing up.

Surfacing again, he took her long wet rope of hair in his hands, drawing her to him more roughly than he'd intended—but he was thoroughly aroused. How could he not be? He had waited so long for her, taken her in his imagination. She looked impossibly beautiful, with water coursing over her, the thick mane of her hair a sleek ribbon down her back, her great luminous eyes tinged with the green of the overhanging trees.

'This is dangerous what we're doing, isn't it?' she whispered to him, even though the light in her eyes was urging him on. 'Reckless. And it was *your* idea.'

He held her hard at the waist, fusing their lower bodies so she could not be unaware of his powerful arousal. For him there was only Francesca. No one else. Her skin in the dappled sunlight was perfection, beaded with tiny sprays of diamonds.

'Why didn't I think of it long before this?' Of course he *had* thought of it, *dreamed* of it, so many times—but Carina had made it her business never to leave them alone together. 'Francesca, you beautiful creature!' he groaned, aware his strong hands on her were beginning to tremble faintly—a sure sign of his monumental desire. The waiting had been impossibly long.

Francesca found her eyelids dropping heavily, her eyes filled with tears. His voice was so warm, so deep, so desiring. Voices were wonderful instruments of seduction. Voices were weapons.

'You're not crying? Francey?' Concern washed over him, and his driving passion was forced to take a step backwards. 'What is it? Tell me,' he urged.

'Tears come easily to me,' she murmured shakily, placing her hand against the tangle of black hair on his chest that had tightened into whorls.

'Why?'

'Pain is never far behind pleasure.' She stared up into his eyes, black as night.

'You think that will happen if we make love?' God knew he didn't think he had any reserve of control left. His sex felt rigid, rock-hard. He was desperate to plunge into her. It was *pain* he suffered, however sublime.

Her thoughts had turned chaotic. Indeed, she sometimes thought her whole existence had been chaotic. Once he made love to her all the secrets of her life would be unlocked. He would know her so intimately. She would have handed over the larger part of herself. Wouldn't it be far safer for a woman if the man was more in love with her than she with him? There was always one who kissed and one who turned the cheek. Great love unreciprocated at the same level could be a disaster. Didn't she have Carrie for a role model?

It's part of his plan. Didn't I tell you?

Out of nowhere Francesca heard her cousin's voice. It was so piercingly clear she even looked swiftly over her shoulder, as though Carina might be standing on the stretch of sand, watching them locked in their watery embrace. Though she was desperate for Bryn to carry her back to the shore, to expose her naked body to his eyes, to reach deep into her yearning body with his own, to claim what was his, fear suddenly overtook her whole person. Carina's warning words rose up like a curse to haunt her.

He'll be everything you ever wanted or wished for, but there'll be a price to pay.

Life had taught her that was cruelly true. She wasn't equal to the power and skill of this beautiful man. Even half submerged in cold lake water his hungry clasp heated her blood. He touched her to her very soul. Didn't that make her his slave? Had his *bid* for her—could she possibly see it as Carina had warned?—come too fast? Here in this enchanted place he knew she would be totally under his spell. It was in the very nature of the man-woman relationship.

Before her body could further betray her, she threw her arms adroitly back over her head, her body half lifting out of the water as she swam a few butterfly strokes away from him.

'Can we stop now, Bryn?' she begged, when she was a distance off. Her insecurities were starkly on show and there was nothing she could do about it. Soaring hearts could just as well fall and be broken. She wrenched the sodden silk bra that encircled her waist back into position, sleekly encasing her breasts. She might be a woman, but she was still frozen in time.

He gave a quick frown. 'Of course.' It wasn't just physical lust that drove him—the need to possess her. He *loved* her. But he could see she was having the fiercest struggle with her emotions. Something was desperately ailing her. But what? She had to be ready for him. He wasn't prepared to force her to overcome her fears, though he knew he could. 'You're always safe with me, Francey. Remember that. Anyway, it's getting late.' He thrust one hand through his glistening raven hair. 'The sun will set soon.'

She rapidly calmed at his tone. What was he thinking? That nothing was ever going to change Francey? 'Let's have our swim first,' she suggested, her voice warm and sweet with conciliation.

He swam up beside her, no hint of bruised male ego in his voice or on his dynamic face. 'I tell you what!' he said, as though she was back to half her age. 'The last one to reach that big moss-mottled rock up there jutting out into the water makes dinner.'

Her heart lifted in a kind of relief. She couldn't bear to have Bryn angry and disappointed in her. 'You're on! Just give me a start.'

'Not *too* much of one,' he scoffed. 'You're fast in short bursts. All right—go!' His voice rang out in that beautiful, secluded place. It startled the parrots. They rose in a vivid rainbow wave, then flew off, protesting, to more distant trees.

CHAPTER SIX

SHE HAD ALMOST finished dressing. Paradoxically, she had dressed herself up as a woman might for the man she loved. Now she sat in front of the dressing table, staring sightlessly at her own image, as captured fragments of the afternoon came back to haunt her. Or more accurately to *taunt* her. She had been over and over her behaviour of the afternoon, and the causes for it. She wanted to hold on to those lingering sensations of rapture when she had been so magically transformed, but her sharp withdrawal from Bryn's embrace, her renouncement of bliss, kept interfering. How easy it was to lose one's way! She had blown her chance, maybe her *only* chance.

A deeply entrenched habit of hers, her mind resorted to Shakespeare. *'There is a tide in the affairs of men—'*and presumably women?*'—which when taken at the flood leads on to fortune. Omitted, all the voyage of their life, is bound in shallows and in miseries...'*

Who was going to argue with arguably the greatest literary genius in the history of mankind, with his sublime understanding of human nature and the power to express it? If she had missed the tide, then maybe she deserved it. Fortune favoured the brave. Fear was her weakness. She had to break free of it, haul herself up. Now Bryn had reverted to the easy companionship of her childhood and adolescence, apparently accepting she was harbouring myriad anxieties. The pounding passion of that episode in the water might not have happened. It was just one of her daydreams that went on for hours.

Slowly she drew her hairbrush through the rippling length of her long hair, listening to its electric crackle. It reminded her of the times when Aunt Elizabeth had brushed her hair as a child. They had been very close. Far closer than her own blood. Satisfied with the result, she set the brush down, giving vent to a sigh.

'The arrow of time flies in only one direction.' Some other genius had said that. She had an idea it was Einstein. Einstein would no doubt have gone on to point out the enormous pulling power of the past and its impact on the future. But in the end one could only go *forwards*. Not backwards. She could never live this afternoon over again; only in memory. Consciousness was the crucial thing that separated man from beast. Man's ability to relive the past and bring it vividly alive—happy or, in her case, cringe-worthy. The past had shaped her. The past had made her what she was.

She tried to fight off the sense of bleakness that had clung to her since she was a child. It was as if her life since the death of both her parents had assumed a topography of hidden dangers and traps that she had to navigate her way safely through. It was part of the misery of loss—not only of her mother and father, but of her very identity. So much depended on where we were born; who we were born to, our environment, social standing, the kind of childhood we had. Those factors determined so much of life. A well-adjusted adult in all probability had had a happy, stable childhood, with the priceless gift of having being loved. Then there were people like herself, with too many memories of being grief-stricken, lonely, afraid to trust, desperate to unmake tragedy, to turn back the clock when the hands of time only ticked relentlessly on.

Somehow over the years she had learned to work her way out

of her pervading melancholy—which could be part of her artistic nature. The trick to survival, she had found, especially of late, was to focus all her energies on her new life and her plans for the future. For doing *good.* She had been given the opportunity to spread her wings, to take flight. What she now had to do—and she had been overlong at it—was throw off Carina's influence, which she now recognised as a blight. Though she really wanted to believe Carina was changing as a person—it would make life so much better—it was difficult to accept the possibility.

Maybe it was *just* possible to accept that Carina had come to terms with being passed over by their grandfather. After all, the reins of power brought attendant burdens of responsibility, and huge security risks in a world gone mad. Carina was, by her own admission, the quintessential party girl—a social butterfly bent on a life of pleasure and self-indulgence.

Then, there was the crucial issue of Bryn.

It began and ended with Bryn.

How was Carina *really* handling her thwarted feelings and her whole world turned upside down? Carina didn't tolerate loss. The way she had been reared as a pampered princess didn't help. Carina was a very poor loser, even over a game of tennis. She *had* to win. Mostly she did, but it had to be *all* the time. Carina pushed gamesmanship to the limit. Wasn't it highly unlikely, then, that Carina had accepted the loss of the man she intensely desired? With all Francesca knew of her cousin, Carina would be most likely to covet what she knew she could never possess. She might be forced to accept Bryn was never going to ask her to marry him, but Francesca couldn't see Carina surrendering him to any other woman. And the worst possible scenario would be to a woman like herself.

Carina's jealousy over Elizabeth's affection for her had just about ruined their childhood. Of course Carina had so often played the caricature of the loving, caring older cousin, but she had never felt it had been real. Carina's genius was for fooling people, confusing them, hiding behind an elaborate mask.

The issue of Bryn remained unresolved.

Yesterday, when Carina had come into the office, she had forced on herself a particular role. But what had she hoped to achieve by doing so? A cessation of hostilities, even though the hostilities had been all one-sided? What had she been playing at when she'd insisted she was only looking out for Francesca's interests? When had Carina *ever* looked out for her? Her mind had all but shut down on that traumatic incident of their childhood when she had almost drowned, only for Bryn's miraculous intervention, with Carina standing by screaming…and screaming…as though she had never wanted any of it to happen.

Even now, all these years later, she couldn't bear to think it had been anything other than an accident that could always happen when children were left unattended. Only sometimes in the realm of her dreams she relived that day… The walk along the banks of the lagoon hand in hand, which had come as a lovely surprise, her exclaiming over the beauty of the waterlilies, how she was going to draw them the minute she was home, her scrapbook in her hand… Carina had hated the way she was always drawing… She remembered the danger of the deep water…the way Carina had waded in, which meant she'd had to go too. It was the paralysing feeling of extreme danger that always forced her awake.

What *had* happened that day? Would she find the answer in her dreams if only she could let the nightmare run its course? Would she have that dream for ever? Her lungs bursting…her hands locked around thirteen-year-old Bryn's neck as he waded out, carrying her in his strong young arms. She remembered looking down at the waist-deep water, and then they were safely on the sand. She must have been near choking him, clinging to him the way she had, though he'd told her afterwards she'd weighed no more than a feather. She remembered he'd had algae caught in his thick, gleaming thatch of hair. Lurid green against black. She remembered she hadn't cried. She had been trying so hard to be brave. A look of bewilderment crossed her face—hadn't she whispered something in his ear? It had to have been a secret, but she couldn't remember it.

All she did remember was that Bryn had rescued her as if he'd been sent by the Great Spirit of the Bush. She believed in such spirits, as the aboriginal people did. They moved across the earth, always standing by to give aid to the chosen, though they remained for the most part invisible. Even Bryn, the sanest man she knew, acknowledged the spirits of the Timeless Land and what they could do.

She was ready to go downstairs, still fighting off her demons. Reaching for a pair of silver bracelets, she slipped them on like an amulet. She was wearing one of her new semi-casual dresses for evening. Adele Bennett had picked it out for her. Adele certainly knew what she liked and what suited her. This particular dress was ankle-length, the material a gauzy water colour silk-chiffon. Very Ondine-ish, she thought with a smile.

The dress had a beautiful belt to go with it. Another one of Adele's finds. It curved snugly around the waist, then dipped low in front, elongating her torso. The belt had a gorgeous enamelled clasp, made up like a large open-faced flower, violet in colour, with a yellow centre and petals dotted with deep pink crystals like dewdrops. Lime-green and turquoise butterflies, their wings similarly encrusted, alighted on either side. It was a work of art in itself. A beautiful dress wasn't just a flattering garment that made a woman feel special. A beautiful dress was more like a magic talisman. Great things could happen! This dress would protect her. It had already given her waning confidence a boost.

So much depended not on Bryn, but on *her.* She had been a hair's breadth away from letting him make love to her. She didn't think he would tolerate a rebuff like that again. Rapture turned on, then abruptly turned off? The last thing she wanted was to have a sense of strain between them. Life wasn't a game.

Love was to be taken very seriously. It was the one thing that really mattered.

Needless to say, Bryn had let her win their race—though it must have been hard—and now it was his job to get dinner. She had told him she was no cook just for something to say. She was, in fact, a good cook and proud of it—she had taken courses as part of her education—so she was ready to help out. That was if she was needed. Bryn had always been great at barbecues. A funny thing, the way men liked to take over at barbecues, if nowhere else…

'S-o-o-o!' he murmured on a long drawn-out breath as he turned to face her. 'That's an extraordinarily beautiful dress. Very romantic.'

He dazzled her with the blaze in his eyes. She responded with a low curtsy. 'Glad you like it.'

'Your eyes are more violet than grey tonight. They've picked up one of the colours in the dress. It amazes me when that happens.'

'What happens?' She leaned towards him, giving a funny little theatrical blink.

'The way your eyes change colour.' He let his gaze rove over her, from her lustrous hair to her silver-sandal-shod feet. 'Large eyes. Your eyes and your arching brows dominate your face in the way of certain women icons. Callas, Loren, and of course Audrey Hepburn.'

'The Big League?' She smiled, conscious of the excited pulses that had started up in her body.

She moved further into the mammoth room, with its custom-made cabinetry, black and white marble-tiled floor, marble benchtops and marble-topped islands. Stainless steel pots and pans hung from a stainless steel fitting suspended from the ceiling. The kitchen had been fitted out with every conceivable appliance. Just for the hell of it, she supposed. Only now and again had her grandfather entertained here. Mostly he'd kept well away from his flagship station.

'I'm expecting a really good dinner,' she warned Bryn. 'This afternoon's ride has made me hungry.' She kept her voice light. 'So what's on the menu? Do you need any help?'

He shot her a droll glance. 'Francey, I understood you to say you couldn't find your way around a kitchen?'

'I was never allowed in one,' she confessed with regret, picking up the bottle of chilled white wine that sat opened on the bench and pouring a pale greenish-gold stream into an empty waiting glass.

'Here—I should have done that,' he said, laying down his knife. He had been chopping fresh herbs, releasing wonderfully pungent aromas.

'That's okay. You're busy. I like that. You know the way we lived,' she said, sipping the wine, catching the fragrance of lime blossom. She broke off with a delighted comment. 'This is delicious. It's got quite a snap to it. I prefer a good Riesling over a Chardonnay.'

'That's why I opened it,' he said. Francesca was no drinker, but she had a fine palate. 'I know you and Carrie lived like little princesses.' He made a clicking sound with his tongue. 'Even if you *were* the little princess in the tower.'

'I'd much rather have been treated like a normal person.'

'Only it didn't happen that way. Poor Francey!'

'That's why I took a couple of cookery courses—just in case I got married and my husband expected me to be able to turn out a good meal.'

'Do you think you'd ever have to?' he asked drolly, midnight-dark eyes mocking. 'You're the Forsyth heiress, Francesca, like it or not.'

'And you're the Macallan heir,' she shot back. 'I mean, *you* haven't had a normal life either.'

'True. But I suppose it's normal enough for me. We've been given a lot, Francey. We have to be able to take the good with the bad. Speaking of the good—we're having cucumber rounds with Tasmanian smoked salmon for starters. No, don't interrupt. I found the horseradish cream and the capers after a lengthy search, when they were right in front of me. Jili has left fresh herbs from her garden, as you see: parsley, mint, basil. There are a few others in the crisper. Beef fillet with mushrooms to follow, and there's a chocolate mousse I've taken out of the freezer and put in the fridge about fifteen minutes ago. Jili whipped it up for us before she left.'

'Good for Jili!' she exclaimed. 'Now, Jili really *is* a good cook. But don't let that put you off,' she added with mock kindness. 'So where are we going to eat? I don't like it in here. You could seat an army and still have room for reinforcements.'

'Sir Francis always thought big,' Bryn remarked dryly. 'He was notorious for it. What about—?'

'I know,' she broke in. 'The Palm Room. It's about the only room I like.'

'You took the words right out of my mouth,' Bryn said, twisting the top off a jar of capers. 'You could set the table. You *can* do that?'

'Very funny!' She was feeling so extraordinarily light hearted she felt she could soar.

Francesca found she was every bit as hungry as she'd claimed. The starter was just right—light and crunchy, the richness of the smoked salmon cut by the cucumber, the horseradish sauce and a sprinkle of lemon. The Daramba beef fillet simply melted in the mouth, as did the selection of mushrooms, and Jili's chocolate mousse was flavoured with Amaretto liqueur. Bryn scooped it out like ice cream and dusted it with cocoa powder. His own touch.

'Perfect!' Francesca enthused, laying down her dessert spoon. 'Let me make the coffee.'

'No, sit there.' He shook his head, rising to his feet. 'I'm enjoying showing off.'

'You don't want it to get around how good you are at turning out a meal,' she warned him. 'You'll have to fight off complete strangers.'

'I take it you mean women?' he asked suavely over his shoulder.

'Of course women. God, don't give me a heart attack. As it is your female admirers stretch for miles.'

He didn't deny it. 'Amazing when all I need and want is one.'

Over the beef fillet they had abandoned white wine for red. Picking up her crystal wine glass, Francesca leaned back in her bamboo armchair. The chair was comfortably upholstered in a fabric she liked—an embossed damask in a deep shade of crimson that stood up to all the greenery in the room, the luxuriant palms and tree ferns in their huge pots, and the dark timbers of the Asian furnishings. Smiling dreamily to herself, she drank a little more of the Margaret River Cabernet Sauvignon. It was from their own state of Western Australia, the ruggedly beautiful Margaret River wine region, which had fast become one of the world's viticulture hot spots. This red she loved. It was smooth and elegant, with a succulent blackcurrant flavour.

After the drama of the afternoon, the night was a dream. A huge full moon saturated the enormous panorama of Daramba in its radiance. Through the floor-to-ceiling doors that stood open to the rear terrace the night wind came in deliciously cool gusts, spiked with the native boronia that grew wild. Which brought her to thinking of a garden. She would have to do something about establishing one. Bring in a landscaper capable of turning the desert site into an oasis. Jili had her extensive vegetable garden, which flourished. Her grandfather hadn't minded that. The produce was used in the house and around the station. But he hadn't shown the slightest interest in establishing a garden, either at the Forsyth mausoleum or at Daramba homestead. Didn't that say something about the aridity of his character? It wasn't as though he hadn't been able to spare the money, though she realised it would take a lot. Gardens just hadn't been in his philosophy.

The success of an Outback garden was going to depend on the skill of the landscaper and his ability to choose plants that would thrive in the dry. She had her heart set on date palms—as advanced as could be obtained and successfully transplanted. And she wanted a large water garden. Daramba abounded in underground springs. The University of Western Australia had a magnificent campus of more than fifty hectares, set in a superb natural bush setting. She had always loved the Canary Island date palms in the grounds there. Her home state was dry, yet beautiful gardens flourished. Why not here? She just needed the right person to handle the job. Lady Macallan could help her there. She was something of an authority on gardens. She adored her own magnificent garden, which was open to public viewing at certain times of the year.

'What are you thinking about?' Bryn asked as he wheeled in the trolley.

'Gardens,' she said, turning her jewelled gaze on him.

Bryn smiled with satisfaction. 'I knew you'd get around to it. The homestead is crying out for a proper setting. So too is the family mansion, but Charles and Carrie seem happy enough with the way it is. You need a home of your own, you know, Francey. You weren't left the mansion.'

'Thank God!' She sighed with feel feeling. 'It's such a strange place. More like a public building. Take those monumental pilasters supporting roaring lions at the front gate. What was *with* Grandfather and lions, do you know?'

'Wasn't Leo his star sign?' Bryn poured coffee, placing one in front of her. 'He named one of his sons Lionel. Sir Frank and my grandfather visited South Africa in their youth. They were stationed in Cape Town with friends, but they travelled quite extensively. It's a wonder he didn't try to bag a lion and bring it home.'

'What—shoot it?' she cried, horrified.

Bryn laughed and shook his head. 'No, he'd have liked nothing better than to capture it live, bring it back, then let it wander around the grounds of the family home. You know—start a tradition.'

'At least that's better than shooting such a splendid creature. I plan on asking Lady Macallan's advice regarding a landscaper for here. I want date palms. Lots of them. Desert oaks. Native plants. A big water garden. God knows we've got plenty of room.'

'I'm sure she'll be delighted to help you,' Bryn said.

After coffee he allowed her to help him. Then, when the kitchen had been returned to its immaculate condition and the dishes stacked away, they decided on a short walk.

'Even if it's only around the driveway.' Bryn spoke lightly, though he was acutely aware of his soaring sensory perceptions. As always with Francesca—holding her hand guaranteed sexual arousal. 'Do you remember the stone fountain that used to grace the centre of the driveway when the Frazers used to own it?' he asked, striving for the casual. She was wearing that lovely elusive perfume he always associated with her, and it was really getting to him. 'I don't suppose you do. You were too young.'

'My father and Grandfather were already estranged.'

'Yes,' he acknowledged. 'I wonder what happened to the fountain? The Frazers had it sent out from Italy. Three winged horses supported the main basin with rearing front legs. I think my grandfather tried to find out where it had gone, but Frank was very non-committal. I wouldn't be in the least surprised if he had it reduced to rubble.'

'Oh, surely not?' she cried, dismayed.

'Don't take it personally.'

'How can I not take it personally? Sir Francis was my grandfather.'

'That doesn't make him a saint, Francey,' Bryn said bluntly. 'But better late than never. He left the Forsyth fortune largely in your hands.'

She stared up at his handsome, chiselled profile, gilded by the exterior lights. 'You know what I've been thinking about?'

Going to bed with me? Bryn was in half-agony, half-rapture. How the hell was he going to get through the night without her beside him?

'Couldn't we return one of the Queensland stations, say Mount Kolah, to being a wildlife area?' she suggested persuasively. 'I understand it has quite a few protected species within its boundaries.'

Bryn stopped in his tracks. 'You've been talking to someone from the Bush Heritage Authority?'

'Ross Fitzgibbon. But he certainly didn't suggest it.'

'Ha!' said Bryn, and walked on.

'He *didn't!*'

'Francey, Ross Fitzgibbon spends his *life* spreading the message.'

'Why wouldn't he? He's one of our leading ecologists.'

'We can talk about this,' Bryn said, meaning it, 'but not tonight. I just want to relax. Last I heard they were having trouble on Mount Kolah from feral pigs. As far as that goes, Roy Forster told me they might have to organise a hunt here, for the leader of a dingo pack that hangs out on the desert fringe. It seems the brute has acquired a taste for blood, savaging calves. It's more dangerous than a pure-bred dingo because it has German Shepherd blood in it. Not from a station dog. Some desert traveller either lost a dog or abandoned it. This isn't the city. Out here it's primeval power that reigns. We'll never tame it.'

They were rounding the side of the homestead, out of the broad reach of the exterior lights and their excessive brightness. Unknown to them they were walking towards a dark figure who had broken all the rules by entering the home compound and then, seeing them emerge from the house, swiftly withdrawn to a hiding place behind the stone archway that led to the vegetable and fruit gardens.

* * *

He couldn't make out what they were saying, and his hearing was razor-sharp. Their bodies had drawn close together. He warned himself to be careful. The man was the danger. The woman would present no problem. That was what he'd been told. By the Bitch—that was how he thought of her—who had treated him like scum, instead of as a trained professional whose expertise was unquestioned. Yet she was only too pleased to hire him to carry out her dirty work—like her grandfather before her.

He'd been furious when he'd first found out she knew all about him, what he had done for the Iron Man, how to contact him. He'd thought of it as blowing his cover. Where had she got her information from? He couldn't accept it was from the old man. Forsyth had known better than anyone how to cover his tracks. The Bitch had the same piercing blue eyes that seemed to see right through you. She was a real stunner, but he hated her. Hated her sort. A normal woman would think what she was asking him to do too monstrous to even put into words. Not her!

It hadn't taken him any time at all to land a job on the station and settle in. There weren't many jobs he couldn't handle. He had grown up on a small Outback cattle run, with a father who had beaten the hell out of him and his mother. He'd done what he had to do. He'd joined the army. Served in the world's trouble spots. That was where he had learned how to take care of business. These days he was more of a mercenary—bodyguard, security man, enforcer, contract guy.

Although he was a man of violence, he didn't like hurting women. Especially not one who looked like a Madonna. He had always stopped short of that. But the Bitch had too much on him, and she had only contempt for his fearsome reputation. Her grandfather had raised her in his image. He had to bide his time. He was in. An opportunity would arise. He felt a surge of rebellion. He didn't like it. He didn't like being dictated to by a woman—a woman, moreover, as ruthless as any enemy he had faced. The only good thing—if one could call it that—was that the Madonna wouldn't feel a thing...

Francesca thought she saw a blur out of the corner of her eye. It unnerved her. 'I'd like to go back now, Bryn,' she said quietly.

'Of course.' He caught the anxious note in her voice. 'Is anything wrong?' She had clutched his hand, as though to have him with her was everything.

'No. I just have an odd feeling we're being watched.'

'What?' Bryn jerked his head in the only direction there was cover. 'I'm sure there's no one about, Francey. None of the men would come up to the house at this time of night unless there was an emergency. They would identify themselves, anyway.'

'I know that.' Still she was caught fast in tendrils of panic.

'I'll take you back to the house, then I'll have a look around.' Bryn drew her closer to his side. 'It's moonlight. There's very little cover except for Jili's vegetable garden,' he pointed out. 'Perhaps it's being raided by a bird? Stand on the path and wait. I'll take a look.'

'No!' Her breath shuddered. 'It's like Carrie always says—I have too much imagination.'

'I'll check all the same,' he said.

'Be careful.' Vivid imagination or not, she was certain her internal radar had picked up some signal. Her heart beating hard, she waited for Bryn to return.

'Nothing,' he said, but he was not absolutely sure she hadn't picked up something. Francesca, even as a child, had had an extra sense.

They were back in the house. He checked all the doors on the ground floor, making it appear like a normal nightly ritual. No unauthorised person had ever dared invade the Forsyth privacy. No member of staff would arrive at the homestead unannounced. The men were all known to him, with the exception of the new guy, the big, burly Vance Bormann. He had questioned Roy Forster about the new arrival, but Roy had assured him Bormann checked out. Maybe it had been Gulla Nolan's ghost hanging around? There were many legends woven around Gulla. Maybe he was keeping an eye on the place?

'All right to go to bed,' he said, turning to face her. It wasn't meant as a question—though God knew he wanted it to be. Her beautiful eyes were like saucers, the black pupils enlarged. 'I'll take the bedroom opposite instead of down the hall, if you're nervous.'

'I'm not nervous with you here,' she said gratefully. 'That's if you're not *too* far away. I've never felt unsafe on Daramba before.'

Her tension was infectious. He felt a vague unease himself. Not that any trespasser on Daramba, let alone the homestead, wouldn't quickly see the error of his ways. The weapons in the gun room were kept under lock and key, but he knew where the key was and he was a crack shot. In a world gone mad, with violence escalating at a frightening rate, he'd had to confront the spectre of kidnap himself. It was always a possibility, but he thanked God he lived in a country where such things didn't happen. No one attacked giants of industry. His grandfather and Sir Francis had walked everywhere free as air. Their womenfolk and their offspring had also taken their safety completely for granted. But times had changed.

They were walking up the staircase together when Francesca, oddly off balance, surprised him with a question. 'Why did you tell Carina we were coming here this weekend?'

On edge himself, his answer was short and clipped. 'You're priceless—really.'

'What does that mean?'

'I've no time for all this nonsense about Carina.'

They had reached the gallery and he moved along it swiftly, a panther without its leash, so she had to increase her pace. He wanted to reach out for her. Hold her. His desire for her was pouring off him. Yet she chose to speak about Carina when all he wanted was to brush all thoughts of Carina aside.

'Well?' She caught his arm, feeling a stab of panic at the glitter in his eyes.

He swung about. 'What is it you want me to say?'

'God knows!' She dropped her hand, feeling confused and suddenly terribly lonely. 'I was a little hurt, that's all.'

'You mean you continue to believe *everything* she tells you?' He knew he was getting angrier by the moment, but for once he couldn't seem to get control. He moved off again, opening the door of the bedroom opposite hers. Unlike the one he usually occupied on his visits it wasn't made up, but who the hell cared? He wouldn't be getting any sleep.

'Don't be like this, Bryn,' she pleaded, coming to stand, shimmering, within the frame of the door, tormenting him. Water nymphs didn't have a heart. Yet hadn't he taken her small breast in his hand? Felt the heart beat?

'Ah, give me a break!' he responded. 'Are we *ever* going to be free of bloody Carina? She's fed you so much misinformation and downright lies since you were a child you don't seem able to see through her.'

'Are you saying you *didn't* tell her?'

'I'm not saying anything,' he said. 'If I can't get through to you by now I ought to give up trying.'

She moved a little further into the room. 'Okay, then, she was lying. She said you made the first move. You rang her. It was then you told her we were coming here for the weekend.'

'There you go! It must be true.' If she came any nearer he really would lose it.

She paused at the brilliant glitter in his eyes. 'Bryn…please, Bryn…'

'Don't you *dare* cry. Don't *do* this!'

His eyes blazed at her. Her tears goaded him.

'I'm sorry,' she said. 'I'm a fool. Carrie gets so many hooks into me they not only pierce my skin they drag me down. You must hate me at times.'

'Oh, yes—*hate!*' He was so wound up his tone could have stripped the skin from her. But the pressure inside him was building at a tremendous rate. A part of his brain told him not to frighten her—his job was to protect her, not to take what she couldn't give—but her beauty was all around him, scenting the very air. It stripped him of all resistance.

He thought she began a little glide towards him. Surely she did? He was almost gone.

'Francey!' he groaned. 'Lord, girl, don't you know how much I want you? I can't keep this up any more.'

He couldn't look like that, speak like that, unless he meant it. There was an *ache* in his voice; the worst kind of pain. He was begging her to be true to herself. She extended her slender arm so her fingertips, light and soft as silk, were just brushing his face.

They burned him like a brand. He tensed, every rippling muscle in his body knotting.

'I was betrayed, Bryn,' she whispered. 'You were betrayed... I—'

Frantic now, feeling the throbbing hardness in his body, he pulled her forcibly to him, his head swimming with sexual excitement and his need so intense he turned her in an instant to being utterly pliant in his arms. 'Don't...don't talk, Francey. I can't wait for you any longer.'

Her heart banged against her ribs. He was so strong she felt physically helpless, yet her instinct told her he would never hurt her. 'Then *don't* wait!' she cried. She was able to bring up her hands, locking them around his neck, her hips consciously working themselves against his highly aroused body. 'I can't wait either.' She put everything she felt for him into her emotion-charged admission.

Briefly she had a glimpse of the change that came over him. The anger disappeared, to be replaced by male exultation in all its forms. His physical power, considerable at any time, had increased. Much taller than she, now he seemed to *tower* over her, A fierce not-to-be-denied hunger glowed out of his dark, glittering eyes.

Holding her beautiful mouth with his, Bryn lifted her in one smooth, effortless movement, as though her slender body was weightless, and carried her across the hallway to her bedroom opposite…

CHAPTER SEVEN

JUST ON A WEEK LATER, they all sat in Francesca's office in serious discussion. Francesca had abandoned her position behind her grandfather's massive desk in favour of a comfortable armchair between Elizabeth and Annette.

'Ah—here's coffee!' she said a little time later, looking towards the door.

Valerie Scott, having tapped on the door, now came in, pushing a trolley bearing a silver tray set with a sterling silver coffee service and the finest English bone china. The wonderful aroma was of coffee freshly made, not from any machine. That would have been out of the question. A three-tiered cakestand held delicate sandwiches and a selection of cup cakes, beautifully decorated.

Francesca held up a hand, smiling at the woman who was proving an unobtrusive but very efficient staff member. 'Thank you, Valerie. This looks lovely.'

'I hope you enjoy it.' Valerie returned the smile, which embraced the two very elegant seated ladies, both of whom she knew—as she knew all the families. Mrs Elizabeth Forsyth and Mrs Annette Macallan. If privately she was wondering what they were doing here, she gave not the slightest sign. Valerie knew the late Sir Francis had taken Elizabeth Forsyth's departure from the family very badly indeed. She knew Elizabeth had not been a beneficiary of Sir Francis's will. She also knew the Macallan women loathed her late ex-lover. So here they were all together, Francesca, Annette and Elizabeth, obviously in perfect harmony.

Or they thought they were. Valerie Scott withdrew quietly, shutting the door.

'I'm a bit surprised you've kept her on, Francey,' Elizabeth said after a moment, a vaguely worried frown between her brows. 'You know she was—'

'Yes.' Francesca headed Elizabeth off. 'Actually, it's working out quite well. She's efficient, and very discreet.'

'Really?' Elizabeth raised her eyebrows, a droll expression on her face. 'She didn't exactly keep a low profile with my dear father-in-law.'

Annette swallowed a laugh.

'She's on her own, Elizabeth,' Francesca explained. 'No husband to support her. I didn't have the heart to move her on.'

'God forbid she'd be left to sell real estate, like another ex-member of Frank's club,' Elizabeth said.

'Not Sally McGuiness?' Annette stared at her friend in mild shock.

'So I've been told,' Elizabeth answered breezily. 'But Sally is a happy-go-lucky kind of girl. She'll be okay.'

'Grandfather didn't leave either of them a razoo, for all their grand affairs,' Fra.ncesca said, thinking that wasn't quite fair.

'The word is he gave Valerie more than enough when he was alive,' Elizabeth, the irrepressible, revealed. 'Anyway, let's forget Valerie. But I wouldn't trust her with too much, Francey,' she warned. 'Remember she *was* sleeping with the enemy.'

'Name me someone he *didn't* sleep with,' Annette broke in, uncharacteristically waspish. She rose to her smartly shod feet, a beautiful woman, dark-haired, dark-eyed, still retaining her girlish figure even though she had taken a back seat in life. 'I'll be mother.' She started to pour the coffee. 'Have you spoken to anyone else about this, Francey? Outside of Bryn, that is?'

'No one,' Francesca confirmed. 'I take it neither of you are opposed to the idea? I do so want you aboard.'

'I'm in,' Elizabeth cried in jolly fashion, accepting her exquisite cup and saucer from her lifelong friend. 'Thanks, dear. I'll enjoy it. It's rather thrilling being a defector. A bit like Nureyev. You're not going to let us down are you, Annie?'

Annette suddenly looked nervous, sinking her teeth in her bottom lip. 'I don't know if I could pull my weight.' Carefully she placed a sandwich and a cup cake on each plate. 'I would hate to let you down, Francey. I've been so out of everything. Rather like a woman in a coma.'

'Time now to break out of it, love,' Elizabeth told her friend firmly. 'You're highly intelligent and you're utterly trustworthy. Francey needs people like us around her. That's why she's asked. It saddens me to say it, but you can bet your life my daughter, who doesn't wish to have anything to do with me, would like nothing better than to see Francey come a cropper. Not that it's likely to happen. I've had my ear to the ground, Francey, and the word is you're turning out trumps. Lady Macallan is still a real powerhouse. She can handle the Macallan side of things on her own. Francey and I need you here, Annie. Don't we, Francey?'

'It would make me feel so much more secure.' Francesca turned to Annette with an encouraging smile. 'The whole place is regularly swept for bugs—courtesy of the age we live in—but I still don't have a clue how Carrie found out Bryn and I were flying to Daramba last weekend. *She* told me it was Bryn.'

'She wanted to upset and confuse you,' Annette said, her expression showing a flicker of anger. 'I don't like to speak ill of anyone—' Annette reached out to pat Elizabeth's hand tenderly '—but if I were you, Francey, I'd take everything Carrie says from now on, especially in relation to Bryn, with a pinch of salt. We all know how she feels about him.'

Elizabeth sighed deeply. 'My daughter has never in her life been thwarted. Her grandfather and her father spoilt her terribly. Both of them rode roughshod over me. Charles has actually admitted it.'

'Really?' Annette asked quickly, rounding on her friend.

'A whole new Charles has emerged since his father died,' Elizabeth told them, going a little pink. 'I think he's trying to get back with me.'

'Are you going to let him?' Annette didn't look at all happy about that eventuality.

'We'll see!' Mischief shimmered out of Elizabeth's fine grey eyes. 'Charles was a different man in the early years, you know. It was later, after we lost Lionel when he began to turn into a control freak like Frank. Simply copied him. Though it *was* the way to go. The only one exempt was Carrie, who really needed a firm hand. Free of his father's dominance, and with Bryn taking over the reins at Titan, Charles isn't under tremendous stress every second. He's much better suited to being supportive.'

'Well, he has a way to go before he'll win *me* over, Liz,' Annette said with asperity. 'They gave you a bad time.'

'I know. I know. But it will never happen again!' Elizabeth stoutly raised her coffee cup. 'Of that you can be sure.' She took a long, appreciative sip. 'This coffee is very good. But for now, Annie, we've got to concentrate on helping Francey out. What d'you think?' She spoke briskly, having lived a long time with her friend's reluctance to participate in most endeavours. 'We need an answer, my girl. That means *today!*'

Annette buried her small nose in her own coffee cup. Then slowly she raised her head, her flashing smile lifting ten years off her. 'If you *really* want me, the answer is yes!'

'Let's get Valerie back in with a bottle of champagne,' Elizabeth suggested, full of cheer. She'd had serious reservations about Annette committing when Francesca had first spoken to her of her intentions. They both knew Annette had been letting the days of her life drift away, with time running out. It was enormously heartening to see that beautiful, flashing smile that her son had inherited along with her midnight-dark eyes. With any luck at all, Annette was back!

It was enough to move those who loved her to tears.

Francesca lost no time contacting the highly regarded landscape designer Gordon Carstairs. Lady Macallan had suggested him, and had probably swung the deal as she'd spoken to the designer directly. Carstairs had extensive experience, having worked on large estates in the United Kingdom as well as France, Italy, Austria and Greece. His home bases were London and Sydney. He had just returned from creating from scratch a very large private garden in Sri Lanka, so Francesca was able to approach him at a period when he was blessedly free. At least for a time.

They met several times, over lunch and at the office. Carstairs, in his mid-fifties, was a fine-looking man with a striking head of pewter-grey hair. A six footer, he was very lean and strong, with great ease and a charm of manner which must have worked well with his international clients. He and Francesca got on extremely well, having similar tastes. They soon decided on a date to fly out to Daramba, so Gordon could make a detailed study of the site which, as Francesca had explained to him was 'relatively leafless'. The date was set for the end of the month, which gave them ten days.

Francesca was right in the thick of foundation business, but she quickly found her job was made easier by having Elizabeth and Annette on board. The two women, close friends and on the same wavelength, consequently worked very well together, sometimes in tandem, depending on circumstance. Best of all, they shared a fierce commitment to Francey and an intense dedication—qualities that worked extremely well for Francey *and* the Forsyth Foundation. At the end of the day Elizabeth and Annette, being who they were, knew everyone who was anyone, and everyone knew them.

The big surprise was Annette. She had taken no time at all to break out of her shell. Once she had even joined Francesca and Gordon over lunch, blossoming in their company and asking Gordon a good many pertinent questions. She had been far more animated than Francesca had ever seen her. Indeed, although Francesca had made no comment to anyone, including Bryn, it seemed to her that Annette and Gordon had not only clicked, they had been instantly attracted to each other.

Annette had mourned her late husband for many years. Without a word being spoken, society had accepted that Annette Macallan would never remarry. No one could take her husband's place. No one had the temerity to try. It was as though she had died with him. All over! Such a waste! Her meeting with Gordon Carstairs had opened up a whole new frontier. Gordon was free. An early marriage had failed—with no children—although he told them he was still good friends with his ex-wife, who had since remarried.

Much, much too early to say, but Francesca had her hopes. Life flowed on like a river. Time now for Annette to be happy again.

Early evening, when the deep blue sky was lightening to mauve, Bryn let himself in to Francesca's apartment. He had his own key. Although he spoke to her on a daily basis, and again last thing at night, it wasn't enough since their weekend at Daramba.

As Titan's new CEO—it had caused scarcely a ripple on the stock market and in the business world—he had begun initiating many changes, holding meeting after meeting. Not all of them had gone smoothly. But he had fully expected that. He was still explaining to the new people he had put in place precisely what he wanted. It was a hands-on affair, an all out effort, so he could be sure his new policies would not only be thoroughly understood, but implemented a.s.a.p. There never seemed to be enough time.

He was also part—'an important part', as the Premier of the

State had stressed—of a trade delegation leaving for China in two days' time. China was their major trading partner. He only wished that like his country's Prime Minister he was fluent in Mandarin.

He had a romantic evening planned. A very special night! They weren't going out to dinner. Both of them wanted to stay at home. Francey had assured him she was already stocked up. Not that he cared so much about dinner. It was Francey he was hungry for. Every minute they spent with each other was precious. They didn't want anyone else around.

He put his attaché case down, shrugged out of his jacket, then walked to the drinks trolley, thinking he would have a Scotch on the rocks while he was waiting. Francey had promised him she would be home by seven. He couldn't wait to see her. Her beauty, her intelligence, her emotional capacity overwhelmed him. It was the sweetest, sweetest pain just thinking about her when they were apart.

High time they were at the very least engaged. Maybe six months on they could set a wedding date. He loved her to the point where he couldn't do without her. He wanted her always *there,* at his side. He and Francesca made quite a pair. He and his grandmother were enormously grateful to her for the way she had coaxed his mother onto her team. It had been a huge coup. He hadn't seen his mother so whole heartedly involved in life since before his father had died. Not only had she become entirely 'with it', she had updated every aspect of her appearance. Always beautiful and quietly elegant, her new and more youthful image was drawing a lot of positive attention.

'Annette has come back to us!' his grandmother had said. 'And who do we thank but our little Francey?'

Francesca took a phone call from Carina a bare ten minutes before she wanted to leave the building. It had come as a puzzlement to her, the way Carina had turned virtually overnight into the sort of cousin she had always wanted. They had only met up once or twice since their grandfather's death, and then only for coffee—Francesca had too many demands on her time—but Carina had dropped her hard brilliance in favour of a much softer, more affectionate approach. She rang at least once a week—'just keeping in touch!'—even going so far as to say she was okay with the fact her mother and Annette Macallan were now working for the Forsyth Foundation.

'A little bird tells me Annette has taken a shine to the landscaper Gordon Carstairs,' she announced now, as though imparting a secret pleasing to them both. 'That's lovely. I know how much Annette adored her husband, but let's face it, life goes on. She's still only young. What? Fifty? She deserves some happiness.'

She did indeed, thought Francesca, but there was something not *right* about Carrie's saying it. Carrie had been quite scathing about Annette and her withdrawal from life in the past. 'It's hardly gone as far as that, Carrie,' she answered, brushing Gordon aside. But all in a good cause. 'You're remarkably well informed.'

Carina gave a laugh as sharp as a piece of broken glass. 'For goodness' sake, Francey, everyone knows Mum and Annette are working for you. As for Carstairs—who, incidentally, is quite a hunk for his age—friends of mine were seated at a table not far from the three of you in a restaurant.'

'What restaurant?'

'Gosh, I dunno. One of the top. It's hard to keep secrets, pet. Everyone knows what's going on. What I particularly wanted to ask you is, when next you go to Daramba could I please come too? I'd love to meet Gordon. I've been thinking we need a really first-class landscaper at the house. Dad doesn't care what changes I make. I suppose you know he's trying to win Mum back?'

Francesca swallowed. Carrie at Daramba? 'And how do you feel about that—seeing *you* haven't contacted your mother?' She played for time.

Carina's soft chuckle came over the wires. 'You know I want to. But, look—it ain't easy. As for Mum and Dad getting back together again—I'd be *thrilled.*'

'Nice if you'd ring and tell her that,' Francesca said. 'As for their getting back together, that's up to Liz.'

'Absolutely!' Carina confirmed. 'Now, about Daramba?'

Francesca sat back in her chair, half horrified by the request. 'Carrie, I don't—'

'Please!' her cousin interrupted. 'I don't ask for much. Besides, it will do us both good to spend time together.'

'I'll get back to you,' Francesca promised at last. 'But for now I must fly.'

'Bye-bye, then,' Carina carolled breezily. 'It must be time for you to walk out the door. You know what they say. All work and no play… Dinner at home with Bryn this evening?'

It was very difficult to get a handle on this new and yet familiar Carina. How did she know so much? Or was she simply fishing? On the other hand, it could all be true. Carina had simply turned into a better person. 'No plans as yet, Carrie.'

'Give him my love. And wish him a safe trip from me. Bryn is a wonderful ambassador for this country,' she said warmly, with no trace whatsoever of lingering bitter resentment. 'No wonder you look to him for everything.' There was a pregnant pause, as if Carina was expecting a prompt response. None was forthcoming. 'Lovely to talk to you, Francey,' she said into the void. 'And thanks for everything. For being so understanding. I know my behaviour has caused you a lot of grief. But that's all over now. First cousins are meant by the very nature of things to be close. Don't forget, now. Give me a ring. I feel so much better about our relationship these days, don't you?'

Francesca tried desperately to inject an answering warmth into her voice. 'I always wanted us to be the best of friends, Carrie,' she said. Lord knew it was true. But what would it take? She had glimpsed their grandfather in Carrie once too often. These present overtures could be nothing more than Carina's sugar-coated controlling mechanisms. Uncertain in her judgement, Francesca eased back. Surely Carina deserved a second chance? 'Bye, now, Carrie,' she said gently. 'Take care.'

Carefully she put the receiver down, breaking the connection. The truth was—and she couldn't suppress it—she didn't want Carina on Daramba. Especially not when Annette and Gordon were there. She wanted harmony, not trouble. She knew both Annette and Carina's own mother, Elizabeth, were convinced Carina was merely playing games.

'Happy families!' Elizabeth had remarked, with considerable irony.

It was something of a dilemma. If Carina really had undergone a miraculous sea change wouldn't she be bitterly insulted, perhaps irrevocably, if she were denied an invitation to Daramba? After all it was the flagship of the Forsyth pastoral empire, and Carina was very much a Forsyth. It was quite possible Carina genuinely intended to bring a top-class landscaper in, to create a more beautiful and softening environment for the Forsyth mausoleum.

If she said yes to Carina there could be no going back on it. Saying no would be the truly difficult part. She and Carina were of the same blood.

Only blood had been let.

She was no sooner in the door, calling jubilantly, 'I'm home!' when Bryn appeared—so vivid, so remarkable. In his presence her energies were recharged.

'It's marvellous to see you!'

She laughed. 'How long has it been since I've seen you?'

'Getting on for fifty-eight hours too long,' he replied, drawing her with an electrifying desire into his arms. 'And, God, how I've missed you! Every second of the day, and worse at night!' Black eyes tender but turbulent, he thrust his strong hand into her lustrous hair as he positioned her face at exactly the right angle for his passionate, welcoming kiss.

Predictably, it turned into kiss…after kiss…after kiss…

Delicate, tantalising little nips and nuzzles, starving little exhalations, in between open-mouthed expressions of the deepest desire, rapidly passing to a tension that built so mercilessly high that kissing was nowhere near enough. They wanted to go to bed. Each was bent on seeking the ultimate physical contact, yearning bodies fused, limbs entwined. Consummation was sublime—especially when they had been deprived of each other for even a short time.

'I understand that,' she whispered.

Neither of them spoke again as he began removing her structured black jacket with its nipped-in waist, turning away briefly to place it over the back of one of the antique Regency chairs that stood on either side of the console. That done, he began slowly unbuttoning her silk blouse. The front was ruched, the colour an exquisite teal-blue. Francesca's every last barricade was long since demolished. Bryn had held up a mirror to her own beauty; to its softness, voluptuousness and, for him, its utter desirability. When they made love, which was every time they came together, they did so with a flawless intensity—as if each was desperate to find out what lay behind the flesh of the other. It was truly as though they both sought to be *one.*

He broke off nuzzling the swan curve of her neck. 'Dinner can wait?'

She thought she murmured, 'Yes!' But she couldn't be sure, her emotions were so extravagantly unbridled.

'I'll take that as a yes.' He laughed deep in his throat, a man at peace, but his hands on her were urgent.

Finally she stood naked, as slender as a water reed, her feverish blood colouring her olive skin pink.

'At last we're alone!' he groaned. 'The more I get of you, the more I want!'

'It's the same with me.' The profound truth.

'Wonderful!' He hugged her warm body to him, his hand

pressed against the smooth curve of her lower back. 'Communion like we have, Francey, comes rarely.'

A stab of fear touched her heart. 'Bryn, no—hush!' She stopped him by placing a warning finger against his lips. 'Is it possible to love too much? It could attract the attention of jealous gods.' That flicker of fear—the fear of loss—showed in her beautiful eyes.

'Then we have to draw a magic circle around us,' he answered, wrapping his arms fiercely around her. 'When you go to Daramba at the weekend speak to Jili. She's right up there with the magic potions and spells. Whatever the past, Francey, and our personal tragedies, we have to leave them behind and face the future with confidence. From now on I'll always be by your side.'

Dinner had been forgotten. They lay quietly in bed, in thrall with one another, only the faint echoes of their impassioned moans left inside the room. All energy was spent, so overwhelming had been their lovemaking. Bryn lay on his back, one arm behind his dark head, and Francesca spooned into him, her heartbeat striking into his side, one arm flung across his naked chest, one foot hooked around his ankle.

'You're the most wonderful lover in the entire universe!' she gasped, her fingers working the hair on his chest into tiny curls. 'That was ravishing!'

'*You're* ravishing,' he replied, dropping a kiss on the top of her head. Conversation was out of the question. They were still floating in the aftermath of sexual bliss. After a few more minutes of drifting, Bryn suddenly said, 'By the way, I've got something for you.'

'You've always got something for me.' She smiled. Flowers, jewellery, a beautiful piece of Chinese porcelain to add to her collection…

'You haven't asked what it is.' He slid out of the tangle of sheets, a living sculpture, his naked body lightly sheened with sweat, little scratches from her long nails showing faintly red against the gilded bronze of his flesh. She had never in her life scratched a man before Bryn.

'Show me,' she invited, luxuriously stretching her legs and curling her toes. With the way they made love, she had inevitably began thinking about the children they would have in, say, a year or so. The power they had to make new life she found sacred. So tragically deprived of her parents, and at such an early age, she had the most intense desire to have a family of her own. Bryn's child, her child—their kids. Beautiful children, to reinforce their great love. Her path in life that had once been littered with pain and confusion was now clear. No more dead ends. No more dark alleys. Home was Bryn.

He was saying something. What?

'I have every intention of showing you. First I'll find my robe. I need to look my best.'

'You look your best now!' Her laugh rippled. She was in awe of his superb physique. 'Your robe is behind the bathroom door, where you left it.' She pushed another pillow behind her head. What was it this time? It didn't matter. It could be a cone shell off the beach. She would still love it.

He was back within a minute, wearing the dark red robe that made such a splash of colour against his darkly tanned skin, and carrying a tiny box in his hand.

She sat up quickly, saying tremulously, 'Bryn?'

'You never suspected?'

'No.'

'I don't believe you.' He sat down on the bed beside her.

'It's true.' She felt such a rush of excitement it was hard to stop her voice trembling.

'You *are* going to marry me?' His dark eyes swept her lovely face, seeing her sudden agitation.

'Oh, yes—*yes,* please.' She articulated it as though reciting a vow. 'I adore you.'

'Then we have to get engaged first—don't you agree?' he asked quietly.

'Oh, Bryn!' She tossed her long hair, damp at the temples, from her face, so it cascaded down her bare back. Just as she was thinking herself strong and secure she experienced a tiny frisson of fear about the timing. She had endured too many years of Carina's conditioning to throw off her cousin's influence overnight. Despite Carina's apparent coming to terms with their new lives and status, she felt thoroughly unnerved by the prospect that Carina mightn't be able to handle the fact of an engagement between her and Bryn so soon! Not that Bryn wouldn't be there for her—her rock in life.

'I thought we were going to wait a while?'

'Unacceptable. I live and breathe *you.*'

Such knowledge was thrilling, yet it scared her a little. Certain people were destined for loss. One saw it all the time.

Bryn touched a finger to the beating pulse in her throat. 'You're too tender-hearted for you own good, Francey. You're thinking of how Carina will react?'

She looked away. She couldn't hide a thing from him. He knew her too well.

'No, look at me,' Bryn said, and made sure of it by placing his hand firmly around her chin. 'You feel sorry for her?'

'Of course I do.' Her iridescent eyes pleaded with him for understanding. 'She *is* my cousin. She's been reared to believe in her divine right to have everything she wants.'

'And you're convinced she wants *me*?' He gave a slight and dangerous smile.

'You know she does. When it comes to you she's a bit deranged. All this current stuff, the way she goes on, is false. At least I *think* it's false.'

'Francey, you have to make up your mind. While Carrie has been supposedly so hotly desirous of me she's been living a downright promiscuous life. And she's been quite vocal about it.'

'Just distractions!' Francesca wrote her cousin's multiple short lived affairs off. 'Trying to make you jealous. I don't know. Who knows Carrie? Not even her mother.' Colour swept into her cheeks. 'I love you, Bryn. God knows, I love you. I want to announce our engagement too.'

'You think this is a *ring*?'

'Isn't it?' Her eyes went wide.

'Of course it is!' He dropped a chastening kiss on her mouth. 'Why don't you have a look?'

'You're angry with me,' she said.

'Not yet.' But his look was very direct. 'Open the box, Francey. I love you. I've always loved you. I want to spend the rest of my life with you. I want you to be the mother of our children. But I'm damned if I'm going to let Carina into our magic circle. If she could, Carina would deny you any chance at happiness. She has wanted nothing more than that since she was a child. Not even me. Surely to God you've come to that realisation?'

'Yes, I have. But it's still a bit new. She's so clever. I was starting to think maybe she really *wanted* us to be friends.'

'Then you'd better think again,' Bryn said, his voice bone-dry.

'All I want to think of is you and me.'

'That's my girl!' he said with open exultation.

Her heart contracted at the sight of the diamond engagement ring that sat so proudly inside the silk-lined box. It was glorious! A great ring for a great occasion! The glittering central stone was a flawless white, its brilliance offset by a garland of precious Arygle pink diamonds from their own Western Australia mines in the fabled Kimberley region. Argyle was the world's major source of rare pink diamonds, and this ring's masterly designer had used them to the utmost effect.

'Well?' he asked tenderly, sympathetic to the pile-up of emotions that had to some extent wounded her psyche.

She stared into his dynamic face, half in shadow, half in

gilded light. 'I couldn't have wished for a more perfect ring. I love it. I love *you!*'

'I was aware of that, my darling,' he said gently. 'But hang on!' Swiftly, he rose. 'This calls for a toast. This calls for champagne.'

'It does.' She went to get out of bed to join him.

'No, stay there.' He held up a hand. 'I want you in bed. I'll be back in a moment.'

He returned with a bottle of champagne and two crystal flutes. He put the flutes down gently, then grasped the base of the bottle with one hand, the other stripping away the foil. 'Now, this is a trick of mine, Francey. Watch carefully. I won't lose a drop.' With his thumb he dislodged the cork and it flew away, landing safely on the carpet.

'Bravo!' She clapped her hands. 'I'm impressed.'

'I have other skills.'

'I *know!*' She blushed deeply all over her body.

They sipped their champagne slowly, observing one another with elated and loving eyes. Bryn had already slipped the ring down over her slender finger, where it sat perfectly.

'It may be that you don't want to wear your ring openly until I get back from China,' he said, correctly gauging her transparent expression. 'I understand you want me with you when we announce our engagement.'

'I do.'

'Okay.' He lifted her hand and kissed it, turning it to press his mouth to the inner tracery of blue veins. 'Let it dwell between your breasts,' he said, and bent to kiss that scented spot. 'But when I get back we make the announcement—agreed?'

'Yes,' she breathed softly, holding up her left hand to the light. 'This is something I could only dream about.'

'No dream, my darling.' His sense of purpose and determination showed itself in his voice and the glitter of his eyes. 'Drink up,' he urged. 'I want to make love to you all over again.'

CHAPTER EIGHT

SHE HADN'T FOR a moment expected Annette to want to join the hunt for the killer dingo. Annette was a good rider, but hunting down rogue animals wasn't her thing. For one thing she had never fired a gun in her life, though she had been a guest on great Outback cattle stations many times in her life. No, Annette shied away from any form of violence, especially blood and killing, but violence was being done to Daramba's precious calves, too weak to save themselves, or to old and helpless animals that roamed the desert fringe.

Bloodthirsty dingoes struck terror. The most vicious and powerful had been known to attack a lone man. Daramba's men had by now taken to calling the dingo crossbreed The Ripper, because of the powerful animal's peculiarly brutal manner of ripping open the flesh of all the unfortunate calves it had stalked and brought down. It wasn't simply hunger, the need to sustain itself, the brute had developed a taste for blood.

The new man, Vance Bormann, out rounding up clean skins in the lignum thickets over the past few days, had sighted the dingo away from the pack. He had taken a shot at it—and he hated to admit it but The Ripper had got away, bounding off into the farther reaches of the lignum swamp. At least it gave them a clue as to where the dingo pack was currently hiding out. Bormann had told them he had found, to his disgust, the carcass of a newborn calf at the scene and buried it.

So the hunt was on. Gordon Carstairs very much wanted to be part of it. He told them quite matter-of-factly he was a good shot and an experienced rider. He'd grown up on a Victorian country estate, and although he hadn't been asked to prove it, after ten minutes with Jacob, who was now Daramba's overseer, Jacob had come back to Francesca with: 'He's a damned fine shot, Ms Francey. It'll be good to have 'im along.'

Annette, it seemed, had got caught up in the excitement. Or perhaps more accurately caught up in the excitement of Gordon Carstairs. Francesca was certain Annette had never expected to find love again—indeed she had turned her back on it—but the strong attraction between the two was plain to see. So Annette wanted to come along, but she would ride to the rear, ready if necessary to box the dingo in. That was if they were lucky enough to sight it or the pack.

'What the hell does Annette think she's doing, riding along?' Carina asked Francesca, angry bafflement on her face. She paused for a moment, as though seeking a solution to a serious problem. 'By far the most sensible thing for her to be doing is staying here at the homestead. You should insist. She'll only be a liability.'

Francesca couldn't really argue with that, but she hadn't had the heart to refuse Annette any more than she had found the heart to exclude Carina from this trip. So far everything had gone well, with Carina as charming and accommodating as Francesca had ever seen her. Now she had to intervene. 'Please don't say that to her, Carrie. Annette is the happiest I've ever seen her. I'm not going to allow anyone to spoil that. You've been so nice to her up to date. Don't spoil it now.'

'Sure!' Carina appeared to shrug her bafflement off. 'It's Gordon, of course!' She gave a knowing laugh. 'He's an old-fashioned man in his way—very gentlemanly and so forth. Annette would like that.'

'I like it too,' Francesca said. Were good manners old-fashioned? She thought not.

'Well, you and Annette aren't dissimilar in type,' Carina said, giving her cousin a considering once-over. 'You know—super-refined. I expect that's why Bryn decided you were more suitable than me. I'm too *out there.* It wouldn't have worked with Bryn and me anyway. I suppose that's why I've found it so easy to move on.' She went to press a real kiss onto Francesca's cheek. The first one Francesca had ever received. 'The great thing is that we're talking, Francey. We're friends again. If Carstairs is in favour with poor Annette, then he's in favour with me.'

Half the hunt got away early: Jacob, Carina—who could ride and shoot with the best of them—Vince Bormann, and two of the station's leading hands. Francesca, Gordon, Annette and three aboriginal stockmen-trackers followed. The sun was up and the mirage was already abroad. Francesca made sure Annette's fine skin was protected, swapping her own best cream Akubra with the ornate snakeskin band for Annette's less effective wide-brimmed black hat, and tucking a favourite sapphire-blue and white bandana into the neckline of Annette's long-sleeved cotton shirt to protect her nape. She wore the full-length sleeves for extra protection, but it wasn't long before Francesca saw her turning the cuffs up to the elbow. All in all, Annette looked immensely stylish. As slender as when she'd been a girl in her riding gear—especially the tight-fitting jeans, which looked great on her. Francesca could see Gordon thought so too.

Mid-morning and The Ripper hadn't been sighted—although the party had flushed out a few dingoes, their yellow-brown coats merging with the colour and texture of the scorched grasses. Spotted, they'd made a run for the hill country, moving at top speed, their desert-lean bodies flattened out with the effort. Jacob had waved a hand, which meant let them go. No love was lost on dingoes, but it was The Ripper they were after. They were to concentrate all their energies on that.

They were all strung out over a broad area of hundreds of yards. Francesca and Annette were away to the rear, with Francesca keeping her eye on the older woman. The horses were tiring. Morale was running low.

'What the hell?' Carina was way ahead, with one of the stockmen. When she shouted, her voice carried a long distance on the clear air. She threw up a hand, gesturing towards a dried-up water course with a heavy surround of trees.

What was she shouting for? Francesca had to ask herself. If Carina *had* spotted The Ripper she would only alert the cunning animal. A glance passed between her and Annette. 'Do you want to go back now, Annette?' Francesca asked. 'You could take shelter under the trees.'

'I just might!' Annette said, a look of relief coming over her face.

'It's very tiring,' Francesca said quietly. 'I'm starting to feel a little shaky myself. My muscles haven't had such a workout in ages.'

Annette nodded, then turned her horse's head in the direction of the nearest billabong. 'Are you going on?'

'Just for a while,' Francesca said. 'Stay in the vicinity. We'll come back for you.'

'I'm fine, Francey. Don't worry. I know where I am,' Annette told her with a reassuring smile. 'Good luck now.'

For some reason Francesca didn't take the route the rest of them had taken. She had the feeling she was being led, that her route was charged with more purpose than finding the rogue dingo. She was *meant* to come this way. For most of her life she had had these mysterious intuitions. She wondered if other people did. Surely they must?

Riding deep in under the trees, she saw to her left a waterhole, glittering like a shallow lake, though she knew from experience it would be deep enough at the centre. Something splashed close in to the reed banks. She froze.

Nothing, though her skin was prickling. Gamely she rode on, her face and her neck streaked with sweat, rivulets running between her breasts. The air was getting thicker and danker. Her nerves were crawling. The deeper in she went, the more she thought she could smell dingo. The others were coming back now. Unsuccessful. She could hear raised voices, the thunder of hooves. She even caught Jacob's dejected yell.

'The bastard ain't here, or he got away!'

Her shoulders rode high and tight. She was very nervous. So was Jalilah. Just a few hundred yards on, the dark green undergrowth became thicker, darker and more tangled, making it difficult for her to proceed or continue searching for tracks. But the smell of dingo *filled* her nostrils. Dread began a slow crawl over her skin. This, then, was where their quarry was waiting. She knew it. She had succumbed to the compulsion. Now alone, she was riding right at The Ripper.

It was enormous for a pure-bred dingo. It was difficult to say who took the most fright. The dingo, in a lather of sweat so its matted coat looked a mangy, orange-streaked grey, slunk back, crouching down on its haunches. No use trying to keep it off by shouting or clapping. She could see that wouldn't work. The dingo was intent on her. Teeth bared, it looked at her with what seemed like human hatred, though that had to be her overactive imagination. Nevertheless it made the short hairs stand up on the back of her neck.

The animal began to snarl, its ferocity and sheer size bringing on a moment of sheer panic. She had seen dingoes all her life, but nothing like this. This wasn't the average wild dog. This was a monster. It wasn't going to retreat. But Francesca's nerves had begun to attack, and the mare, spooked by the presence of the dingo, was acting up. Dingo or not, it looked more like a lion ready to spring.

It couldn't reach her upper body—or could it?—but it could savage her foot, or Jalilah's legs and sides. She heard shots. Marvelled at them. One seemed very close. Too close. She hadn't expected that one. Her hands that one moment had been shaky now steadied on the .22 rifle. She had a job to do. This was *her* world, and this was one dingo who had to go.

'All right—come on!' Francesca muttered at the beast, in the process passing on courage to herself. 'Come *on!*'

The dingo needed no further urging. It leapt for her, as though she were no more than its next victim to be ripped to shreds, but Francesca, ice-cool, got off a single shot.

The bullet sped to its mark, penetrating the rogue dingo's brain.

Hey, little one!

Near startled out of her wits, Francesca swung her head sharply. She didn't know the soft voice, but it was aboriginal. There was no one in sight, which her mind found unacceptable.

Hey, little one, can you hear me?

The voice came again. From where? The waterhole? The reeds were flattened over a wide area. The dingo had most probably torn through the area, snapping them off. It seemed to her for a trance-like moment that the grasses were stained with blood. She blinked, by now dumbstruck, and when she opened her eyes again the bloodstains were gone. Incredible! Her body rocked a little in the saddle. The heat and the kill. It was proving too much for her.

'Who's there?' she called, trying to inject authority into her shaky voice. 'Show yourself.'

What did she expect? An aboriginal figure to slide out of the water and into her field of vision? The voice *was* aboriginal. No question. But now, to her further astonishment, the whole scene that had been bathed in a deep green gloom changed dramatically. The sun slanted through the high branches of the Red River gums, vividly illuminating the deep waterhole.

Francesca sat her horse, confounded, watching ripples fan

out wide over the water. There was no wind. No movement in the air. The branches of the trees were still. She felt as if she was having an out of body experience, but curiously she was not alarmed. Someone, some entity, was trying to tell her something. Make her pay attention. A vivid imagination was part of her. She had to accept that. It worked supremely well for her as an artist, but sometimes it could work against her. She listened a little longer. Nothing. She tried to remember who had called her *little one.* The 'one' had been clearly articulated. Taree Newton had always called her *little 'un.* It wasn't Taree's voice. Aboriginal, but more city-educated. She would have been very glad to see him, but Taree hadn't come on the hunt. At his age, he wasn't up to it. A memory long forgotten stirred, then as quickly faded out.

'I'll come back,' she promised, though she couldn't begin to explain why she said it, or to whom.

The mare delicately skirted the body of the dead dingo, hoofs high, returning almost of its own accord along the rough trail Francesca had blazed. It wasn't until she reached the open plain that she saw Carina, riding towards her as if a gang of cattle rustlers was hot on her trail. Her mount looked almost out of control, though Carina was an experienced rider. When she and Francesca met up, a hundred yards off, Francesca saw her cousin's face was streaming with tears. Carina was sobbing, struggling for breath. In an instant Francesca's heart went cold with fear. She had never in her life seen her cousin in such a state.

'There's been an accident,' Carina gasped, swiping the wetness from her face, her hand like a washcloth. 'Annette. She's been shot.'

'Dear God, no!' A fine trembling started up in Francesca, spreading from her chest into her stomach and limbs. Had Annette been brought down by the shots that had preceded her own? Sick to the point where bile was rising to her throat, Francesca kicked her mare into action. Unless she had shifted out of the designated area, Annette should have been perfectly safe.

* * *

Annette had been extremely lucky. The only reason she was still alive was at the last moment the man sent to terminate Francesca Forsyth's life had realised he was targeting the wrong woman. Abruptly he had changed aim, so that the bullet glanced off her arm, high up, near the shoulder. Fool that he was, he had mistaken Annette Macallan for his target. The woman was of a height, with the same very slender build, and she was wearing the cream Akubra and the blue bandana he had been alerted to look for. Even when she had turned her head she had momentarily confused him. She was a beautiful woman, but at the very least twenty or more years older than his target. There would be no pay-off for killing the wrong woman.

Swiftly Bormann had remounted, then ridden like the wind. When the woman was found he would be nowhere near her. Some of the others had got off a few shots. Hadn't he and the Bitch been the ones to incite them? This whole thing was an accident. The woman could hardly say otherwise. She hadn't even been aware of him.

It was Bryn when he returned home—he had cut short his China trip—who hit on his own theory for the shooting 'accident'. It came to him the instant his mother mentioned in passing that she had been wearing Francesca's Akubra, and that Francesca had also lent her a blue bandana to protect the vulnerable skin of her nape. He took time to think it out. His mind searched for alternative explanations for the bizarre incident, but nothing carried the weight or the logic of his own scenario.

Francesca had been the target. Not his mother. Not that he could alarm Francesca by telling her that. What proof did he have, anyway?

His mother had started walking the length of the lagoon when she had heard shots being fired. There had been a lot of shouting as well. She had grown afraid. Everyone in the party had an alibi, if indeed an alibi was needed. He could be wrong. There were no witnesses to anything. Quite a few shots had been fired to flush out the animal. No one else believed for a moment it was anything but a near tragic accident. There was no reason in the world for anyone to want to hurt Mrs Macallan. She had been in the wrong place at the wrong time. The stray bullet had mercifully glanced off her shoulder. All the flowing blood had made the injury seem much worse than it actually was.

His mother was already on her way to a full recovery, with Gordon Carstairs dancing attendance, seemingly unable to get back to work. Annette would bear a scar, but nothing cosmetic surgery couldn't fix. Everyone on the station had been extremely upset. Carina had needed sedation, so severe had been her reaction. Francesca had astonished herself by taking charge. No police had been called in. It would have taken hours for them to get there in any case. Daramba had always looked after its own. A doctor well known to them had been flown in to attend to Annette.

Even so, Carina had been quite right. Annette should have stayed back at the homestead, where she would have been perfectly safe. Francesca felt she had to bear a lot of the blame, though Annette wouldn't hear a word of it.

'My own fault, Francey,' she said, gently holding Francesca's hand. 'You told me to stay put, not walk into the danger zone.'

Still her son was not convinced. And what the hell was that? Carina requiring sedation? Carina and his mother had never got on. More likely Carina was hiding from a plan gone wrong. Bryn thought back to how at the end his grandfather had come to believe his partner had got rid of Gulla Nolan. Frank Forsyth would have had his reasons. Gulla might have had something on him. It had been no accident at all. Carina had more than a dollop of her ruthless, unforgiving grandfather's blood. And she was an excellent markswoman. When she'd realised she had the wrong target in her sights, she'd veered off before making her getaway. No one was likely to suspect let alone question a Forsyth. A woman, moreover, so distressed she had to be sedated.

All the more reason to get Carina to admit it, Bryn thought. Francesca had to be protected at all costs.

It was Elizabeth who gave him the lever. She was the one to unmask the mole in their midst. She had gone to Valerie Scott to ask for the schedule for any upcoming meetings Francesca was to have with those seeking potential grants. She had, in fact, fully expected to have the schedule on her desk that morning. Not finding Valerie in her place, Elizabeth had decided the schedule was most probably in a drawer. When it was not easily sighted amid the paperwork, Elizabeth had pulled out an entire drawer to give it a thorough search. It was then she'd come upon what she'd at first thought was a state-of-the-art mobile phone. She had never come across one like it.

She was busy examining it, frowning in a troubled fashion, when Valerie returned from a visit to the restroom.

Elizabeth looked up and met the other woman's eyes. Immediately it struck Elizabeth like a bolt of lightning. Valerie Scott was their mole. It wasn't simply Valerie's violent flush that gave her away. Elizabeth had had her doubts about Mrs. Scott right from the beginning. Her loyalty could well have been given to her ex-lover's immediate family and not to Francesca, whom she must have thought of as a usurper. Elizabeth was certain that with this sophisticated gadget Valerie Scott would have been able to monitor all of Francesca's calls and pass on information. She might even have been able to relay the calls directly, for all Elizabeth knew. Right now it was a matter for security.

Elizabeth lost no time getting them up to the executive floor, motioning to the Scott woman—stricken now she was found out, and making no attempt to brazen it out—to sit down and await her fate.

* * *

'I can't believe it. I can't deal with it.' Bryn had just finished telling Francesca of his suspicions, and the reasons for them. 'Carrie couldn't want to *kill* me. She couldn't! That's a great sin.' Shock and revulsion were in Francesca's voice. 'Was she trying to frighten me off, do you think?'

'Frighten you off the planet,' Bryn retorted grimly, keeping his arms around her. 'I had Elizabeth ring her with a message from you saying you'd like her to come to the apartment this evening around seven, if she can make it. She told Liz she could.'

'But that's in twenty minutes.' Francesca's head shot up in agitation. 'Are we going to confront her?' She searched Bryn's brilliant dark eyes. 'What if you're wrong?'

'I'm not wrong, Francey,' he told her bluntly. 'I've spoken at length to my grandmother about Gulla Nolan. There's a tie-up here. She and I have never had this discussion before, but I guessed that towards the end my grandfather had come to believe Sir Francis had played a part in Gulla's disappearance. My grandmother said—and this stunned me—Gulla had once saved her from Frank's highly unwelcome advances. Apparently he'd always had a thing for my grandmother, since before my grandparents were married and they were all friends. Gulla threatened to shoot Frank on the spot. Just imagine it! He meant it too. Frank would never have forgotten. It was his way to get square. It's Carina's way as well. She's always wanted to get square with you. Did you tell her we were engaged?'

'No, no—of course not.' Her emotions were in tumult. 'I've told no one. We announce it together, as planned.'

'We announce it to Carina *tonight,*' Bryn told her. 'Or rather *you* announce it. Be wearing your ring. I'll be behind the scenes. You won't tell her I'm here until we're ready to confront her. By the way, Bormann has gone missing. Big surprise! He was part of the plot. He would have to have made contingency plans. We know about Valerie Scott's part in things. I intend to string it all together for dear Carrie.'

'This is a nightmare.' Francesca groaned. 'I couldn't face it without you, Bryn.'

'You're not without me. We're together.' Bryn kissed her hard.

His rage at Carina and her actions would never in a million years drain away. She really shouldn't be allowed to go free. She deserved jail. But the scandal! Francesca would hate that.

'The best way to get rid of a nightmare like Carina is to banish her somewhere she can't ever seek to harm you again,' he said forcefully. 'She's always loved Monte Carlo, hasn't she? All the money and glamour. She can take up residence there. We can't have a huge scandal. The smartest thing Carina can do is transplant herself to the other side of the world. It's just big enough. She has the money. She's in no position to fight us.'

Francesca lifted her head to stare into his masterful face. 'This is shocking, Bryn. The most obscene thing possible. Annette could have been killed.'

'Don't!' A shudder passed directly from him into her. Fears for the two of them—his mother and the woman he so desperately loved—hadn't yet subsided.

'I think I know where Gulla's remains are,' she said gently.

'Francey!' He sat there stunned, and more than a little spooked. She'd said it as if it was fact.

'When this is over I'll show you, as Gulla showed me. His people will want to give him a ceremonial burial.'

Urgently he pulled her across his knees, burying his face in her neck. 'Oh, God, Francey, you're the best, the bravest, the most beautiful woman in all the world.'

'And a little crazy?' For the first time that evening she smiled.

'Never! You're protected by the Light.'

It was something that would draw people to her all her life, Bryn thought, but it was only for him, her future husband, to bask in its flame. Carina was the one who was crazy. The time had come for her to be held responsible—at least in part—for her actions.

EPILOGUE

LADY MACALLAN HAD insisted on giving the official engagement party. The news had swept the city, causing widespread coverage, a deluge of congratulations, expressions of delight and a good many hastily-got-together gala parties.

The general opinion was that this was the best possible outcome for the Macallan-Forsyth clans. Not only that, the best possible outcome for the city and for the giant state of Western Australia. Many benefits would flow from the union between these two very powerful families.

It wasn't all that much of a surprise for the city to learn that Carina Forsyth had decided to quit 'the backwater of Perth' for the glamour and culture of Europe. If more than a few people responded with 'good riddance', Carina was not to hear it. She had lost no time quitting the country of her birth, with a cold and haughty, 'I don't expect to return.' She would, however, in the fullness of time, marry a bogus Italian prince…

The beautiful one-shouldered gown Francesca had chosen for her engagement party, a one-of-a-kind silk-satin in a vibrant shade of cerise, couldn't have been more perfect for such an occasion—nor more perfect as a showcase for her very slender, supple body When she arrived with Bryn at the great, graceful

Macallan mansion blazing with joy and pride, Lady Macallan took her aside to pin an heirloom sunburst of diamonds high on the gown's shoulder.

'It's gorgeous!' Francesca breathed, consumed with gratitude. She stared at her glowing reflection in the tall gilded mirror. 'I love it.'

'It looks wonderful on you!' Lady Macallan exclaimed, her beautifully coiffed head tipped to one side. 'And I think I always knew the girl I was going to pin it on.' She smiled. 'Welcome to the family, Francey.' Lightly she kissed Francesca's cheek. 'I couldn't be more happy for you and for Bryn. I adore my grandson. He is the light of my life. And I know he has loved you literally from childhood. Annette and I both knew. What I hadn't counted on was Annette finding a new love to fill *her* days,' she said with a chuckle. 'I expect she and Gordon will be married next, but I insist it's you and Bryn first.'

And that was exactly how it happened.

Charles Forsyth, happily reconciled with his wife, gave his beautiful niece away.

In front of the altar, with the Archbishop waiting to conduct the ceremony, the bride, exquisite in her bridal gown, a bouquet of white roses in her hand, her smile radiant, and the groom, in his finery a fitting match for his glorious bride, looked at one another with perfect understanding. Their love and happiness was so great it overflowed. It surged down the aisle and along the lavishly beribboned pews, so that the entire congregation was bathed in it, absorbing its wonderful glow.

Everything was absolutely *perfect.* Francesca even fancied she saw a shining vision of her parents. They were smiling at her, waving in silent valediction, before merging with the blaze of bejewelled light that poured through the cathedral's stained glass windows. Knowing herself blessed, Francesca turned her head to smile radiantly into the face of her soon-to-be husband.

His soul so beautifully complemented her own.

Love was the elusive key that opened up the door to an earthly happiness that made life complete.

* * * * *

Outback Doctor, English Bride

Leah Martyn

Leah Martyn loves to create warm, believable characters for the Medical™ Romance series. She is grounded firmly in rural Australia, and the special qualities of the bush are reflected in her stories. For plots and possibilities, she bounces ideas off her husband on their early-morning walks. Browsing in bookshops and buying an armful of new releases is high on her list of enjoyable things to do.

Recent titles by the same author:

THE DOCTOR'S PREGNANCY SECRET
A MOTHER FOR HIS BABY
DR CHRISTIE'S BRIDE
THE BUSH DOCTOR'S RESCUE
CHRISTMAS IN THE OUTBACK
THE DOCTOR'S MARRIAGE

CHAPTER ONE

FRUSTRATION WAS EATING him alive.

The regular flight for the week had been and gone and his locum hadn't been on board. So, where the hell was he?

Impatiently, Jake Haslem pushed a hand through the dark strands of his short hairstyle. 'Ayleen!' he yelled through the open door of his consulting room.

Ayleen Sykes, loosely titled Practice Manager, tipped a long-suffering gaze towards the ceiling, before swinging off her chair and walking across the corridor to Jake's consulting room. 'There was a reason we spent all that money and had the intercom phones installed, you know?' she said dryly from the doorway.

'Mmm. Forgot.' Jake gave one of his repentant twisted smiles. 'Could you call the agency in Sydney and see if they have any word on our locum's movements, please? He was supposed to be on today's plane.'

Ayleen glanced at her watch. 'Haven't you noticed the time, Jake? They'll have all gone home.'

Jake swore under his breath. He hadn't realised. Outback Australian summers meant daylight went on and on into the evening, until darkness fell as profoundly and quickly as a cloak thrown over the sun.

'I suppose I could email them,' Ayleen compromised. 'We'd possibly have an answer first thing tomorrow.'

'Sounds like a plan.' Jake gave a resigned open-handed shrug. 'Thanks.' As his receptionist disappeared back to her desk, he swung to his feet and went across to the open window, looking out at the heat-hazed landscape.

There was the smell of smoke in the air today. And smoke meant bush fires. Jake exhaled a long slow breath. Not *that* on top of everything else.

He was trying to do the best for his patients but he was finding it more difficult every day. Tangaratta was dry and dusty, struggling through the worst drought in memory. And just lately he'd begun doubting his sanity in relocating here shortly after he'd returned from England two years ago.

But with his dreams for the future in tatters, he'd wanted out of Sydney and the predictability of working civilised hours at the state-of-the-art medical centre. And that had been when he'd chosen the hard physical grind that went with practising medicine in a remote rural area. In a place where he could actually feel needed by his patients. He huffed a rueful grunt into the silence. Sometimes, like today, he wished he didn't feel quite so *needed.*

But, then, he had to admit that nothing had gone to plan since he'd arrived at what was supposedly a two-doctor practice. When he'd been in Tangaratta for only a month, a family emergency had driven his partner Tom Wilde back to the city. So now, many months on, Jake was still the sole family practitioner for the district, with the nearest large medical facility over two hundred kilometres away.

He reached up and rubbed a crick in the back of his neck. He couldn't go on like this. Every day the situation became more critical. And if *he* fell by the wayside then his patients would have no one. And now, more than ever, the welfare of his patients had to come first. He blew out a low, weary breath. And in the same breath made a decision. To hell with trying to entice a locum to come here. He needed something much more permanent.

He needed a partner.

A murmur of conversation from Reception had him turning and frowning. He didn't conduct an evening surgery and if someone was under the impression he did, they could think again. Unless it was an emergency, of course. But by the lilt of female conversation, it didn't seem so. Possibly one of Ayleen's tennis friends had come to collect her for their weekly night game…

Jake got no further with his speculation. Suddenly Ayleen was back at his door. 'Someone to see you, Dr Haslem,' she said formally. And sensing something private and of a confidential nature between her boss and his visitor was about to happen, she twinkled a finger wave and fled.

'What the—?' Jake's muttered response was cut short as a young woman stepped forward into the doorway, looking squarely at him across the space that divided them.

For a second Jake couldn't believe the evidence of his own eyes or the weird kind of sexual energy that rose out of nowhere to slice the air between them. His throat convulsed in a dry, deep swallow. His eyes weren't deceiving him. It *was* her.

In the flesh.

As gorgeous as he remembered. Tall and leggy, her cloud of red hair drawn back from her face and gathered loosely under the sassy little cap perched on the top of her head, the peak almost hiding the green of her eyes. In deference to the heat, she wore a white vest top and fatigue-styled pale olive cotton trousers.

Jake felt his heart go into freefall, the nerves in his stomach twist and grind painfully.

'What the hell are you doing here, Maxi?' he said into the nerve-crunching silence.

'Well, hello to you, too, Jacob.'

His mouth compressed and something like pain, no more than

a flicker crossed his face. No one, not even his mother, called him Jacob but on *her* tongue, with its precise little English accent, it sounded perfect. And suddenly he was pitched back to another time and another place.

And a lover he would never forget.

Had she expected way too much? That his attitude might have softened in the two years they'd been apart? Maxi felt the composure she'd drummed up slide away and be replaced by a tangling disquiet in the pit of her stomach. Even just *seeing* him had elevated her pulse to drumming proportions, her body humming like a high-energy electricity grid.

She bit hard on the inside of her bottom lip and harnessed her wayward thoughts. He obviously wasn't pleased to see her. That was an understatement. He wasn't far off oozing hostility, riveted to the spot, the vibe of tension around him almost palpable.

Maxi frowned uncertainly. This Jake Haslem hardly seemed the same man who had arrived at the emergency department of her London hospital as part of a six-month doctor-exchange programme. Then he'd seemed big and brash, loaded with self-assurance, his Australian accent and his tan in the middle of an English winter setting him apart. And she'd decided huffily that his manner had bordered on arrogance. He'd annoyed her, confused her. And she'd avoided him like the plague until the duty rosters had changed and they'd been thrown together shift after shift.

And she'd begun to know a different Jake Haslem.

He'd told her he was from Sydney, his mother was an MP.

'And your dad?' she'd asked him.

'Left us when I was thirteen.' He'd got a closed-in look about him suddenly. 'Went back to the States. He's big in mining. You might have heard of him, John J. Haslem?'

She'd shaken her head. 'And he's not been back to see you since?'

He'd given a one-shouldered shrug. 'Mum divorced him.

But he had the grace to settle an obscene sum of money on us. I'm a rich kid,' he'd added with his charm-laden grin. 'So what about you, Maxi Somers? What's your story?'

'My parents have a small farm in Kent.'

'Siblings?'

'Twin brother and younger sister. Large extended family.'

He'd made a face. 'Curse or blessing?'

Maxi had felt herself bridle and responded sharply, 'Always a blessing.'

'Hey, bear with me.' He'd held up his hands in self-defence, sending her a little-boy-lost look. 'I know nothing about big families and how they operate.'

'Then you'd better come down to Kent on your next days off and meet mine,' she'd said, almost cringing at the sudden huskiness in her voice.

And so it had begun. A love affair that had lasted three glorious months and ended in a mixed-up, emotional mess the day he'd flown back to Australia.

Now Maxi swallowed deeply, running a quick, critical gaze over him in case it told her something. He looked older, harder, but his tanned leanness was still there. She blinked a bit. There was no mistaking the fatigue in his eyes. He was obviously worked to death. Perhaps that accounted for the new look of hardness about him.

A lump came to her throat. Would he be receptive if *she* moved closer and gave him a hug for old times' sake? Probably not, if his body language and that narrowed steely blue gaze were anything to go by.

At last Jake found his voice. 'How did you find me?'

She moistened her lips. 'It wasn't too difficult. At first I thought I'd have to start calling every Haslem in the Sydney phone book. And then I remembered you'd said your mother was an MP. After that…' She flexed her hands. 'Easy as.'

Jake lowered his gaze. Why *now* suddenly had she come

here? Thousands of miles from everything that was familiar to her and for what?

Nostalgia for the past…? Hope for a possible future…? After the soul-destroying way they'd parted? Unlikely.

With a flick of his hand he motioned for her to take the chair at the side of his desk and then threw himself back into his own chair. 'So, Dr Somers.' His mouth twisted slightly over the formal use of her name. 'It's been two years. I don't imagine you've come for the scenery?'

Her heart gave an extra thud. How did she answer that? Honestly, if they were to have a chance of a reconciliation. 'I wanted to travel, see some of the world. I haven't come to apportion blame, if that's what you're thinking.'

In a second she saw a flash of his old arrogance. 'It hardly matters now, does it? As I recall, you dumped me at the airport barely an hour before my flight home.'

Maxi felt faintly sick. She hadn't expected them to get into it so immediately or so intensely. But then what had she expected? It was never going to be easy. 'You'd sprung a marriage proposal on me the day before,' she reminded him. 'You expected me to just up and follow you to the other side of the world.'

'I didn't have time to hang about while you made up your mind, Maxi,' he dismissed with a sharp thrust of his hand. 'My work visa had run out. I had to leave.'

'That's your excuse, Jacob,' she threw at him. 'You could have extended your visa. The hospital admin would have sorted that.'

He looked disconcerted. 'I had a job waiting for me in Sydney—a job I *wanted*. In the best clinic with the best facilities. Did you expect me to turn that down?'

She shook her head. 'But you expected to add *me* to your list of *must-haves*—just like that!' She clicked her fingers for effect and he gave a hard laugh.

'I practically begged you to come to me when you were ready. And you had a thousand excuses why it couldn't work.'

Maxi sighed. 'You're exaggerating, Jacob. I asked for time to sort out my feelings, my life. You were asking me to leave my family, everything I knew and...loved.'

Jake's gut clenched with huge uncertainty all over again. 'More than you loved me, obviously.'

'Well, if that's the way you want to see it, so be it.' Maxi looked down at her clenched hands. She could only imagine that for a man like Jake it must have been a shock and a bitter frustration to discover he couldn't make life happen the way he wanted it to, that even his money couldn't get him what he clearly wanted—for her to up and follow. Because he'd simply asked her to.

Jake was shaken to his boots. Losing Maxi Somers had been the hardest lesson he'd ever had to learn. He'd been so angry she hadn't seen it his way. And seeing her again here, it seemed the anger hadn't died. It had catapulted back at him and now it had nowhere to fit. He dragged his thoughts together. Maybe they still had something to say to each other, maybe they didn't. He wasn't sure he wanted to find out. But she was here and somehow he'd have to deal with it. He dragged his brain into gear and asked the first mundane question that came into his mind. 'So, how are your travels going, then?'

'Good.' Maxi drummed up the briefest smile. 'I've been to New Zealand already.'

'And how was that?' he asked levelly.

'Green, beautiful, folksy.'

He lifted an eyebrow.

'I loved it.'

Jake leaned back in his chair and studied his fingertips. 'So, then what? You decided to flip over the Tasman to Oz?'

'Something like that.' She hesitated. 'And when I called your mother, she told me where you were working. I thought it was probably my only chance to see something of the outback and catch up with you...'

So there it was. Jake felt his gut clench even harder. She'd put it straight on the line. But letting her stay would mean his life would be turned on its head. He didn't want it and he certainly didn't need it. He opened his mouth to speak, but then just shook his head. 'You shouldn't have come, Maxi.'

She gave an uneasy half-laugh. 'Well, thanks for the unwelcome. Why shouldn't I have come? Your mother said your workload was horrendous. I actually thought perhaps among other things, I could help out…'

He snorted. 'Don't be ridiculous! You'd last a week and then you'd be screaming for the air-conditioned comfort of a city hotel.'

'I'm tougher than I look,' she protested, and he actually gave the semblance of a dry smile. 'And you know we work well together.'

'Maxi, listen,' he said, serious now. 'Living out here is light years from what you're used to. And just now it's hell on wheels. The drawbacks for you would be onerous.'

Her face had disbelief written all over it. 'Like what?'

His heart revved. He *couldn't* have her here. Not after all the hurt. Hell, did she think he was made of stone? He dragged his brain into gear. 'Your complexion, just for starters. You'd be a sitting duck for melanoma.' He warmed to his hastily invented excuses. 'Believe me, I wouldn't like to be responsible for anything as ugly as skin cancer happening to you.'

'That's a totally spurious argument,' she countered in her smooth, well-modulated voice that had always played hell with his senses. 'The actual cause of melanoma is unknown. And unlike you, Doctor, I didn't run around with my skin exposed to harsh sunlight as a child when it's assumed the damage is done.'

'We lived five minutes from the beach. Everyone ran around in the sun. And I did wear sunscreen.'

She arched an expressive brow. 'How do you explain those two lesions on your back, then? They could have turned nasty.'

'Just as well you excised them for me,' he dismissed with a shrug.

She felt a gentle tide of warmth wash over her skin at the memory. He'd been barely a week in her department. For a man she had been doing her level best to avoid, the intimacy of seeing him half naked while she'd operated had almost undone her.

'And they turned out to be benign,' he reminded her now.

'You were lucky.' And this was an absolutely crazy conversation. 'Look.' She held out her arms in front of her. 'My skin hasn't suffered so far. And I'll cover up while I'm here.'

He shook his head. 'You're not staying. How did you get here, anyway? You weren't on the plane.'

'I hired a car in Sydney and drove here.'

He felt a glitch in his heartbeat. She'd driven over a thousand kilometres on some of the most isolated roads in the country just to see him again? 'I can't believe you did that.'

'Oh, I took it in easy stages,' she countered lightly. 'It was… fun.'

He looked at her broodingly. 'It was downright dangerous. What if you'd been targeted by a low-life?'

'I wasn't.'

'Or had a flat tyre in the middle of nowhere?'

She gusted a small impatient sigh. 'I have a mobile phone.'

'And there was I, imagining you needed a *jack* to change a wheel,' he said with a deadpan expression.

She poked a small pink tongue at him. 'I stopped for petrol here and there. I asked the garage guys to check things. They were great.'

'I'll bet,' he observed, studying the rosy mouth into which her tongue had retreated. A mouth with its tiny freckle on her bottom lip. A mouth that was made for kissing. And in a second some instinct, entirely male and protective, swamped him and locked itself around his heart.

He had no choice here. No choice at all. He couldn't risk her turning temperamental on him and taking off into the sunset. 'All right. You can stay for a week until the next flight out.'

'That's pathetic. I can't do anything useful in a week!'

He got to his feet. 'Well, it's all I'm prepared to let you have.' And, please, heaven, by then he'd have acquired the gumption to be able to handle this situation with Maxi with cool detachment.

'Fine, then.' Maxi shrugged and spun off her chair. But she was by no means giving up on this. 'The pub looks pleasant enough. I'll stay there.'

'You'll stay with me,' he countered, the glint in his narrowed gaze as it skimmed over her, confirming her impression that he wasn't about to let her out of his sight.

She bit back a smile. Well, that might work to her advantage. They still had something wildly unfinished between them whether Jake admitted it or not. She tilted her head and said innocently, 'I appreciate you letting me stay with you. But won't people talk?'

'Talk, schmork,' he dismissed. 'Tangaratta is in the middle of a drought. Folk are too busy just trying to survive and keep food on the table to be concerned about their doctor's living arrangements.'

'I did notice the country looked rather parched,' she said seriously. 'How bad is it—really?'

'It's bad.' He rolled back his shoulders as if to slough off an aching weariness. 'Depression, exhaustion and stress everywhere. We're already trucking water in for general use in the town.'

She nodded, moving closer to him, as if in some way to share his load. 'So, I guess folk are pretty desperate.'

He nodded. 'Farmers especially. Outlaying money they don't have to plant crops that die before they're barely out of the ground. In some cases selling up and getting nothing for their livestock. Families having to split up to go after jobs elsewhere. There certainly aren't enough to go round locally.'

'Suicides?' she asked with some perception.

'Couple.' Jake dipped his head, the muscle in his jaw pulled tight. 'One only recently.' He stopped, unwilling to burden her with the harsh reality of it all. And especially he didn't want to tell her about how it had affected him personally and made him question his worth as a rural doctor.

But Maxi, being Maxi and knowing him far better than he gave her credit for, soon sensed his need to unload his self-doubt. 'So, tell me about it,' she encouraged gently. 'Was it someone you knew personally? A patient?'

He gave a hard-edged laugh. 'Still the counsellor, I see.'

A flood of colour washed over her face. He'd made it sound almost an insult. 'Call it debriefing, if that will assuage your medical ethics.'

Jake rode out the implication of her words with a small lift of his shoulders. He couldn't deny it would help to talk and only another doctor, one with the special qualities that Maxi Somers possessed, would understand where he was coming from, when you agonised that perhaps you could have listened more closely, done more…

'It was a friend, a local grazier.' Jake scrubbed his hand across his cheekbones and went on, 'When he was in town we'd usually make time for a beer and a chat. I knew he was concerned about the future. The bank was squeezing him and his property had generated little income with the prolonged dry.'

'So, awfully difficult times,' Maxi commented thoughtfully.

'Yes.' His moody gaze raked her face. 'And it didn't help that he was the fourth generation to inherit the property and felt an enormous burden to try to keep it in the family. But I guess things finally folded in on him. One morning he just upped and wrapped himself and his motorbike around a tree.'

'Oh, lord…' Maxi's hand flew to her throat.

'He should have come to see me,' Jake emphasised tightly. 'Maybe we could have talked things through. I'd encouraged him often enough…'

'But he never came?'

'No.' In the brittleness of the silence that followed, Jake said hollowly, 'This is no place for you to be, Max.'

She brought her chin up. 'On the contrary. I'm a doctor. At a rough guess I'd say you could do with an extra pair of trained hands. And so could the people of Tangaratta, by all accounts. And I'm accredited to work here. I arranged all that before I left the UK. Put me on the staff and let me help.'

'No.'

She hesitated infinitesimally. Jake was not a man you could bulldoze. She knew that. But there were other ways. More subtle ways… Closing the small gap between them, she went on tiptoe to kiss his cheek. 'OK, then,' she murmured. 'If that's what you truly want.'

Jake took a shaken breath as her hair fluttered a lacy pattern against his skin and he found himself surrounded by the delicate floral scent of her. God, it was magic to be this close to her again.

And in a rush all the old disconcerting feelings of his feet not seeming to quite touch the ground when she was this close were back, engulfing him.

He stepped away, breaking the mood quickly, before it turned into something wild and bitter-sweet. Sweeping down to collect his medical case from the floor beside his desk, he said briskly, 'Let's get you settled in, then, shall we?'

They arrived outside Jake's place which Maxi observed was a big old sprawling timber home with verandahs all round.

'Here, let me help you with that,' he said gruffly when she opened the boot of her hire car and dragged out an overstuffed backpack. 'Is this all you've got?'

She wrinkled her nose at him. 'You expected seven suitcases, didn't you?'

'Probably.' His mouth twisted wryly. 'I thought you might have even brought your feather-down quilt as well.'

Maxi chuckled. He'd always taken the mick. She'd finally got immune to it after being tetchy at first. 'I've brought everything I'll need and this thing has a thousand pockets.'

'Hmm. Is that it, then?'

'That's it,' she confirmed. 'I have all my really important stuff in here.' She tapped the large leather satchel she'd swung over her shoulder. 'Oh—who's this, then?' she laughed as a black Staffordshire terrier tore from the region of the back yard to wait inside the gate, thumping his tail on the cement path.

Jake opened the gate. 'Get down, boy.' He shooed the dog away with a nudge of his knee. 'This is Chalky. He came with the practice so I'm stuck with him.'

Maxi bent and fondled the Staffy's blunt head. 'Chalky? Oh, I see.' She gusted a laugh. 'Upside-down logic—Chalky because he's black.'

'I didn't name him so don't blame me.' With the dog glued hopefully to his side, Jake led her up onto the verandah and produced a key to the front door.

'Do you take him for walks?' she asked, as Chalky followed them inside, his claws clipping across the polished floor.

Jake snorted. 'Of course I don't take him for *walks*. 'He's got a huge back yard to run in. And when would I get the time?'

'I suppose… It's a nice house,' Maxi changed tack, her gaze flying over the simple furnishings.

'It comes with the job. You'd better have this room,' he said abruptly. 'It has its own en suite bathroom.'

'Oh, lovely.' She lifted a hand to tug off her cap and shake out her tangle of hair. 'I'd kill for a bath.'

'No baths.' Jake went into the bedroom and dumped her backpack on the end table. 'Three-minute showers are all that's allowed.'

'Oh, of course.' She frowned a bit. 'I imagine it's imperative to use the least amount of water as possible.'

'You're going to hate it,' He said flatly.

'Don't go making assumptions on my behalf, Jacob,' she responded sharply. 'Now, do you have spare linen? I'll need to make up the bed.'

Jake's eyes glazed over and he took a deep, very deep breath. This was never going to work. 'Sheets and towels in the built-in cupboard in the hallway. Help yourself. Marie Olsen is employed by the hospital to come in once a week and keep the place clean and aired so you should find everything else is OK.'

'Fine, thanks. Um, you mentioned a hospital.' Maxi's curiosity was piqued. 'What's the bed capacity?'

'These days, ten,' he replied, a slight edge to his voice almost as though he thought it was none of her business. 'Four are designated nursing-home beds. We're funded differently for those.'

'The same the world over, then. Doctors being slaves to management number-crunchers wherever they work.'

Jake gave a noncommittal grunt and glanced at his watch. 'Speaking of the hospital, I have to make a quick round. Couple of patients to check.'

Maxi's eyes brightened. 'I need to stretch my legs,' she said. 'Give me a minute to freshen up and I'll come with you.'

Jake sensed he was never going to win here so he'd better just go with the flow. Or go nuts. 'Whatever makes you happy.' Shaking his head, he turned and left her to it.

Maxi spritzed water on her face and then ran a brush through her hair. It needed cutting and shaping again, she thought ruefully, disentangling a couple of strands until her brush ran smoothly.

She looked in the mirror, feeling an expectant throb in her veins as she twisted her hair up into a presentable knot. She'd found him again. Now, somehow, some way she had to make him want to reclaim all they'd had.

Impossible as it appeared on the surface, she had to get Jake to tap into his feelings again. Realise that what they'd shared together in England they could have again here on the other side of the world—his world in the Australian outback. She had her fingers firmly crossed as she left her bedroom and went to find him.

His efforts at hospitality left a bit to be desired, Jake thought thinly as he poured fruit juice into two tall glasses. She was probably dying from thirst after being on the road for most of the day and he hadn't even offered her a drink of water. His mouth clamped.

He still found it unbelievable she was here. Under his roof. The time they'd spent in England suddenly seemed pitched into sharp focus. And he knew now that meeting her had changed the whole course of his life. And it hadn't just been the intimate moments they'd shared, although they had been magic. No, it had been the way she'd made him feel, the way she'd made him laugh. In fact, it had been the whole damn package that was Maxi. His Maxi?

Well, she had been. For a while.

Suddenly, he felt as though his heart had been squeezed with terrible force and hung out to dry.

CHAPTER TWO

RETURNING THE JUG to the fridge, he swung back just as Maxi popped her head in and then joined him at the breakfast bar.

'Cheers.' She lifted her glass, tilting her head in that alert, bird-like way he remembered. 'Who do you need to see?'

'One of our seniors who was admitted with heatstroke earlier today and a third-time mum. Delivered twenty-four hours ago.'

Maxi looked surprised. 'I've been doing a bit of homework about Australian rural medicine. From what I've been reading, most bush doctors decline to take midwifery cases. Because of the litigation tangle if things go wrong,' she elaborated. 'I mean, you're so far from specialised help.'

'We operate on a slightly different premise here.' Jake lifted his glass and downed half his drink. 'One of our nurses, Sonia Townsend, is a midwife. If the pregnancy looks straightforward, we like to deliver women here. Otherwise it's a huge disruption for the family if the mum has to travel ahead of time and hang about for the birth at Croyden. That's our closest regional hospital and it's over two hundred Ks away.'

Maxi thought that through. 'So, what else do you do?'

Jake sent her a wary look. 'Medically?'

'Of course.'

'Let's just say a broad-based training has helped me out more times than I care to recall. But there's also an internet hook-up for rural doctors where we can consult with a specialist if we get desperate.'

Maxi slowly drained her glass and then placed it carefully back on the countertop. 'It's a different world out here, isn't it?'

He gave a hard laugh. 'You noticed?' Without giving her time to answer, he swept the glasses off the bench and into the sink. 'Let's go and do this round,' he said briskly. 'And then I might buy you tea at the pub.'

'Tea?' Maxi took off after him as he strode to the front door. 'As in cucumber sandwiches?'

'More likely steak and chips.'

She sent him a speculative look, wondering if she was being sent up. 'So, you actually mean you'll buy me *dinner*?'

His smile was gently wry. 'Something like that.' Ushering her through the front gate, he began striding off along the concrete footpath.

'Hey!' Maxi trotted to keep up. 'Aren't we driving?'

'Hospital's just next door.' Jake indicated the low-set weathered brick building some hundred metres up the road. 'Years ago, the town council bought up acreage to build the hospital and then the doctors' residence came after. Apparently in those days, when Tangaratta was a thriving rural community, there was a permanent medical superintendent on staff and several GPs in the town.'

'So, what happened?' Maxi asked, increasing her strides to match his.

'Technology, probably. The needs and skills of the workforce change. And then a kind of domino effect sets in. Folk have to relocate to go after jobs and towns as small as this go into a kind of recession. But apparently, a couple of years ago, people were beginning to trickle back to start new ventures in the district. Gem fossicking, tourism and the like.'

'And then the drought hit,' Maxi surmised quietly.

He nodded, tight-lipped.

As they neared the hospital, Maxi began to look about her. There was a strip of lawn, faded and burned from the harshness of the sun, but along the path to the front entrance a border of purple and crimson shrubs was vividly in flower. 'They look like hardy plants,' she commented.

'Bougainvillea.' Jake huffed a laugh. 'Can't kill them with an axe. They thrive under these kinds of hot, dry conditions.'

'The hospital itself looks quite a spacious building, at least from the outside.' Maxi cast an interested glance around. 'And I love those verandahs.'

'In the summer they bring a sense of coolness. Conversely, they're great for catching the morning rays in the winter months. The walking wounded love them.'

She shot him a brief smile. 'So the architects of earlier times knew what they were about, then?'

He grunted. 'More than they do now in lots of cases. This is where the CareFlight chopper lands when we have an emergency transfer.' Jake led her across to where a windsock hung listlessly at the far end of large unfenced paddock.

Maxi's gaze stretched across to the distant hills, muted into diffused greys and blues as the evening light softened their stark outlines. 'It's so quiet…'

'Mmm. It kinds of enfolds you. You stop noticing it after a while.'

'I guess you would, yes. Oh, look!' Surprise edged Maxi's voice and she pointed skywards, watching as a flock of large birds thrummed by on urgent wings, calling harshly to one another as they passed overhead. 'What are they—wild geese?'

'Wild duck. There's not much water in the lagoons for them these days. They're leaving in numbers now to fly towards the coast.'

'Will they come back?'

'When the waterholes and lagoons are full again. Come on, Doctor.' He touched a hand to the small of her back. 'Enough of the local commentary. Let's do this hospital round.' He shot her a questioning look as they went through the front entrance. 'I'm assuming you still want to accompany me?'

'Yes, please.'

Loretta Campion, the charge for the shift, was just coming out of her office as they approached the nurses' station. 'Evening, Jake.' She tilted her fair head enquiringly. 'We expected you much earlier. Was there a problem?'

He gave a short laugh. Only the female one beside him. 'Got held up a bit. Loretta, this is, Dr Maxi Somers. She's—'

'The new locum,' the charge guessed, smiling as she extended her hand to Maxi across the counter. 'We expected you on today's plane.'

'Ahh…' Maxi took a moment to think on her feet, her green eyes sparkling with mischief. 'I'm afraid I rather surprised Dr Haslem. I drove here.'

Jake almost choked. He could see what she was up to. 'Maxi's here on a trial basis,' he counter-claimed swiftly, trying to salvage something that had some semblance of truth.

Loretta's eyes widened in query. 'I thought the tenure was for three months?'

'I'm sure we'll sort something out that will benefit us both,' Maxi came in smoothly. 'Jacob's just being his usual cautious self.'

Loretta's gaze skittered curiously between the two medical officers. 'Am I missing something here?'

'We worked together in England,' Maxi said, keeping the patter going but flicking Jake a *don't-you-dare* look. 'But I'm sure I'll settle in here. I love the place already.'

'Well, it's not at its best at the moment,' Loretta said sadly. 'But what a godsend to have another doctor—and no offence, Jake, but my guess is that the ladies of Tangaratta will be making a beeline for Dr Somers's surgery.'

'Excellent.' Maxi beamed. 'I'll look forward to meeting my new patients.'

Jake bit back a squawk of unbelief. She'd outgunned him

without blinking an eye. Hell! And he'd thought she needed protecting! He turned to the charge, his expression carefully neutral. 'Loretta, do you have the charts for Bernie Evans and Karryn Goode, please?'

'Mr Evans has perked up. We've pushed fluids into him for most of the afternoon,' Loretta said, proffering the files. 'But I think we should keep him overnight. He was in a right old state when the meals-on-wheels folk found him. If it hadn't been their day to call...'

Maxi opened her mouth and closed it again quickly. She was full of questions and suggestions but wisely kept them to herself. She guessed she'd already stretched Jake's patience a little too far.

'And Karryn wants to go home.'

'We'll have to see about that.' Jake ran his eyes over his patient's chart. She'd recovered well after the birth of her baby boy. Maybe he'd let her go and maybe he wouldn't. 'OK, thanks, Loretta.' He lifted a hand in acknowledgment. 'We'll find our way.'

'Where to now?' Maxi asked eagerly. They'd walked from the nurses' station and turned the corner into a short stretch of corridor.

'Nowhere.' In a quick, precise movement Jake angled himself in front of her so she was almost pressed against the wall. He stared down at her, his look unreadable. 'Just what are you trying to prove here, Maxi?'

'Sorry?' She blinked uncertainly at him.

'Pretending to be the locum. And what's with the "I love the place already",' he mimicked.

Maxi winced. Had she really sounded like that? Almost simpering? She shook her head, biting the soft inside edge of her bottom lip. 'It was a silly, spur-of-the-moment thing.'

His dark brows came together. 'You've hardly been in the place five minutes. How could you have formed *any* opinion?'

She shrugged, wrapping her arms over her chest and kneading her upper arms.

'Max, this isn't some kind of mind game!' Jake's voice was laced with frustration. 'This is about real patients with real needs!'

Maxi's heart thumped. Had she gone too far? 'I know that, Jacob.' She swallowed uncomfortably. 'I *know*.'

'Then why give Loretta the impression you're the locum?'

'Your receptionist happened to mention the locum hadn't arrived and I thought...well, I thought, why not? It was out of order,' she admitted, her green eyes soulful and large. 'I'll rectify things with Loretta before we leave.'

'You won't,' Jake said, his tone implacable. 'If you want to be taken seriously, just start thinking of a plausible explanation for your sudden departure, when the time comes.'

'But—'

'Maxi...' he warned.

She hesitated. Then lifted her shoulder in a dismissive shrug. 'Whatever you say.' A beat of silence. 'So, do you want me to just make the tea while I'm here or am I allowed to speak to the patients?'

'Just drop it, please.' Jake's gaze narrowed on her flushed face, the angry tilt of her small chin. 'For the time you're here, you're a VMO—a visiting medical officer. With all the responsibility the title carries.'

'Oh.' Emotions began clogging her throat. His generous approach to what could have turned into a messy situation took her by surprise. And yet it shouldn't have, she allowed. He'd always played fair. 'I appreciate that—thank you,' she said quietly.

'You're welcome.' He began walking again. 'Now, come and meet Karryn.'

Maxi felt a sudden overriding sense of caution. 'I wouldn't want the midwife to feel I was going over her head.'

'You wouldn't be. Sonia's not around anyway. She left this morning to check on a couple of expectant mums on outlying properties.'

Maxi inclined her head towards the files. 'May I see Karryn's notes, then?'

Handing the chart over, Jake said, 'I'm not sure I want her to go home just yet.'

They held a mini-consult in a nearby small treatment room. After Maxi had speed-read the patient's history, she said musingly, 'Karryn's twenty-nine and this was her third pregnancy, right?'

'Yes.'

And the delivery had been straightforward, Maxi noted. There'd been no excessive bleed and only a minor repair necessary. And twenty-four hours post-partum, her obs were well within the normal range. Maxi brought her gaze up. 'So, why don't you want her to go home?'

'They live miles out of town, for starters.' Jake hitched himself against the treatment couch. 'She has a child of six and another four. The eldest, Belinda, goes to school. The four-year-old, Nathan, is home with Mum. Plus now she'll have the new baby. And no one around for back-up.'

'Are you concerned she'll overdo?'

'No question.' Jake rubbed a finger along the bridge of his nose. 'Karryn and her husband Dean are trying desperately to keep their property viable. For the last few months Dean has been away most of the day sinking water bores, and right up until she delivered the baby Karryn had been doing the feed drop for the cattle.'

'I see.' Maxi made a moue of conjecture. 'So, fill me in here, Jacob. What does that entail? And when you say cattle—how many does that mean, a dozen or fifty?'

'Nearer four hundred head.'

'OK…' Maxi refused to be thrown. 'So, how physical is it for Karryn, then?'

'It's physical, time-consuming and iffy with the set-up they have to use. She takes the Land Rover with a trailer attached. She's had to take Nathan with her. Now she'll have to take the baby as well. They'll be in safety harnesses but just the thought of it scares the hell out of me.'

'It's obviously a struggle,' Maxi agreed. 'But it's the physical part that alarms me. Karryn is not hauling bales of hay out of the trailer, is she?'

Jake shook his head. 'Not quite. The method they use is to put the vehicle into the lowest gear and secure the steering-wheel so it can't deviate. The idea then is that the vehicle crawls along while Karryn walks behind, throwing out armfuls of hay from the trailer.'

'It must be exhausting in this heat.' Maxi's heart went out to the young mum. 'And Dean, the husband, can he not take over the chore until Karryn's quite fit again?'

'He'd like to, I'm sure,' Jake said. 'But their present bores are drying up and they have to sink for more water sources on the place. The alternative is that they sell their livestock, getting a pittance for it because there's a glut on the market. And then basically…' Jake paused for effect. 'They'll walk off their farm.'

Maxi winced. 'I'm beginning to get a handle on things now. Could they buy in water, perhaps?'

Jake shook his head. 'Not when every spare dollar has to go to buy feed for the cattle.'

'I understand your concern as Karryn's doctor, but realistically how far can you interfere?'

'Maxi, credit me with a little sense. I've no intention of interfering. I just need a reason to keep Karryn for another few days. And then to think of a possible solution to ease her workload when she gets home.'

Maxi frowned, beginning to understand just how swamped he must be feeling with his patients' stress rapidly becoming his own. And obviously Karryn and Dean were just one of many families facing similar scenarios.

But Maxi had a few ideas of her own. 'Does the town have a physiotherapist?'

'Not any more. She left a month ago. And I know where

you're going. Some appropriate exercise would up Karryn's fitness considerably.'

'Yes, it would. But we can get round that. I have the basics to know what I'm doing. But I'd like a chat with Karryn first. And I promise I won't go over the top.'

Jake's mouth crimped at the corners in a dry smile. 'Can I trust you, though, I wonder?'

'Give me a break, Jacob.' Maxi hastily turned towards the door. 'You've told me I have a job here—for the present, at least. So just let me get on with it, please?'

Jake pushed himself away from the couch, his jaw working for a moment. 'I'll introduce you to Karryn, then leave you to it,' he said, grabbing the swing door before it slammed in his face. 'And, Max?'

Maxi felt an odd little dip in her stomach as her gaze flew up to meet his. 'Yes?'

He shrugged a bit awkwardly. 'Just—thanks, I guess.'

She huffed a jagged laugh. 'I may need that in writing later.'

Jake was as good as his word, taking his leave as soon as he'd courteously introduced Maxi and adding for good measure that she'd come from England on a working holiday.

Maxi shrugged inwardly. It wasn't quite the truth but it would do for the moment.

'You must be wilting in our summer weather,' Karryn said shyly, pulling herself higher on to the pillows.

'Just a bit,' Maxi admitted with a smile. 'But, then, I gather it's not been an easy time for you either. How's your bub doing?'

Karryn's gaze went softly to the downy head in the cot beside her. 'Really well. He seems a placid little guy. After Nate, that's a blessed relief, I can tell you.'

Maxi husked a low laugh. 'Handful, was he?'

'Like you wouldn't believe. Always on the go. Still is, for that matter.' She blinked, her eyes filling suddenly. 'I hate being away from my kids…'

Maxi placed her hand on the young mum's shoulder and

squeezed. 'I'm sure you do, Karryn. And that's what I want to talk about. How best and how quickly we can get you ready to go home to them. Dr Haslem has told me a little of your circumstances. I hope that's OK?'

Karryn nodded, palming the wetness away from her eyes. 'It's hard for everyone around here at the moment. Not just our family.'

'So I believe. How about you, though?' Maxi persisted gently. 'How do you feel in yourself?'

'It's been good just to be able to stay off my feet, I reckon,' Karryn said honestly. 'But I have to get back to help Dean. I don't really have much choice.'

'Perhaps you do,' Maxi's voice firmed. 'If we put our thinking caps on.'

'How do you mean?'

'Well, how would you feel about having a few more days with us?'

The young mother looked torn. 'I don't know...'

'I promise we'd use the time well,' Maxi coaxed. 'For starters, I could give you a daily massage.'

Karryn bit her lip. 'I've never had one of those.'

'I used to do it back home for my new mums. They always found it brilliant.'

'My tummy is a disaster area,' Karryn mourned.

'Hey, that's only to be expected,' Maxi returned bracingly. 'At this stage your tummy will naturally lack muscle tone. And don't forget, it's your third pregnancy.'

The young mother laid a hand across the tummy in question. 'It just seems a bit more wobbly this time,' she reflected.

'Your ligaments and joints will be loose for about three months,' Maxi explained. 'But in the meantime I could show you a series of exercises to get you on the right track again.'

Karryn looked uncertain.

'It would all be very low-impact,' Maxi promised.

'What kinds of things would I have to do?'

'Nothing more taxing than sitting and keeping your lower back flat,' Maxi illustrated. 'Then breathing out and drawing your belly button towards your spine, holding the position for a count of ten and then repeating it. Think you'd be cool with that?'

Karryn grinned. 'I reckon. And I could keep the exercises going when I got home.'

'That's the general idea,' Maxi affirmed with a smile.

A flicker of uncertainty crossed the young mum's face. 'But… I couldn't afford to pay much. Would this extra stuff cost a lot?'

'Well, I certainly won't be charging anything,' Maxi dismissed. 'I'd guess you'll simply transfer from Jake's list to mine so I'll be treating you. If that's all right with you, of course?' And all right with Jake, she willed silently.

'Oh, yes,' Karryn asserted quickly. 'I mean, Jake's always very kind and I don't know what the district would do without him—but sometimes it's just nice to be able to speak to a woman doctor. We only ever had another one out here and that was when I was having Belinda. But she left soon after. I don't think she really took to the place…'

Maxi grinned. 'She wasn't from England, too, was she?'

'Melbourne, I think,' Karryn replied guilessly.

Maxi got to her feet, deciding she'd gained enough of her new patient's confidence to go forward with her plan. 'I'll let you get some rest now, Karryn. But I'll pop back first thing in the morning and we'll get cracking, all right?'

'That'd be great. I hope you stay in Tangaratta, Dr Somers,' the young woman added earnestly.

'Oh—thanks. Me, too.' Maxi felt incredibly touched. A wild kind of expectancy hurtled through her veins. Now she only had to convince Jake to let her stay…

Somehow she had to, she resolved as she left Karryn's room and made her way slowly back to the nurses' station. She just couldn't allow herself to be gathered up like so much nuisance baggage and put on the plane out.

Just the thought of it made her insides twist sickeningly. And suddenly it was all happening again, the absolute need she felt around Jake Haslem—the need to be held, *loved*. The need that had driven her here, belatedly, to this quaint little outback town in Australia.

In her mind's eye she relived the first time they'd kissed. It had been halfway through his six-month exchange in England. Such an unromantic time and place for it to have happened. They'd been in Casualty at the end of a particularly gruelling night shift. Their patient had been stitched up and released and they'd been standing side by side at the basins in the treatment room.

Jake had washed his hands and dried them quickly while she'd only just elbowed the taps off, her hands dripping wet. And out of the blue he'd leaned his body towards her, turning his face to meet hers. And just like that he'd kissed her.

And after a little gasp at his audacity, her body had gone to meet his like a river returning to its source.

Circling her arms around his neck and keeping her wet hands out of the way, she'd anchored her body closer until they'd been hard against each other.

And it had felt wild and wonderful, as if it had been destined to happen from the moment they'd set eyes on each other. He'd printed kiss after kiss on her mouth, the way he'd gone about it almost imperious, so damned confident. Yet his lips had been teasing and meltingly sweet…

'Touch me, Max,' he'd whispered gruffly against her mouth. '*Touch* me.'

'My hands are all wet…'

'Who cares?' He'd folded her more closely to him, more tightly, driving a wild kind of passion through her veins until she was giddy with power. And wanting to kiss him all night long.

They'd heard the rattle of a trolley outside and pulled back from each other, and her heart had caught in her throat at the look in his eyes. 'Next weekend?' he'd whispered urgently. 'The Cotswolds? Can you get away?'

She hadn't even tried to pretend it was a casual invitation to go walking. 'Yes.'

CHAPTER THREE

MAXI GUSTED A small sigh. Backtracking her thoughts had left her mind in a muddle, her spirits flagging. Perhaps she was just travel-weary. On the other hand, perhaps it had been one huge mistake, coming here at all. She moistened her lips as if trying to dampen the panicky feeling that had surfaced out of nowhere.

And suddenly and uncomprehendingly she felt homesick for everything familiar. For winter and the grey skies of England. For the sharpness of the outdoors stinging her cheeks when she'd taken the dogs for a run. For the warmth of her parents' old-fashioned kitchen, the comfort of her mother's hearty soup at teatime. For a heart-to-heart with her brother, Luke, and shopping with her little sister, Freya…

She shook her head as if to clear away the shards of retrospection. This was no time to be wallowing in the past. Jake hadn't run her out of town—yet. Like a squirrel methodically gathering nuts for the winter, she pulled all her mental resources around her, her manner purposeful as she crossed to the nurses' station.

'Oh, hi, Doctor.' Loretta looked up from her paperwork. 'Like a cuppa?'

'Not just now, thanks.' A trapped smile nipped Maxi's mouth. 'Jake's buying me tea at the pub.'

'That'll be right,' Loretta confirmed. 'Thursday's his night to eat there. It's steak night.'

Maxi felt her cobbled-together courage drop to the floor. So he hadn't meant the invitation as anything special. Why on earth had she let herself imagine he had? She swallowed the knot of disappointment, instead working the muscles in her face into the semblance of a smile and making herself focus. 'Loretta, does the town have a WI?'

The charge looked blank.

'A Women's Institute,' Maxi enlightened her.

'Ah. Don't think so…' Loretta frowned a bit and then brightened. 'But we do have a CWA. A Country Women's Association—any use?'

'That's just what I'm looking for. Is there a head person I could contact?'

'Now, there I can help you.' Loretta looked pleased. 'Liz Maynard. She runs the local craft shop. It's is in the main street just a few doors along from Jake's surgery.'

'Excellent.' Maxi nodded her thanks. 'I'll pop in and see her tomorrow. Couple of things I want to run by her.'

'Steak not to your liking?' Jake asked later as they sat over their meal at the pub.

'It's fine.' Maxi sent him an over-bright smile. 'There's rather a lot of it, that's all.'

Jake lifted a shoulder dismissively. 'They do tend to think in servings of half a cow. Just leave it.'

'I wouldn't be offending anyone?'

'I doubt they'd even notice.' He met her widened gaze, his blue eyes mocking her with their trace of wry laughter. 'Beef is the one thing there's plenty of at the moment.'

Maxi looked at him doubtfully and then gave a reluctant smile. 'If you're sure it's OK…'

'Perfectly.'

With a neat co-ordinated movement, she moved her plate aside and leaned across the table towards him, her eyes alight with purpose. 'Would this be a good time to talk about my patient list?'

'Who said anything about you having a patient list?'

'I already have the beginnings of one,' she informed him smartly. 'I have my new mum, Karryn.'

'So you do.' Jake acknowledged dryly. 'And what did you come up with?'

'I've outlined a programme of massage and gentle exercise for her and she seemed pleased with that and agreed to stay an extra few days.'

'And?'

'And what?

'I don't imagine you stopped there.'

She shrugged away his cryptic taunt. 'I'm working on a way of perhaps making things a bit easier for when Karryn gets home from hospital.'

'Oh?' Jake's eyes narrowed at her earnest expression and the tiny dimple in her cheek that gave the impression she was always on the brink of a smile. Damn and blast. If he lowered his guard for just a second, he knew he'd be leaving himself open to heartbreak again. He gave a rather curt nod of his head. 'Tell me.'

'Loretta's put me onto the CWA.' Maxi's voice was laced with enthusiasm. 'And from what she told me, their funding guidelines would seem to cover what I have in mind for Karryn and her family. Anyway, I'm going to pop in on Liz Maynard in the morning. I think between us we can work something out.'

Jake's mouth pleated at the corners. 'Just don't get your hopes too high. There may nothing at all Liz can come up with. The CWA's funds aren't limitless and neither is their capacity to help people.'

'I'm not about to give in to pessimism,' Maxi declared stoutly. 'I still believe in successful outcomes. I would've thought you did as well. You used to,' she reminded him.

He gave a bleak kind of smile. 'We're in desperate times here,

Maxi. Sometimes, no matter how much we wish it otherwise, there really *is* nothing we can do to change things.'

Maxi took a thoughtful swallow of her wine. She didn't believe in giving up easily. There would always be *something* they could do. And for whatever time she had here in this tiny community, she resolved to find a way to do that something.

As they left the pub, she realised they still hadn't discussed her patient list. Baby steps, then, she decided philosophically. She had enough to be going on with. And with a bit of luck, the rest would follow.

When they got back to the house, Jake unlocked the front door and stood aside for her to enter. In the lounge room, he tossed his keys on the coffee-table and swung round a bit awkwardly. 'I'll get house and surgery keys cut for you tomorrow. Meanwhile, do you have everything you need?'

Unfolding her clenched hands, Maxi held her palms against her thighs. 'Yes, thanks. Um, what time do you usually have breakfast?'

He gave a hollow laugh. 'I *usually* just grab a banana as I go. That's breakfast.'

She gave a disapproving little shake of her head. 'You can't possibly start your day on a banana! How early do you leave for the surgery?'

'Seven-thirty-ish,' he said, his voice curiously gruff. 'If there are patients to see at the hospital, I do a round first and then go on to the surgery.'

'I could do your hospital round,' she offered. 'I'll be going there anyway to start Karryn on her programme.'

He seemed to hesitate and then he said, 'Fair enough. Thanks,' he added, almost as an afterthought.

'Then what?' Maxi prodded. 'I'll come to the surgery?'

'Will that be before or after you've seen Liz Maynard?'

She sent him a brief exasperated look. 'After, I imagine.' And, please, take me seriously, she wanted to add, but didn't. She turned away. 'I'll say goodnight, then.' Suddenly, it was all just too difficult.

* * *

Maxi couldn't sleep. And it wasn't as though the bed was uncomfortable. It wasn't. And the sheets and pillowcases were of softest cotton, sweet and sun-dried. But she'd been overtired, she realised now, her thoughts all over the place.

She sighed and turned over, plumping up the pillow yet again. The absolute quiet was getting to her, unnerving her. That was until the cicadas started their concert outside her window, of course. It was driving her nuts. But that was nothing compared to the fright she'd experienced when a long mournful howl had pierced the night air and had had her jackknifing up, her heart banging inside her chest. Now, *that* was the stuff of nightmares.

Oh, lord… Closing her eyes, she began some relaxation techniques… Surely Australia didn't have wolves, did it? But the howl had sounded like a wolf. And so close—so close…

She finally slept, rising early and strangely more in control. And under the needling warmth of the shower, even a three-minute one, she felt her body revive and her mind begin to focus.

Dressed for work in well-cut linen trousers and crisp white figure-hugging shirt, she made her way along to the kitchen, surprised that Jake hadn't surfaced yet. She'd give him a surprise and fix breakfast.

Her eyes tracked around the kitchen. It was lovely, homely. She'd hardly had time to register anything last night, she thought, going forward to place her hand almost reverently on the scrubbed pine table, touching her fingers to the tiny dips and grooves in its surface and speculating about the doctors, young and possibly not so young, who had sat here. What stories they could tell now.

She moved across to the pantry and peered inside, raising an eyebrow in surprise. It was well stocked. And obviously down to the lady who came in—Marie. The fridge was similarly well provisioned and Maxi made a little sound of annoyance in her throat. There was no need for Jake to be skipping meals at all. Or as good as.

But, then, it wasn't much fun cooking for one, she guessed. And wondered anew just how lonely and isolating it was for him here.

Locating bowl and whisk, she broke in several eggs and began to fluff them. A tiny frown pleated her forehead. Had disillusionment from their break-up driven him here? she wondered. Had her inability to join him really done that to him? She turned the beaten eggs into a pan and adjusted the heat.

'What's going on here?'

Maxi spun round from the cook-top and shot Jake a haughty little look. 'Good morning. I'm fixing breakfast. And don't tell me you don't have time to eat.'

A little bemused, Jake leaned against the doorframe, watching her. She looked so absolutely right here, he thought, his mind sharpening with memory. Until he cautioned himself bleakly, silently, Just don't get used to it, chum. There may be history between him and Maxi but there was definitely no future. He wasn't about to set himself up to be hurt all over again.

'Well, don't just stand there, Doctor.' Maxi beckoned him in. 'I could use your help here. We need some toast to go with these scrambled eggs.'

Jake pushed himself away from the door and moved across the kitchen to look over her shoulder. 'You really didn't have to do this, Max.' His voice was edged with a gruff quality, his hand of its own accord coming up to rest fleetingly at the nape of her neck.

Maxi felt warning signals clang all over her body and turned her head a fraction. With only the merest encouragement from him, she could have flung herself into his arms. Instead, she took a steadying breath, finding herself breathing in the fresh tang of his sandalwood shower gel. 'I was up early,' she improvised quickly. 'It seemed logical to start breakfast.' She swallowed a laugh. 'You can take your banana for your play lunch instead.'

His chuckle was a bit rueful. 'Perhaps I will. Anything would be better than Ayleen's scones.'

'Oh, dear.' Maxi's mouth turned down at the corners. 'That bad.'

'They give a new perspective to the meaning of rock cakes.'

Maxi chuckled. 'I guess she's just trying to be kind.'

'Oh, she is,' Jake agreed, sliding bread into the toaster. 'She thinks I need looking after.'

Well, I'm your woman, then. Maxi bit her lips together on the words before they could tumble out. 'So, if you don't eat the scones, what do you do with them? I can't imagine you'd want to hurt Ayleen's feelings and chuck them in the bin?'

'Lord, no.' He pretended to shudder. 'I'd never talk my way out of that. I smuggle them out and bring them home for Chalky.'

'Is that good for him?' Maxi seemed shocked by the very idea.

Jake shrugged. 'Chalky loves them. They're so hard, I think he cleans his teeth on them.'

Listening to his crazy banter, Maxi felt a strange sense of lightness. *This* was more like the man she'd known and—*loved.* Her mind stumbled over the word. To distract herself, she quickly got plates off the shelf and watched as Jake buttered the toast. 'Please, tell me Ayleen doesn't bring scones in every day.'

'Only on a Friday.'

'But that's today!'

He gave a crooked grin. 'Better brace yourself, then.'

Maxi felt a swirl of pleasure, watching Jake obviously enjoy the simple meal they'd more or less prepared together. She poured the tea and handed his mug across. 'So, am I going to be seeing some patients today or are you intending to keep them all to yourself?'

Very deliberately, Jake took a mouthful of his tea. 'I'll sort out a few for you to see.'

'Good.' She smiled, activating the tiny dimple in her cheek. 'I'd like a nice mix, then, please. Don't feel you have to give me all the females.'

Jake put down his mug and wrapped his hands around it. 'Be aware, Maxi, some folk will present with physical ailments that are purely manifestations of stress.'

'So an unexplained pain somewhere but in reality they need to talk?'

'Exactly.' He gave her a brief nod of approval, seemingly pleased with her grasp of things. 'There's also been an upswing in drug and alcohol use. So use your own judgement but if you're in doubt at all, check with me before you prescribe anything.'

'I think I can manage that.'

It was just on ten o'clock when Maxi arrived at Jake's surgery. Ayleen was, of course, in attendance, beckoning Maxi to the end of the counter out of earshot of the waiting patients. 'Jake thought you might like to settle in a bit, Doctor, and then see a couple of patients after lunch.'

Maxi nodded. 'That sounds fine. And, please, don't let's be formal. Call me Maxi.'

They exchanged a smile. 'And I'm Ayleen. So now that's settled, I'll show you where to go and you can start getting your bearings.'

'Brilliant.'

'This'll be you.' Ayleen opened the door on a reasonably sized consulting room.

'Oh, wow.' Maxi blinked a bit, seeing a well-equipped, although impersonal domain. It set her thinking and she turned to the receptionist, a query in her eyes. 'So, was this always a two-doctor practice?'

'Oh, yes.' Ayleen was only too happy to supply the information. 'Jake joined Tom Wilde a couple of years ago but then

Tom and his family had to leave for various reasons and Jake's been soldiering on alone ever since. Such a relief you can stay for a while.'

Yes, but for how long? Maxi's gaze clouded slightly. 'The locum's not turned up, then?'

Ayleen shook her ash-blonde head and gave a little sniff of disgust. 'Changed his mind, according to the agency.'

'There's no chance he'll change it back?'

'Not when he's accepted a job on the Gold Coast instead! Some people have no sense of personal responsibility these days,' Ayleen proclaimed. 'It all boils down to lack of respect, of course. In my younger days, you wouldn't dare *not* turn up if you'd been offered a job.' She flapped a hand around the consulting room. 'This'll be better once you get your own bits and pieces around. But plenty of time for that,' she added cheerfully. 'Now, come through and I'll give you the rest of the tour.'

Her thoughts very mixed, Maxi followed.

'Treatment room through here,' Ayleen said, pulling back a screen.

'Looks a good work area.' Maxi was impressed with the array of equipment and would have liked to linger but Ayleen was on the move again.

'Staff kitchen and other facilities along here. And talking of kitchens,' Ayleen said with a smile, 'what about some tea and scones? I brought my usual batch in this morning.'

Oh, dear, the dreaded scones. Maxi thought quickly. 'Uh, thanks, Ayleen, but I already had a cuppa with Loretta over at the hospital.'

'Next Friday, then.' The receptionist-cum-practice manager beamed. 'Now, I'd best get back and leave you to settle in. I usually make us a sandwich for lunch. Can I count you in?'

Maxi nodded around a smile. 'Wonderful, thanks, Ayleen.'

'So, how was your morning?' Maxi asked. She and Jake were in the staffroom and Ayleen had just cleared their lunch things away and returned to her desk to get ready for the afternoon surgery.

Jake lifted his gaze, his eyes narrowing. 'Much as usual. How was yours?'

'Oh, pretty good, I think.' Her teeth caught on her lower lip as she smiled. 'I got a good hearing and a promising outcome from Liz Maynard,' she added, leaning forward and warming to her subject. 'Apparently the welfare of women and children is the main priority of the association so doing something for Karryn and the new baby comes well within their guidelines.'

Jake raised a dark eyebrow. 'So, materially, what can they do?'

'Liz is going to ask some of their members to cook and freeze some meals so Karryn won't have to worry about getting everyone fed the moment she gets home, and Liz said they'll get together and make up a basket of goodies, baby stuff and so on, as a gift for Karryn. Hopefully throw in some toys for the older children as well.'

'That's brilliant. I'm impressed.' Jake's mouth pulled down. 'Why couldn't I see all that was possible?'

Maxi made a throw-away movement with her hand. 'Don't beat yourself up. It's hard to be objective when you're the one having to deal with everyone's stress day after day. And sometimes...' she sent him a trapped smile '...it needs a woman-to-woman approach. Anyway, that's not all my good news. Liz's two teenage sons are home from boarding school early. Apparently the college needs the dorm for a group of overseas students on a study trip. Liz said the lads are bored already so she's going to suggest to Karryn and Dean that the guys go out to the farm and do the hay drop for the next couple of weeks.'

Jake frowned a bit. 'I doubt the Goodes will be able to pay the lads much.'

'They won't have to. Liz said once she's explained things to the boys, they'll be happy to volunteer. And the elder, Heath, has his driver's licence so they can drive out and back each day—' Seeing his expression, she broke off and bit her lip. 'What?'

'Nothing.' Jake's lips twitched thoughtfully. In just a few short hours this woman had begun to weave small miracles. And it felt as though a huge weight had been lifted from his shoulders. There was no denying her input would make a huge difference to the practice, to the patients. But it had taken him ages to close down his feelings about her. Did he really want them dragged out and opened up for inspection again? And that was bound to happen if he let her stay...

'You don't think I've gone over the top, do you?' Maxi spoke uncertainly, interpreting his continued silence as disapproval.

'Sorry?' he said, looking completely startled. 'Do I think what?'

'That I might have gone OTT with the Goodes?'

'No.' He raked his fingers roughly through his hair. 'It's good stuff. Just keep me posted. Uh, I've to go out to one of the properties shortly,' he said, changing the conversation jerkily. 'Farmer's had a confrontation with a cranky bull. Looks like a suturing job. I could be a while so I'll leave you to take the afternoon surgery. There are only four patients booked.'

'No problem.' Maxi sat higher in her chair, hardly able to believe his turnaround.

'You can get me on my mobile if you need to consult about anything.' Jake got to his feet. 'Ayleen will know where I am. I could be pretty late,' he emphasised.

'I'll cope.' Maxi rose with him and followed him out. 'I'll make a start on dinner as well. And don't panic.' She flapped a dismissive hand. 'I'll make sure it's something that will keep.'

He seemed amused, although in an edgy, brittle kind of way. 'Don't go getting too settled, Maxi. We haven't decided anything yet.'

'Meaning *you* haven't decided anything yet,' she retorted. 'But, then, I don't believe you'd run me out of town, Jacob. So any decision as to whether I go or stay will ultimately be mine, not yours.'

He stared at her in silence for a long moment, his jaw

clenched, a muscle jumping. 'We'll see,' he said, his mouth twisting in the parody of a smile. 'Just don't start something you can't finish. That's all.'

CHAPTER FOUR

WITH HIS NOT-TOO-SUBTLE warning ringing in her ears, Maxi tamped down the rolling nerves in her stomach. Perhaps she shouldn't have said what she had—called his bluff like that. But it was done now and one part of her was glad. But if it came to the point where he actually asked her to leave, what then…?

With this unsettling scenario in her mind, she made her way along to Reception, addressing Ayleen, who was busily sorting files. 'I believe there are only four patients booked for this afternoon, Ayleen.'

'Mmm, so far.' The older woman made a small face. 'But folk wander in off the street so don't be surprised if your list gets a bit longer.'

Maxi smiled. 'No worries. And I prefer to come out and call each patient in when it's their turn, if that's OK?'

'Perfectly.' Ayleen beamed. 'Jake likes to do that as well. Anything else I can do for you?' she asked as Maxi still hovered.

'There is, actually.' Maxi tapped a finger to her chin. 'I wondered if we have a supply of health literature, suitable material I could hand out to patients?'

'Oh, heavens, yes!' Ayleen got to her feet. 'Come with me.'

Maxi's first patient, Erin Langley, was right on time. 'Have a seat, Erin,' Maxi invited. 'I'm Dr Somers—Maxi.'

'Hi. I wanted to ask you about Bonnie.' The young mother tumbled the words out awkwardly, indicating the toddler on her knee.

Maxi hitched her chair closer and tickled the little girl under the chin. 'What seems to be the problem?'

'She won't eat properly. And I'm worried she'll starve. And she throws her food around and I'm continually cleaning up after her. And her father's no help.'

And you're at the end of your rope, Maxi decided as Erin's eyes filled. 'Is Bonnie your first child?' she asked gently.

'Yes—and I never thought it would all be this hard.'

'Toddlers can be hard work,' Maxi agreed. 'But Bonnie looks particularly healthy and bright. And some kids are natural grazers around food.'

'I guess…' Erin set the little one down on the floor and watched as she made her way towards a basket of toys in the corner. 'Is that OK?' she asked anxiously.

Maxi tinkled a laugh. 'That's what they're there for.' Maxi didn't add she'd run around the cheap and cheerful shop earlier and gathered up a selection of toys and picture books suitable for any small patients she might encounter on her list. 'Tell me a bit about your lifestyle, Erin,' she invited, needing to get an overview of the family's situation.

The young mum's head came up defensively. 'What do you want to know?'

'Just a general outline of your day perhaps? Do you do paid work?'

'No.' Erin shook her head. 'There's no work here even if I wanted a job. We've only been here three months. My husband, Craig, was transferred here. He's a police officer. I hate the place. I had my group of friends in Sydney and a playgroup for Bonnie. And I've had to leave it all behind…'

'And you're feeling a bit isolated and lonely?' Maxi homed in gently.

Almost defiantly, Erin blinked the sudden tears away from her eyes. ‘I suppose you think that’s pathetic.’

‘Not at all.’ Maxi shook her head. ‘I think it’s pretty normal. But perhaps it’s why Bonnie’s erratic eating habits have seemed like the last straw for you. I guess your husband works shifts, does he?’

Erin nodded. ‘It’s hard. I have to try to keep the baby quiet while he sleeps or go out. And there’s nowhere to go.’

‘You haven’t tried to find a playgroup here?’

Erin’s mouth turned down. ‘I’ve looked in the library and on the notice-board at the supermarket but everyone just seems caught up in the drought.’

‘What about the CWA?’ Maxi asked with her new-found store of information about the association. ‘They might have some contacts you could tap into.’

‘They’re all older women, aren’t they? I mean, would they even know about playgroups?’

‘Oh, I think they would,’ Maxi refuted lightly. ‘Do you know the craft shop in the main street?’

Erin looked puzzled. ‘I’ve had a look in there a few times. I like to do quilting.’

‘I like to knit when I get time,’ Maxi said. ‘But quilting looks quite challenging.’

‘Not once you get the hang of it.’ Erin brightened. ‘I’ve actually won a few prizes here and there,’ she added shyly. And then a look of uncertainty brushed her gaze. ‘Why did you ask whether I knew the craft shop?’

‘Because Liz Maynard, who runs it, is the contact person for the CWA. And they do have younger members. And with your ability at crafts, you’d be a real asset.’

‘You think?’

Maxi shrugged a shoulder. ‘From what Liz told me, they’re always on the lookout for women who can pass on special skills. Why not pop along after I’ve checked Bonnie over and we've had a chat about her diet? I promise you'll find Liz very friendly.'

'I suppose I could…' Erin looked diffidently at her small daughter. 'But if I joined I'd have to go to meetings. And what would I do with Bonnie?'

'They're bound to have childminding,' Maxi said expansively, hoping like mad that they did. 'In fact, their whole chapter is about nurturing women and children. At least it would be a good place to start, don't you think?'

Erin drummed up a tentative smile. 'It might be nice.'

'Good.' Maxi got to her feet. 'Now, let's check this little one over, shall we?'

Maxi's examination was gentle and thorough. 'She's up to date with all her vaccinations?'

'Yes. We're very particular about that,' Erin said.

'Well, she's seems a very healthy little girl,' Maxi smiled. 'And her height and weight are well within the general range for her age.' She met Erin's gaze and smiled. 'I guess in her own way she's getting enough food. Remember, children don't have huge stomachs but somehow they won't let themselves starve either.'

'She's very savvy,' Erin admitted. 'And I do offer her a variety of foods.'

'That's the way to go.' Maxi finished her examination and swung back to her chair. 'Is she keen on vegetables?'

'Not really.'

'There is a sneaky way you could try to interest her,' Maxi said. 'Most kids like chips so perhaps you could make some chunky oven chips but for variation, try some pieces of sweet potato or pumpkin—even beetroot. They're all very rich in vitamins.'

Erin bit her lip. 'I never thought of that. So, any suggestions how I could get her to eat fruit? Usually she just chucks it.'

'As they do.' Maxi chuckled. 'Maybe you could give her a little party platter—say a selection of fruits cut small, even slip in some carrot and celery sticks and add a little bowl of yoghurt she could dip into. And sit down and share it with her. Kids like company when they eat.'

'It all sounds so easy when you say it.' Erin's mouth turned down. 'I think I've been a bit slack.'

'Hey, don't beat yourself up. It all comes with experience. And every child is different.' Maxi reached across to the hastily erected magazine rack beside her desk. 'Take some of these leaflets,' she invited. 'They're mostly reader-friendly and they've some excellent suggestions about toddler health in general and you might even find some recipes there as well.'

'Thanks so much, Dr Somers.' Erin took the printed matter and tucked it into her big shoulder-bag. She rose to her feet, taking Bonnie by the hand. 'You've been great,' she added shyly. 'I really thought I'd be in for a lecture on proper parenting.'

'No lectures here,' Maxi said with a smile. 'I can guarantee it.' She touched a finger to Bonnie's little cheek. 'Take care of yourself, too, Erin.' And remembering Jake's cautionary advice about monitoring the stress levels of their patients, she added, 'And come and see me any time you need to talk.'

'Thanks.' For the first time Erin really smiled. 'I will.'

Maxi's last patient for the day was sixty-two-year-old Les Fielding. He'd come to get a repeat of his prescription to reduce his blood pressure.

'Your BP is up a bit today, Mr Fielding,' Maxi told her patient, after carrying out the necessary checks. 'Anything bothering you?'

'Just the bloomin' drought, Doc. It's enough to make anyone crook.'

'You're a farmer, then?' Maxi asked.

'Nah—run the general store out at Emerald Crossing. But folk can't pay their bills so I let 'em tick up stuff where I can. And they pay eventually, but you know…?' He came to a halt with a dispirited shrug.

'I'm sure it's very difficult,' Maxi commiserated, pulling out a prescription pad from her desk drawer. 'I see from your notes that Dr Haslem calls you in every six months for a review.'

'That's right.' Les frowned a bit, pulling his feet back under his chair and sitting up straight. He'd caught the new doctor's English accent. He hoped she didn't want to suggest some new-fangled treatment…

'Don't be alarmed.' Maxi had immediately picked up on her patient's body language. 'I'm just a bit concerned about the jump in your blood pressure.'

'Jake's told me it goes up and down a bit,' Les offered. 'But it was nothing to worry about.'

'It's probably not.' Maxi smiled as she signed the script and handed it across. 'But let's be cautious and have you back in a month. Can you manage that?'

'If you say I have to, then I'll be here.' Les folded the prescription into the top pocket of his shirt. 'Will I see *you* then, Doc?'

In a reflex action, Maxi's hand went to the small medallion at her throat, as if touching a talisman. Would she even be in the place in a month's time? But, then, hadn't she already decided that particular decision would be down to her? Determinedly, she lifted her chin and dragged every positive thought into her head. 'If that's all right with you, Mr Fielding. But I'll understand if you want to stay with Jake as your doctor…'

Les shook his head. 'You'll do fine, Doc.' He rubbed a hand across his cheekbones and gave the glimmer of a smile. 'And it's Les. Only the wife calls me Mr Fielding.'

Maxi's surprise showed in her raised eyebrows and then she realised. He was ever so gently taking the mick. She waggled a reproving finger at him and gave a low laugh. 'Les it is, then. See you in a month.'

Jake drove back to the town centre. It was late and he was whacked. All the way home his mind had been pulling his thoughts further into disarray.

He wondered how Maxi had coped with the afternoon surgery. Brilliantly, he imagined. His mouth tightened. She'd slotted into the practice as easily as a duck took to water.

So why was he about to cut off his nose to spite his face and insist she leave in a week's time? His dark thoughts scuttled to the front of his mind and took over. You know why, they insisted. Because you'd have to start dragging up the past, open the lid on your feelings and risk Maxi walking away from you again. And just why had she come anyway?

It certainly wasn't about a casual *catching-up* with him, as she'd said. That much he knew with certainty.

Maxi's nerves were shredding. She'd heard swish of tyres as Jake had driven his Land Rover along the car tracks at the side of the house and slid into the carport.

He was home at last.

The reality sent her heart swooping like a drunken butterfly, the sweet sting of anticipation tiptoeing up her spine.

Almost mechanically, Jake hitched up his medical case from the passenger seat and swung out of the vehicle, wishing the insistent fantasies in his head would just butt out and leave him alone.

Making his way across the gravel path towards the back steps, he brought his head up sharply, sniffing the air. It had to be a home-cooked meal and it smelt wonderful. Suddenly, he felt a lightness in his step, a twist of wild anticipation that almost choked him. Swallowing convulsively, he made his way up the steps and across the verandah towards the kitchen.

'Maxi?'

'In here.' Maxi's throat was so dry her voice came out like a croak.

'Hi…' Jake slid his case into a corner and looked around him. He blinked a bit. 'Are we having a party?'

'What *this*?' Maxi's laugh was edged with nerves as she

flapped a hand at the elegantly set table. 'It's just dinner, Jacob. I said I'd cook.'

Hell's bells. Jake stared at the white cloth, the gleaming cutlery and long-stemmed glasses and drew in a sharp breath. Just what kind of statement was Maxi making? More to the point, what kind of response did she expect from him? Strands of emotion unravelled, knotting his gut. 'You didn't have to go to all this trouble.'

She took up her stance beside the worktop. 'You'd prefer I'd set out paper plates?'

He ignored her question. Instead, he went to the fridge and took out a can of light beer. Pulling the ring-top, he gulped down several deep swallows. 'How was your surgery this afternoon?'

'Fine. How was your patient who'd tangled with the cranky bull?'

'Not so fine.' Jake's dark brows kicked together in a frown. 'The wound was a few days old so it was too late to stitch it. And he seems to have an infection brewing.'

'Tsk!' Maxi shook her head, the action sending highlights bouncing off her freshly washed hair. 'So now, instead of being on the way to healing, he's put himself out of action for longer. Why did he delay?'

'It's a sad fact but men in this country and rural men in particular are apt to set the state of their health at a very low priority.' Jake took another swallow of his drink. 'They keep putting off seeing a doctor until they can't stand their wife's nagging any longer.'

'That's a dreadful situation,' Maxi said. 'Have you tried running a specific gender-based health programme?'

'Last year. Only one guy turned up.'

Maxi's mouth pursed into a thoughtful moue. 'Perhaps it needs a fresh approach.'

Jake jerked a shoulder self-deprecatingly. 'Be my guest.'

'You mean you'd let me run it?' Maxi's eyes flew wide in astonishment.

He laughed shortly. 'Why not? You seem to be achieving miracles everywhere else. With a bit of luck, you might pack the local hall.'

Maxi could feel herself flushing. Was he being facetious? It was difficult to tell. She decided to take his words at face value. 'How would I set about letting everyone know it was happening?'

His brows rose slightly. 'From what I've gathered after a couple of years here, the women are the best communicators. You could start with Liz Maynard. The news will be on the phone wires before you've left the shop.'

'OK…' Maxi nibbled her lower lip thoughtfully, 'Then could we sit down and work out something at some stage? Like the most appropriate topics to cover and so on?'

Jake met her gaze steadily. 'This is your idea, Doctor. You run with it.'

'You don't want any involvement? Is that what you're saying?'

'That's right. You've suggested men's health issues require a fresh approach…' Turning away dismissively, he crushed his empty can and sent it flying towards the recycling bin. 'Do I have time to grab a shower before dinner?'

Maxi waved away his question as if it was of no consequence. 'Oh, by the way, Les Fielding came in for his check-up. I wasn't happy about his BP reading so I've scheduled him to come back in a month.'

'Fine,' Jake said flatly. 'I'll put him through his paces then.'

'Actually…' Maxi felt her heart pick up its rhythm, her hand going automatically to her chest as if to still its beat. 'Les indicated he'd like to stay with me—' She broke off and swallowed dryly, expecting Jake to begin sounding off about her taking liberties with his patients and with attempting to strengthen her tenuous hold on her job.

But he didn't.

Instead, he looked past her to the bright pots of cacti on the window ledge and then back to her face. 'What are we having for dinner, then?'

Maxi just resisted poking her tongue at him. Obviously, he wasn't prepared to get into any discussion about her staying in Tangaretta. A new thought struck her. Perhaps after all, he was coming round to the idea—and perhaps not. She breathed in and told herself to stop trying to speculate. 'We're having lasagne and a salad.'

Jake returned to the kitchen a little later, showered and dressed in cargos and a navy polo shirt.

'You were quick.' Maxi looked up from lighting the tall church candles on the dinner table, registering his questioning look. 'I found these in the laundry cupboard.' Her laugh was fractured, nerves gripping her insides like tentacles. 'It's OK to use them, isn't it?'

'It's fine.' Jake looked on in dark amusement. 'We keep them in case there's a power cut.'

Maxi's heart gave a little flutter. 'Well, I think it's…nice to have candles. Civilised.'

'Mmm.' Jake's mouth pleated in a dry smile. 'Did you find the wine?'

'I actually bought some at the pub. I hope it's all right.' She flicked him an uncertain smile. 'It's a Chardonnay from the Hunter Valley.'

'Good choice. They make some of the finest wines in the country.'

'I haven't eaten so well in yonks,' Jake complimented her, as the tangy smoothness of a warm lemon pudding slid over his tongue.

Maxi shrugged. 'The kitchen here is so user-friendly. I quite enjoyed myself, preparing everything.' And there was something very sensual about cooking for your lover, she reflected. Except Jake wasn't her lover any more…

'Why are you really here, Max?' As if he'd defined the direction of her thoughts, Jake slowly lifted his gaze from the glass dessert bowl to her face.

With fingers that shook, Maxi crushed her serviette and dropped it on the tablecloth in front of her and thought it was now or never. 'I did want to travel a bit. And I thought, Why not Australia? Besides, I couldn't stand not knowing any longer. How you felt about things. I…hated the way we parted.'

'In was in your power to change that.'

Her heart twisted painfully. Were they back to that? 'It was all too quick. You expected too much, Jacob.'

'You think a marriage proposal was too much?' He lifted his chin, the action emphasising the stubborn set to his jaw. 'I would have thought that proved my intentions were at least honest.'

'The timing was wrong,' Maxi responded thinly. 'And I don't want us to keep going on and on about it.'

His gaze narrowed over her. 'So what *do* you want now you're here, Max—a casual tumble between the sheets?'

She winced at the rawness of his language, her response coming out in an almost husky undertone. 'I'd like you to show some respect for what we had in England. Stop feeling so…*intense* about me being here.'

He laughed harshly. 'Know what, Max? Right now, I don't think I'm feeling anything about you.'

Then why was he so filled with barely concealed angst? she thought with sad perception. If he doesn't *feel* anything about me? Her heart was hammering and she dragged in a shallow breath and tried to regroup. She'd made a huge leap of faith in coming here to find him. And she hadn't used most of her savings and travelled twelve thousand miles just to cave in and run away because he was making things a bit tough for her.

She had to give him space. She guessed he was still in shock mode at her sudden arrival. But if he'd only bend a little, give her a chance to explain… She looked down, shading her eyes with her hand, too churned up with emotion to look at him. A bleak kind of silence settled over them.

When his mobile phone rang, it took several seconds for either of them to register the fact. Then Jake swung to his feet and picked up the phone from the countertop where he'd left it earlier. Without looking at her, he stepped outside to the verandah to answer the call.

'That was Brian Forrester, the nurse manager at Lakeview, the retirement home,' he said shortly, coming back into the kitchen and pocketing his phone. 'A couple, Violet and Trevor Hawthorne, are presenting with symptoms of gastro.'

Maxi pulled her ragged thoughts together, getting to her feet and automatically beginning to stack their used dishes. 'When did it start?'

'This afternoon. Came on very suddenly, apparently. Both are quite frail and Brian doesn't want to hang around speculating. So I'll go over and check them out now. I may have to admit them.'

'Finding out what's causing the illness will have to be a priority,' Maxi said, her professional instincts overriding her personal unhappiness. 'Could it be food contamination?'

'Possibly,' Jake agreed bluntly. 'And if it is, we can expect a few more to go down.'

'Perhaps investigating what they ate for lunch might be a good start,' Maxi pointed out practically. 'But on the other hand, bugs can be picked up anywhere.'

'You're right, of course,' Jake replied brusquely, reaching down to collect his medical case. 'Uh, will you be OK?'

As if he cared. She watched as he shifted from one foot to the other, as if hesitating about leaving her. 'About what?'

'I don't know how late I'll be.'

Maxi hardened her heart, dismissing his look of concern. 'Just go on about your business, Jacob, and I'll get on with mine.' Deliberately, she turned her back on him and took the dishes across to the sink.

* * *

With a jagged sigh, Jake slammed his vehicle into gear and took off on the one-kilometre drive to Lakeview. Dammit! He'd acted like a carping adolescent suffering from wounded pride.

His circular thoughts tightened like knots. Instinctively, he pressed his fingertips to his temples and increased his speed. Dark thoughts of self-reproach invaded his mind. He'd trampled all over Maxi's feelings.

Again.

CHAPTER FIVE

NEXT MORNING.

Jake rose early. His insides felt as though they were tied in a thousand knots. And he wished he could have crawled back into bed and shut the world out indefinitely. But there was one thing he had to do before the day got any older.

He had to apologise to Maxi.

He went through to the kitchen, hoping he'd find her there, as he'd done yesterday. But one glance told him that hope was spent before it could take flight.

A strange unease settled on him. Suddenly, the house felt too quiet, eerily so. And the cold possibility struck him. Had his rant and blame-shoving driven Maxi away?

Heart pounding, he pivoted on his heel and strode quickly along the hall to her bedroom. Raising his hand, he knuckled softly on her door. And again, louder. No response.

Damn. He squeezed his eyes shut and leaned his head against the door. What the hell had he been thinking of? Whatever the truth of their past relationship, she was after all a visitor in his country. Alone. Her welfare should have been at the top of his priorities. Instead…

He swore under his breath, stark visions of her driving along that lonely highway stabbing into his mind with the intensity of a horror film. Suddenly, he brought his head up. He took a deep breath and tried to collect his thoughts.

In his panic, perhaps he was jumping to conclusions. That was always a possibility. He let out the breath he'd been holding and placed his hand on the doorknob. 'Maxi?' he called softly, pushing the door slightly open. 'You awake?

There was no answer and he pushed further into the room. The bed was neatly made. His stomach dropped to his boots. Had it even been slept in? His gaze spun wildly to each corner of the room and slowly, very slowly, his heart returned to its rightful place.

Her things were still there.

He felt the guilt and panic ease a little. But where was she? His throat felt dry as he swallowed.

Had she gone across to the hospital? That must be it. Dammit, she could at least have left him a note. He surged out to the verandah, a truckload of mixed emotions threading through his mind. Shaking his head as if to clear it, he gripped the railings, staring down at the few hardy shrubs that were still standing despite the drought. And then he heard the click of the garden gate as it was opened, the relief he felt verbalising in accusation. 'Where the hell have you been?'

Slowly and deliberately, Maxi raised her gaze. 'I took the dog for a walk,' she informed him flatly, bending to release Chalky from his lead.

'Where did you go?' he demanded, the words slashing harshly between them.

'The field next to the hospital. Chalky had the time of his life.' Maxi watched indulgently as the dog ran in joyful circles around her and then took off towards the back yard. 'Attaboy!' she whooped, coiling the lead and placing it back on a hook next to the hosepipe where she'd found it. Mission accomplished, she ran lightly up the steps. 'Why the face? All your chickens die?' She directed the flippant comment to Jake as she slipped past him.

He glowered, following her inside. 'Why did you disappear like that?'

She gave a click of exasperation. 'Like what, Jacob? I was up early, earlier than you, obviously. I fancied a spot of exercise and some company.'

'You chose the dog for company?'

'Yes, I chose the dog.'

'In preference to me?'

She gave a hard laugh. 'I figured my company would be the last thing you'd appreciate at the moment. Now, if you'll excuse me, I need a shower.'

'Maxi, wait…' Jake hovered awkwardly, his hands jammed into the back pockets of his jeans. 'I was looking for you to apologise for last night. I was totally out of order. I acted like a clod.'

More like a self-righteous adolescent, Maxi would have substituted, but held back. Instead, she gave a dismissive little shrug, reaching up to pull the sweat band from her hair.

Watching her action, Jake felt tightness in his groin as her skinny little T-shirt rode up from her shorts, revealing the feminine curve of her tummy and a strip of skin as pale and delicate as porcelain. Memories of how they'd been together flooded his mind. He almost groaned out loud.

Maxi felt hot suddenly and it wasn't just from her run with Chalky. Her body was tingling and she felt the weight of Jake's gaze all over her. It was all the fault of this stretch fabric in her T-shirt, she lamented silently. It showed *everything* underneath it. 'Apology accepted,' she said in a little rush.

'Thanks.' Jake felt as thought a ton weight had been lifted off him. 'Have your shower.' He shooed her away. 'I'll fix breakfast.'

'Full English?'

Cheeky monkey. He dipped his head to hide a relieved smile. 'I'll see what I can do.'

* * *

'Afraid there weren't any mushrooms.' Jake set the cooked breakfast in front of Maxi.

She eyed the heaped plate of bacon, egg, sausage and tomato hungrily. 'No baked beans either?'

'I don't do baked beans.'

She wrinkled her nose at him. 'They're very good for you.'

'Mmm.'

She laughed softly. 'I remember now.'

'What?' His brows peaked in question.

'Your aversion to baked beans. It was after we'd had all those school kids in with—'

Jake held up his hand. 'Max, if you mention the V word, I swear I'll send you out to eat with the dog.'

She showed him the tip of her tongue. 'Wuss.'

'Eat,' he said gruffly. 'And then we'd better take time to sort out a few things, don't you agree?'

'That sounds good,' she said softly, her mouth making a little pout like the shape of a kiss on the last word.

A muscle pulled in Jake's jaw, desire rocking him like an earthquake. He couldn't take his eyes off her. She looked sexy and sweet all at once, fresh from the shower, her white cheese-cloth shirt open all the way down and the snug little vest top underneath showing just a peep of cleavage—

Maxi shivered as if he'd actually touched her. Her body ached for his. Ached for his touch and his heat, his breath on her skin. His whispered words, husky, deep, filling her mouth as they kissed.

'Our food's getting cold,' she said around an edgy little laugh, dragging her thoughts back from the brink and picking up her cutlery.

'Do you have any more on the seniors with the suspect gastro?' Maxi asked. They'd finished breakfast and were now sitting over their second cup of tea.

'It looks like we might escape an epidemic,' Jake said. 'Apparently, Violet and Trevor were the only ones at the retirement village for lunch yesterday. The rest of the folk had gone on a bus trip.'

Maxi looked up expectantly. 'So, if we can narrow down what they ate for lunch, we could find our source there?'

'That's what Brian thinks. No one else appears poorly.'

'Did you admit Mr and Mrs Hawthorne?'

'To be on the safe side.' Jake's blue gaze shimmered across her face. 'I called the hospital while you were in the shower. They've had a reasonable night. I'll check them over a bit later. Probably let them home this afternoon.'

'I'll come over to the hospital with you, then. I have to do Karryn's massage.'

Jake looked at his watch. 'Fifteen minutes?'

'Fine.' Maxi whirled to her feet. 'I'll wash up seeing you did breakfast.'

'Shove everything in the dishwasher.' Jake scooted his chair back and began to help gather up the dishes. 'It's supposed to use less water that way.'

'At that rate, I guess we should just do one load every couple of days. Lord knows, there's not much with just the two of us.'

'Unlike back *home*?' Jake gave full rein to a grin. He'd spent several weekends at her parents' farm and had loved the warmth of her big extended family. And her mother's cooking. 'Are they all well?' he asked now, coming up behind her as she began to stack the dishwasher.

Maxi went cold for a second. 'Yes, they are.' *Now*, she added silently. But she couldn't go into any of that with Jake. Not yet, when they'd only just got their communication lines open again. 'Miffy's had pups.'

'Little Miffy?'

Maxi choked a laugh. 'Not so little these days. But there were only four and Mum's found homes for them already. Well, that seems to be done.' Closing the door of the dishwasher, she straightened and turned abruptly, almost spinning off balance.

In a reflex action Jake stuck out his hands to catch her, the impact of her soft femininity sending a thousand volts of electricity zapping through him. He brought his head up, his gaze darkening as her lips fell softly apart on a whispered little 'Ooh...'

In a second they both knew what the other was thinking, stomach-churning awareness leaping between them. It went on and on, tightening until it seemed something would snap.

Jake swallowed the dryness in his throat and very slowly, as if already savouring the exquisite climax of his quest, he bent, his mouth touching one corner of hers, imprinting her skin with his taste and warmth. 'Maxi...?'

'Oh, yes...' She made the tiny plea in her throat, sighing into his mouth. Oh, *yes*. She began evoking every fantasy she'd ever had about this moment, her knees almost buckling with the intensity of the avalanche of emotions that swept through her.

Her rapture already on a knife-edge, heightened as Jake deepened the kiss, the sweetest pain lancing downwards, conveying heat to the very core of her femininity. It had been so long...

Why hadn't he known it would be like this? Jake was starving for the taste and feel of her, his arms wrapping her closer so that her breasts were pillowed against his chest and he could feel the beating of her heart through the fine cotton of her top.

Desire hammered into him, making the nerves low down in his belly tighten with erotic torture. He couldn't believe he had his arms around her again, her taste in his mouth again, and it still almost overwhelmed him.

Just as it had two years ago.

But now everything was different. The thought catapulted its way into Jake's head and he drew back sharply, his breath jerky and shallow.

What now? Maxi saw the beginnings of doubt in his eyes. Was he already regretting their kiss? Well, she wouldn't let him. In just a few seconds they'd come a thousand miles. She wasn't going back to square one. She'd defuse things anyway she could. It would kill her but she'd do it.

'Hey…' she said throatily. 'It was just a kiss, Jacob.'

'Was it?' Was that what she really thought? Jake wasn't prepared for the ball of disappointment that landed in his stomach. He tilted his head, brought his mouth to within a centimetre of hers. 'I don't think either of us believes that, Maxi,' he refuted softly. 'Let's not kid ourselves.'

'OK…' She backed away from him to lean against the countertop, her breathing uneven. 'Let's not, then. It doesn't need to change anything,' she added.

And that was pie in the sky. So what should he do? Send her packing before they both got hurt all over again? His mouth kicked up in a self-mocking little twist. At least then his guts might return to something like normal. 'Are you saying we shouldn't start analysing it, then?'

Maxi made a huge effort towards rationalism. 'It's done and we can't take it back. So…let's just get on with our day and—'

'Pretend it never happened? That's not being very honest.'

She gave a short, almost tragic little laugh. 'That's rich, coming from you, Jacob. You've been running away from *honesty* from the moment I landed in your surgery.'

'You're right,' he said, deadpan.

'So, what do we do now?' she blurted after an agonising beat of silence. 'Start being honest with each other?'

'OK.' His jaw was suddenly hard and square. 'Let's do that. You first. Why did you come here?'

'I've *told* you,' she insisted.

She heard the hiss of his breath between his clenched teeth and an impatient mutter low in his throat. 'That you decided to *catch up* with me, like we were never more than friends? I don't buy that.'

Maxi could feel her control slipping by the second. She could hardly say, *I've come to tell you I still love you. And to find out if there's still a chance for us...* Instead, she said abruptly, 'Look, let's save ourselves any more angst. Do you really want me to leave?'

'Since we're being honest...' Jake gave a short, harsh laugh. Then added softly, 'No, I don't want you to leave.'

'Oh...' Maxi felt such relief at that point she could have cried. But managed not to. 'So, when did you decide this?'

'It's just crept up on me,' he said, and realised that here at least he was speaking honestly. 'Already the town's buzzing with news of your arrival. And for the women, at least, having a female doctor in the place is equivalent to winning the lotto. Well, as good as,' he added with a twisted smile. 'And as for me, I know you're an excellent doctor so for that reason alone I'd be crazy not to keep you here to share the load.'

But not because he was still in love with her and wanted her in his life again? Was that what he was saying? Or not saying? Suddenly the terrible uncertainty of what she was about to take on materialised in a flood of nerves to her stomach, as though an entire aviary of hummingbirds had been let loose and were trying to escape.

But she couldn't turn back now. She had Jake's approval to stay and surely that was the biggest hurdle overcome?

She forced an off-key little laugh. 'In that case, we should get over to the hospital, so I can start earning my salary.'

'We'll take my vehicle,' Jake said. 'I may have to drive the Hawthornes home. Our only ambulance is off the road for a service this morning.'

'How do you keep track of all this?' Maxi asked as they made their way outside to the garage.

Jake looked into her eyes and saw her confusion. A dry smile nipped his mouth. He'd have to keep reminding himself she was on a steep learning curve here. Practising medicine in outback Australia was light years away from what she was used to. 'Ayleen keeps me up to date so I know what's happening. Hop in,' he directed.

'So she'll include me in the loop as well?

'Of course.' He put the four-by-four into gear and reversed out. 'You're part of the practice now. Like me to give you a run-down on the staff at the hospital?'

'Please.'

'Loretta you've already met and we've several assistants in nursing who rotate as the second person for each shift, as well as a couple of RNs who work on call and come in as needed. David and Bron Walker work as a team as joint nurse managers. Professionally they do an excellent job and personally they're trusted friends.'

Maxi thought that over. 'I guess that would mean a great deal out here where you're so isolated.'

'Yes.' Jake's reply was muted.

'Do they have children?'

'A daughter, Katie. She's fifteen. Presently away at boarding school for her higher education.'

'Do most folks out here have to send their kids away?'

Jake shrugged. 'Not necessarily. There is a high school here but obviously more choices are offered by schools and colleges in the city. And that aspect and the extra-curricular activities offered appeals to some parents. Especially if they've been away to school themselves. But it also costs money, of course. And recently some kids have had to be brought home because of the family's changed circumstances in the big dry.'

So, stress upon stress piling up and affecting the children as well, Maxi thought, and understood more clearly now what Jake had meant by the domino effect of the drought. She sent him a sideways glance. 'As the only doctor in town, you must feel like you're carrying the weight of the whole place on your shoulders.'

He gave a twisted smile. 'Lucky they're broad, then, hmm?'

Maxi laced her fingers across her lap. 'I'll do everything I can to help, Jacob.'

'I'm counting on it,' he said as he brought his Land Rover to a stop in the hospital car park.

'So, in view of our new arrangement, is my status still that of a VMO?' she enquired as they made their way along the brick path to the entrance.

Jake flexed a shoulder dismissively, dragging his attention from the fullness of her just-kissed mouth. 'Does it matter, as long as we pay you properly?'

'I suppose not…'

'Maxi, it's no big deal.' Jake said, pushing open the heavy plate-glass door and ushering her through. 'Folks here will just be glad to have a competent doctor. They really won't be concerned with putting labels on you or worrying about your status, so relax, would you?'

Both David and Bron were at the nurses' station, looking smart and professional in their navy trousers and crisp khaki shirts. Jake made the introductions, stating calmly that Maxi would be helping out for the next little while.

'Welcome, Doctor.' Bron smiled. 'We heard you'd arrived.'

'And from all accounts, the big fella here has had you working hard already,' David added, as he shook hands, his laughing blue eyes magnified by silver-framed spectacles. 'You're a long way from home and family, Doc.'

'Yes. And it's Maxi, please.' Maxi felt herself almost basking in the nurses' warm welcome. 'I've been blown away by the friendliness shown to me here already. Um, Jake tells me you have a daughter at boarding school. You must miss her.'

'Oh, we do.' Bron looked wistful. 'But she won a scholarship to do her higher education in Sydney so we really couldn't hold her back.'

Jake parked his elbows on the countertop. 'She'll be home soon for holidays, won't she?'

'Only for a week.' David's mouth turned down. 'She's been invited to spend some of the break with one of her friends from school. The family live at the beach so we decided to indulge her. Tangaratta at the moment can't compare with Bondi,' he finished with a rueful smile.

'But we'll try to do something special when she's home,' Bron enthused. 'A nice big lunch party or something. You'll both come, won't you?'

Maxi looked instinctively at Jake. 'I'm sure we'd love to.'

'Barring emergencies as always,' he replied, his drawled response careful and hard to read. 'But right now I'd like to check on the Hawthornes, please.'

David pulled the charts. 'Brian's been beavering away on that. Violet and Trevor prepared their own lunch yesterday and he's pretty certain it was some pre-packed chicken they ate on sandwiches. It was well past the use-by date.'

'Oh, the poor things!' Maxi put a hand to her stomach in sympathy. 'So, is it sorted now?'

'Let's hope so. One of the staff at Lakeview has been through their fridge for any other possible culprits but there was nothing suspect apparently.'

'I'll check Violet and Trevor now,' Jake said, handing the charts back. 'If they're fit to go home, I'll drive them.'

'And I'll pop in on Karryn, if that's OK?' Maxi said, linking the two nurses with an expectant little smile.

'I'll accompany you,' Bron offered, coming out from behind the station. 'I'd like to observe your massage technique, if you've no objection.'

Maxi gave a quick smile. 'None at all.'

'Thanks. Oh, by the way, Karryn's had a gorgeous basket of goodies delivered from the CWA. Bucked her up no end.'

So Liz had come through. Maxi basked in a sense of achievement as she fell in with Bron's brisk nurse-stride along the corridor.

Watching the two women go, David turned to Jake, saying quietly, 'Must be a hell of a relief for you, mate, having someone of Maxi's calibre here.'

'Uh, yes…' Jake felt his heart rev uncomfortably. 'We worked together in England.'

'And the place is buzzing with speculation,' David hinted knowingly.

'It's a small community.' Jake resisted the urge to roll his eyes. 'You and I both know *anything* out of the mundane is news.'

Yeah, right. David gave his friend a narrowed look. There was history between Jake and his new locum or *he'd* completely lost the plot. He decided to help things along. 'The place is looking pretty quiet. Why don't you show Maxi a bit of the district? Despite the drought, there's still a decent picnic spot out at Wonga Springs.'

Jake looked at his watch. He didn't know how he felt about that at all. But, then, he could hardly leave Maxi to her own devices when she was so new to the place. He guessed in some way he'd made himself responsible for her well-being.

Seeing his hesitation, David came in persuasively, 'It's only a thirty-minute ride out there. If there's an emergency, you're on your mobile. How long is it since you've had a real day off? Even half a day?'

Oh, hell. Jake was tempted but his relationship with Maxi was still on a knife-edge. And a picnic in a secluded spot with just the two of them could lead to more complications. More than he was ready for.

'Shove some food together and take off.' David upped the pressure. 'I'll take the Hawthornes home, if you're happy to release them. I'm not officially on duty, just here for a stocktake.'

'OK, OK.' Jake held up his hands in surrender, his mouth compressing on a wry grin. 'You've sold me. Now, let's hope we can spring Violet and Trevor out of here.'

'I gather from Bron this is a bit of a turnaround for you—taking time off, I mean.' Maxi gave a brittle laugh as she slid into the passenger seat once more.

'She's exaggerating.' Jake sent her a moody look, reaching forward to start the engine. 'I just don't flag *everything* I do with my so-called leisure hours, that's all.'

Feeling put in her place, Maxi felt her nerves tighten. Oh, lord… A new thought struck her. Did he have a girlfriend here? Someone the locals knew nothing about? Suddenly she felt awkward, almost in the way. 'Whose idea was the picnic?'

'David's, actually. Does it matter?'

'I think it does, if you felt pressured to—to spend time with me when you'd rather be seeing—that is, *doing* something else.'

He flashed her a mocking kind of look. 'You're way off target, Max. Anyway, what's wrong with having a picnic together? You should see something of the place while you're here. I saw parts of England I'd never have seen without you acting as my guide.'

'I suppose so,' she agreed, slightly mollified.

'And just for the record, Maxi, while we're on the subject of sightseeing, don't ever go haring off on your own without telling someone where you're going. Is that clear?'

She shot him a look. 'I'm not devoid of common sense, Jacob. I have actually gathered *something* of the vastness of this country.'

And yet she'd thrown caution to the winds and embarked on that horrendous drive from Sydney. To find him. And he hadn't given her even the semblance of a welcome. A bolt of something like shame zapped through him.

'Sorry, Max.'

A tiny frown notched her forehead. 'For what?'

'My lack of good manners, if nothing else. I want you to make the most of your time here.'

Maxi hadn't expected that. A wild ripple sparked her veins, powering to a waterfall when he stretched out his hand to capture her fingers, carrying them all the way to his lips. 'Forgiven?'

She nodded ruefully and he smiled. 'For now let's just enjoy our picnic, shall we?'

For a while they travelled in silence, Maxi a little amazed at how some inner part of her had already begun to respond almost unconsciously to the rich, bold colours of this huge landscape. 'Drought and all, it's really something special in the outback, isn't it?'

'Certainly is.' Jake spun his head towards her and lifted an eyebrow. 'Feel the quiet?'

'I'm beginning to—especially at night. Do you have wolves here, Jake?'

'What?' He spluttered a laugh. 'Who gave you that piece of misinformation—another English tourist?'

She poked her tongue at him. 'Well, what makes that blood-curdling howl at night, then?'

'Dingos—Australian wild dogs. They're tawny-coloured, quite shy really.'

'They didn't sound too shy to me,' Maxi countered. 'In fact they sounded just outside my window.'

'They probably weren't,' Jake said seriously. 'But they are coming closer to town, probably because their natural food sources are diminishing with the drought.'

Maxi frowned a bit. 'What do they normally eat?'

'They're carnivores for the most part. They'd normally be hunting smaller animals but in times like the present nature kicks in, urging those smaller animals to look for other more hospitable areas. Then the dingos start looking for kills amongst larger animals, like lambs. But we don't graze sheep here so hunger will be driving the pack closer to civilisation as they hunt for food.'

Maxi suppressed a shiver. 'How close?'

'Stop worrying, Doctor.' Jake began to cut back on his speed as a thin line of spindly she-oaks came into view. 'The rangers will have it sorted.'

'Well, I hope so.' Maxi didn't sound convinced. 'Is that our picnic spot over there?'

'Mmmm.' Jake took a well-worn track off the road. 'There's a spring-fed creek still in existence, green grass to sit on, even a rock pool if you want to swim.'

She sent him a wary look. 'I didn't bring a swimsuit—did you?'

Jake didn't answer but his grin was wicked and the glint in his blue eyes was even more wicked as he eased the Land Rover down a short incline and braked.

Maxi felt her heart skitter. Surely he wasn't thinking of skinny-dipping? They may be in the middle of nowhere and they may be no strangers to one another's nakedness, but there was no way she was ready for that!

'This is as good a spot as any,' Jake said, swinging out of the four-by-four and busying himself spreading a groundsheet and rug on the grass.

'What can I do to help?' Maxi hovered uncertainly.

'Drag out the esky, thanks. Most of our picnic is in there. The ice-box,' he clarified as she hesitated. 'And there's a large paper bag with some bread rolls.'

Maxi dropped to her knees on the rug and peered inside the esky. 'Oh—this looks good, and I'm famished. Should I start putting stuff out?'

'Give us a minute, Max. I'm going for a swim.' Raising his face to the sky, he inhaled a long breath, then another. 'Smell the eucalypts?' He'd turned to her, a teasing glint in his eyes.

Maxi scrambled to her feet. Following his action, she breathed in. 'I'm not sure—but it's lovely, whatever it is.'

'Ah, Max.' Jake moved closer and gently took her by the shoulders. 'You're such a diplomat. You can't discern a damn thing, can you?'

'I can, so! It's a bush smell—nice.'

He chuckled. 'Like that tells me anything. Look over here.' He guided her closer to the waterhole. 'See those red blossoms dipping down into the water? They're bottlebrush. The birds swing on them to get the nectar. Now, over there are the gum trees, or eucalypts.'

Maxi tipped her head back, her gaze travelling up the long mostly white treetrunks, some of which looked more than a hundred feet high. 'They're gumtrees?'

'Ghost gums. Did you happen to get up to the Blue Mountains while you were in Sydney?'

'No.' Maxi shook her head. 'But your mum mentioned them. A real tourist spot, she said. Are they really blue?'

'Oh, yes. No mistake about that. Their blueness is caused by the natural light catching the evaporating oil from the leaves of the gum trees. Come on.' Jake tugged her hand. 'There are young leaves shooting out of the main trunks all over the place, we'll break off a leaf and you can smell the real thing.' Reaching up, Jake snapped off a couple of the pale green gum leaves and rubbed them between his hands. He held them out to her. 'Now, smell.'

Maxi sniffed the leaves obediently. 'Oh, yes!' Her eyes were shining. 'It's gorgeous! A bit pungent but nice…'

'You'll do.' Jake knuckled her cheek playfully, then dropped his hand as if he'd been stung and turned away quickly. 'Uh—I'm for that swim now.' In a jerky movement he peeled his shirt over his head and flung it on the ground, his trainers and jeans following quickly until he was down to his black boxer shorts. Throwing his watch down on the heap of clothes, he sent her a rakish grin. 'Care to join me?'

'Not this time.' She gave a breathless little laugh, pulling back the almost overpowering urge to reach up and run her hands from his neck to his wrists, up to the bareness of his chest and around to encircle his back. She swallowed deeply. His body seemed just as blindingly beautiful as she remembered, hard and tanned and male. And once it had belonged exclusively to her. 'I'll, um, settle for a paddle,' she said quickly, and kicked off her shoes.

'The rock pool's too deep to paddle,' he said. 'But there's a handy log you can sit on and dangle your toes in.'

'Sounds good.' Maxi grabbed at the reprieve, following him across to the edge of the pool. 'Do you come out here a lot?'

'Used to, when I first came to Tangaratta. Now I hardly get time to do much else besides doctoring.' That said, he pointed out the log where she was to sit and with the caution 'Don't fall in' he lowered himself into the water and began striking out strongly to the other side.

'This has been such a lovely afternoon, Jacob.' Maxi looked up, her face dappled by the shade from the canopy of leaves. They'd eaten their crusty bread rolls stuffed with ham and cherry tomatoes and finished with coffee from the flask he'd brought and some chocolate biscuits. 'Thank you.'

Jake shrugged her thanks away. Today his thoughts were all over the place. One part of him wanted to lower his guard, let her back in. The other part cautioned him to take things slowly. His gut clenched with uncertainty. Had he after all been way too judgmental about her? He'd thought back then she'd simply not cared enough—not as much as he had. Perhaps he'd been a bit arrogant in his thinking. Perhaps, perhaps…

'I guess we'd better head back.' He got abruptly to his feet, holding out his hands to help her up from the rug. 'Had fun today? he asked, brushing the backs of his fingers gently across her cheek.

She nodded, her throat suddenly too dry for speech. Time had slowed and there was an almost tangible sense of expectation hanging in the drowsing late-afternoon air. A tingle flooded her spine.

She looks so beautiful, Jake thought, looking down at the little flecks like gold dust in her eyes. He wanted to kiss her again. And again. But kisses weren't going to solve anything. Only prolong the uncertainty of where they were heading. If anywhere.

His chest rose in a long sigh and he slowly let his hands drop. 'It'll be dark soon. We should get back.'

'Could we come again some time?'

'Yes,' he said simply. Lifting a hand, he ran a finger lazily down from her throat to the edge of her little top. 'And perhaps next time you'll swim with me.'

CHAPTER SIX

IT WAS A Friday two weeks later and there was a full waiting room at the surgery. Maxi scattered a quick smile among the patients on her way through to Jake's consulting room. Knowing he hadn't started for the day, she tapped and went in. 'Hi, got a minute?'

Jake finished something on his computer and then his dark head came up. 'Yep.' He waved her to a chair.

Maxi shook her head. 'Can't stay. I just wanted to run something past you.'

He leaned back in his chair and folded his arms. And waited.

Maxi got straight to the point. 'It occurs to me, in this environment, I may come across a case of snakebite. What's the latest in the way of treatment?'

'This may take a while. Sit down so we can talk properly,' Jake said a little tetchily. 'I can't keep craning my head to look at you.'

She all but rolled her eyes but did as he asked.

'If you're not doing it already,' he said, 'you should be carrying a broad bandage in your medical kit.'

'I'll check but I don't think I have one.'

'Then ask at the hospital. They'll set you up. The bite usually occurs on one of the limbs. So you bandage the whole limb, groin to toes or alternatively armpit to fingertips, according to where the puncture wound is located.'

'So…' Maxi spread her hands in query. 'In the case of a bandage not being available, then clothing torn into strips would do the job, right?'

Jake nodded. 'Anything like that. Even pantyhose will suffice. It's essential to immobilise the limb. Whatever you do, don't allow the wound site to be washed. The venom is used to identify the snake.'

Even though she'd settled in and found her niche here, Maxi freely admitted there were some things about working in an outback practice that terrified her. 'Have you treated any cases while you've been here?'

'A few. The hospital keeps a supply of anti-venin and usually the patient recovers after a few days in hospital. But where they haven't responded in a reasonable time, we don't take chances. We chopper them out for specialist treatment in the city.'

'Thanks.' Maxi got to her feet and stepped round her chair, placing her hands across the back. 'Ayleen tells me we have a full list.' She smiled. 'Should be a good day.'

Jake felt something shift in his chest. Hell, she was practically glowing at the prospect of her morning's clinic. 'Haven't forgotten it's Friday, have you?' he reminded her dryly. Swinging off his chair, he moved to stand quite close to her.

'The dreaded scones?' she said in a stage whisper.

Jake made a cutting motion across his throat.

An air of mischief gleamed in her eyes. 'Prepare yourself for a treat, Doctor. I'm supplying double-chocolate muffins instead.'

Jake's head went back in disbelief. 'How did you manage that?'

She put a finger to her lips. 'Told Ayleen I was missing being able to bake some of my mum's recipes. She's such a softie. She insisted I take over the Friday morning tea in future.'

'Hallelujah!'

'I made the muffins early this morning when you went out on your call.'

Jake stared at her, his fingers flexing, aching to free her hair from its ponytail. The thought of its silkiness gliding through his fingers was enough to set his body on fire. He took a deep controlling breath. Sweet God, she was lovely. So full of life, her presence like a breath of sweet, clean air in this place. 'You're really flying, aren't you?'

If he meant was she enjoying being part of this bush community, of being able to use her medical skills where they were needed, then, yes, she supposed her spirits were certainly up. And so far their living arrangements were working out and they were communicating—not as openly as she would have liked but then again the wariness he'd displayed around her seemed to have taken a hike. And she was glad about that.

Slowly and surely they were rebuilding their relationship brick by brick and this time she hoped with all that was in her that it would stand the test of time, be good and true… She lifted her chin, the motion a slight challenge. 'Did you think I'd not fit in?'

'No…' His answer came out low and soft. Lifting his hand, he stroked back a tendril of hair from her cheek. 'Not for a moment.'

Maxi felt the heat flow through her body like a river, so utterly aware of him, of the very essence of him—the sheer power of his body, the faint scent of soap and warm masculine skin, the way his shirt moved over the lean, muscled contours of his shoulders, the neat hips and long muscular legs encased in moleskins so well cut they merely hinted at all that masculinity.

She swallowed heavily. 'We've patients waiting…'

'Mmm… Shame, that.' His dark head swooped towards her, his mouth teasingly urgent against her lips, the corner of her mouth, her lips again. 'Off you go, then,' he said, regret in his gruffness.

Her legs felt like jelly but she made it to his door.

'Max?'

She turned, eyes widening in query. 'Something else?'

Jake's eyes glinted with dry humour. 'Just thanks in advance for the muffins.'

She nodded, slipping out and scurrying back to her consulting room as though she was being pursued by those wild dogs he'd told her about.

Maxi's first patient was Brandon McCall. She opened his file, deciding she'd better try to get a handle on things before she called him in. For heaven's sake, focus, she directed herself, brushing her fingertips across her forehead.

It seemed that six months earlier the seventeen-year-old had been out riding on his family's property when his horse, startled by a snake, had bolted into thick bush, throwing Brandon. According to his notes, he'd landed on a tree stump, a branch of which had pierced his chest, grazing the back of his lung and lodging behind his heart.

Maxi shook her head at the bizarre nature of the accident and read on. Brandon had been air-lifted to St Vincent's in Sydney where surgeons had removed the branch. He was now home, supposedly fully recovered. So had something else gone wrong? Maxi wondered as she went out to the waiting room to call him in.

'Take a seat, Brandon,' she said, ushering him into her room and closing the door. 'How can I help you today?'

The youth sat gingerly on the edge of the chair. He was obviously right out of his comfort zone, batting his Akubra back and forth between his jeans-clad knees. 'Uh, Mum said I should come in and talk to Doc Haslem.'

Maxi sent him a quick smile. 'Dr Haslem's list is pretty full this morning. Will I do?'

The youth coloured, shifted his feet awkwardly and after a long moment said, 'Guess so…'

Silence again.

Well, this was getting them nowhere fast, Maxi thought. Perhaps it was just youthful male reticence on Brandon's part but she had a feeling it was something else entirely. On the other hand, she didn't have all day and they had to start somewhere. 'Let's give you a quick check over for starters, shall we? I've read your notes,' she continued, snapping the blood-pressure cuff around the lad's arm and beginning to pump. 'That was some accident you had.'

The lad shrugged. 'Everyone at the hospital said I could have died.'

Maxi frowned a bit. Who on earth had been responsible for that kind of inappropriate language in front of a vulnerable young patient? But perhaps he'd inadvertently overheard the gossip. Whatever, it was too much information. 'How are you sleeping?' she asked, releasing the cuff.

Brandon's dark lashes made half-moons across his cheeks as he looked down. 'Not great.'

'What about when you were recovering in hospital?'

'No chance. Old guy next to me sounded like he was snoring for the Olympics.'

Maxi smiled in commiseration. 'What about now you're home though—any reason you're not able to sleep?'

'Keeps going round in my head…'

'The accident?'

He nodded, his young gaze filled with uncertainty.

Had he not had any counselling? Maxi's intuition sharpened. She hastily perused his notes again. There was no mention. So were they looking at post-traumatic stress? She was aware it could happen after shark attacks, even dog bites.

So why not, after the extraordinary nature of Brandon's accident and its aftermath? It was possible. In fact, it was probable. Her bottom lip pursed and tightened momentarily. She had to get this lad to begin the long journey back and start to talk about things. 'When you were injured, was help long in getting to you, Brandon?'

'Took a while.' Suddenly, the youth seemed eager to talk. 'I staggered to the Berwicks' place—they live on the farm next to ours and it was closer than trying to make it home.'

'That was good thinking,' Maxi said approvingly. 'But I'm surprised you weren't out of it.'

He shrugged. 'Couldn't let myself go under but I could hardly breathe or talk,' he replied, with a grin that was more a grimace. 'Mrs B. got a hell of a fright when I turned up at her kitchen door.'

'I imagine so. Were you bleeding?'

'Nah. The paramedic on the rescue chopper told me my shirt had been pushed so far into the wound that—'

'It automatically sealed it?' Maxi came in, somewhat in awe of the cool behaviour this youngster had exhibited. 'That's amazing.'

He nodded. 'Doc Haslem came out and stayed with me until the chopper got there. They took me straight to Sydney.'

'And apart from the sleeping, you're doing OK now?'

'Not too keen to get on that damn stupid horse again,' he drawled.

Well, that was understandable. Maxi put her head on one side and asked, 'Don't you usually muster on motorbikes out here?'

'Sometimes.' For a second Brandon seemed to retreat into himself. 'Mum's not too keen on them. Like to see my scars?' Almost proudly, he pulled up the front of his shirt and Maxi was able to see the curved outline of the scar under his right nipple and another running horizontally down the lower part of his chest.

'Neat job,' she approved.

'I reckon. The doc in Sydney told me the branch had gone about seventeen centimetres into my chest.'

'Ouch!' More than six inches. Maxi drew back in her chair. 'I have to say I'm pretty impressed with your gutsy behaviour when you were injured. I doubt I'd have been so cool.'

'You're a woman,' he dismissed with the brashness of youth, and began tucking his shirt back in.

'Hey, women can be brave,' Maxi protested laughingly. 'Do you have a girlfriend, Brandon?'

'Kind of…' He reddened. 'Don't see her much. She's away at school.'

And the school holidays were coming up so in all probability Brandon would quickly regain his equilibrium in the company of someone around his own age. Especially a girl. Suppressing a wry smile, Maxi got to her feet. 'I'll just be a minute, Brandon. I need to get something.'

When Maxi returned, she handed her young patient a small plastic bottle. 'These are some mild sleeping tablets, seven in all, one for each night for a week. Hopefully they'll get your sleeping pattern back into its normal rhythm. And I want you to come back and see me in a week. It might be a good idea to make an appointment with Ayleen now as you leave. And I think we should let your mum know about this as well—is that OK with you?'

The youth's expression clouded and he looked down at the bottle resting in the palm of his hand. 'I won't do anything stupid.'

'I know that. But as your mum is the one who sent you in, she'll want to know how you got on and support you through this rough patch. That is, if she's anything like my mum,' Maxi added wryly, a tiny dimple flowering in her cheek as she smiled.

The boy returned a half-grin. 'No worries. I won't need the pills for long anyway,' he ended with a forced kind of bravado.

'I'm guessing you won't either.' Maxi got to her feet to see him out. 'You can update me when you come in next week.'

'Yep.' Brandon shouldered his way out. 'See you, Doc.'

'Yes. See you, Brandon.'

Maxi had just finished her call to Brandon's mother when Jake rapped and strode in. 'I just saw young Brand McCall leaving,' he said without preamble, throwing himself into the chair beside her desk and locking his arms across his chest. 'What's the deal?'

'Deal?' Maxi frowned in query.

'He should have been on *my* list.'

Maxi felt the waves of his disapproval crashing over her. Was he suggesting she'd had no business treating his patient? Well, she'd soon sort him out about that. 'Brandon arrived without an appointment. He seemed ill at ease and Ayleen felt he wouldn't hang about and asked me to see him first. Which I have done,' she finished coolly.

'I know Brand's history. I would've seen him.'

'You'd told Ayleen you were on a long consult and didn't want to be disturbed for *anything*,' Maxi pointed out with calm logic. 'Ayleen used her discretion.'

'She should have known I'd want to see him.'

'What point are you making, Jacob? For heaven's sake! If you're going to be so protective of all your patients, then I have to wonder why you agreed to have me here at all.'

Jake's jaw tightened. He was beginning to wonder about his sanity regarding that as well. 'Brand's family background is pretty complex,' he gave out stiffly. 'You wouldn't have known about it. That's the only point I'm making.'

'I read his history as far as it went,' Maxi said defensively. 'Today he seemed to need a friendly ear so I provided that, and in the process found out he wasn't sleeping. I gave him some mild sedatives just to—'

'How many?' Jake cut in sharply.

'Seven—one for each night until I see him again in a week.'

'You did impress that on him *one* each night?'

'Of course!' Maxi hissed. 'Just what is going on here, Jacob?'

He went very still. 'Brand's father, Harley, was the recent suicide I told you about.'

Oh, lord… Maxi dragged in a breath. And immediately it all came back to her—her young patient's sudden glance when she'd mentioned motorbikes and his expression as he'd looked at the pills, declaring he wasn't about to do anything stupid. She rallied. 'I didn't detect anything flaky about Brandon's behaviour. In fact, for a youngster, he seemed to be handling things pretty well. He even showed me his scars.' She tried for lightness but found none in return. OK, if that's how he wanted to play it she'd keep it wholly professional. 'However, in my opinion, he still has some residual trauma from his accident.'

'PTSD?'

She nodded. 'I'm surprised he received no counselling at the hospital.'

Jake's dark brows kicked together in an unforgiving frown. Was she finding fault with Australian hospitals now? 'I know for a fact he did.'

'There was nothing on the file.'

'Then you should have checked with me before you went assuming things. And it just proves my point—I should have been the one to see Brandon.'

Maxi's heartbeat surged to a sickening rhythm. Spots of colour glazed her cheeks and she felt ill. *Arrogant pig.* What the hell was he playing at? Grandstanding like some petty bureaucrat—as though she'd broken some cardinal rule for daring to see his patient. In one fluid movement she threw her pen sideways so it landed on the floor next to his feet and swung out of her chair, glaring across the desk at him. 'Then, perhaps, Dr Haslem, you should have indicated *mind-reading* was a requirement to work here!'

Jake's jaw dropped and he hauled it back up. Then with a savage yank he retrieved her pen off the floor, replacing it on the desk next to her prescription pad.

Watching him, Maxi shook her head. She wanted to yell and throw the entire contents of her desktop at him. Instead, she spun round and marched across to the window, looking out, her breath coming hard and fast. All her efforts to come here to find him seemed worthless now. If they couldn't even *work* in harmony, what was the point of any of it?

Jake sat frozenly. His gut resembled a receptacle for heavy metal. He'd acted like a smart ass from a cheap movie. Damn and double damn. Was the matter with him? Maxi would walk if he didn't get his act together.

He swallowed the sudden ache in his throat. He blamed his foul mood—in fact, *everything*—on their present untenable situation. Sharing a home with Maxi, yet sharing nothing at all. Having her so close but wanting her *closer* was like a never-ending nightmare. From early morning she breathed life into his day, smelled like the sweetest wild flowers as she flitted about the place, loving life itself.

If only she loved him. But she wasn't giving anything away on that score.

His mouth pulled tight. Each night while he lay sleepless, he'd vow he would talk with her. Really talk. Try to unravel the mess they'd made of things.

Like, why it had taken her so long to come to him?

For that matter, why hadn't he pocketed his pride and gone back to England to her? He could have done. He'd had the money. Hell, he'd always had the money to do whatever he'd wanted. But money with all its uses couldn't buy happiness.

Some hard lessons had taught him that.

He scrubbed a hand roughly across his cheekbones. Brooding over the past wasn't going to solve anything. Shooting his chair back, he went to stand beside her at the window. 'Uh, about Brand…' he said, his voice coming out scratchy and not quite even. 'I overreacted. You obviously handled things. Thanks.'

Could he spare it? Maxi held back a snort of disgust—just. 'Don't do this again, Jacob.' She hoped she sounded cooler and calmer than she felt. 'I won't be taken to task about something that is not my fault. Is that clear?'

'Quite clear.'

It wasn't until the door closed behind him that Maxi realised she'd been digging her nails into her palms. The outline of four purplish indents mocked her from each hand. And they felt sore. But not as sore as her heart.

It felt like a football that had been battered and kicked through the longest, meanest grudge match.

She fell back into her chair and closed her eyes. Drawing a deep breath, she forced herself to relax. She had a long list to get through.

Maxi's next patient was a little three-year-old, Harrison Pender. 'What seems to be the trouble?' She dug deep and drummed up a smile for the anxious-looking mother.

'He's been complaining of pain in his ears,' Christy Pender said, swooping a kiss across the top of her son's fair head and holding him closely to her.

'Off his food?' Maxi asked.

'Yes, and blowing bubbles in his milk when usually he slurps it down. I looked for a rash but there wasn't any. What could it be, Doctor?'

'Let's examine Harrison and we'll have a better idea,' Maxi said gently.

'Do you want him on the bed?'

'No, he's fine on your lap,' Maxi said, beginning her examination, deftly requesting further information about the child's symptoms along the way. Fever, sore throat and obviously not feeling well, poor little guy. 'Has Harrison had a problem with his ears before, Mrs Pender?'

'Christy—and he did last year. I was staying with my parents at the coast. The doctor at the hospital gave him some antibiotics. It cleared up. Shh, now, Harry,' she hushed, as her son began to grizzle.

'OK, sweetheart, that's all for now.' Maxi put her laryngoscope aside and went to wash her hands at the basin, collecting a picture book from the pile before she took her chair again. 'Do you like animals, Harrison?' She proffered the book and the little lad reached out a chubby hand and tentatively accepted the picture book, looking at the bright, shiny cover. 'Tiger,' he said clearly, before turning away and burrowing into his mother's breast.

'Mmm, that's a tiger all right.' Maxi chuckled, watching in gentle amusement. Sweet little boy. Her look was soft and she felt the faintest glitch in her heartbeat. Children were precious. And it would be so special to have a family with the man you loved. As long as he loved you in return.

'So, Doctor, what do you think?'

Christy's soft, anxious query jolted Maxi back to her role as a family practitioner. 'Harrison appears to have a middle ear infection.'

'That's the same thing he had before.' Christy worried her lower lip. 'Will he get them all the time now?'

'He may do,' Maxi said, 'but fortunately his eardrums appear intact so that's a plus.'

Christy brought her head up, asking fearfully, 'You mean they could burst?'

'In severe cases they can rupture, yes. But I think we've caught Harrison in time. I'll prescribe an antibiotic and I'd like to check him again in forty-eight hours.'

'And if it's not clearing up?'

'We'll monitor him carefully but we may need to refer him on.'

'To a specialist?' Christy raised worried eyes. 'And what would be the worst-case scenario—I mean, what if the eardrum ruptured?'

'Christy, we're a long way from that.' Maxi leaned forward earnestly. 'If this kind of infection becomes chronic, a specialist would insert little tubes called grommets into the eardrum to allow draining of the middle ear.'

Christy swallowed. 'And would these…grommets have to be there for the rest of his life?'

'Goodness, no. More often than not they drop out after about six weeks or so when the ear is healthy again.' Maxi pulled her prescription pad towards her. 'It's a very common procedure amongst children.'

'Thanks for explaining things, Dr Somers.' Christy took the slip of paper, hitching Harrison on to her hip as she stood. 'We'll see you in a couple of days.'

Maxi was halfway through her list when Ayleen arrived with morning tea. 'Time for a break,' she declared, slipping the little tray onto the desk. 'And your muffins are delicious. I had two,' she confessed guiltily.

'Take some home,' Maxi insisted. 'I made heaps. They'll freeze well.'

'Oh, what a good idea.' Ayleen was all smiles. 'I'll take some along to my tennis club. I know the girls would appreciate a change from my scones. I'm not much of a cook,' she confessed ruefully. 'My husband, Gavin, reckons I'm heavy handed with everything except corned beef and potatoes.'

'Ayleen, I'm sure that's not true.' Maxi had to chew down on the inside of her cheek to stop herself from laughing. 'You're a brilliant practice manager anyway.'

'Oh…' Ayleen pinked a bit. 'I do try to look after everyone's needs.' She made a small face. 'I guess Jake would soon have something to say if I didn't.'

And she'd have something to say if he *did*, Maxi decided in an inner voice that echoed her own resentment and displeasure with the man. Her shoulders lifted in a dispirited sigh. A short time ago she'd felt so hopeful about things. About her decision to come here to Tangaratta, about her relationship with Jake. About life in general. Now…

'There's me chatting on.' Ayleen sensed Maxi's change of mood and began to take her leave. 'I'll let you get back to things.'

Maxi managed a small smile. 'Thanks for cheering me up, Ayleen.'

'Oh, rubbish,' the practice manager replied lightly. 'Don't let your tea get cold now.'

Jake closed the door behind his last patient. Lord, what a morning. Except it was already afternoon. Raising his arms, he stretched, working his shoulders and neck muscles. What he wouldn't give for a decent massage. At the thought, he took in a jerky breath, a shiver prickling his skin.

Maxi gave the best massage.

If only.

He closed his eyes, almost feeling his muscles beginning to loosen and unknot under her skilful kneading and smoothing…

Who was he kidding? Right now she hated his guts. She wouldn't want to be within a mile of him.

A gravelly sigh dragged itself up from the depth of his lungs. With no chance of a massage in the offing, he'd better settle for smashing some balls around the squash court instead.

Moodily he contemplated the rift between himself and Maxi—mostly his own fault, he reminded himself grimly. He'd better eat crow before things got any worse. Hell, it was all he seemed to do lately.

He felt the tightening in his throat again. So tight he could barely swallow. He swore under his breath, scrubbing the heels of his hands across his eyes. He couldn't remember when he'd felt so grim and it was all such a mess. But, by heaven, it didn't have to stay that way.

Emotionally, whatever it took, he had to stop living a life of indecision.

Buoyed by his resolution, he pushed his way through the swing doors into the staff kitchen.

Ayleen was doing a last flick around the benchtops. 'At last! I'd just about given up on you.'

'Where's Maxi?' Jake's dark brows flexed impatiently.

'Liz Maynard invited her to a working lunch with some of the CWA committee. It seems we have a batch of "new poor" in the district. Liz is after ways to help so I guess she's hoping Maxi might be able to contribute.'

Jake snorted. 'Maxi's got more than enough to do here.'

Ayleen's mouth pursed and she shook her head. With quick, deft movements she set Jake's lunch in front of him and switched on the kettle. She was quite certain these two had had a falling out. And she'd had such hopes for them, too. Jake needed someone like Maxi, sweet, natural, a lovely young woman. 'You're *both* working too hard, Jake, and you especially are jaded. Cut yourself a bit of slack, for heaven's sake!'

'If only.' Jake dug into his corned beef and salad hungrily.

'Perhaps the surgery hours could do with a bit of streamlining,' Ayleen said carefully.

Jake looked up, brows raised in query. 'How do we manage that?'

'Shouldn't be too difficult.' Ayleen's enthusiasm revved. She wasn't about to let this opportunity slip by. Pulling out a chair, she sat facing Jake across the table. 'Some days we run right over and it's not because there's an overload of patients. It's because some folk think its OK to wander in twenty minutes late for their appointment.'

Jake looked less than convinced. 'As doctors, Maxi and I can't *not* see patients, Ayleen.'

'But you don't have to put up with stragglers, or with patients turning up without appointments and expecting to be seen,' Ayleen countered earnestly. 'A case in point was Brandon McCall this morning.'

Not that again. Jake shrugged dismissively, his broad shoulders shifting under his shirt. 'Maxi saw him, didn't she?'

'And I'm well aware he should have gone to you.'

'Who's been talking?' Jake raised the question quietly and lethally. He wouldn't have thought Maxi would want to air their personal grievances. But then again…

'Oh, for heaven's sake! Do you think I'm blind? I saw the way you stormed into Maxi's room after Brand had left. And your face when you came out,' she tacked on for good measure. 'Maxi only did what was asked of her. My instincts were telling me Brand was about to do a runner if he wasn't seen quickly. And we wouldn't have wanted that, would we?'

'No.' Jake's mouth twisted ruefully. 'I should have known you'd have had the situation in hand, Ayleen.'

'Of course you should,' Ayleen declared, not ready quite yet to let her boss off the hook. 'You and Maxi make a great team. Be sure you're not the one to wreck it.'

'Women power, is it?' From somewhere deep inside him Jake found a jaundiced grin. He'd had that coming, he supposed. 'I'll make amends,' he promised Ayleen.

'Good.' The receptionist got to her feet. 'And if Catherine McCall had had the gumption to phone for an appointment for her son, none of this would have happened.'

'The family have had more than their share of grief lately,' Jake said quietly.

'And that's precisely the reason I didn't want to add to it and made sure Brand was seen promptly.'

'OK, point taken.' Jake raised a hand in surrender. 'Just sort out a time when you, Maxi and I can get together and nut out this streamlining, would you, please?'

'My pleasure, Doctor.' Ayleen left, quietly triumphant.

CHAPTER SEVEN

'MAXI', LIZ SAID, as the women took their places around the table in the workroom at the rear of her shop. 'These are my co-committee members, Dawn, Alison and Jennifer. Girls.' She smiled. 'This is our wonderful new addition to Tangaratta, Dr Maxi Somers.'

Dawn, mid-fiftyish and with the suntanned complexion of her outdoor lifestyle, looked at Maxi over the rim of her tea mug, her clear blue gaze registering slight disbelief. 'And you've come all the way from England to work *here*?'

'Must be nuts,' Jennifer, blonde, cute freckles, the youngest of the group laughed. 'But good on you.'

'That goes for me, too,' Alison, the shy one said quietly. 'And thank you. It's an answer to prayer to have a woman doctor right out here. Not that Jake isn't caring—he is—but you know how it is…' She broke off and went a little pink.

Maxi nodded. She did know how it was, when you'd rather confide your problems to another woman, doctor or not. But acknowledging the welcome from this group of bush women, she felt almost like a fraud. After her run-in with Jake earlier, she'd seriously considered abandoning the place and just packing up and going home.

Except, when she'd thought about it, the idea hadn't filled her with the joy it should have. And she'd realised with something like amazement that this quaint little outback town was already beginning to feel remarkably like *home*. At least it would do, if Jake would only learn to trust her again…

'What do you think, Maxi?' Liz was asking. 'Any ideas where we could go with this?'

'Uh…' Maxi snapped back to reality, surveying the expectant faces of the women around her. She knew the gist of what Liz was aiming to achieve but she'd had no time to think of anything specific—unless… 'Perhaps we could begin with the schoolchildren?' she said off the top of her head, linking the assembled group with a questioning look. 'Would there be a possibility of forming a breakfast club, feed any child who's hungry for one reason or another?'

'It would certainly be a start,' Liz acknowledged thoughtfully.

'And we could use the facilities at the school tuck shop,' Jennifer chimed in enthusiastically. 'They're more than adequate and it would mean we could keep an eye on things.'

'Even though my family have all left school, I'd be happy to take a turn at supervising,' Alison said.

'I'm hoping all the CWA members will rally round in some capacity.' Liz took up her pen and began making notes. 'We should probably approach the school authorities first, though,' she added on a cautionary note.

'No need to worry about that, Liz.' Jennifer flapped a hand in dismissal. 'I'm on the P&C committee. I'll square it. Just let's get Maxi's plan up and running and get the kids fed. I'd be happy to act as facilitator, order the food and so on.'

'Do you have the time?' Maxi frowned a bit. 'It would be quite a big undertaking.'

'I'd make the time,' Jennifer said. 'I've four kids at the school and I'm already spending lots of my time there helping with the reading and stuff. And if it gets too much, I'll delegate.'

'Sounds like you've acquired the job, then,' Maxi said. 'As long as the rest of the committee is in favour, of course,' she said diplomatically.

Murmurs of agreement echoed around the table. 'What kinds of things should we serve the children?' Dawn asked practically. 'Kids can be a bit fussy.'

'Not when they're hungry,' Jennifer declared. 'But let's keep it simple. Cereal, fruit and toast with a nourishing spread.'

'And milk,' Alison came in helpfully.

'And if it takes off, we could even run to grilled tomatoes or scrambled eggs.' Jennifer's voice bubbled with enthusiasm.

'We'd have a small amount of funds to kick it off but they're not unlimited,' Liz reminded them. 'And that's where we'd like you to come in, Maxi.'

Maxi blinked and realised everyone was looking speculatively at her. Oh, heavens, did they expect a monetary contribution? She had the tiniest bit put by but lawks! Her hand went to the fine gold chain at her throat. 'Uh…in what way, Liz?'

'Hey, don't look like that!' Laughingly, Jennifer reached across and gave Maxi a comforting pat on the forearm. 'We're not about to bleed you dry. We'd just need you in your capacity of medical officer here, to add your weight to our petition for government funding for the project.'

'Oh.' Maxi gave an embarrassed look around the table. 'Of course I can do that. And if you need any facilities at the surgery, just ask. I know Ayleen wouldn't mind sending off the odd fax or email for you.'

There were smiles of satisfaction and little nods of approval from all the women. 'I can see our new doctor is going to be a great asset to the district,' Jennifer declared with an infectious grin. 'Liz, at the next meeting of the CWA, I'd like to nominate Maxi for membership.'

Liz positively beamed. 'And I'll be honoured to second it myself.'

A few minutes later Maxi was on her way back to the surgery. She'd just acquired some new friends and there was a spring in her step and a very warm glow in her heart.

But all that dissipated when she stepped through the front

doors at the surgery. There was an air of urgency about the place and Jake was hovering. 'Oh, good,' he said shortly. 'You're back.'

Obviously. Maxi felt her hackles rise. 'I'm not late, am I?'

His expression sharpened. Hell, she was still on the warpath apparently. 'I don't have a stopwatch on you, Maxi,' he responded heavily. 'But we do have an emergency out at the skydivers' club at Rossvale. One of the jumpers has been caught up in a freak wind. Took a pretty bad tumble, from all accounts. We'll need to get out there.'

Immediately, Maxi felt put on her mettle. Her mind raced ahead. 'What do we do about this afternoon's surgery?'

'I've had a look through the list. They're all regulars. At first glance I'd say they could be seen either tomorrow morning or Monday. Ayleen is doing a ring-around now. Whatever's needed, she'll sort it.'

'As she does.' Maxi offered a tentative smile.

'Mmm.' Jake met her eyes, returning a wry, fence-mending kind of smile. Later, it seemed to imply.

Maxi took a thin breath. Well, she could live with that.

'We'll need to collect a trauma kit from the hospital.' Jake reined in his thoughts abruptly. 'Do you have a jacket of some kind with you?'

'Yes. I brought one in and left it here.'

'Good. We could be out late and even though it's summer, it can get freezing further west.'

Maxi felt a swirl of nervous tension in her stomach. Attending the scene of an accident never got any easier, wherever they happened. 'I'll just grab my coat and catch up with you, then.'

His eyes narrowed and he nodded. 'Meet you outside.'

'How far is this Rossville?' Maxi asked. She'd been astounded how quickly things had been co-ordinated and now they were out on the highway and travelling at speed.

'Rossvale,' Jake corrected. 'And it's about forty k's. It won't take us long to get there. There's very little traffic, as you see.'

He was right there, Maxi thought, her gaze going to the dun

colour of the grass of the paddocks on either side of the road. It was so silent and there was still something oddly untouched about Australia's wide open spaces. Something fearless—if she wasn't being too fanciful. She sent Jake a quick, enquiring look. 'So, do we have any more details of the injuries?'

'Fractures for sure and possible head injury. The ambulance should be right behind us.'

'So the patient will have to be airlifted to Sydney?'

'The CareFlight chopper's been alerted.' Jake's response was clipped. 'They'll land at the hospital strip and we'll meet them there with the ambulance and, hopefully, with a stabilised patient onboard.'

Maxi heard the thread of disquiet in his voice. She didn't blame him. They were so isolated out here and in medical terms flying by the seats of their pants for the most part. The responsibility was almost crippling…

'Someone has to do it, Max,' Jake said quietly.

Her head spun towards him, her eyes widening in disbelief. It was almost spooky the way he'd somehow been able to tap into her thoughts. 'You must feel like you're always being tested.'

He lifted a shoulder. 'We can only do what we can do, given the circumstances we're faced with.'

'And if all doctors were so philosophical, there'd be no burnout in the profession, would there?' Maxi's voice was laced with faint cynicism. 'Tell me more about this freak wind you mentioned,' she said in an effort to take her mind off what lay ahead.

'It's like a huge whirlwind,' Jake explained. 'Certain weather conditions can trigger them. In today's incident, the jumper was only about nine metres from the ground when the wind caught him up, shook him to blazes and then literally dropped him like a stone.'

Maxi suppressed a shudder. 'It would be something like being dumped by a huge wave, then?'

He grunted. 'It's the parachuting equivalent of being struck by lightning.'

Oh, lord. Maxi inhaled deeply, recognising the flutter of uncertainty in her stomach. This idea of delivering medicine on the trot was surely the stuff of nightmares.

Aaron McEvoy, the chief instructor from the Rossvale Ramblers was waiting for them. 'Thanks for coming, Jake,' he said, his expression a bit grim.

'This is my practice partner, Dr Maxi Somers.' Jake made the introductions briskly. 'Do we have a name for the injured man?'

'Brett Hosking, nineteen. Only his fifth jump. Poor blighter didn't know what hit him.'

'Conscious?' Jake snapped.

'Just.' Aaron began leading them across to where a temporary tent-like shelter had been erected over the injured jumper.

'Right. Thanks, Aaron.' Jake pulled back the tent flap and waited for Maxi to precede him. They made straight for the huddled form of their patient and dropped down beside him.

'Hi, Brett.' Jake slid the emergency kit off his shoulders. 'I'm Jake and this is Maxi. We're doctors. Can you tell us where you are?' he asked, beginning a simple test of their patient's competency. Brett's answers were strained but he got them out. 'Torch, please, Maxi.'

Jake's face was set in concentration as he flicked the light into the young man's eyes. 'Equal and reacting,' he relayed.

Thank goodness. Maxi gnawed at her bottom lip. They could administer a painkiller without the risk of destablising him. 'His leg seems at an odd angle, Jacob.' In fact, Brett's right leg appeared several inches shorter than the other and now sat painfully out of joint. 'Fractured NOF?'

'Looks like it. We'll need a doughnut dressing over that protruding bone. Take it easy, mate.' Jake's hands were gentle as he lifted Brett's head and applied an oxygen mask. 'Breathe away, now. We'll give you something for the pain. Chopper's on its way. You'll be heading off to hospital pretty soon.'

'I'll check his breath sounds.' Maxi flicked a stethoscope over the young man's chest. 'Bit raspy,' she murmured, putting the stethoscope aside. Carefully, she began palpating Brett's stomach. 'Tummy's soft,' she reported.

So no spleen damage, Jake interpreted, and gave Maxi a quick acknowledgment. 'I'll get a line in.' It took only a few seconds to whip a tourniquet around Brett's arm. 'Blood's a bit slow…' He began tapping gently to prompt a vein to the surface. 'Finally!' Letting his breath go in relief, he slid the cannula into the young man's arm.

Maxi kept a watchful eye on their patient. 'Are we going with morphine for pain relief? If so, I'd prefer to under-prescribe. He's a fairly slight build.'

'Let's play it safe, then. Draw up morphine five milligrams.'

'And something to settle his tummy. Do we have an anti-emetic with us?'

'Maxolon,' Jake confirmed. 'Give ten. And we'll follow with fifty of pethidine. That should get him through transportation to the hospital.'

Maxi began preparing the drugs. 'Are you allergic to anything you know of, Brett?'

Eyes dulled with pain, the young man shook his head.

'Hang in there, mate.' Jake's voice was gentle. 'You're doing great.' He glanced at Maxi. 'Ready?'

She nodded, swabbing the cannula and shooting the first two drugs home, praying the injection would work, and soon. This young man was in a lot of pain.

'Splints now, Max.' Jake's instruction was clipped. 'The sooner we can get him aboard that ambulance, the better.'

Maxi felt the tightness in her temple ease marginally. Please, heaven, they were almost out of the woods and soon Brett would be on his way to specialist care in Sydney.

Jake's hands were quick and sure as he placed the supportive splints between the young man's legs and expertly bandaged Brett's injured leg to his good one. 'Right, he's ready to move now. I'll just duck outside and ask the ambos to bring the stretcher. Time for that peth dose now, please, Max.'

With the reassuring presence of Jake gone, Maxi felt the suffocating silence of the small tent close in on her. She swallowed, impatiently brushing a strand of hair away from her cheek with the back of her hand. This was no time to start wondering what the heck she was doing here, miles away from the back-up support of an emergency department. Suddenly some sixth sense made her pause over the drug pack. Her hand froze. Her gut clenched. Dear God…

One look at Brett told her that they had trouble of the worst kind.

'Jac-ob!' Maxi's piercing cry was anguished.

Brett was gulping, his eyes rolling back in his head, his colour a ghastly grey. Please, no. Maxi gave a little whimper of distress in her throat. But if she didn't act quickly, they'd have a death on their hands. In one swift movement she ripped Brett's shirt open and began chest compressions.

Jake's shadow fell beside her. 'Bloody hell… He's throwing a PE!' A pulmonary embolism. The worst possible complication. He grabbed for the lifesaving equipment. He would have to intubate. *Damn it to hell.*

Why hadn't he seen this coming? All the components for a PE had been staring him in the face. A serious fracture. Fat escaping from the break, gumming up the arteries. Hell's teeth! Why did he do this job?

He deliberately steadied his breathing. Don't lose it, you idiot, he cautioned himself darkly, skilfully passing the tube down Brett's trachea, attaching it to the oxygen. 'Breathe now!' he grated. 'Come on!'

Maxi lifted her gaze, watching with mounting dread as Jake checked and rechecked the carotid pulse in Brett's neck. He shook his head.

'For God's sake, Jacob.' Maxi's voice shook. 'Zap him!'

Jake got into position. 'Be ready to take over the bag when I defibrillate,' he snapped.

'Just do it!' Maxi found added strength from somewhere. Brett's life could depend on their teamwork now. Almost in slow motion she reached out and took over the Air Viva bag.

'And clear!'

Maxi dropped the bag and spun back, praying the volts of electricity would do what they were supposed to do and kick-start the heart's rhythm.

'Damn all…' Jake spat the words from between clenched teeth. 'I'm going to two hundred. Clear!'

Maxi felt panic claw at her insides and the slow slide of sweat between her breasts. The trace was still flat.

'Start compressions again, Maxi.' Jake looked haunted. 'I'm giving him adrenalin.' His mouth clenched into a thin line and his fingers curled around the mini-jet already prepared with the lifesaving drug. 'Work for me, please!' he implored, sending the long needle neatly between Brett's ribs and into his heart.

'Clear!' He activated the charge and their combined gazes clung to the monitor. The trace bleeped, faded and then staggered into a rhythm. 'Yes…' Jake's relief was controlled. 'We've got him, Max. Well done.'

'Oh…' Maxi felt the tight lens of tears across her eyes. Hastily, she blinked them away, gathering her composure.

'Hey…' Jake's voice was hushed and his arm came round her shoulders. 'It's OK, Max… It's OK.'

'I…thought we'd lose him.' She hiccuped a sob and turned her face into Jake's shoulder.

'No way…' Jake cleared the lump from his throat, pressing a kiss to her temple and hugging her to his side.

They were still entwined when Tony Jones, the senior ambulance officer, poked his head in, towing the collapsible stretcher. 'Nice work, guys,' he said quietly.

Maxi felt as though she'd been to hell and back. Swallowing hard on the tightness in her throat, she eased herself away from the protective warmth of Jake's arm and pulled herself upright. 'I'll just give Brett a shot of midazolam to ease him over the shock, Tony. And then he should be ready to move. He's back in sinus rhythm but he'll need careful monitoring.'

'Understood, Doc.' Tony was no novice to the job. He knew well how easily the dice could have fallen the other way and they could have been facing a whole different outcome. 'Right.' He cleared his throat awkwardly. 'Let's get this youngster on his way, then. If you're ready, Jake, on my count.'

'Here's where our responsibility ends,' Jake said with feeling, as they stood, tracking the blinking lights of the rescue aircraft across the pale sky.

Maxi roused herself. Brett was at last on his way to hospital and now she just wanted to go home.

Once they were in Jake's vehicle and on their way, Maxi, to her disgust, felt herself folding like a wet tissue. 'I hate this part of being a doctor.'

'It was a bit hairy today,' Jake admitted, throwing her a discerning glance out of the corner of his eye. 'But you coped, Max. That's what matters.'

'And if I hadn't been there?'

'Tony would have filled in where he could, but I can't tell you enough how good it felt to have another doctor on my team.'

Maxi stifled a bitter laugh. So he only needed her for her medical skills—was that what he was saying? But right now she was too weary to find out.

Maxi blinked against the light as they came through the front door and into the hallway. It seemed an age since she'd left for work that morning. 'I'm off for a shower.'

Jake eyed her critically. She looked shattered and he had a fair idea it wasn't all down to the harrowing few hours they'd just spent. 'Do that,' he said quietly. 'I'll grab a shower as well and then I'll rustle up some food.'

'I'm not hungry.' Her mouth drooped. At the moment food seemed inconsequential compared to the rest of her problems.

'You have to eat,' he insisted. 'We both do. I'll knock an omelette together. Off you go.'

Feeling dismissed, Maxi turned into her bedroom and closed the door. She went through to her en suite, peeling off her soiled clothes and shoving them into the hamper. Stepping into the shower, she let the hot stream of water ease her aching muscles, then realised she'd stayed well beyond the mandatory three minutes.

One slip-up didn't constitute a major crime, for heaven's sake, she allayed her conscience, closing off the taps. Drying herself quickly, she returned to the bedroom, eyeing the plumpness of her pillows wistfully. Right at this moment she craved nothing more than to crawl into bed and blot out her relationship with Jake and everything about the whole day.

But, of course, she couldn't do that. She had a fair idea Jake would come looking for her if she tried that ruse. Half-heartedly, she dug out some three-quarter-length trousers and a T-shirt and pulled them on.

When she walked into the kitchen, Jake indicated the glass of chilled white wine on the breakfast bar. 'Thanks.' She lifted the glass and swallowed a mouthful. 'You having one?'

For answer, he pointed to his opened can of lager on the worktop. 'Anything you want to debrief about?' he asked, setting about preparing their food, assembling eggs, bowl and whisk.

She looked down, running the pad of her thumb across the raised pattern on the base of the glass. 'We did everything we could, didn't we, Jacob?'

His dark head snapped up, a frown lodging between his brows. So that's why she'd been so quiet on the way home. Was she doubting herself and her skills? 'We got to the accident scene as soon as we possibly could. We carried out appropriate emergency procedures as competently as our circumstances allowed. What else could we have done?'

Maxi's hand tightened around the stem of her glass, remembering those few seconds when she'd felt frozen to the spot. 'I never felt so isolated in my professional role, or so vulnerable…'

Jake knew those kinds of feelings only too well. His moody gaze raked her face. 'Don't start second-guessing everything you do out here or you'll end up on the shrink's couch. We got our patient stable enough to travel to specialist help. I think we can forgive ourselves a few moments of panic here and there.'

She returned his gaze uncertainly. Had he guessed? 'If you say so.'

His brows lifted slightly but, instead of commenting, he merely said, 'You did well. Now, if there's anything else you want to unload, just hit me with it.' He turned away and began to whisk the eggs with undue vigour.

'I could use a hug,' she said in a low voice.

'Sorry?' He tilted his head back towards her.

Maxi felt put on the spot, feeling the tension between them wind a little tighter. Was he pretending not to have heard? She didn't know, couldn't guess. Whatever, she wouldn't play his games. She pointed to the mixing bowl. 'I said, that will make them tough.'

'What will?'

'Attacking them like that. You need a light hand with eggs.'

He lifted a shoulder dismissively and went on with his task. 'See if there's something to make us a green salad, hmm?'

So, end of debrief. Maxi shrugged inwardly, sliding off her high stool. She went to the crisper part of the fridge and dived in. 'Marie's left a huge bunch of rocket. Isn't she a gem? It must be from her own veg garden.' She broke off one of the peppery leaves and popped it into her mouth. 'Mmm, gorgeous. We could probably grow a few herbs and things, couldn't we?'

'As long as you intend to be around to nurture them,' Jake threw the words out as a kind of challenge. And wondered whether tonight would be the time when they could actually talk about whether or not they had a future together.

Maxi went on preparing their salad. Had he guessed just how unsettled she'd been feeling after today's run-in about Brandon? 'A few plants wouldn't take up much of anyone's time. Even yours,' she added, and her heart gave a little flutter.

Jake's mouth tightened. Was this her way of telling him he could go to hell? Chasing the little knob of butter around the pan, he waited until it melted and then poured in the beaten eggs. 'We may as well eat out on the verandah,' he said gruffly.

'Fine with me.'

Their mobile phones rang simultaneously when they had almost finished their meal. Jake rocked off his chair and went to the end of the verandah to take his call.

When he came back to the table, Maxi bubbled excitedly, 'That was Liz. Karryn Goode's invited some of the CWA girls out to her place tomorrow. She asked Liz to include me.'

A beat of silence and then his throat made a convulsive movement. 'I'm glad you're making friends.' He hitched his hands across the back of his chair. 'My call was from Ayleen. Appears there are several patients who'd like to be seen in the morning. I'll go in. You've more than earned a day off.'

'Thanks.' Maxi stood and began clearing their dishes. She thought she had, too. 'I'll just load these and then I'm off for an early night. Not sure when I'll be back from Karryn's tomorrow, so I'll see you when I see you.'

Jake let her go without further comment. Were they ever going to find the right time to actually *talk*? he wondered grimly.

CHAPTER EIGHT

MAXI FOUND JAKE on the verandah when she arrived home. He was sitting at the outdoor table, in semi-darkness, the space lit only by a lantern. 'I'm a bit later than I thought,' she said by way of greeting.

'Maxi…' He lifted his head, blinking as if he needed to regain his focus. 'Drink?' He held his glass aloft.

'What are you having?'

'Mineral water.'

She made a small face. 'I'll get a white wine.' She touched his shoulder. 'Don't move. I want to tell you all about my day at Westwood.'

'And the birdsong was almost deafening.' It was quite a bit later and Maxi's voice still held a breathless quality as she recounted her impressions of her day on an outback property. 'And the kookaburras! We had a barbecue lunch and would you believe one of the cheeky young things flew down and snatched a piece of raw steak off the plate where Dean was cooking?'

'Much of their natural food is caught live,' Jake said quietly.

She chuckled. 'Karryn said they'd eat the nose off your face if they thought it was tempting enough.'

'See any cockatoos?'

'Dozens. What a chatter! They were flapping around one of the big gumtrees. And then we saw this huge lizard trying to climb the trunk.'

'That would be a goanna,' Jake's mouth twisted wryly. 'Black and pale green?'

'Something like that. Karryn said there was probably a nest up there and he was after the eggs. The birds kept swooping on him until he finally came down and lumbered off into the bush. And a couple of king parrots came to lunch. Their feathers were brilliant red and emerald green. Male and female apparently. They sat like sentinels on the railings while we were eating. I took pictures. They were amazing.' She shook her head. 'I can't believe how everyone out here takes such fabulous wildlife for granted.'

Jake flexed a shoulder. 'From growing up with it, I guess. What else did you do?'

'Earned my keep.' She laughed, lifting her tangle of auburn hair and letting it fall away. 'I checked Karryn and the bub over. They're doing well. Karryn's still working far too hard, of course. Dean took me for a run around the property in the Jeep. It's so vast, mile after mile. And so dry. But Dean said there's been good rain on the coast and it may move inland—did you know?'

'No…'

'Oh, help.' Maxi swallowed an embarrassed laugh. 'I've been rabbiting on. I never thought to ask. How was your day?'

Jake's mouth lifted in a brief half-smile that ended in a grimace. 'Pretty ordinary.'

Maxi frowned a bit. 'Was the patient list longer than you thought? I could've stayed and helped.'

'No—surgery was fine.' He took a deep breath and let it go. 'I was called to an MVA. Young woman dead at the scene. Took some sorting. She'd run her car over an embankment, lost control and it had overturned. She'd broken her neck.'

'Oh, no…' Maxi's throat made a compulsive movement. 'Was she local?'

'No.' Jake would have shaken his head but it hurt too much. Instead, he took another mouthful of his mineral water and waited until the nausea subsided. 'It was a hire car from interstate. The police found some ID. They're handling things. I wrote out the death certificate. Medically, that was about all I was able to do in the end.'

So, he'd obviously had an awful, soul-destroying kind of day. And coming on the back of yesterday with Brett… 'Any clues about whether or not the woman had a family?'

'There were photos of kids in her wallet.' Jake lifted a hand to the side of his head and groaned, recognising the sudden blur in his vision and the sickening throb of pain in his temple. Oh, hell. He didn't need this.

'Jacob?' Maxi's gaze flew wide and she recognized his sudden pallor, the strained lines of his face.

'Migraine. Sorry,' he muttered, shielding his eyes and leaning forward to support his head in his hands. 'Haven't had one since final exams.'

Maxi moved quickly, grabbing a small plastic bucket she used for saving the vegetable peelings for the compost. At least it was clean, she thought inconsequentially, holding it out towards him. 'Do you want to be sick?'

For answer, he groaned, grabbed for the bucket and promptly threw up. 'Hell!' he said hoarsely, and tried to clear his throat. 'Sorry.'

'Don't be daft. You should lie down. What do you normally treat it with?'

'I'll sleep it off.'

'And I'll give you a jab to speed things along.' Maxi helped him to his feet. 'Lean on me. And take my bedroom. It's closest and I changed the linen this morning.'

'Shame…' He tried to smile and couldn't.

'Are you OK in those clothes?' she asked as he sank down

on the side of her bed. He was wearing loose cargo shorts and a battered T-shirt.

'You want to strip me, Max?' He tried to lift his head but the pain was too much.

'Don't think I couldn't.' She bent and eased off his deck shoes and then rolled him onto the bed. Going back out into the hall, she took a cotton blanket from the linen cupboard. 'Back in a tick,' she said softly, unfolding the blanket over him. 'I'll just get my bag.'

He was still lying where she'd left him when she returned, his eyes squeezed shut. 'Remember, you're not tranquilising a buffalo...' he reminded her hoarsely, his brow wrinkled with pain.

She chose to ignore that. 'Just a little sting now,' she said gently. 'And I'll be here if you need anything.'

'Anything...?' He made a mock-grimace as she shot home the dose of painkiller and anti-emetic.

'Within reason, Jacob.' Her mouth moved into a prim little moue. 'Now, try to sleep.'

Maxi checked on him during the next couple of hours. He wasn't sick again and finally he became less restless, his dozing easing into sleep. She could safely leave him now, she decided, blocking a yawn.

She had a quick shower and then, with Chalky on the floor beside her, she settled onto the big divan in the lounge room, pulling a sheet over her. There was no way she could face going into Jake's room and sleeping in his bed.

She woke at about six and tiptoed in to check on him. Some time during the night he'd obviously shucked off his T-shirt and the blanket but he was still fast asleep, his hands splayed on either side of the pillow, head turned to the wall, his tanned, strong legs sprawled apart, his right knee slightly bent.

Maxi leaned over him, touching her hand to his neck and forehead. He seemed quite cool, normal. Thank heavens.

She stayed beside him, watching almost entranced. He looked

so vulnerable in sleep. Her mouth dried. Almost helplessly, as though she was watching from outside herself, she followed her hand as it slid across his back, all pretence of treating him as her patient vanishing like leaves in the wind as she acknowledged the wild beat of her heart, her breasts achingly aroused. She took a swift indrawn breath. His skin was warm, smooth, like the pelt of an animal. And stroking him gave her such pleasure. A pleasure she'd denied herself for two long years.

She rose slowly from her crouched position. Could she do what she wanted to do so badly? She bit her lips together, stifling the whimper of need that would have spilled from her mouth. Driven by something beyond her power to explain, she went to her stash of oils. Quietly and deliberately she coated her palms with a refreshing light mixture of lavender, camomile and ginger.

Should she be invading his privacy like this? Had she crossed the line from being professional to very, very personal? She beat back her unease. A massage would help him relax, she justified silently. Help him recover from the crippling pain of last night.

She kept her movements light and delicate so she wouldn't wake him but even that didn't stop her from enjoying the sleekness of his skin, the fluid power of his muscles.

She felt a quiver low in her abdomen. Once she'd known his body as well as she knew her own.

Once.

Now she had the chance to rejoice in looking at his body up close, anew. Almost mesmerised, she followed the ridge of his backbone, letting her fingers drift slowly over the symmetrical bumps and hollows. And then wander across to the shallow curves of his ribs and along the indentations between them.

It was only when her fingertips slid beneath the waistband of his shorts and he stirred that she pulled back.

Enough was enough.

She hurried along to the main bathroom and threw herself under the shower. Heavens, their water bill would be sky high at this rate. But she needed the soothing warmth to still her turmoil.

Out of the shower and towelled dry, she looked around for something to wear. The morning felt sticky, the temperature climbing already. She sighed, pulling on a pair of shorts and a sleeveless top. Taking up a brush, she tamed her hair and tied it back into some semblance of order.

She looked in the mirror, watching in dismay as two spots of colour rose in her face and stained her cheeks. She shouldn't have done what she'd done. And Jake would know. Once he'd smelt the trace of oil on his body, there'd be no way he'd *not* know.

She shook her head and swallowed the lump in her throat. She'd face him. There was nothing else to do. And perhaps it was about time they clarified things. Did they want to be lovers again—or not?

Perhaps today would be the day she would find out.

She walked back through the lounge room and Chalky looked directly at her, lifting his head, his mouth opening in a huge, doggy yawn, showing his teeth and pink gums. Then he stood and stretched, clipping along beside her as she went through to the kitchen.

'Outside, now,' Maxi commanded, opening the screen door for him. 'When you come back, I'll get your food.'

'Any tea going?'

Maxi spun round, feeling her face flood with colour. Jake stood, arms folded, leaning against the doorframe. 'Oh, you're up. How do you feel?'

'Better—thanks to your massage.'

Her gaze flew wide. 'Dammit, Jacob! You were awake, weren't you?'

He rocked a hand. 'Drifting a bit.'

'You could have stopped me.'

'Why?' His eyes glinted and there was a brief taut silence before he added, 'I enjoyed it—didn't you?'

'Yes.' She held her head high. There, she'd said it. 'I'll…make that tea.' She caught her lower lip between her teeth, concentrating on the practicalities. 'And you need to keep up your fluids.'

'Yes, Doctor.' He wandered over and took one of the high stools. 'Thanks for everything, Max. I was a cot case.'

She hitched a shoulder, getting down tea mugs and placing them on the breakfast bar. 'You'd have done the same for me.'

'Don't know whether I'd have managed the massage quite so expertly.'

Her throat constricted. 'I thought I might have overstepped—'

'I'm all for overstepping,' he challenged.

Maxi took a shallow breath, felt the tingle of awareness down her spine. She felt his gaze on her as she made the tea and handed his mug across. 'It occurs to me I may have been rather selfish yesterday.'

'In what way?' Jake lifted his mug, lapping thirstily at the black sweet brew.

'Taking off like that. You deserved a day off, too. In fact, Dean asked where you were. He said he thought you would have understood the invitation included you—after you'd finished surgery, of course. He was the only male among all the women.'

'And he was complaining?'

Maxi dimpled. 'Out of his depth a bit, I think.' She placed her mug back on the counter and wrapped her hands around its warmth. 'I should have stayed and helped with the surgery. After all, we're supposed to be a partnership, aren't we?'

'Don't beat yourself up about it, Max,' he reproved softly. 'You needed a break—from me, as well as from the practice. I was totally out of order about Brandon. I undermined you. You deserved much better.'

'Oh.' It was more, far, far more that she'd hoped for or indeed expected. 'I was pretty miffed at the time,' she admitted candidly. 'So,' she said after a minute. 'What's the future for Brandon and the family now? Are they going to be able to keep the property or are they still on the bank's hit list?'

'A relative of Mrs McCall's has helped out with a sizeable infusion of funds, I gather.'

Maxi frowned a bit. 'And that help wasn't forthcoming before…'

'Harley didn't like to ask, I suppose. He felt enough of a failure without having to go to his wife's family to bale him out.'

'If only they'd just talked about it.' Maxi shook her head at the futility of it all. A few words could have saved the man's life.

'*We* need to talk as well.' Jake's gaze narrowed on her face. Almost without her noticing, he'd slid off the high stool, skirted the end of the breakfast bar and come to stand very close to her. He put out a hand and touched her cheek.

Maxi felt her throat tighten, fluttering her eyes closed as his fingertips idled, taking their time, delicate, like the finest strands of silk. And when they reached her lips she parted them, in thrall to their exquisite touch which sent shock waves right through her body.

'Max…open your eyes for me…' She did, every part of her aware of the heat of his body against hers, of that fathomless blue gaze and of a need as basic as her own. Lifting her hands to the back of his neck, she gusted a tiny sigh and drew his face down to hers.

At last the kiss ended and they drew slowly apart.

They looked at each other for a long moment, unmoving until Jake reached out to slide his fingertip up her cheek and tucked a wayward curl behind her ear. 'I want all this to end, Maxi.'

End! Maxi's gaze flew wide. Was this the kiss of goodbye? Had he finally made the decision? Was he actually sending her away? Well, she wouldn't go. Even if he dragged her to the plane, she wouldn't get on. Her throat convulsed as she swallowed. 'End?' she said thickly. 'How, *end*?'

'End the uncertainty between us,' he said softly. 'If that's what you want, too.'

'Oh! Yes… I thought…'

'What did you think?' His mouth lowered to her throat, his lips on the tiny pulse point that beat frantically beneath her chin.

She thumped him on the chest with a small fist. 'That you were about to truss me up like a chicken and dump me on the plane out.'

At that, a wave of laughter rose in his chest and he gathered her in. 'I want you to stay, Max. Let's find out if what we shared in England has some basis for something more than a holiday fling.'

If she was being perfectly honest, it wasn't exactly what she'd wanted to hear, but for now it was plenty to be going on with. A frown touched her eyes. 'It wasn't a fling.'

His head tipped back and he looked at her, the expression in his eyes fathoms deep. 'No…but in hindsight it was a bit surreal, wasn't it?'

'I suppose it was,' she admitted slowly. 'We tried to pack too many emotions into so little time.'

Well, that was one way of putting it. Jake's jaw worked for a second. And it was probably the reason she'd panicked about following him to the other side of the world. Although it didn't explain why it had taken her two years to change her mind and come to him. But she was here now and that was all that mattered.

'Let's do the real deal, then.' Leaning forward, he pressed a brushstroke of a kiss on her lips. 'Give ourselves time to see what we've got going for us.'

'Fine with me,' Maxi responded jerkily, suddenly feeling vulnerable and uncertain under his gaze. Gently, she pushed away from him and collected their tea mugs. 'Would you like some breakfast?'

His eyes crinkled in soft amusement. Breakfast didn't rate on the scale of what he'd really like. But he wouldn't ask for anything she was unready to give him. It would probably kill him but he'd waited for two lonely years. He could afford another little while, until it was absolutely, perfectly right. 'Uh, just some toast, I think.'

'And you should probably allow yourself a stress-free kind of day.' Maxi had her doctor's hat on again. 'I'm on call anyway.' And if she got a call to somewhere at the back of beyond, she'd have to go, she decided resolutely. She was an outback doctor now and she'd do whatever it took to keep the privilege.

With the uncertainty of her tenure in Tangaratta lifted, Maxi threw herself into preparing her talk on men's health. Jake still didn't want anything to do with it so she decided to approach David and Bron with her ideas. She glanced at her watch. It seemed as good a time as any to go across to the hospital and sound them out. She found them at the nurses' station.

'What exactly did you have in mind?' David looked up from the files he was sorting, his expression wary.

'Something non-threatening, low key but informative. And I want to cover all age groups. The general word out there is most men only see their doctor after being *encouraged* by a female.'

'Well, how pathetic is that?' Bron gave her husband a knowing look.

'Fair go!' David held up his hands in self-defence.

'I'm a nurse. I know when I need to see a doctor.'

Maxi leaned her elbows on the countertop. 'But you'd have to agree, men of all ages, even when they have symptoms, put off seeing their doctor.'

'Of course they do.' Bron clicked her tongue. 'Or they front up when it's far too late for anything useful to be done or complications have set in. Anyway, I think what you're suggesting is worth a go, Maxi. I'll help.'

'Thanks. I'd hoped you would.' Maxi's tone was heartfelt. She'd had visions of having to pull the whole thing together on her own. 'David, are you in?'

'Ah...' He scrubbed a hand across his cheekbones, looking

ambushed. 'I'll help in the background—whatever's needed in the way of organising seating and whiteboards, portable screen.'

'That would be a great help. Then I can run most of the audio-visual stuff from my laptop.' Maxi paused. 'I'm not sure of a suitable venue, though…'

'What about the local hall?' David warmed to his newly created role.

'Hmm.' Maxi's mouth turned down. 'Jake said he tried to run something similar there but hardly anyone showed up. There's plenty of room here at the hospital but I don't imagine the guys would turn up if we held it here.'

Bron chuckled. 'We'd probably be choked by the dust as they stampeded out of town.' Pursing her lips, she thought for a moment. 'What about the pub? There's a reasonable room upstairs where they have the odd wedding reception. Shouldn't be too difficult to transform it into a suitable venue for a seminar.'

'Hey, that could work!' Maxi flicked a querying look between the nurses. 'Couldn't it?'

'As long as the guys don't take it as an excuse to get plastered,' David cautioned.

'That's easily dealt with,' Bron countered. 'We'll stipulate no alcohol to be brought in and offer only tea, coffee or soft drinks when they arrive. Besides, many of them will be coming in from their properties. They certainly won't want to be drinking and driving.'

'OK.' David spread his hands in compliance. 'The pub it is.' He slanted a query at Maxi. 'Want me to organise that part for you?'

'Super.' She smiled. 'And I may yet get Jake to co-operate.'

Bron lifted a brow. 'He doesn't want to be involved?'

'Not so you'd notice. Said maybe it needed a woman's approach to get the guys along.'

'Poor babies.' Bron rolled her eyes. 'How soon do you want to do it?'

'Soon. I've collated most of what I need to speak about. And

I want to leave time for a Q and A session. Got some great cartoon stuff as well.'

David laughed. 'About to take the fear out of the rubber-glove syndrome, are you? Heck, if we can get the right kind of publicity out there, you just might get the guys to actually turn up.'

Maxi felt suddenly uplifted, as though she was really earning her place here in this rural setting. 'Spread the word, then, would you please, Dave? As soon as we confirm a venue, I'll fix a date.'

'Then we can get some flyers into the shop windows,' Bron said eagerly. 'And if I leave a pile at the post office, Maggie will ask the mail contractor to shove one in all the farm boxes when he delivers their post.'

'Terrific.' Maxi beamed. 'And, Dave, let me know about the pub as soon as you can, won't you?'

'No worries, Doc. Leave it with me.'

'Oh, before you go, Maxi,' Bron said quickly, 'Katie's home. We're having a barbecue lunch next Saturday. We'd love it if you and Jake could come.'

At the thought of spending some quality time with Jake among their friends, Maxi's heart gave a little skip of happiness. 'That sounds wonderful. We'll be there. Anything we can bring?'

Bron flapped a hand. 'Just yourselves.'

'And your bag,' David chimed in with a dry smile. 'A mob of teenagers mucking about—anything could happen.'

'Done.' Maxi waggled a finger wave. 'And thanks, both of you. You've made my day.'

CHAPTER NINE

IT WAS GOING to be a lovely day, Maxi decided, surveying her newly styled hair in the mirror and nodding happily at the results. Bron had put her onto Kimberley, Tangaratta's 'only decent hairdresser', who'd understood exactly the look Maxi had wanted.

And today she and Jake would be attending their first social occasion together since she'd come to the outback. It was a delicious yet stomach-churning feeling…

'Maxi?'

Maxi jerked back to reality as Jake banged on her bedroom door. 'One second,' she called, taking a last glimpse in the mirror, before stepping outside into the hallway and almost tripping over a hovering Jake.

'Ready? 'He blinked a bit, his eyes widening, darkening, his mouth tucking in at the corners. Hell. She looked amazing. *So... sexy.* He swallowed the sudden thickness in his throat. Her hair, burnished with highlights, tumbled around her shoulders. Her complexion was glowing, her mouth redder without lipstick…

'What?' she managed, her throat drying on the word. The temperature felt as though it had suddenly rocketed up to ten degrees higher, twenty, thirty. Oh, lord… She licked her lips, achingly aware of the almost tangible sense of expectation hanging in the air between them. 'Sh-should we go, then?'

Jake gave a bare shake of his head. 'I want you,' he said starkly.

Maxi's eyes glazed. 'Now?'

'It just seems…right.' He pressed his forehead against hers and sighed out his breath. 'As long as you…'

'Oh, yes…' Her words spun out on a raspy little cry.

It was enough for Jake. His hunger for her glittered in his blue eyes, and his impatience showed in his hands as he wound her hair through his fingers, using the impetus to draw her close and find her mouth.

And she went to him, needing his strength against her body. 'Jake…' she murmured against his mouth. 'Jacob…'

'You taste like fresh mint from the garden.'

'So do you…' She felt his smile on her mouth, until his lips firmed, opened, deepening the kiss, tangling his tongue with hers. It was wild. Like the charge of an electric current between them. Urgency shot through her and she wanted to pull off his clothes and wrap herself around him, claim him again, feel his heat, hold him and never let him go.

'I've so wanted you…' His voice husked on the words as he slid the straps of her top from her shoulders, peeling them lower with aching slowness.

Maxi mewed a tiny inarticulate sound in her throat. Soon, soon he would touch her breasts and feel just what this was doing to her.

'We need the bedroom,' he murmured, raw emotion carved into his features. 'Yours?'

She swallowed dryly, nodding assent.

In seconds they were naked. And Jake was drawing her down with him onto the bed. She shivered, feeling the slick of his skin against hers, felt his body tensing with the effort to control it. So close but not close enough. Not yet. He made a deep, dry sound in his throat. 'Protection?'

Maxi pressed her mouth into the hollow of his throat. 'All covered.' And then the rapturous journey of rediscovery began.

They were both achingly aroused, hungry for the taste and touch of each other and thinking only that after the long seperation they were about to be become lovers again.

But through the haze of her ecstasy Maxi felt ragged memories pushing at her that wouldn't be held back. She stiffened in Jake's arms.

His face close to hers, Jake felt her warm tears. 'Max, what is it?'

Nothing. Everything. She trembled against him. 'I keep remembering…that awful day at the airport…'

'Don't!' He spoke in a fierce undertone. 'It's gone. Forget it and come to me…*please*.'

In an instant their passion was recharged and his body claimed hers. Filling her. The long nights of longing faded into insignificance.

Maxi arched under her lover, urging him to take her even more deeply, wrapping her legs around him. When his final thrust touched her soul, she heard his groan of release, whirlpools of sensation dragging them both under, before tossing them higher than the highest star.

For a long time they lay silent, replete. Jake had shifted to lie on his back, curving his arm round her so her head was pillowed on his chest.

Maxi draped her arm across the flat plane of his stomach, curving into him. She felt almost weightless, drenched with feelings she couldn't begin to describe. Good, though. All good. For both of them.

At least she hoped so, prayed so. Because she loved him in every way a woman should love her man. And would do so for the rest of her life.

Finally Jake spoke. 'You OK?'

'Mmm.' She sniffed the last of the tears away on a strangled laugh, tiptoeing her fingers along his chest. 'We still make great music together, don't you think?'

'Magic.' His chest rose as he chuckled. 'Symphony orchestra stuff.'

She sighed happily. 'We're going to be awfully late for the party.'

'Doctors are notoriously late for social functions.'

She gave a soft laugh. 'Is that so?'

'Mmm.' He turned to her, brushing her lips once and then again. 'Goes with the lousy profession we've chosen.'

'Poor us.' She burrowed against him. 'I'll need another shower.'

'And I'll join you…'

Almost in slow motion, she lifted a hand, running her forefinger over his mouth until he parted it and gently bit her on the nail. 'Jacob…' Her voice trembled on a jagged little breath and suddenly their passion was reignited as swiftly and as forcefully as a shooting star into the heavens.

Jake lowered his head and they kissed slowly, completely. Until kissing was no longer enough.

'We're so late,' Maxi lamented as they drove towards Bron and David's home.

'Stop worrying.' Jake reached out a hand to her thigh and squeezed. 'They'll have kept us some food.'

Maxi felt her stomach lurch. Food was the last thing on her mind. Surely everyone would know she and Jake had been to bed. She knew for a fact that she herself had that *look* about her.

Her cheeks were flushed and her eyes were shining. And she couldn't stop smiling. Oh, help. She bit her lips together but the smile just wouldn't go away.

The Walkers' home was a sprawling timber structure with wide verandahs. A lovely, old-fashioned country home, Maxi decided, taking a deep breath. She turned to Jake. 'Do you have the drinks?'

'Right here.' Jake hitched the insulated wine cooler over

his shoulder. 'We'll go round the back. That's where the action will be.'

'There seem to be quite a few cars here.'

'They'll just be friends and neighbours. Out here, folk think nothing of travelling miles for a party.'

Maxi's insides heaved crazily with anticipation and nerves as Jake unlatched the wooden gate that led into the back garden. 'Perhaps we should have arrived separately.' She cast a worried look at him. 'And don't laugh!' she threatened, watching him slyly rub the back of his hand across his mouth.

But she had no time to agonise further when their hostess spied them from her position on the deck. 'Hello, you two,' Bron called, popping down the stairs to greet them. 'What kept you?'

'Uh…' Maxi drew in a long ragged breath. 'Something came up.'

Jake gave a slow grin. 'Bit of an emergency.'

'Ah, one of *those* emergencies.' It was David this time, his blue gaze warm behind his silver-rimmed glasses. He'd strolled across the lawn to greet them, still carrying his barbecue tongs. 'Plenty of food left, guys. Help yourselves.'

'Thanks, mate.' Jake clapped him across the shoulders. 'I'm starved, actually.'

Maxi felt her skin warm and prayed no one noticed her heightened colour. 'We've brought some champagne,' she said in a breathless little rush. 'It's the good stuff. The last the pub had. Left over from a posh wedding apparently.'

'Crikey,' David said blandly. 'What are we celebrating? The drought hasn't broken, has it?'

Maxi smiled around a strangled laugh. 'Just thought we could drink to—to good friends…'

'And lovers,' Jake murmured in a low tone meant only for her to hear.

'Lovely idea.' Bron stepped in quickly and led the way to where the tables were set out under dark green umbrellas. 'Now, come and meet our Katie.'

* * *

'You've made such a lovely home here, Bron.' It was a couple of hours later and Maxi and her hostess were relaxing on outdoor chairs in the garden.

'Well, we decided long ago that Tangaratta, warts and all, was where we wanted to make our lives together,' Bron said matter-of-factly. 'So we went all out to make our home our haven away from our responsibilities at the hospital.'

'Well, it's certainly worked. And you've gone to so much effort to make it a lovely party.' Maxi's gaze took in the white picnic tables with their brightly coloured serving platters and salad bowls, the striped fabric bunting and big rainbow outdoor floor cushions.

Bron's look was wistful. 'Well, it's for Katie, really. All the trimmings, I mean. She'll be gone again in a few days.'

Maxi looked across to where Bron's bright, bubbly daughter was the centre of a group of her teenage friends. And she'd noticed something else. Katie's constant shadow was Brandon McCall. And now and again the two had shyly linked hands and exchanged very meaningful looks.

So that's the way it was, Maxi thought indulgently. Katie Walker was the girlfriend the young man had referred to. And he looked happy and relaxed in Katie's company. And that could only mean her young patient was well on the way to recovering his equilibrium in full.

Two seconds later Maxi heard the summons of her mobile. 'Sorry.' She made a small face at Bron. 'I'm on call today.'

She rescued the phone from her little straw basket on the table, listening as Loretta outlined the emergency. 'That was the hospital, Bron. I'll have to go.'

'Of course you will.' Bron pulled herself upright from the lounger. 'Loretta's on duty today, isn't she?'

'Yes.'

'So you'll be fine. Thanks so much for coming today.'

The two hugged briefly. 'No, *thank you*. It's been a wonderful day.' In more ways than one, a cheeky imp whispered inside Maxi's head. 'Uh, we came in Jake's car.' She looked towards the group of men relaxing in an untidy circle near the barbecue. 'I guess I'll have to drag him away as well.'

'Go, then.' Bron made a shooing motion with her hand. 'We'll catch up soon, no doubt. At work, if nowhere else,' she added dryly.

'So, what do we have?' Jake asked as they headed back to the town a few minutes later.

'A young couple have arrived at the hospital.' Maxi outlined what Loretta had passed on. 'The woman is twenty-nine weeks pregnant, torn membrane and amniotic fluid leak.'

Jake's mouth compressed. 'Could be iffy.'

Maxi beat back a feeling of unease. Seeing their lack of high-level neonatal facilities, *iffy* didn't even begin to describe what lay ahead of them.

Once again they were flying by the seats of their pants.

Loretta met them at the nurses' station. 'Oh, good, you've both come,' she said, as if seeing them as a couple was no great surprise.

'What can you tell us, Loretta?' Jake's voice was clipped.

'Our patient is Alex Vellacott, husband is Zane. Apparently they've been on the road for several weeks while Zane looks for work.'

'He could have chosen a better time,' Jake muttered. 'Or gone on his own, instead of dragging his pregnant wife around with him.'

'These are hard times, Jacob,' Maxi reminded him quietly. 'Just let's see what we can do for Alex, shall we? Is Sonia around, Loretta?'

The charge shook her head. 'In Sydney for the weekend—her mum's sixtieth.'

Maxi sent a trapped smile in Jake's direction. 'So, it's just us, then.'

'I've put Alex in the treatment room for the moment,' Loretta said. 'And I've alerted the CareFlight chopper for her transfer to Croyden.'

And there didn't seem any doubt a transfer to the larger hospital would be needed, Maxi decided after she'd examined her patient. The trickle of amniotic fluid hadn't stopped and was, in fact, stimulating intermittent but painful contractions.

Maxi held a mini-consult with Jake and then they both went to speak with the couple.

'Can you do something for me and the baby?' The young mother-to-be looked at them with wide, fearful eyes.

Maxi placed a comforting hand on patient's shoulder. 'Alex, if it were just a matter of bed rest and monitoring you for any infection, we could keep you here.'

'But it's not—?'

'No, Alex, it's not,' Jake came in gently. 'The amniotic sac is leaking. That means you could go into premature labour over the next twenty-four to forty-eight hours. We don't have high-tech neonatal equipment here and if your baby was born now, he or she would be unlikely to survive. I'm sorry to have to be so blunt.'

'No, it's OK,' Zane came in quickly. 'We'd rather know.' His throat convulsed as he swallowed. 'W-what should we do, then?' He reached for his wife's hand and held it tightly.

'We'll transfer Alex by air ambulance to Croyden,' Jake explained. 'You'll be able to go with her. The chopper's already on its way so it should get here within the hour.'

'But what if I have the baby mid-flight?'

Maxi heard the trepidation in her patient's voice and hastened to clarify the situation. 'It's a relatively short flight, Alex. You'd be very unlikely to deliver the baby during the journey.'

Alex bit down on her bottom lip. 'If the baby does come early, would it have a chance at the bigger hospital?'

Maxi nodded. 'Your baby would be placed in a special neonatal intensive care unit so it would have every chance of surviving.'

'And if you can hang onto the pregnancy for even another couple of weeks, the chances of your baby having no ongoing problems would be lessened even further,' Jake added.

The young woman's face crumpled. 'I don't know if I'll be able to. I can feel another contraction…'

'What can I do to help, babe?' Zane muttered through pinched dry lips.

'It's fine.' Alex hiccuped a jagged laugh. 'It's gone already. Only a light one. And I hadn't had one for a while.' She cast a determined look at her husband. 'We'll make it, Zane. We have to…'

'Just thought you'd like to know—chopper's ETA is fifteen minutes.' Loretta popped her head in.

'Thanks, Loretta,' Jake acknowledged. 'We'll go ahead and prepare Alex for the transfer.'

Maxi stood beside Jake, steeling herself against the shudder in the air as the helicopter took off. How she wished she could have done more for Alex and her baby.

As if he'd tuned into her thoughts, Jake said quietly, 'We'll just have to pray the baby is a little battler.'

Maxi sent him a quick look as they turned and began making their way back to the hospital car park. He seemed subdued, even a bit grim. Perhaps, like her, he already had a mental picture of the infant, born far too early—translucent, fragile, so delicate. 'Under-developed lungs will be a problem.'

'Along with myriad others. If the team at Croyden can buy some more time, it might give the baby a fighting chance. I guess that's all we can hang on to at the moment.'

'Alex told me she'd had hardly any prenatal care,' Maxi said bleakly.

'And it's not *our* fault, Max. She could have been living in the heart of Sydney and this could have happened anyway,' Jake pointed out. 'As a doctor, you should know by now you can do only what you can do given all the circumstances.'

'But out here…'

'Out here, what?' Jake stopped, a frown notching his forehead as he took her hands, linking his fingers through hers and tightening their hold.

'When it comes down to it, medically, there's so little we can do. It's so harsh, so raw. So *far* from everything.'

Her words, so heartfelt, so desolate-sounding, bombarded Jake like shrapnel. An uneasy chill traversed the length of his spine. Was she ready to chuck it all in and leave him? Just when they'd found each other again? He sighed. 'You can't compare it with working as a GP in England, Max.'

'I know…' Maxi tried to make light of her mood, tried to smile, but her mouth got all out of shape in a jumble of emotions. 'I know.'

'What's that you have there?' Jake asked. It was Sunday afternoon and they'd slept in their separate bedrooms last night. Maxi had said she wanted an early night and disappeared and he hadn't liked to presume anything. Now he wondered if the intimacy they'd reignited was already a one-off in her mind. Were they back to being merely housemates? His chest tightened.

But he wasn't about to beg.

'I'm collating stuff for my men's health seminar.' Maxi turned her head up, meeting his questioning look as he leaned over her shoulder. 'Dave thinks we can get a room at the pub to hold it. Bron's helping as well.'

'Great. Like my input?'

She blinked. He'd sounded brisk, impersonal. But she wasn't about to quibble. 'I would,' she said simply.

'OK, then. 'He yanked up another chair to the outdoor table and dropped his length beside her. 'Tell me what you have in mind.'

'It'll probably be nothing like yours.' Maxi shielded her A4 pages defensively.

He shot her a wry grin. 'Let's hope not. Mine wasn't exactly a roaring success, was it? Come on, then,' he coaxed.

'You'll probably think it's quite unsuitable.'

'No, I won't. Show me what you've got so far.'

Maxi took a deep breath. 'Well, originally, I thought it would be good to separate the information into age groups, say, young, middle age and then fifty and upwards, and finally sixty-five plus. But then I thought it'd be better to keep it general.'

'Probably,' Jake agreed. 'In the first place, we've no idea how many will turn up, let alone their age groups. So, yes. Let's keep the information general. Go on,' he encouraged.

'I think we should emphasise the importance of a yearly check-up, even if the men are feeling well,' Maxi said, gaining confidence. 'Make the guys aware of the things that can impair men's health in general.'

'OK, but let's not make it too daunting.' Jake rubbed a hand thoughtfully over his chin. 'First we need to get them along to the surgery and then the rest will follow—with a bit of persuasion on our part.'

Maxi nodded. She could see his point. 'So, we'd explain tests for cholesterol and BP are simple and straightforward, but necessary. And I'd like to stress the need for a skin exam every year, especially for those men who have high exposure to the sun in their working day. And with their very physical lifestyles out here, we should include a review of their immunisation status—for instance, tetanus.'

'Sounds fine. What else?'

'Well, it goes without saying they need to know they can discuss anything with their doctor in strictest confidence.'

'Of course. That's a good point. Stuff like relationship difficulties, drug and alcohol issues and so on.'

Maxi twirled her pen in her fingers. 'And I really don't think we can ignore speaking about male-related cancers. Testicular is more prevalent in the eighteen to thirty age group than we like to imagine. And prostate, of course.'

'We don't want to frighten the daylights out of them, though,' Jake warned. 'But I agree the subject has to be addressed.'

'I've some excellent stuff on disk I can show them,' Maxi said enthusiastically. 'It's in cartoon form, non-threatening, and I think it will get the message through. I brought it with me from home.'

A beat of silence.

'It sounds like you're well prepared, then.' Jake hadn't missed her emphasis on *home*. If her heart and her loyalties were still back in England… He clamped down on the bleakness of his thoughts.

'I've yet to decide when to hold the session.' Maxi looked thoughtful. 'What time of day do you think would suit most of the men?'

'Not sure. Have a chat to Ayleen. She's usually got her finger on the pulse.'

'OK.' Maxi nodded. 'I'll do that.' She got to her feet. 'I think I'll marinate some chicken pieces for an early dinner. Suit you?'

'Uh, count me out.' Jake spun off his chair and replaced it neatly at the table. 'I want to go over to the hospital. I need a word with Dave. And I want to catch up on some paperwork as well. I'll grab a bite to eat somewhere.'

In other words, he didn't want her company.

A knot of uncertainty tightened in Maxi's stomach. Life, *her* life, had seemed so good yesterday. And now her thoughts were all muddled.

'I wondered…' She bit her lip and went on, 'Would be in order for me to call Croyden and find out how Alex is doing? It's been twenty-fours hours…'

'Of course,' Jake said with complete professional detachment. 'Better still, I'll make the call from the hospital and let you know.'

'Thanks,' she replied huskily, and held up two crossed fingers.

With Jake gone about his business, Maxi decided she

wouldn't bother with cooking dinner. If she was forced to eat alone, she'd open a can of baked beans.

With this bleak thought in mind, she went along to the room Jake reserved as an office and began to transfer her written notes to her laptop. After half an hour, she stopped and sighed. She just couldn't get into it.

Alex and her baby were on her mind.

Out of nowhere, Maxi imagined herself in the same predicament. How awful it would be. Miles from specialist care, her child's life in jeopardy. A lump came to her throat. She couldn't bear it.

Oh, get a grip, her saner self protested. Jake would be the only man you'd consider having a baby with and he wouldn't let anything untoward happen to you. Or your baby.

But sometimes things just…happened. Maxi knew that better than most. Things you had no control over. When her mobile rang, she jumped back to reality. It was Jake.

'Alex is holding her own,' he said carefully. 'She's on a drip, of course, and they're monitoring the baby closely. So far the scan shows it's still viable.'

Maxi let her breath go. A tiny ray of optimism shone inside her. 'I guess that's the best we can hope for, isn't it?'

'Yes, it is.' His voice deepened. 'I'll be a while. Don't wait up.'

CHAPTER TEN

'I KNOW WE decided we wouldn't take patients without appointments any more,' Ayleen said apologetically. She'd come quietly into Maxi's surgery on Monday afternoon, closing the door behind her.

'What is it, Ayleen?' Maxi looked up from her computer.

'I have sixteen-year-old Lily Carpenter in Reception. She's come straight from school and asked especially to see you.'

'Is she already a patient?'

'She is.' Ayleen proffered the file.

Maxi got the message. The youngster obviously wanted to see a female doctor. Well, that was what her role here was all about—to give the patients a choice. 'It's no problem, Ayleen. I have a short list today. I'll just take a sec to run through Lily's notes and then I'll come out and call her in.'

Maxi speed-read the file. There was nothing out of the ordinary to cause concern and nothing outstanding that needed follow-up. So possibly the young woman needed a chat about something personal.

Maxi's first impression of Lily was that her patient was a very pretty girl, with dark blonde hair that was thick and shiny. Her demeanour was polite but any semblance of a smile was entirely missing. It put Maxi on her mettle, raised her doctor's antennae. 'So, Lily,' she encouraged. 'How can I help you?'

'It's a bit of a long story,' Lily said awkwardly.

'That's all right. You're my last patient for the day. Take whatever time you need.'

'Well…' Lily linked her fingers tightly across her midriff. 'I'm staying at the student accommodation at the CWA hostel at the moment. Mrs Maynard said I should come and talk to you.'

Liz. Maxi raised an eyebrow. 'That's fine. Go on.'

'I'm not getting on with my mother. In fact, I think she hates me.'

'That's a very strong statement, Lily.'

'Please, don't put it down to teenage angst.' The youngster's throat jerked as she swallowed. 'It's been going on since I can remember. Nothing I do seems to please her and when I achieve at school, and I do, you'd think she'd be over the moon…'

'But she's not?' Maxi pursued gently, thinking they were about to open a Pandora's box here.

Lily shook her head.

'What about your dad?'

'He loves me to bits.' Lily's mouth trembled infinitesimally. 'And that just makes Mum even more jealous. Lately, I'm finding it hard to get to sleep and when I do I have nightmares—awful ones where I'm trying to find my way to somewhere and every way is blocked and I walk and walk…' Her voice became husky. 'And when I wake up, I'm so scared.'

'I see…' Maxi said slowly, dragging together every counselling skill she'd ever acquired. 'Lily, I have to tell you at the outset I'm not a therapist but we'll talk a bit more and then perhaps we'll be able to come up with some strategies to help you.'

Lily gave the semblance of a relieved smile. 'Mrs Maynard said you'd be able to.'

Thanks a bunch, Liz! Maxi shrugged mentally. I only wish I had such confidence in me. Rising from her chair, she went to the cooler to get herself and her patient a glass of water. It was going to be a long session. 'Tell me a bit more about your mum,' she coaxed.

'She was adopted when she was a baby.' Lily took a mouthful of water and set her glass back on the desk. 'She's always been quite bitter about the fact her real mother didn't or couldn't keep her. Dad said when I was born she doted on me.'

'And when did that change?'

'I can't really remember but I know I felt a bit…*hemmed in* around Mum even from when I was a little kid and I guess I'd run to Dad instead. That just made Mum angry and she and Dad would row. I remember once she yelled that he'd *stolen* me. I didn't understand it then but as I've got older I'm starting to understand Mum needs help…' She swallowed and tears brimmed.

Undoubtedly. And Lily had obviously decided it was time to be pro-active, which only went to prove her maturity for one so young. Maxi put her practical hat on. 'When did you move out to the hostel?' she asked.

'Couple of weeks ago. Dad arranged it. It's good 'cos I've got more time for study and after-school stuff.'

'So you live out a bit, then?'

'Twenty-five K's. It's a small farm. Isolated. Dad runs a few head of cattle but he works away a lot and Mum was getting on my case more and more so he just upped and moved me out. I really wish I could go away to school.' Lily lifted a hand, agitatedly, curling a strand of blonde hair around her finger.

'And that's not an option?'

'Dad couldn't afford it. About Mum…' She brought her gaze up, drawing in a long shaky breath. 'I can't help wondering if I did something wrong to make her so unhappy with me…'

Oh, lord. Maxi's intuition sharpened. She had to find the right words here or Lily would be left feeling even more confused. 'You did nothing wrong, Lily. Your parents possibly had a complex relationship even before you came along. We don't know what emotional issues either or both brought to the marriage. That would be for a skilled professional to work through with them.'

Lily's pretty mouth flattened in resignation. 'Mum wouldn't have a bar of that.'

'Not yet, perhaps,' Maxi said gently. 'But in the meantime, you've done the right thing in trying to get help for yourself. And that in turn may lead your parents to take stock.'

Lily began blinking fast. 'I feel sad for Mum…'

'Of course you do. Possibly, a crisis in her own past meant she needed your love desperately for reassurance but something in her caused you to turn to your dad. It's complicated but it's certainly no one's *fault*.' Maxi felt the youngster's anguish and got a mental picture of this mother living in some kind of quiet desperation. But until she was ready to seek professional help, no one could force it on her. 'Would you feel you could write to your mum explaining why you felt it best to move out?'

'It's a bit soon for that,' Lily said defensively. 'But maybe someday…?'

'Well, that's a good start,' Maxi said. 'And something positive for you to take away. Now, about getting off to sleep. I've a tape here I can loan you. It's relaxation music. Do you have a player?'

Lily nodded.

'And I'd like you to go along to Mrs Maynard's shop, when you leave here and ask for some scented candles you can burn. Lavender is good. And while you're there, select some comfy cushions and whatever else you'd like to make your new room cosy.'

Lily bit her lip uncertainly. 'I don't have much pocket money…'

'That's OK.' Maxi waved away the youngster's disquiet. 'The CWA's funds will cover that. Care and concern for families is a large part of their brief.' And if it came down to it, Maxi herself would pay for Lily's little comfort items. 'Just select what bibs and bobs you fancy. I'll call Liz and tell her to expect you and if the parcel is too bulky for you to carry, I'm sure she'll deliver it for you. If not, I'll pop over with it to the hostel some time this evening. OK with you?'

'Thank you.' Lily gave a tentative smile. 'For the talk and everything…'

'You're very welcome, Lily.' Maxi's eyes were gentle. 'Now, what about popping back to see me in a couple of weeks for another chat?'

'I can do that.' Lily swung gracefully to her feet. 'I'll make an appointment now, as I leave, shall I?'

'That would be good,' Maxi smiled, the intense nature of the consult lifting. 'Now, just hang on a tick and I'll get that tape for you.'

As soon as she'd seen Lily out, Maxi called Liz. The matter of Lily's shopping settled, she replaced the receiver and thought for a moment before she picked it up once more. This time her call was to Bron. 'Can I come and see you on a confidential matter?' she asked when Bron answered.

'Of course you can. I'll put the coffee on.'

Maxi drove across to the Walkers' home, knowing Bron was taking the week off to spend it with Katie.

'You look like you could do with this.' Bron's mouth turned up in a wry smile as she took the tray of refreshments out onto the back deck.

'Ah…' Maxi looked around anxiously. 'I was hoping for somewhere a bit more private, Bron…'

'Not to worry.' Bron rested the tray on the outdoor table. 'There's just us chickens here. David's at the hospital and Katie's spending the day at the McCalls'. Brand called and picked her up this morning. She's staying out there for tea so I don't expect her back before nine or so.'

Maxi gave a jagged laugh. 'Sorry to sound paranoid but it's to do with a patient and I wouldn't like her to think I'd broken her confidentiality.'

'Discretion's my second name,' Bron said, deadpan. 'Now, try one of my jam drops.'

After a few leisurely minutes, while they talked and drank their coffee, Bron refilled their cups and said, 'Now, what did you want to run by me?'

Maxi outlined Lily's situation, divulging only as much detail as she felt the teenager would be comfortable with. 'Do you know the family at all, Bron?'

'Well, I know *of* them,' Bron said thoughtfully. 'They've a small property out at Willow Bend. Myles Carpenter has been in to Casualty now and again. Needed a tetanus jab once, I recall. Seemed an OK guy. Janine, the wife, I don't know at all. She came to a few things at the school when they first moved here but she didn't get involved. I do know Lily, though. She's a year ahead of Katie. Sweet kid. Very bright, from all accounts.'

'That's what I wanted to ask you about,' Maxi said quietly, and their eyes linked in a moment of feminine understanding. 'Lily mentioned she'd love to go away to school but that the fees would be a problem. I just wondered about the possibility of her applying for a scholarship somewhere in Sydney. Somewhere…nice.'

'Lots of the private schools offer scholarships,' Bron said helpfully. 'It would be just a matter of doing a quick search on the net. I'll collate some names for you, if you like.'

'That would be a great help.' Maxi looked thoughtful. 'You're happy with Katie's school, aren't you?'

'Yes, it's lovely. In fact, I think their scholarships are about to be advertised for next year's intake. Lily could try there, along with any others she fancied. There would be an entrance exam involved so she'd need to speak with her form teacher and take it from there. And have her parents' permission, of course.'

Well, they could get round that somehow. Maxi chewed on her bottom lip. Should she be getting so involved with her patient, though? Jake would probably tell her to back off and let the family sort themselves out. She gave a silent huff. They hadn't done much of a job of it to date. And Lily deserved so much better.

'Do you know, I still have all the guff from when Katie applied last year.' Bron got to her feet. 'I think I've stashed it in the so-called file cabinet somewhere. Take it home and read through it. Then you could run it by Lily when you see her. It will be a starting point at least.'

Jake came out of his office and placed the last of his patient files on the counter at Reception. Ayleen looked up and he asked, 'Maxi still about?'

'She left ages ago.' Ayleen took the files and tapped them neatly together. 'Said she had some urgent business to attend to.'

Jake felt the tentacles of fear grip his insides and squeeze. Was she about to do a runner home to England? He didn't know where her head was any more. Sure, they'd made love but now they seemed further apart than they'd ever been. He shook his head. He couldn't wait any longer. As soon as she got home, they'd talk. And they'd sort things out—even if it took all night.

'Oh, poor baby,' Maxi crooned, as Chalky came joyfully to greet her when she arrived home. She glanced at her watch. There was still time to take him for a run before dark. Collecting her medical case from the boot, she ran lightly up the back stairs to the verandah. And stopped. Jake was leaning back on one of the loungers, a can of beer propped on his chest.

'Hi.' Maxi took a dry swallow. 'You're home early.'

'I *am* allowed an early mark sometimes.' Dark humour spilled into his eyes and pulled at the corners of his mouth.

'That's not what I meant.' Soft colour licked along her cheekbones and she added throatily, 'I think I'll change and take Chalky for a run.'

'The dog's fine.' Jake gave an impatient twitch of his shoulder. 'I ran countless laps of the yard with him when I got home. Get yourself a glass of wine and come join me.'

Suddenly Maxi felt vulnerable. There was something implacable about his manner that had her antennae twitching uncomfortably. 'Oh…' she said after a moment, then cleared her throat and tried again. 'Fine. I'll do that.'

'Good result?' Jake asked innocently.

'Result?'

'Ayleen said you were off about some urgent business.'

Jake watched as the smoky hue in her green gaze disappeared, instantly replaced by something else—not guilt exactly but something akin to it.

'Oh, that.' Maxi flapped a hand as if to dismiss his question. 'Tell you all about it in a minute.' With that, she beat a hasty retreat across the verandah and into the kitchen beyond.

Jake looked after her moodily. Then he lifted his arm in a swift, jerky movement, draining the last of his beer. His thoughts were churning at the speed of light. Had she already made plans to leave? And when the hell was she going to tell him?

As Maxi poured her wine, she realised her hand was shaking. She had to calm down. But her tummy was turning back flips at the possibility of perhaps another confrontation—like the one they'd had over Brandon McCall.

But surely this time it was different. There'd been nothing on Lily's file to suggest caution. Unless, like Brandon, the information was still in Jake's head. But surely she had some autonomy when it came to treating her patients?

Hardened by this resolve, she picked up her glass and made her way back out to the verandah. Seeing Jake's crushed beer can on the table, she said with false brightness, 'I could have brought you another from the fridge.'

'One's my limit when I'm on call.'

Well, she already knew that. She gave him a guarded smile and decided to plunge straight in. 'Do you know the Carpenter family?'

Jake seemed taken aback by the question. His head came up

and he thought for a second. 'As the doctor, you gradually get to know most everyone in a small town. I've a slight acquaintance with Myles and the daughter…'

'Lily,' Maxi supplied. 'She came to see me today. She appears to be carrying the weight of a very dysfunctional family on her young shoulders.'

'Fill me in.' Jake frowned a bit, straightening to sit upright in his chair.

Maxi outlined what Lily and she had spoken about, ending, 'So that's what I've done.'

Jake stayed silent, his mouth pursed in thought. 'If what Lily has told you is only half-true, then what's happened is not far removed from child abuse.'

Maxi felt a wave of unease. The last thing Lily would want would be intervention from Social Services. 'I think Lily has been able to handle things so far with her father's help, and now she's out of the picture perhaps her parents will manage to start resolving their problems. Ideally, they should be referred along to a psychologist—or at least a family counsellor. But there's no hope of that happening *out here*.'

Jake's lips thinned into a hard seam. There she went again. And he didn't relish criticism heaped on *him* about the inadequacies of the system under which they worked. He knew them backwards.

But delivering medicine to rural communities in a country as big as Australia was a hard call, always would be. Unless nature took it into her head to radically change the geography of the place, he thought cryptically. He set a steely look on Maxi. 'So there are holes in the system. Just what the hell do you expect me to do about it?'

Maxi looked shocked. She hadn't expected that kind of reaction from him. She licked suddenly dry lips. 'Nothing, I suppose. I…guess I'm just venting. It's frustrating, trying to work like this.'

'Tell me something I don't know,' he growled. 'This kind of

situation would be frustrating wherever you worked. Until the Carpenters seek help for their problems, what could any MO do? But for crying out loud, Maxi, by now you should be aware of the shortcomings of practising medicine *out here*. And if you're not, perhaps you should be asking yourself what you're doing here at all?'

Had that been a challenge or a blatant personal attack? Either way, Maxi felt the stinging impact like a hail of stones. Her heart was hammering. But she didn't let it sway her. If he wanted answers, she'd give him answers. 'I came to the outback because of *our* relationship, Jacob. I thought even you would have known that.'

He laughed and it was a harsh, angry sound. 'After two lousy years of not knowing anything? Just what am I supposed to *know* now? Only hours ago you made love with me as though you were dying of thirst. Now it's as though it never happened. You're off somewhere with the fairies. I may as well be invisible. In my book it doesn't add up to much of a relationship.'

'I've...had a few things on my mind,' she defended inadequately. 'And despite what you think, I did have valid reasons for not coming to you sooner.'

His eyes narrowed. 'Like what? You'd met someone else in the meantime and you waited to see how it panned out?'

'No! It was nothing like that. I *wanted* to come to you.'

In a gesture of a man almost at the end of his tether Jake raised his hands, ploughing his fingers through his hair and locking them at the back of his neck. 'So, what kept you? If it was money, I'd already offered to pay for your flight.'

Maxi shook her head. She realised she'd come to some kind of watershed. She'd just have to spit it out and let him make of it what he would. But not here with him looking like a jungle cat about to pounce. 'Could we go inside?' She got to her feet, leaving her wine untouched on the table. She needed a clear head for what she had to tell him.

They went into the lounge and sat on the sofa, taking opposite ends. Like two combatants, Maxi thought with grim humour. She licked her lips. 'This may take a while.'

He lifted his hands in a gesture that might have indicated, just get on with it.

She took a shuddery little breath. 'Barely a week after you left, Luke was diagnosed with Ewing's sarcoma.'

Ewing's? Jake's brows peaked. Oh, hell. The cancer was a rare type that usually began in the bones or soft tissue. But Luke? Her twin? Sweet God. He took in her painfully clamped jaw, a sliver of terrible unease ripping through him. Was her brother…dead? Oh, please, no. He shouldn't be putting her through this, he thought, ashamed at his unremitting stance. His mouth tightened, before he scooted along the sofa towards her. Reaching out, he touched her cheek drawing his fingers over her skin. 'I'm so sorry, Max…'

'It was awful,' she said thickly, her voice shaking.

Jake's emotions began to show as well. 'He's not…?'

'No.' She managed a fluttery kind of smile. 'We're a tough lot, it seems. Luke's still in remission.'

'Why did you not tell me!' The words were wrung from him.

Her shoulders lifted in a shrug that spelt desperation. 'What could you have done, Jacob?'

'I could have *been* there for you.'

'After the way we parted, I didn't think I had any right.'

'No right? No right, when I'd asked you to marry me? Had asked you to make a life with me?' A ragged sigh came up from his boots. 'You had no trust in me at all, did you, Maxi?'

'That's where you're wrong.' Maxi felt as though her heart would crack wide open. 'I always trusted you. It was the situation between us at the time I didn't trust. The compelling suddenness of how it happened. And whether it had any real substance…' she ended in a low voice, staring down at their clasped fingers.

A long silence, after which he said quietly, 'With hindsight, I guess I can see it from your point of view. We were on opposite sides of the world. It was…difficult and I didn't offer you much reassurance at the time, did I?'

'No.' And that didn't even begin to cover it.

His grip on her fingers tightened. 'It must have come as a total shock when Luke was diagnosed. Ewing's usually attacks a younger age group.'

'Usually.' Her mouth turned down. 'But when Luke drew my attention to the lump at the back of his knee, I told him we couldn't hang about speculating. I got him straight in to see Marcus Blanford at our old hospital.'

'Good move,' Jake approved. 'I guess then it all snowballed into the inevitable practicalities.'

'Yes.' In medical shorthand, she outlined her brother's treatment, the endless hours of sitting with him, watching him try to make light of the wretched aftermath of the chemo. And fighting so hard to get well. Living in a kind of limbo until he was cleared.

Tight-lipped, Jake asked, 'What's the success rate of it not recurring?'

'At present around eighty-five percent.'

'And he's in remission now?'

'Yes.' She gave a fleeting smile. 'But with cancer you never really know, do you? But he's determined.'

'Like you.'

She laughed in surprise. 'Perhaps about some things.'

'About most things,' he countered. 'You came twelve thousand miles to me. That had to take some kind of determination.'

If only he knew. But, then, perhaps he did. She moved her hands, shifting them to his forearms and holding on. 'For a long time I had to put all thoughts of joining you out of my head. I had to stay. I was the one with the medical knowledge so everyone in the family turned to me for answers.'

'Of course,' Jake said quietly. Knowing Maxi, she would have run herself ragged supporting not just Luke but their whole family. Despite the many joys they brought, extended families could be hard work. Not that he was any authority. Apart from his mother, he had practically no one who gave a damn about him.

Except now, maybe…there was Maxi.

His eyes were fixed on her face, wanting to take the lingering pain from her eyes, faintly ashamed at his almost petulant attitude earlier. He could only imagine the strength she'd had to summon up to be the rock for her whole family. 'I could have helped, if you'd let me.'

'With hindsight, I know that.' Leaning forward, she raised her hand and stroked his shoulder tentatively, ending at the ropey hardness of his forearm. 'The good part is Luke is back at work—still in the drawing office at the moment, but I don't imagine they'll keep him off-site for much longer.'

'Hotshot architect like him? I wouldn't think so.' Jake's mouth twitched into a dry smile. 'And everyone's coping now?'

'Pretty much. And that's why I felt free to come to you.'

'Without knowing just what you'd find when you got here,' he said, his voice gruff and not quite even. 'I could have gone and got married.'

'You could. I had to wait until I got to Sydney to find you hadn't.'

He looked taken aback. 'How come?'

'When I phoned your mother, she asked me to lunch. She told me then.'

'I see…'

'I hope you do.' Maxi felt her eyes drawn helplessly to his. 'I didn't come here on a whim, Jacob.' His blue gaze shimmered over her face and she added silently, *I came because I love you. Because I'll always love you.*

CHAPTER ELEVEN

THREE WEEKS ON and Maxi and Jake were sitting at the long kitchen table.

'I can't believe how quickly things have come together. All we need now is an audience,' Maxi said. She was speaking about the men's health seminar that was taking place on the upcoming Friday evening.

Jake's mouth flickered in a controlled smile. Her face was a study in bright anticipation. He just hoped enough of the local males would turn up to make all her efforts worthwhile. 'I've had my ear to the ground. I haven't heard anyone say they won't come.'

'I suppose that's something.' Maxi twirled her pen thoughtfully. 'But it doesn't mean we'll get numbers, does it?'

'Having the pub as the venue is a good start.' Jake infused enthusiasm into his voice. 'The guys who normally come into town for a drink and a game of snooker on a Friday night may just be curious enough to poke their heads in and see what's happening. And it takes only one or two and the others will follow.'

'Like sheep.'

'Reluctant sheep,' Jake countered with a wry grin.

'Oh, well…' Maxi's mouth turned down. 'I guess we'll just

have to wait and see. I'm so grateful you decided to give me a hand on the actual night, Jacob.'

He lifted a shoulder in a shrug. 'Everything deserves a second chance.'

Even them? Maxi wondered, a tiny flicker of unease shadowing her eyes. Their relationship had come a long way but instinctively, she knew they were taking nothing for granted. They were closer than they'd ever been. Yet neither had sought commitment. She tried not to analyse that, letting what they'd rediscovered be enough to be going on with.

Jake wished he knew what she was really thinking. He studied her mouth, unaware his eyes had darkened with need. He loved her, wanted her, wanted to build his life around her. But could she say the same about him? Or should they just keep blundering along, grateful for what they had?

For the umpteenth time his thoughts edged towards asking her to make a formal commitment. Because otherwise what were they having here? A hot affair? Mentally, he winced at the suggestion. It was much more than that, surely? But he couldn't rush her. Every instinct was telling him that. He'd tried that once and look where that had got them—a two-year separation that had almost killed them emotionally.

'I happened to bump into Myles Carpenter at the barber shop yesterday.' He switched his thoughts back to the present. 'He was actually reading one of the flyers you'd left there.'

'He was?' Maxi's vice rose in surprise. 'So, did he mention he might come along on the night?'

Jake's eyes glinted with soft amusement. 'Rural males don't flag those kinds of decisions, Max. But I casually mentioned it should be a good night,' he confessed a bit sheepishly. 'If only Myles could begin to seek some help, even in this roundabout way, he could find it a jumping-off point to begin solving his family problems.'

Maxi nodded. If, and it was a very big *if*, he did attend, and somehow it helped his family, it would all have been worth it.

* * *

'Has anyone turned up yet?' Maxi asked of Bron. It was Friday evening and they were at the pub, in the little annexe adjoining the room where the seminar was being held.

'Couple,' Bron said guardedly. 'Heaps of time yet.'

Maxi checked her watch. 'Perhaps if we'd held it earlier, or later…' Or not at all.

Bron made a sound of dismissal. 'We couldn't have made it earlier. We had to allow the guys from the outlying districts time to get home from their farm work, shower and change and drive here. And anything later wouldn't have worked either.'

'I know, I know. We discussed it a thousand times.' Maxi took a steadying breath and let it go. 'Thanks for being the voice of sanity, Bron.'

'Any time. I don't charge for friends,' she said dryly.

'Where's Jacob, though?' Maxi was all but wringing her hands. 'He said he'd be here.'

'He's downstairs at the bar.'

'At the bar!' Maxi could feel her control of things slipping by the second. 'What on earth is he doing there?'

'Don't panic.' Bron flapped a hand. 'If I know Jake, he'll be drowning in orange juice and networking like mad to get a decent roll-up. Can't have all your good work going to waste, can we?'

Maxi felt her heart squeeze tight. How generous of Jacob. And he was doing it all for her sake so that she wouldn't be disappointed. 'He's a very good rural doctor, isn't he?'

'The best,' Bron agreed quietly. 'Totally tuned into the special needs of the folk out here.'

Maxi's heart began beating like a tom-tom. So, how on earth could she ask him to leave—if ever she had to?

'Well, what did you think of the evening?' Jake asked. It was several hours later and they were on their way home.

'Um… I thought it turned out quite well.'

'Quite well?' Jake imitated her crisp little accent to a T. 'Lady, you were terrific.'

'Was I? Really?' Her hand went to her throat. 'Most of it turned out pretty good fun, didn't it?'

'It *was* good. In fact, I think we may have quite an increase in our list of male patients as a result.'

'*You* might. I somehow doubt they'll come to see me in droves.'

'They might surprise you there.'

'You think?'

'Mmm. They like your style, Doctor. As I do.' Jake placed his hand over hers and squeezed.

'Thanks, Jake.' Maxi spun him a soft look.

'For what?'

'For tonight—rallying round, getting the men to at least look in.'

'And *stay* for the most part,' he reminded her. 'Even Myles Carpenter shoved his head in for a while. I hope he took something positive away with him.'

'Lily's applied for several scholarships. She's hopeful of getting one. Just the thought of perhaps going away to school has made such a difference to her outlook.'

'And it's all down to your intervention.' Jake brought her knuckles to his lips.

She gurgled a laugh. 'Now, if I could just make it rain, they'd put up a statue after I'm gone.'

Jake felt the weight of her words knocking in his chest. What an odd thing to say. Was this her roundabout way of telling him she now saw her time here as limited? He formed the words to challenge her but his throat dried before he could get them out.

He wouldn't ask her. Because deep down he didn't want to know.

Maxi was midway through her morning surgery on Monday when Jake made a surprise announcement over their inter-connecting phone. 'I've just had a call from Croyden. Alex Vellacott delivered her baby by C-section this morning. A little girl. She's small but they're hopeful.'

Maxi gave a delighted cry. 'That's wonderful news! Those extra few weeks will have been the kick-start the bub needed. Oh, Jake, let's send some flowers—could we?'

His chuckle was indulgent. 'Talk to Ayleen. She'll organise it. Uh, it's a short list today. Why don't we take off to Wonga Springs this afternoon? Feel like a swim?'

In a second Maxi was contrasting the heat of the day against diving into the deliciously cool spring water. It would be heaven. 'Um, I guess…' She felt oddly flustered, hesitating over her reply. 'I'll just need time to duck home and change into my swimsuit.'

'If you must.' Jake gave a dry laugh. 'It doesn't mean I'll let you keep it on, though,' he ended throatily.

'Promises, promises…' Maxi hardly recognised her voice. She'd sounded positively giddy. Her lashes fluttered down and she felt her face heat almost as if he was watching her instead of being on the other end of the phone line. 'See you at home a bit later, then.' She ended the call quickly. Sitting back in her chair, she fanned the sudden heat from her face.

He'd obviously been only teasing her, Maxi decided some time later, as they swam lazily up and down in the crystal-clear rock pool. There'd been no further hint of skinny-dipping and Jake, to her relief, was wearing a pair of baggy swim shorts.

Suddenly, she wondered uneasily whether he thought her a bit of a prude. Surely not. Heavens, they made love often enough for him not to think that. She was just being modest, she consoled herself. But would it matter here, with only a few cows looking on, if she slipped out of her swimsuit and swam nude with him? Would he like her to? More to the point, would *she* like to?

Still mulling over her options, she turned over and began

to float, observing that Jake had done the same. 'Lovely, isn't it?' she sighed, a feeling of pure gladness twisting inside her.

'Mmm.' Jake turned his head. She was here with him in the way he'd always dreamed about, and nothing had ever felt so right. Suddenly, he wanted to share everything with her—right down to the deep blue canopy of sky, the cool depth of the water, the sharp tang of the eucalypts and the other more elusive bush smells that charged his senses. This is my country, he wanted to shout. My country.

'Max?' Scooping a hand into the water, he scattered droplets over the creaminess of her throat and the peep of cleavage above her swimsuit. 'Open your eyes.'

She sent him a droll look. 'They're open.'

'What do you see?'

Maxi gazed upwards between the lacy pattern of overhanging branches. What on earth was she supposed to say here? Oh, well, if it meant so much to him. 'I see leaves and sky, sky and more sky.'

'And that's it?' Jake pretended outrage.

She stuck out her tongue at him. 'You want poetry?'

'You bet I do.'

Laughing, she made a lunge at him but he was too quick. He ducked her and she came up slicked with water, her hands clasped around his neck. They pressed foreheads, touched noses and kissed playfully once, twice.

Just when it changed into something else, Maxi wasn't sure. She heard her name on his deep exhalation of breath and then he was reclaiming her mouth in a searing kiss, stripping away the top of her swimsuit in one swift movement. The rest followed and she wriggled her hips as though she couldn't wait to be free of the restricting garment.

And, oh, it was heaven. As the water welcomed her nakedness in its cool embrace, she wondered why on earth she had ever hesitated.

Jake noted her wonderment with a touch of arrogant male

satisfaction. In a second he'd discarded his swim shorts, sending them in an overhead arc towards the bank. 'Good?' He turned back to her.

'Magic.' She went into his arms, loving the feel of his maleness, of skin against skin, the soft caress of the water and the whisper of the trees above them. She made a husky whimper in her throat as he kissed her sweetly. And slowly, as if prolonging the pleasure, she let him part her lips, allowing his insistent tongue to enter. He tasted of the outdoors, cool and fresh and something else…something of the drowsing late afternoon and the mood.

And the essence of hard-muscled masculinity.

'Maxi…' Jake's hands fell to the round curves of her backside, pulling her in to feel his maleness, moulding her body to his.

She shuddered, her senses spinning her off-centre.

Jake groaned her name hoarsely, lowering his head to kiss her, lifting her, joining her body to his. He could feel her tighten around him, heard her moan as though poised on the edge of her release.

Jake's response was electric. In an instant, pulses began rocking his body from head to toe as he became lost in the taste and texture of her, his passion climbing to fever pitch, fuelled by her guttural little cry and then shattering as she arched back, exposing her throat, white, like the finest porcelain.

At some point they eased apart but only enough to hold each other. Maxi felt her feet touch the sandy bottom of the pool as he lowered her.

'Could it ever get any better than this, Max?' Jake hooked his chin across the top of her head and wrapped her more closely.

'I wouldn't think so.' She pulled back and smiled shakily up at him, the breath catching in her throat as he parted her hair a little to kiss just behind her ear. She looked around dazedly. The sun had shifted. 'How long have we been here?'

He grinned. 'A couple of lifetimes? Want to get out?'

She nodded quickly, suddenly conscious of her nakedness, her vulnerability. At Jake's invitation, she locked her arms around his waist, allowing him to tow her up the steep incline to the grassy bank above.

Maxi made a beeline for her towel. With her back to him, she wrapped herself firmly into its folds, tucking the end into the hollow between her breasts. That felt better.

'Don't tell me you're still shy!' Jake's disbelieving bark of laughter rang out.

'I was cold,' she defended, refusing to look at him, scuttling off behind the vehicle to get dressed.

Jake was still chuckling when she emerged a few minutes later, dressed in her jeans and T-shirt and towelling her hair dry. 'What?' she sent him a haughty glance.

'Nothing,' he countered, laughter still in his throat as he gathered up their wet swimmers and stuffed them into a sports bag. 'You about ready to hit the road?'

'Sure.' Maxi shook her hair out, finger-combing it into a semblance of order. When his mobile phone rang, she looked at him with a sense of resignation.

'I'd say that's the end of our perfect afternoon.' Jake's smile was rueful as he whipped the phone from his back pocket and held it to his ear.

Watching him, Maxi felt the thread of resentment. For a couple of hours they'd been able to forget the responsibilities that went with being outback doctors. But then, whatever way you looked at it, they were never really off duty.

Never.

And what kind of emergency were they facing now? she fretted, settling herself quickly into the passenger seat of the Land Rover while Jake finished his call.

Seconds later, he threw himself into the driver's seat and started the engine. 'Young Nathan Goode's gone missing,' he said, his voice clipped as he reversed in a swift arc and took off back towards the main road.

Maxi felt the tentacles of an unknown kind of fear grip her insides. 'How long has he been gone?'

'Karryn's not sure.' Frustration sounded in Jake's voice. 'Usually Nate and Belinda have some outdoors playtime in the late afternoon when it's cooler, but apparently today Belinda left Nate to his own devices and came inside to play with the baby.'

'And she didn't tell her mother?'

Jake shook his head. 'Karryn was busy in the kitchen. When she went to call the kids for their bath, Nathan was gone. And it seems the dog's gone with him.'

Maxi looked uncertain. 'Is that good or bad?'

'Could work either way.' They'd reached the junction and Jake took the main road out of town, aiming the Land Rover in the direction of Westwood. 'The most logical scenario is that the dog will be apt to just run and run, looking for adventure, and Nate will try to keep up with him.'

'So, you're saying they could already be miles away by now?'

Jake frowned. 'It looks that way.'

'But Nathan's only four. Surely his little legs will give up and he'll simply plonk himself down somewhere. And wait to be found.'

'He won't realise he's lost,' Jake said heavily. 'And if the dog scents cattle, he'll be gone like the wind, and Nate with him.'

'But if he's a good dog, he'll protect Nathan.' Maxi tried to bolster her hopes.

'Stay with him? Maybe.' Jake's mouth tightened. 'But parts of the property are steep and scrubby. Nathan could take a bad tumble and we'd be ages trying to find him. And we've barely an hour of daylight left to search.'

Maxi cast her fears aside. 'On the other hand, if that's what happened, the dog could alert the search party by barking—couldn't he?'

'There is that,' Jake agreed. He didn't want to play devil's advocate but he had to prepare her for the seriousness of the situation. The Outback was no place for a small child. There were waterholes and dams all over the property. And even though they were drying up, there'd still be enough water to entice an adventurous little boy like Nate. He could be out of his depth in seconds. And unfortunately accidental deaths by drowning on farms were still too numerous for Jake not to feel a measure of unease. He took a steadying breath. He wouldn't allow himself to go there. Not yet.

Maxi knitted her fingers together across her chest. 'So, as doctors, what exactly is our role here, Jacob?'

'To help where we can. I'll go out with the search party, of course—it's just a precaution in case Nathan has sustained an injury.'

Or worse. Maxi felt her stomach churn. 'Ok—I'll stay with Karryn at Westwood, shall I?'

'That's the general idea. The homestead will be the headquarters for the search. People will turn up from everywhere to help. The CWA will be there very quickly to support Karryn and get food and hot drinks laid on for the search parties.'

'Have you been involved in searches before, then?'

'Plenty of times. Usually it's a foolhardy tourist who's gone missing. It can be a pretty daunting experience being lost in this kind of country.'

'I can imagine…' Maxi's voice faltered.

Looking at the group already assembling around the Goodes', outbuildings, Maxi felt tentacles of fear grip her insides. Somewhere in the back of her mind she'd cherished a hope that by the time she and Jake arrived, Nathan would have been found.

But the stark reality was all there before her eyes. The search was about to get under way. Somewhere out there in the vastness of the outback there was a lost little boy. She turned to Jake as he brought his vehicle to a stop beside a farm utility. 'If Nathan hasn't been found by dark, what will you do—abandon the search and wait till morning?'

'No way. The team will have equipment that seeks out body

heat. If we get within cooee of Nate or the dog, it will go off and alert us.'

'Will you please be careful?'

'I'm not the one you have to worry about.' In one fluid movement Jake threw open the car door, his impatience to be gone evident. 'Just keep a friendly eye on Karryn and Belinda. That's all you have to do.'

'Good luck!' Maxi called out to him, but he was already out of earshot, jogging across to where the first party of searchers was about to head out.

Maxi's feelings were very mixed as she alighted slowly from the four-by-four. She lifted a hand, batting away several persistent bush flies, the heat of the early evening pressing down on her. She brought her gaze up, suddenly conscious of the backdrop of scenery. There were no two ways about it. This was harsh country. Unforgiving country. A man's world. And Jake slotted into it like a hand into a well-fitting glove. The thought gave her no comfort.

With a tiny shake of her head Maxi pulled her thoughts together. She'd better stop wallowing in her own misgivings. Karryn had to come first here. And she must in pieces with her little boy missing.

The farm kitchen was probably the hub of things, Maxi decided, and with her knowledge of the layout of the place from her previous visit, she made her way straight there.

'Oh, Maxi!' Liz looked up from wrapping cling film around a tray of freshly made sandwiches. 'Is Jake with you?'

'Gone with the searchers.' Maxi looked around the friendly faces of the women present, most of whom she already knew. 'I'm not sure what help I can offer…'

'Just having you here is tremendous reassurance for everyone,' Liz said kindly, and a soft, 'Hear, hear,' echoed from the other women.

Maxi bit her lip. That kind of praise didn't sit well with her when part of her seemed reluctant to be there at all. 'I thought perhaps I could have a word with Karryn.'

'She's feeding the baby.' Liz quickly washed and dried her hands. 'I'll come with you.'

'How is she coping?' Maxi asked quietly, as they made their way along the hallway to the little bedroom being used as a nursery.

'Karryn's a woman of the outback,' Liz said, as if the question was irrelevant. 'She'll find strengths most of us could only dream about.'

Maxi went quiet for a few seconds. She felt suddenly out of her depth. She and Karryn may as well have come from different planets, their life experiences were so diverse. And even as a doctor it seemed presumptuous to think she, an English doctor, had anything to offer this Australian bush mother in her time of crisis.

Liz raised her hand and knocked softly on the bedroom door. 'Karryn is quite concerned about Belinda,' she whispered. 'Poor mite thinks she's to blame for not watching out for her little brother.'

Oh, lord. Maxi pressed her lips tightly together. How did she handle this new complication? 'Where is Belinda now?'

'With two of Jennifer's young brood. They're watching a video. Karryn?' Liz opened the door to the bedroom and popped her head in. 'Welcome visitor for you. Our wonderful English doctor's here.' She nodded towards Maxi. 'Go in,' she urged gently. 'I'll bring you both a cuppa directly.'

'OK to come in?' Maxi moved quietly into the bedroom.

'Hi, Maxi…' Karryn gave the ghost of a smile. 'Thanks for coming all the way out here.'

'That's fine, Karryn.' Her gaze soft, Maxi watched as the young mother eased her infant son from her breast and kissed the top of his downy head. 'All done?' she asked gently, holding out her arms for the baby. 'I'll put Christopher back in his cot, shall I?'

'Thanks... I'm trying to keep things as normal as possible for Belinda's sake. Otherwise I'd be out searching...' Karryn's voice faltered and she looked blankly at her hands, as if they belonged to someone else. 'I...can't help wondering if I'll ever hold Nate again, read to him, give him his bath—all those things...'

Maxi swallowed. 'Of course you will, Karryn. Nate will be found. Our men will find him.'

Karryn summoned up a brave kind of smile. 'I know they will. And he's wearing a light-coloured T-shirt, thank heavens.'

Maxi looked disconcerted. 'Is that a help?'

'It'll stand out against the landscape far better than a dark colour.' Getting to her feet, she looked around vaguely. 'I think I'll go and spend some time with Belinda. We'll go for a little walk...'

Maxi floundered again. 'Would...you like me to come along?'

'That'd be nice. I'll just ask Jen to listen out for the baby.'

Ten o'clock, and hope which had been high in the early evening had fallen progressively.

Rubbing her hands up and down her arms, Maxi felt she'd stepped into a nightmare, her time with Jake at the springs that afternoon seeming some kind of dream. Had it happened at all? she wondered, watching as a new team of searchers was preparing to go out, allowing the first team some respite. Except for Jacob and Dean. Her face tightened. She knew instinctively that wild horses wouldn't drag them back until they'd found Nathan.

She blew out a calming breath. The utter stillness of the night on top of the uncertainty of the situation were beginning to unnerve her. At least Belinda had gone to sleep but although Maxi had offered a mild sedative to Karryn, the young mum had refused, remaining resolute, looking endlessly out into the night.

The ringing of Maxi's mobile phone startled everyone.

'Is there news?' Karryn had come running, new fear in her eyes as she watched Maxi depress the key to speak.

'It's Jake…' Maxi reached out to grab Karryn's hand and pressed the phone into it. 'He wants to speak to you.'

As she listened to Karryn's murmured responses, Maxi wrapped her arms around her midriff, a ring of ice numbing her lips. Oh, lord, what if…?

'They've found him!' Karryn's face broke into a shaky smile that flickered and then crumpled. 'My boy is OK…'

Immediately emotions boiled over.

The group of woman who'd been waiting for news surged together into a huge hugging circle, laughing and crying at the same time. Finally, they broke apart.

'Jake said they'll be here in twenty minutes,' Karryn choked, rubbing her eyes fiercely.

'Right, let's top up the tea urns,' Liz said practically. 'The men'll be starving.'

Lights came on all over the house, a breathless kind of expectancy overtaking everyone as they flocked outside to wait for the searchers' return.

'There they are!' someone called, long before Maxi was aware of their approach. But she certainly joined in the cheer when the search party walked out of the night, the light from their powerful torches strobing the trees with yellow brilliance.

Maxi stood back. This moment was for Karryn and Dean and their little boy.

'Max…you OK?'

She jumped, goose-bumps running up and down her spine. It was Jake, barely recognisable under a mask of grime.

'I think so,' she said shakily. 'Are *you* OK?' Tears of relief were running down her cheeks and she had no idea how painfully her arms were around him. 'Nathan?' Drawing back, suddenly embarrassed, she scanned his face in the pale moonlight.

'Twisted ankle. Slowed him down for a bit.' Jake's mouth folded in on a rueful smile. 'And you were right about the dog. He'd stayed with Nate. And once he'd got our scent, his barking would have woken the dead. Smart little mutt.'

'I guess he'll be Nate's friend for evermore.' Maxi tried to smile, groping for a sense of lightness, but it wasn't there. Perhaps it would come later, she thought. After all, the child had been found and wasn't that the best outcome they could have hoped for? She turned to Jake, urging him towards the back verandah. 'Get some hot food inside you. I'll take over now.'

'Thanks. Good to have you here, Max,' he added, his voice rough with weariness.

The complimentary words left a hollow ring in Maxi's ears. She checked Nathan over and, finding nothing more serious than the ankle and a few scratches from the brambles he'd tumbled into, gave him the all-clear. 'Nate's ankle will mend pretty quickly,' she said to Karryn. 'But it would help if he didn't run around on it for a couple of days. I know it's a big ask.'

'No.' Karryn shook her head. 'I can manage that. I won't let him out of my sight. It could have all turned out so differently…' she continued, speaking faster, sounding scared. 'Thanks so much, Maxi.'

Maxi made a helpless sound. 'I hardly did anything.'

'You were here—as the doctor. That means such a lot in a rural community.'

And the responsibility was crippling. Maxi paused, biting her lip. Suddenly she felt drained and completely out of her depth. She dragged her professional skills to the fore. 'Nate's ankle may ache a bit tomorrow, Karryn. He'll probably complain of it feeling sore.'

'I've children's paracetemol I can give him. Is that OK?'

'It's fine. But if you're worried about him at all, please don't hesitate to call the surgery.'

Karryn nodded, her smile a bit wobbly. 'I'll give this young rascal a sponge now and pop him into bed. I guess I should say a little prayer as well.'

Handing Nathan over to the care of his mother, Maxi sent up her own silent prayer of thanks for a little boy delivered safely back to his family.

* * *

'How do those women cope, Jacob?' They were on their way home from Westwood and it was late, very late.

'They just do, Maxi,' Jake confirmed wearily. Why on earth had she brought this up when they were both emotionally spent and physically exhausted? 'You're seeing Tangaratta at its worst, with the drought and all its implications.'

'It must take such a terrible toll on people…' She turned her head away, her voice cracking.

Jake lifted a hand from the steering-wheel and scrubbed it across his eyes. 'For the most part this is the lifestyle they've chosen, but it takes people with big hearts to survive here.'

But did that include her? Maxi wondered bleakly. The isolation of the outback rammed home loud and clear in her head. Keeping her face averted, she blinked fast, containing the tears that threatened to fall.

They were quiet for the rest of the way home.

CHAPTER TWELVE

SOMETHING WAS WRONG. Jake looked broodingly across at Maxi as she made a pretence of eating breakfast. 'You look shattered,' he said. 'Why don't you take the morning off? I can manage surgery.'

Maxi opened her mouth to protest, then closed it. 'OK, thanks,' she accepted throatily. 'I might do that.'

'Good.' Jake scraped a hand slowly around his jaw. 'Any plans?'

Her gaze jerked up. 'Plans?'

'For your time off.'

Maxi felt her pulse accelerate. Was now the time to tell him? She'd been awake for most of the night and now finally she knew what she had to do. 'I've...a few things in mind.'

His dark brows rose. 'Would you like to borrow the Land Rover?'

She shook her head. 'I won't be driving anywhere. Just... doing other stuff.'

Hell's bells. Jake's mouth tightened. She looked uncomfortable, almost hunted. 'Is there something you want to talk to me about, Max?' he asked, watching conflicting emotions on her face as she grappled with her thoughts.

She looked down briefly. He knew her too well. 'I guess so.' She took a deep breath and plunged in. 'I'd like to go home.'

Jake's heart hurtled into a nosedive and his mind began clamouring. 'You want to go home? To England?'

Maxi nodded hesitatingly, as if searching for the right words. 'I want you to— That is, could you come with me?'

'Hell, Max. You expect me to just ditch my patients and go on holiday with you?' Jake's shock gave his words a harsh edge.

'Surely it's not too much to ask, is it?'

His mouth a tight line, Jake shook his head. 'It's totally unrealistic. I can't just up and trot off on a whim. I have responsibilities here.' His gaze narrowed. 'How long have you been planning your own get a way, then?'

'I…haven't been actually planning it.' She stopped, her teeth closing on her bottom lip. 'It's just something I need to do. I need to feel centred.'

'I see.' Jake's mouth snapped shut, his tightly clamped lips a harsh line across his face. With all that was in him he wanted to ask whether she intended coming back, but the words jammed in his throat.

The silence between them lengthened and became thicker. Until Maxi asked carefully, 'Couldn't you get a locum?'

His harsh laugh cracked out. 'You've just no idea, have you? Doctors don't want to work out here—it's all too hard. Hell, you've just proved that point yourself. And especially now, with the drought? What calibre of locum would be attracted, do you imagine?'

Her eyelashes fluttered down. 'I don't know, but I'm sure you'll tell me.'

'I'd get someone barely competent who can't get a job anywhere else, or maybe even a drunk.'

'That wouldn't happen.'

Jake's lip curled. 'Oh, believe me, it has. I can't come with you, Maxi,' he said after a moment of heavy silence. 'It's out of the question.'

So what about *us*? Maxi picked up her tea-mug with shaking fingers, her insides suddenly twisting as the truth hit. He just didn't care enough. Otherwise he'd move heaven and earth to go with her.

Jake felt a lump the size of a lemon in his throat and even the act of swallowing hurt. His hunch had been right all along. She wanted out. Obviously what she felt for him hadn't been enough to hold her. And that made him feel like garbage. 'When do you want to go?' he asked stiffly.

'I'm not sure yet. I'll look up some flights on the net this morning.'

The catch in her voice tore at Jake's emotions but he hardened his heart. He'd done all the pleading he intended to do. Leaning forward, he extracted his wallet from his back pocket. He opened it and took out his credit card, placing it in front of her on the table. 'Book business class. It's a hell of a long journey and you'll be much more comfortable.'

'I don't need your money, Jacob,' she protested. 'I haven't spent much of my salary here. I can afford to fly economy.' *Just*, she added silently.

Jake stared at her, just watched her, and then said flatly, 'Use the card, Max.' He pushed back his chair and got to his feet. 'If it will make you feel better, treat it as a bonus for all your hard work.'

Maxi made her booking and clicked off-line. In less than a week she'd be home. She closed down her laptop and got to her feet. She still had things she had to do. And then she had to get over to the surgery.

And face Jake.

Ayleen looked up with a smile when Maxi walked into Reception. 'Feeling better?'

Maxi's gaze clouded.

'Jake said you were having a sleep-in.'

'Oh. Yes.' Maxi managed a tentative smile. 'Much better,

thanks.' And if that didn't quite ring true, nobody here would know that. 'How's this afternoon's list looking, Ayleen?'

The receptionist made a small face. 'Pretty full, actually. Thank goodness it's a two-doctor practice now. Did you want a spot of lunch? I made sandwiches but Jake hardly touched anything.'

Maxi felt her throat close. He was obviously upset and she could understand that. But she'd asked him to go with her. And he'd refused point blank. What more could she do? 'I've already eaten, thanks, Ayleen. Is… Jake in his room?'

'Mmm.' Ayleen looked up from her filing. 'He's not in the best of moods,' she warned, as Maxi turned away.

The walk to his consulting room seemed endless. Maxi paused for a moment outside his door, her heart hammering. Then, taking a deep breath, she knocked and went in.

He was standing at the window, looking out. At her knock he looked back over his shoulder, his expression carefully controlled. 'All set for the off?'

She nodded, too close to the edge to answer. She went forward and placed his credit card on his desk. 'Thanks for that, Jacob. I will pay you back, though.' And she would, she vowed, every cent.

He turned fully then, folding his arms and leaning back against the window-sill. 'When do you fly out?'

'Early next week. I'll make sure I'll leave everything in order.'

Something flickered in his eyes briefly. 'Do that.'

Maxi felt as though her heart was splitting in two. If he was going to change his mind and make a snap decision to go with her, he would have done it the moment she'd walked in. But his whole attitude was distant. Leaning on his desk, she pressed one hand on top of the other to stop herself from trembling. 'Please, try to understand, Jacob. I need to see my family.'

Jake's expression remained neutral as he took her information on board. 'You should aim to be in Sydney by Monday at the latest, then. Give yourself time to relax a bit before the flight.'

'I realise that. I'll drive.'

'You won't have to. I'll get in touch with John McIlwraith, one of the better-off graziers. He has a private plane. He and his wife are only too happy to have an excuse to head down to Sydney. They'll be glad to give you a lift.'

Sudden pain welled in Maxi's heart. It sounded as though he couldn't wait to get shot of her. Well, as least she knew now. 'I've moved my things across to the hotel. I'll stay there for the few days until I leave.'

Jake frowned. 'Why did you do that?'

Maxi bit the inside of her bottom lip. 'It just seemed simpler.' And it wasn't as though they had anything left to say to one other, she thought bleakly. 'Folk are going to talk anyway.'

'Do you think I care about that?'

Maxi felt her insides twist painfully. She didn't know what he cared about any more. It certainly wasn't her.

Jake felt his chest tighten so much, it hurt to breathe. He didn't understand any of it. More and more recently, he'd thought they belonged together…

Seeing his closed expression, Maxi sighed and made to turn away. 'I'd better head back to my room. Ayleen says we have a full list this afternoon.'

'I never took you for a quitter, Max.' There was bitter resentment in Jake's voice.

Maxi felt her throat almost close. 'That's not fair, Jacob. I've given this place my very best. And you. We've had some wonderful times together…'

Had. Already she was speaking in the past tense. Jake's gut wrenched. He'd carried a torch for her for two long years. She'd re-ignited it briefly. Now she'd well and truly blown out the flame. And stamped all over it.

How dumb can you be, Haslem?

CHAPTER THIRTEEN

IT WAS A month later and early evening and Maxi was home on her own. She put the finishing touches to the chocolate cake she'd made, thinking it would be just the thing for supper when her family got home from the fundraiser in the village.

Besides, the activity had occupied her hands and mind. And for a while at least stopped her thinking about Jake.

She'd spoken to him only once since she'd left Australia. He'd called to ensure she'd arrived home safely. But the conversation had been brief, his impersonal, far-away tones leaving her unsettled. And even though she'd been surrounded by her family, she'd felt lonelier than she could have imagined.

But some time very soon, maybe even tonight, she was going to have to pluck up the courage to call him. And tell him of her plans. Whether or not he'd even be interested, she didn't know, couldn't guess…

Her thoughts were miles away when the doorbell rang. Sliding off her kitchen stool, she went to answer it. And when she did, a whimper of disbelief escaped from her mouth.

'Hello, Max,' her visitor said quietly, and looked straight into her eyes.

'Jacob…?' Maxi's voice shook. 'Tell me I'm not dreaming.'

'I'm right here. Feel me.' He held out his arms and in a second she was flying into them, being cradled against the solidness of his chest.

'Let me look at you…' He tilted her head up, his voice a murmur against her lips until his mouth caught her own breathy sigh, swallowing it, savouring it, before he claimed her fully with a passion that shook them both.

'Is it really you! And what are you doing here!' She buried her face against his throat, breathing in the warm male closeness of him like life-giving oxygen.

He gave a laugh deep in his chest. 'If we can get past the front door, I'll tell you.'

'Oh…sorry.' She managed a strangled laugh. 'I'm in the kitchen. Come through.' Leading the way but still holding his hand, she asked, 'Are you starving? I could rustle up some food.'

'No, thanks. I'm fine. Coffee would be welcome, though.'

'Let me take your coat,' Maxi offered.

For answer, he burrowed more deeply into its folds and moved closer to the Aga. 'Just give me a few minutes to thaw out a bit, Max.'

She rippled a laugh of sheer happiness. 'Poor you. Actually, it's quite mild for this time of year.'

Jake snorted. 'It might be to you. But I've been sweltering in forty-degree heat until recently.'

She handed him a big mug of coffee, watching as he drank in huge gulps. As he always did. She blinked back a sudden rush of tears. She'd missed him so much…

Oh, hell. Jake put down his coffee-mug hurriedly and reached for her. 'Don't cry, Max. I never wanted to make you cry.' Wiping away her tears with his thumb, he tightened his arms around her.

'They're happy tears,' she told him shakily. 'How did you get here, though?' She locked her hands around his neck. 'I mean, what about the practice? Did you manage to get a locum?'

He tipped his head to one side. 'It's a long story. Got time to listen?'

For answer, she thumped him lightly on the chest.

They went through to the lounge. Jake shrugged out of his coat and draped it over the back of a chair. Holding out a hand, he guided her down beside him on to the sofa. 'My former practice partner, Tom Wilde, arrived back in Tangaratta last week.'

'So, he's covering for you while you're away?'

'In a manner of speaking.' Jake hesitated. 'He wants to take over the practice again and he has a partner who's keen to come in with him.'

Maxi's eyes flew wide. 'Is that what you want? To sell the practice?'

He shrugged. 'Depends on you, Max. I'm quite happy to set up practice here if it will mean I can have you back in my life.'

Maxi's mouth dried. Was he saying what she thought he was saying? And if he was… 'You'd do that for me?' she said, her voice not quite steady. 'Leave your own country and settle in mine?'

'I'll do whatever it takes, Max,' he said throatily. 'You make me whole.'

'Oh, Jacob…' Her voice broke. 'What a lovely thing to say. But you won't have to give up your outback practice. I've made some plans, too.'

'Plans?' Jake heard the snap in his voice but he didn't care. A fire of rebellion began building inside him, flaring with incredible speed. He'd just confessed his *love* for her or as good as, and she was telling him she'd made her own plans!

'Jake, don't look like that.' Maxi felt her heartbeat increase sickeningly. 'Just let me explain.'

'Hell, you'd better.'

'I want to go back to Tangaratta.'

'Uh…!' The breath went out of him as if he'd been struck.

Maxi licked her lips, biting them uncertainly. 'That is…if you'll have me?'

'If I'll have you!' Jake made a grab for her hands, intertwining them in a fierce grip and holding them over his heart. 'I've spent the last month feeling as though a very bad surgeon had been let loose on my guts. I finally decided that if I loved you I'd better damn well get over here and convince *you* of the fact. And find out if you loved me back.' His voice softened suddenly. 'Do you love me, Max?'

'Oh, Jacob…' Maxi felt as though a huge crippling weight had been lifted from her. Tears sprang into her eyes again and she blinked them back. 'Of course I love you. I thought I'd proved that over and over again.'

He pressed his forehead against hers. 'I guess neither of us actually said the words, though, did we?'

'No. Awfully slack of us,' Maxi agreed, snuggling against him.

Jake felt the knot in his chest begin to unravel. It was going to be all right. 'So, Dr Somers, are we getting married, then?'

'I want to make a life with you, Jake.' She touched his face, stroking the marks of strain around his eyes with gentle fingertips. 'You need a holiday anyway.'

'*We* need a honeymoon,' he corrected, his mouth quirking into a crooked familiar smile. 'And let's not hang about. Do you want to get married here or back home?'

She looked into his eyes, hers alight with love and giving. 'I never thought I'd ever think of Tangaratta as *back home* but I do. Isn't that amazing?'

He laughed. 'You're amazing, that's why. Everyone's been asking when you're coming back?'

'Everyone there was so kind to me.'

'Why wouldn't they be? You were like a breath of fresh air in the place. You went all out, got things done—initiated projects that people were crying out for. It took a fresh eye. Most of all it took courage, Max. And even for the short time you were there, you touched lives. The people of Tangaratta aren't likely to forget that in a hurry. And best of all we've had rain, glorious rain. The place is green again and instead of cicadas we now have frogs croaking all over the place and keeping us awake at night.'

She chuckled. 'That I have to hear. When can we fly out?'

A wry smile tilted his mouth. 'Whenever you like. It'll be so good to have you back, Max.'

Maxi dipped her head. 'I'm—sorry about the way I just… took off. But I just needed the reassurance of being with my family again, checking on Luke again. That kind of thing, you know, before I announced to the world I was staying in Australia.'

Jake groaned his frustration. 'If only you'd explained that to me, I would have done everything in my power to go with you. As it was, I thought you'd just plain had enough of me. You should have *talked* to me,' he said deeply. 'We should have *talked* to each other.'

'I meant to… I wanted to,' she said miserably. 'But you seemed so…locked up.'

He gave a snort of harsh laughter. 'Perhaps that's what I should have been—locked up. You needed me to hold you and reassure you but I stood back like a wounded adolescent. And instead let you go without a word.'

'But you're here now.' Maxi took a ragged little breath, running her fingers lingeringly over his cheekbones, around his jaw and then stroking his bottom lip.

'Yes,' he echoed deeply. 'I'm here now.' Lifting his head, he looked around. 'Where is everyone? I expected to be greeted by the Somers family en masse.'

'There's a fundraising do on at the church hall. They've all gone there. You'll stay, though, won't you?' She looked up, a searching question in her eyes. 'Spend a bit of time with us?'

'If it's OK with your folks.'

She tutted as if that didn't deserve an answer. 'I expect you hired a car. Do you have luggage?'

'Mmm. I'll get it presently. But there's something I need to do right now.' Propping his hands beneath her elbows, he levered them upright.

'Now what?' Maxi gave a nervous laugh.

His eyes glittered. 'Have a little patience, hmm?' Moving across the room, he reached into the pocket of his overcoat and drew out a small gift-wrapped package.

"Oh." Maxi's hand went to her mouth and her heart began pounding like a drumbeat inside her chest.

'I had a day in Sydney before I flew out,' Jake said casually. 'I did a bit of shopping. And this, my love, is for you.'

Maxi swallowed deeply and took the gift with trembling hands. 'It's so beautifully wrapped…'

Jake rolled his eyes. 'Honey, the idea is to pull the ribbon undone and open it.'

She did, her throat drying further with every movement. The ribbon fell away and then the gold-embossed paper until she was left holding what was unmistakably a jeweller's box.

'Oh… Jacob,' she sighed.

'Oh, Maxi,' he mimicked, but gently.

She lifted the lid and stared, speechless at what she saw.

'They're Argyle diamonds from Western Australia,' Jake said proudly. 'I wanted you to have something from my country because it will always be a reminder of where we finally rekindled our love.' He took the ring and slipped it on her finger. 'So, I'm asking now formally, Max. Will you marry me?'

'Oh, Jacob.' She swallowed, blinking back the tears of joy. 'What lovely sentiments and what a beautiful ring. And of course I'll marry you.'

'Come here, then,' he said throatily and drew her into his arms.

In a while they resumed their place on the sofa and began making plans.

'How long can you stay?' Maxi asked, adrift in something so delicious she wanted to stay floating there for ever.

Jake kissed her tenderly. 'Tom said he'll hold the fort as long as necessary. And about the wedding—I really don't mind where, as long as it's soon.'

Maxi looked down at her ring, her eyes suddenly misty. 'I think it would be lovely to have an outback wedding.'

Jake shook his head. 'You never cease to amaze me. Are you sure?'

She nodded.

'Then we'll fly your whole family over for the occasion. And they can have a holiday afterwards in Sydney. Mum will be happy to show them around. And I've a feeling Bron and Dave will want to host our wedding at their place.' Jake bent his head and kissed her gently. 'If that's all right with the bride, of course.'

'Perfectly.' She fluttered a hand towards the window and the twilight outside. 'When you think about it, home really isn't a place at all, is it? It's people. And for us it's our people of Tangaratta.' She stared into his eyes, so blue and steady. 'We'll have a lovely wedding.'

'That we shall,' Jake said, indulging her.

'And I just love my ring.' Maxi lifted her hand from his clasp, watching as the diamonds caught the light.

'Thought you would.' There was a youthful grin on Jake's face. 'We had to have diamonds anyway.'

Maxi lifted her gaze and looked at him tenderly. 'Tell me why.'

'Because they're for ever.' Jake's eyes glittered briefly. 'And that, my love, is what we're all about.'

'Oh, Jacob…' Maxi thought her heart would burst with joy. She blinked, looking into his eyes and seeing a reflection of what was surely in his heart. And in hers.

What she'd thought they'd lost had been found, only now it was so much more. Their hearts were safe in each other's keeping. And very soon their lives would be joined in marriage. 'There's just one small thing, Jacob.'

His brows knitted sharply, betraying a tiny residue of vulnerability. 'What is it, Max?'

'Would you kiss me again?'

He gave a short grunt of laughter, then drew her close, very close. 'It would be my absolute pleasure,' he said, his voice gruff, and bent to capture her lips.

* * * * *

Keep reading for an excerpt of
Unlikely Lover
by Diana Palmer.
Find it in the
Texas Honour anthology,
out now!

CHAPTER ONE

WARD JESSUP WENT to the supper table rubbing his big hands together, his green eyes like dark emeralds in a face like a Roman's, perfectly sculpted under hair as thick and black as crow feathers. He was enormously tall, big and rangy looking, with an inborn elegance and grace that came from his British ancestors. But Ward himself was all-American. All Oklahoman, with a trace of Cherokee and a sprinkling of Irish that gave him his taciturn stubbornness and his cutting temper, respectively.

"You look mighty proud of yourself," Lillian huffed, bringing in platters of beef and potatoes and yeast rolls.

"Why shouldn't I?" he asked. "Things are going pretty well. Grandmother's leaving, did she tell you? She's going to stay with my sister. Lucky, lucky Belinda!"

Lillian lifted her eyes to the ceiling. "I must have pleased you, Lord, for all my prayers to be so suddenly answered," she said.

Ward chuckled as he reached for the platter of sliced roast beef. "I thought you two were great buddies."

"And we stay that way as long as I run fast, keep my

mouth shut and pretend that I like cooking five meals at a time."

"She may come back."

"I'll quit," was the gruff reply. "She's only been here four months, and I'm ready to apply for that cookhouse job over at Wade's."

"You'd wind up in the house with Conchita, helping to look after the twins," he returned.

She grinned, just for an instant. Could have been a muscle spasm, he thought.

"I like kids." Lillian glared at him, brushing back wiry strands of gray hair that seemed to match her hatchet nose, long chin and beady little black eyes. "Why don't you get married and have some?" she added.

His thick eyebrows raised a little. They were perfect like his nose, even his mouth. He was handsome. He could have had a dozen women by crooking his finger, but he dated only occasionally, and he never brought women home. He never got serious, either. He hadn't since that Caroline person had almost led him to the altar, only to turn around at the last minute and marry his cousin Bud, thinking that, because Bud's last name was Jessup, he'd do as well as Ward. Besides, Bud was much easier to manage. The marriage had only lasted a few weeks, however, just until Bud had discovered that Caroline's main interest was in how much of his small inheritance she could spend on herself. He had divorced her, and she had come rushing back to Ward, all in tears. But somewhere along the way Ward had opened his eyes. He'd shown her the door, tears and all, and that was the last time he'd shown any warmth toward anything in skirts.

"What would I do with kids?" he asked. "Look what it's done to Tyson Wade, for God's sake. There he was, a contented bachelor making money hand over fist. He married that model and lost everything—"

"He got everything back, with interest," Lillian interrupted, "and you say one more word about Miss Erin and I'll scald you, so help me!"

He shrugged. "Well, she is pretty. Nice twins, too. They look a little like Ty."

"Poor old thing," Lillian said gently. "He was homely as sin and all alone and meaner than a tickled rattlesnake. And now here he's made his peace with you and even let you have those oil leases you've been after for ten years. Yes sir, love sure is a miracle," she added with a purely calculating look.

He shivered. "Talking about it gives me hives. Talk about something else." He was filling his plate and nibbling between comments.

Lillian folded her hands in front of her, hesitating, but only for an instant. "I've got a problem."

"I know. Grandmother."

"A bigger one."

He stopped eating and looked up. She did seem to be worried. He laid down his fork. "Well? What's the problem?"

She shifted from one foot to the other. "My brother's eldest girl, Marianne," she said. "Ben died last year, you remember."

"Yes. You went to his funeral. His wife died years earlier, didn't she?"

Lillian nodded. "Well, Marianne and her best friend, Beth, went shopping at one of those all-night department store sales. On their way out, as they crossed the parking lot, a man tried to attack them. It was terrible," she continued huskily. "Terrible! The girls were just sickened by the whole experience!" She lowered her voice just enough to sound dramatic. "It left deep scars. Deep emotional scars," she added meaningfully, watching to see how he was reacting. *So far, so good.*

He sat up straighter, listening. "Your niece will be all right, won't she?" he asked hesitantly.

"Yes. She's all right physically." She twisted her skirt. "But it's her state of mind that I'm worried about."

"Marianne..." He nodded, remembering a photograph he'd seen of Lillian's favorite niece. A vivid impression of long dark hair and soft blue eyes and an oval, vulnerable young face brought a momentary smile to his lips.

"She's no raving beauty, and frankly, she hasn't dated very much. Her father was one of those domineering types whose reputation kept the boys away from her when she lived at home. But now..." She sighed even more dramatically. "Poor little Mari." She glanced up. "She's been keeping the books for a big garage. Mostly men. She said it's gotten to the point that if a man comes close enough to open a door for her, she breaks out in a cold sweat. She needs to get away for a little while, out of the city, and get her life back together."

"Poor kid," he said, sincere yet cautious.

"She's almost twenty-two," Lillian said. "What's going to become of her?" she asked loudly, peeking out the corner of her eye at him.

He whistled softly. "Therapy would be her best bet."

"She won't talk to anyone," she said quickly, cocking her head to one side. "Now, I know how you feel about women. I don't even blame you. But I can't turn my back on my own niece." She straightened, playing her trump card. "Now, I'm fully prepared to give up my job and go to her—"

"Oh, for God's sake, you know me better than that after fifteen years," he returned curtly. "Send her an airline ticket."

"She's in Georgia—"

"So what?"

Lillian toyed with a pan of rolls. "Well, thanks. I'll make it up to you somehow," she said with a secretive grin.

"If you're feeling that generous, how about an apple pie?"

The older woman chuckled. "Thirty minutes," she said and dashed off to the kitchen like a woman half her age. She could have danced with glee. He'd fallen for it! Stage one was about to take off! *Forgive me, Mari,* she thought silently and began planning again.

Ward stared after her with confused emotions. He hoped that he'd made the right decision. Maybe he was just going soft in his old age. Maybe…

"My bed was more uncomfortable than a sheet filled with cacti," came a harsh, angry old voice from the doorway. He turned as his grandmother ambled in using her cane, broad as a beam and as formidable as a raiding party, all cold green eyes and sagging jowls and champagne-tinted hair that waved around her wide face.

"Why don't you sleep in the stable?" he asked her pleasantly. "Hay's comfortable."

She glared at him and waved her cane. "Shame on you, talking like that to a pitiful old woman!"

"I pity anyone who stands within striking distance of that cane," he assured her. "When do you leave for Galveston?"

"Can't wait to get rid of me, can you?" she demanded as she slid warily into a chair beside him.

"Oh, no," he assured her. "I'll miss you like the plague."

"You cowhand," she grumbled, glaring at him. "Just like your father. He was hell to live with, too."

"You sweet-tempered little woman," he taunted.

"I guess you get that wit from your father. And he got it from me," she confessed. She poured herself a cup of coffee. "I hope Belinda is easier to get along with than you and your saber-toothed housekeeper."

"I am not saber-toothed," Lillian assured her as she brought in more rolls.

"You are so," Mrs. Jessup replied curtly.

Lillian snorted and walked out.

"Are you going to let her talk to me like that?" Mrs. Jessup demanded of her grandson.

"You surely don't want me to walk into that kitchen alone?" he asked her. "She keeps knives in there." He lowered his voice and leaned toward her. "And a sausage grinder. I've seen it with my own eyes."

Mrs. Jessup tried not to laugh, but she couldn't help herself. She hit at him affectionately. "Reprobate. Why do I put up with you?"

"You can't help yourself," he said with a chuckle. "Eat. You can't travel halfway across Texas on an empty stomach."

She put down her coffee cup. "Are you sure this night flight is a good idea?"

"It's less crowded. Besides, Belinda and her newest boyfriend are going to meet you at the airport," he said. "You'll be safe."

"I guess so." She stared at the platter of beef that was slowly being emptied. "Give me some of that before you gorge yourself!"

"It's my cow," he muttered, green eyes glittering.

"It descended from one of mine. Give it here!"

Ward sighed, defeated. Handing the platter to her with a resigned expression, he watched her beam with the tiny triumph. He had to humor her just a little occasionally. It kept her from getting too crotchety.

Later he drove her to the airport and put her on a plane. As he went back toward his ranch, he wondered about Marianne Raymond and how it was going to be with a young woman around the place getting in his hair. Of course, she was just twenty-two, much too young for him. He was thirty-five now, too old for that kind of child-woman. He shook his head. He only hoped that he'd done the right thing. If he hadn't, things were sure going to be complicated from now on. At one time Lillian's incessant matchmaking had driven him nuts before he'd managed to stop her, though she still harped on his unnatural attitude toward marriage. If only she'd let him alone and stop mothering him! That was the trouble with people who'd worked for you almost half your life, he muttered to himself. They felt obliged to take care of you in spite of your own wishes.

He stared across the pastures at the oil rigs as he eased his elegant white Chrysler onto the highway near Ravine, Texas. His rigs. He'd come a long damned way from the old days spent working on those rigs. His father had dreamed of finding that one big well, but it was Ward who'd done it. He'd borrowed as much as he could and put everything on one big gamble with a friend. And his well had come in. He and the friend had equal shares in it, and they'd long since split up and gone in different directions. When it came to business, Ward Jessup could be ruthless and calculating. He had a shrewd mind and a hard heart, and some of his enemies had been heard to say that he'd foreclose on a starving widow if she owed him money.

That wasn't quite true, but it was close. He'd grown up poor, dirt poor, as his grandmother had good reason to remember. The family had been looked down on for a long time because of Ward's mother. She'd tired of her boring life on the ranch with her two children and had run off with a neighbor's husband, leaving the children for her stunned husband and mother-in-law to raise. Later she'd divorced Ward's father and remarried, but the children had never heard from her again. In a small community like Ravine the scandal had been hard to live down. Worse, just a little later, Ward's father had gone out into the south forty one autumn day with a rifle in his hand and hadn't come home again.

He hadn't left a note or even seemed depressed. They'd found him slumped beside his pickup truck, clutching a piece of ribbon that had belonged to his wife. Ward had never forgotten his father's death, had never forgiven his mother for causing it.

Later, when he'd fallen into Caroline's sweet trap, Ward Jessup had learned the final lesson. These days he had a reputation for breaking hearts, and it wasn't far from the mark. He had come to hate women. Every time he felt tempted to let his emotions show, he remembered his mother and Caroline. And day by day he became even more embittered.

He liked to remember Caroline's face when he'd told her he didn't want her anymore, that he could go on happily all by himself. She'd curled against him with her big black eyes so loving in that face like rice paper and her blond hair cascading like yellow silk down her back. But he'd seen past the beauty to the ugliness, and he never wanted to get that close to a woman again. He'd seen graphically how big a fool the most sensible man could become when a shrewd woman got hold of him. Nope, he told himself. Never again. He'd learned from his mistake. He wouldn't be that stupid a second time.

He pulled into the long driveway of Three Forks and smiled at the live oaks that lined it, thinking of all the history there was in this big, lusty spread of land. He might live and die without an heir, but he'd sure enjoy himself until that time came.

He wondered if Tyson Wade was regretting his decision to lease the pastureland so that Ward could look for the oil that he sensed was there. He and Ty had been enemies for so many years—almost since boyhood—although the reason for all the animosity had long been forgotten in the heat of the continuing battle over property lines, oil rigs and just about everything else.

Ty Wade had changed since his marriage. He'd mellowed, becoming a far cry from the renegade who'd just as soon have started a brawl as talk business. Amazing that a beautiful woman like Erin had agreed to marry the man in the first place. Ty was no pretty boy. In fact, to Ward Jessup, the man looked downright homely. But maybe he had hidden qualities.

Ward grinned at that thought. He wouldn't begrudge his old enemy a little happiness, not since he'd picked up those oil leases that he'd wanted so desperately. It was like a new beginning: making a peace treaty with Tyson Wade and getting his crotchety grandmother out of his hair and off the ranch without bloodshed. He chuckled aloud as he drove back to the house, and it wasn't until he heard the sound that he realized how rarely he laughed these days.

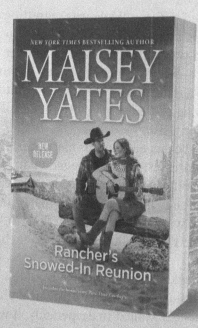